BEAST
BY DAY

BEAST BY DAY

HORRIFIC FAIRY TALES BOOK 2

ELIZABETH K. KING

Published in the United States by Elizabeth King. For inquiries, please visit the author's website: www.elizabethkking.com

Cover Art by Miblart.

Map by Saumya Singh (@Saumyasvision/Inkarnate).

The text for this book was set in EB Garamond. This book was formatted with Atticus.

The Library of Congress Control Number: 2023924736

ISBN 979-8-9888121-4-2 (hardcover)

ISBN 979-8-9888121-5-9 (paperback)

ISBN 979-8-9888121-3-5 (ebook)

First Edition, March 2024.

For David, who always listened.

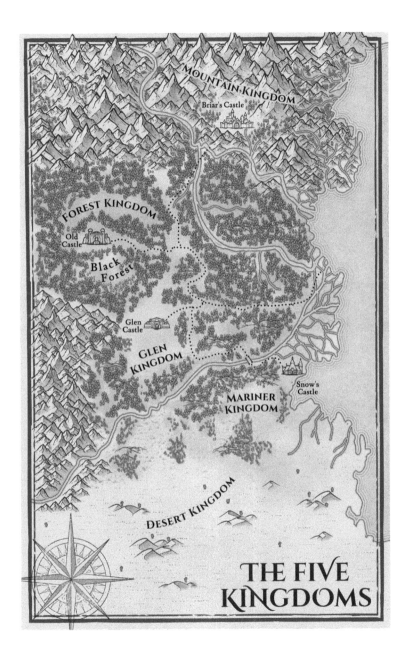

MOUNTAIN KINGDOM

Briar's Castle

FOREST KINGDOM

Old Castle

Black Forest

Glen Castle

GLEN KINGDOM

Snow's Castle

MARINER KINGDOM

DESERT KINGDOM

THE FIVE KINGDOMS

1

CURSED

I SABELLE FLINCHED AS THE splintering oak door slammed
shut behind her, closing out the scowls and mutterings of
the tavern workers inside. An icy gust blew past, and Isabelle
shivered, pushing her windswept curls from her face. Not even
her snug wool coat was enough to guard against the bitter chill
of the Black Forest. The village tavern may not have been very
friendly, but at least it had been warm.

This was the third village she'd come to in the past week, and
so far, no one knew of a castle in these woods. But Isabelle had
become suspicious of this professed ignorance. The villagers'
fearful eyes and curt responses told a different story. There *was*
a castle in this forest. But no one wanted to talk about it. Which
did not bode well for Isabelle.

Standing outside the tavern now, Isabelle peered up at the slate
blue sky. It was not dawn yet—the sun rose late and set early this
time of year, especially so far north—and she wondered if she
should wait for daylight before setting out. The village here was
small: a cluster of houses, a business or two, and the one tavern,

all pitched on either side of the road. Beyond the village, the road ended, leaving no clear way through the tangled wood.

Isabelle wound the gears on her lantern, and as the bulb flared to life, she raised it high, throwing a circle of bright white light ahead of her. The road ended, but perhaps there was a path, Isabelle thought, as she ventured past the final stone houses. The wooded land rose just ahead, obscuring what lay beyond—more forest probably. Indeed, the air was scented with the musty fragrance of cold, muddy earth and dead leaves.

Isabelle hesitated. Her lantern's cold, metal handle bit into the crevices of her palm as she shifted her grip. Sunrise must have been close, because the world around her had begun to lighten, the black veil of night lifting. But the way forward was still concealed, murkier than ever in the pre-dawn gray.

A shadow shifted ahead, something moving in the dark.

Isabelle froze. Her spine felt rigid, as though something had clamped it tight. The movement could have been anything—a hawk winging beneath the forest canopy, the wind rustling the furry branches of a spruce tree. But something about the way that shadow undulated in the gloom—with uncanny grace—put Isabelle on alert.

"Heard you're looking for the old castle."

Isabelle gave a start, her heart leaping in her chest.

A woman glided out of the forest, materializing from the darkness.

Isabelle's breath sank out of her. "*Stones*."

"Sorry. Didn't mean to frighten you." The woman gave her the briefest of smiles, her glinting teeth a flash of white. As she stepped into the light of the lantern, Isabelle took in the sight of her. She had thick, fiery red hair, bound in a complicated mass of braids. Her skin was wintry fair, her cheeks pink with cold. And she was tall. Isabelle was tall, but thin and bony. This woman had a heft to her, a muscled litheness.

She must be a woodswoman, Isabelle realized, perhaps a trapper, living off the woods. She didn't have the air of a villager, and she dressed in rough clothing—brown trousers tucked into well-worn boots, a thin scarf stuffed into a leather vest. And a wool sack coat—a garment often worn by men rather than women.

"Well?" the trapper said. "Are you?"

"What?"

"Looking for the old castle?"

Hope seized Isabelle by the throat. "Yes, I am. If it's real, anyway."

"Of course it's real." The woman gave a short laugh. "This forest used to be one big kingdom. And a kingdom's got to have a castle, doesn't it? Though I understand your skepticism. People around here don't like talk of that castle."

"So I've gathered," Isabelle said.

The woman smiled again. There was something off about her smile—as though it meant to convey something more than friendliness. Something sinister.

Isabelle shook off a chill as a cutting wind sliced through her black coat. The mistrust of the villagers, the darkness of the early morning—it was putting her on edge. If there *was* something off about this woman, well, Isabelle knew people who lived alone could be a bit strange. She herself was, after all.

"So the castle?" Isabelle prompted. "Where can I find it?"

The woman turned, shrugging for Isabelle to join her. "There's a path you can start on. I'm headed that way myself—I'll show you."

Isabelle followed, relieved. She'd begun to think this entire venture was a fool's errand. That the telegram she'd received had been nothing more than a cruel prank. The telegram had contained news of Isabelle's brother, claiming he was being held prisoner in an old castle here in the forest. But the details had been vague, and as Isabelle delved further into the forest, she'd begun to think it was all for nothing. But now, as Isabelle trekked up the sharp rise in the land and down a dirt path, she felt hopeful for the first time since leaving the Glen Kingdom.

The forest was formless in the early darkness, shadows blurring together. Bulging fir trees were like sleeping giants and barren alders like twisted monsters, their branches grasping and grotesque. Isabelle kept her gaze on her guide, wary of wandering off the path.

"This is just an old deer path," the trapper told her. The ground began to level out. "It winds through the woods here and eventually disappears. But the castle isn't far beyond that. You should reach it today."

"This castle then." Isabelle stepped over a mossy rock jutting up from the ground. "It's the seat of the old Forest kings?" Even concern for her brother couldn't dampen Isabelle's interest in such an intriguing historical site.

"Sure is," the trapper said.

"And it's still standing?"

"Was the last time I saw it." The woman came to a halt, rounding on Isabelle. "Did anyone in the village tell you *why* they don't speak of it?"

"Hardly. They refused to acknowledge it exists."

"Sounds about right," the trapper muttered. "Well. If you're going there, you should know. People say the castle is cursed."

Isabelle felt an icy hand grip her heart. She was not typically a fanciful person. She believed in what was rational, what was recorded, and what could be proved. But she also knew very well that curses were real. They *had* been recorded and proved. "Cursed? In what way?"

"No one really knows." The trapper studied Isabelle as though appraising her mettle. "There are all sorts of rumors. But the story generally goes that—back when the kingdom still stood—a witch cursed the last Forest king. Him and his family. Even their descendants."

A shiver rattled through Isabelle. Enough time had passed that the sun should have risen by now, shedding morning light. But the Black Forest was true to its name. The dark fir trees soared overhead, blocking out the sky. Even the bare-limbed alders loomed, their knobby branches snarling together in a tangled canopy. A thin layer of snow lay over it all, dusting the fir trees and clumping in the crevices of the alders. The snow should have lent the landscape some beauty, but even its glossy sheen was overshadowed by the dim forest.

"Why did the witch curse them?" Isabelle asked.

"Who knows?" the trapper replied. "Some say the king slighted her. Some say they were lovers, and he broke her heart. Others claim the royal family was involved in something dark—forbidden rituals and blood magic and all sorts of madness."

Isabelle mulled this over, her usual skepticism breaking through the sordid corners of this tale. Forbidden rituals? The old Forest kings had been pagans, and their citizenry allowed to worship whoever they chose. And it was hard to believe a witch would care if the king was involved in dark magic.

"Some of the stories are outlandish, I'll grant you." The trapper turned, scanning the way before them. "But *something* happened that night the king fell. The stories agree on that. It was no invasion or famine that toppled this kingdom. Something struck down the royal family in one swoop. And the castle has been abandoned ever since."

There could be some truth to it, Isabelle thought, watching a tiny critter scurry across the path. There was little historical evidence to say why the kingdom fell, and no one knew what had become of the last Forest king. "And their descendants?"

The trapper turned to her. "What?"

"You said the witch cursed the king's descendants as well. Or *were* there any descendants? If everyone was killed—"

"I didn't say they were killed. I said they were *cursed*. Including their descendants." The wind picked up, soughing as it blustered through the fir trees. The trapper's red hair blew in the wind, but she stood still, untouched by the cold. "Some people say they fled to the mountains. But others say the descendants still walk these woods. Haunting the forest. Living out their curse." Her gaze settled on Isabelle with a smile that did not reach her cool gray eyes.

Isabelle swallowed. She suddenly wanted to be on her way—and leave this woman behind. "So the castle itself isn't cursed then."

"I suppose not."

"And it's not abandoned anymore?"

"No. It's not. But the one who lives there now—some disgraced lord—doesn't much like visitors." The trapper's tone turned bitter.

The one who lives there now. Isabelle reached for the crumpled paper tucked in her pocket, the transcript of her telegram. The paper felt brittle in her hand, the well-worn creases grown sharp. According to the telegram, her brother had stayed at the castle as a guest—until he'd done something to offend the lord of the castle. Now he was a prisoner. Though she hadn't seen him in three years, Isabelle knew her brother, and she could well believe Ansel had done something stupid or criminal. But that didn't mean she wasn't worried about him.

"Well, whatever he likes," Isabelle said, trying to make her voice light, "I need to get to that castle. So, I just follow the path?"

"Yes. Follow the path through the woods. When it ends, you've got about three miles before you reach the castle. But it's a straight shot through the forest. Due north." The trapper stepped aside. "I'll leave you here. I'm headed elsewhere." A smile played at her lips as she watched Isabelle pass. "Good luck. And you really *should* try to reach the castle before dark."

Isabelle stilled. She turned back towards the trapper.

"Why?" she asked.

"Oh. You know. There are those stories. The cursed descendants haunting the woods." The trapper smiled. "And wolves."

"Wolves?" Isabelle echoed, trying to hide her alarm. She'd lived most of her life in the woods, but in the southern kingdoms, where wolves were scarce.

The trapper waved a hand. "Yes, they're all about this forest. And at this time of year, food gets scarce. They get hungry. But not to worry." She tipped her head. "You'll be fine. So long as you reach the castle before dark."

Then she was gone. Vanishing through the trees, the deep foliage swallowing her up.

Isabelle let out a long breath after she'd gone, feeling shaken. *Nonsense*, she told herself, heading down the path. *She's just a strange woman.*

Still. That didn't mean Isabelle wasn't in danger. Whether it was unfriendly villagers or the merciless winter weather—or wolves or curses or this "disgraced lord"—Isabelle knew she was risking a lot, coming here alone. She probably should have asked Prince Garrett for some soldiers to accompany her. Garrett, the crown prince of the Glen Kingdom, was Isabelle's closest friend (strange as that was, since Isabelle herself was a commoner). Garrett was also an adventurer. Searching for an abandoned castle in the Black Forest was just the sort of endeavor Garrett loved. He would have helped her in a heartbeat, had she asked.

But the girl who'd sent her the telegram—a servant at the castle—had insisted she come alone. And besides, this was a family matter. Estranged though they were, Ansel was family—the only family she had left.

Isabelle pressed on, following the scanty deer path through the wood. The ground beneath her feet grew soft and doughy, the untraveled path awash with fresh mud. Once or twice, the path almost disappeared, and Isabelle thought it was at an end. But then it appeared again, and she realized it had only been eaten by the forest—by the dense clusters of trees and overgrown bramble. As the hours passed, Isabelle cast uneasy glances overhead, looking for glimpses of sky through the trees. How much farther did this path go on, and how long left until dusk?

Finally—her relief so thick it clogged her throat—she came to the end of the path. Another three miles due north, the trapper had said, and she would reach the castle.

But she'd only gone about one mile when she heard it. She'd just slipped over a slick patch of mud, mumbling a curse as she caught herself. But her curse was drowned out by a long, keening howl—a howl that quivered through the air and ghosted past the back of Isabelle's neck.

Isabelle's breath snagged in her throat. *Wolves.*

Another howl sounded out, and before it was done, a second one, joining the first in an otherworldly symphony. Isabelle licked her cracked lips. The stillness that had come over her seeped through her bones, settling on the inside like a hardening lump of clay. Hardening into fear.

Those wolves sounded close. Much too close.

Isabelle turned around. She scanned the forest behind her, her gaze roving over the darkening wood.

And latched onto a pair of yellow eyes, smoldering like embers in the shadows.

Isabelle's breath froze in her chest.

She turned and ran through the woods, and the cries of the wolves raced after her.

2

BEAST

THE WOLVES HOWLED AS Isabelle tore through the forest, her chest tight with fear. Perhaps she'd imagined those yellow eyes, but she didn't dare slow her pace, not even to glance over her shoulder. Gelid air rushed at her as she ran, biting her chapped face and making her eyes water. But she didn't stop, not until she reached a clearing in the woods where the land ended in a sudden drop.

Isabelle panted, skidding over the frozen ground. She caught herself around the emaciated trunk of a scarred silver birch, the tree swaying as she lolled to the side. She finally tossed a glance behind her, scanning the trees, but she saw nothing. No yellow eyes. No wolves.

She didn't think she could go much further. Her legs burned, her throat was raw with cold—

Then she saw it.

A castle. A stone castle with narrow windows and pointed spires, just over a bridge spanning the rugged gorge before her. Like a mirage in the snowy white landscape.

The seat of the old Forest kings. Where her brother was being held prisoner.

A harsh wind gusted, dead leaves skittering over the forest floor. Isabelle shivered, though not from the cold. The castle stood stark and remote in the dead winter woods. It was like a dead thing itself, a desiccated ruin mocking the grandeur it once held. The Forest Kingdom had fallen over a century ago, long before Prince Garrett's great-grandfather led a host out of the woods and into the Glen Kingdom.

All that was left of that old kingdom were the people scattered throughout the Black Forest, in the villages and the wood. And this ruin of a castle. A cursed castle, if the rumors were true.

Standing here, shivering in the snow, Isabelle felt her *alone-ness* more than ever. A profound sense of disquiet slipped over her. The wind gusted again, icier now the sky was darkening. But still, Isabelle didn't move. She only gazed at the castle.

The gorge before her was not wide, but it looked steep, a jagged scar in the snow. The bridge spanning the gorge was dark wood, but stone pillars reinforced it, stretching down into the gully. It looked stable enough. And yet Isabelle stood, clutching her birch tree. Paralyzed by a fluttering in her chest—an eldritch *pitter-patter.* Like spider legs crawling over the tender walls of her heart.

Another howl rent the air. A chilling whine, like rusty hinges on a door.

Isabelle jumped away from her tree. Steeling herself against the ominous fluttering, she started across the clearing. As she took her first ungainly step onto the wooden bridge, yet another howl rang out behind her. Isabelle whipped around.

She did not imagine anything now.

A pair of yellow eyes stared at her from the shrouded woods.

Isabelle leapt into a run down the bridge. Her boots *thunked* against the solid wood, her shallow breaths so loud, they echoed inside her head from one ear to the other.

The bridge led beneath a stone archway, smeared black with lichen, and straight up to a broad wooden door gilded in silvered metal. Isabelle ran until she slammed into the door, half-hoping it would buckle open beneath her. But, of course, it did not.

"Come on." Isabelle beat at the door with both fists. "Come on, come *on*—"

Suddenly, the great door shuddered and swung open. Isabelle fell forward, her knees crashing into stone. She winced but lurched to her feet, her mind still full of wolves as she stumbled into an open courtyard.

There was a grating *squeal*, as startling as the wolves' cries. Isabelle whirled around. A silvery portcullis lowered from the stone arch in front of the open door. Isabelle leaned forward, her fear of the wolves dissipating as she took in the sheen of the portcullis. The metallic coating gleamed even in the fading daylight. Was it real silver? Or just painted to look that way? If so, the coat of paint was new, which seemed extravagant for a ruined old castle.

As the portcullis settled upon the courtyard, rattling in place, another long howl cut the air. Isabelle peered through the portcullis with unease. Though it stood between her and the wolves, she could not help but stare down the long stretch of bridge, looking for another glimpse of yellow eyes.

"Don't worry. It's only wolves."

Isabelle bit back a yelp and spun around.

Standing before her was a man. He was tall, as tall as Prince Garrett, and around the same age. He was fair like Garrett too, though his hair was a sandier, dirtier blond, and his eyes dark and penetrating. He stood with his hands clasped behind his back, his weight shifted lazily to one side. And yet there was something intimidating about him—as though his casual air was a pose. Like a wolf putting its victim at ease.

"Only regular wolves, I mean," the man clarified.

The oddity of this statement didn't reach Isabelle. She was too distracted by the sudden appearance of this man—though now she thought of it, someone must have lowered the portcullis. But there was something about him. Something that put Isabelle on guard.

Perhaps it was his face. Three deep scars were carved into his skin, running diagonally from left temple to the right side of his jaw. One of the scars nipped the corner of his eye, while the middle one cut a craggy groove through his lip. They were old scars, yet red all the same, as though too violent to heal.

Isabelle tried not to gawk at his scars. He was dressed like a hunter, in brown breeches and leather boots with soles made to be silent upon the forest floor. His single-breasted coat looked warm enough, though it was patched and ragged, as was the wool scarf wrapped around his neck, the ends tucked in like an imitation cravat.

"You must be Isabelle," the man said. "Ansel's sister."

"Yes. Are you—the lord of the castle?" Doubt colored Isabelle's words. Given this man's rough appearance, he didn't seem much like a lord, even a disgraced one.

The man snorted. "No. I'm not the *lord*." He didn't provide a name of his own. "I just work here."

"Oh." That made more sense. "Is he all right? My brother, I mean, not your lord. The telegram I received from...Ellery?...said he was sick. And that he'd landed himself in your dungeons."

"He's hanging on." This terse response was not very reassuring. But the hunter only glanced across the courtyard, unconcerned. "I don't suppose you want to get inside? It's cold out here."

It was a small courtyard, just as the castle itself was small. Two short turrets guarded the southwestern corner, the ramparts flanking them lined with stone gargoyles. The gargoyles were blackened by the same crusty growth that stained the entryway, their grimacing faces spotted and grimed. A single, lofty tower rose from the back of the castle like a coiled serpent.

Isabelle stepped carefully as they crossed the courtyard, for the flagstones beneath her feet wobbled, unseated by gobs of slimy moss. The castle seemed darker and more menacing as they approached the front doors, and Isabelle eyed it with deepening foreboding. It was a very old, very medieval structure, and in another time, she might have found it fascinating. But all she could think about now was Ansel, and where he might be in the bowels of this gothic place.

The hunter led her up a flight of broad steps into the castle. Isabelle found herself in a cavernous entrance hall, made more so by its stark emptiness, like a cave beneath a mountain. Old-fashioned candelabras, brassy and dull, sat in sconces carved into the stone walls, but only two were lit. Their flames capered, making shadows dance over the bare floor. Something loomed at the back of the hall, something monstrously huge. It wasn't until Isabelle's eyes adjusted to the dim light that she realized it was a grand staircase.

"You'll have to wait here," the hunter said. "You need to talk to the lord before you can see your brother. I'll get him, but you'll have a bit of a wait." He picked up his pace as he left her, his footsteps a whisper against the floor. "You're early," he tossed over his shoulder.

Isabelle gaped after him. *How could I be early? They sent me a telegram, and I came as soon as I could.* Which wasn't even all that soon; it had taken her nearly a month to come all this way. If there was some timetable she was meant to adhere to, she hadn't been informed of it.

With a groan, Isabelle dumped her pack onto the floor. It *thumped* and *clattered*, the noise ringing out in the hall. Her sore muscles begged for respite, but there was nowhere to sit. The hall was devoid of furnishings. Isabelle eyed the staircase, but it seemed so far away at the back of the hall...and so forbidding. She couldn't make out the top of the stairs; they seemed to lead up into a well of shadows.

So she stood, exhausted and alone, waiting. She would have plopped down on the floor if she'd had any confidence about getting up again. Drumming her fingers against her thighs, she cast an impatient glance down the corridor. She wondered how long she would be expected to wait for this *lord*, and as she wondered, her apprehension grew.

Isabelle felt as though she'd spent most of her life getting her brother out of trouble. Ever since he was a boy, he'd attracted it. Falling in with crowds too rough to handle, making stupid wagers and promises he couldn't keep, taking on jobs far beyond his skill set. And yet, Isabelle had never stopped caring about him. Even after they'd parted ways, her worry for him had not abated. It became a constant thing, a parasite she carried inside her, gnawing with questions. *Where is he? Is he all right? Is he hurt? Is he even alive?*

Now, for the first time in two and a half years, she had answers. But they had done nothing to banish that parasitic worry.

Why had Ansel come to this old ruin? What had he done to get himself thrown in the dungeons? Until now, Isabelle had not thought on that too much, weird as that might seem. Ansel was no stranger to trouble, after all. But now that she stood here, waiting and worrying, she wondered—who *was* this lord of the castle? What if Ansel hadn't done anything wrong? What if the "lord" was just a mad person or a criminal or—who knew what else?

Isabelle shifted her weight from one foot to the other. And if he *was* mad or criminal, what would this lord do to *her?* What if he threw her in a dungeon too?

A sudden *squeal* cut through the silence, the eerie noise reverberating throughout the castle. Isabelle jumped, looking around, but there was no one there. She waited another moment, wondering if that had been the hunter, passing through a creaking door on his way back here. But the hunter did not appear.

That decided Isabelle. The sooner she found Ansel—and the sooner they left—the better. She needed to find him now. She wasn't going to wait around for this lord.

Since dungeons were usually on the lower level of a castle, Isabelle crept around until she found a staircase—narrow, stone, and shrouded in shadow—leading below the ground floor. The staircase wasn't immediately apparent, closed off by a locked door, but Isabelle had the lock picked in a matter of minutes. She sent a silent thanks to Prince Garrett for teaching her such a skill, then peered dubiously down the staircase. It wasn't completely dark, and as Isabelle began the descent, she found there were flaming torches set in sconces on the walls. They were few and widely spaced apart, but Isabelle was grateful for them—not just for the light, but because their presence meant someone had been down here recently. Hopefully to feed and check on her brother.

The bottom of the stairs opened into a dank corridor. An iron candelabra hung over the passage, filled with thick candles, but the scant light was little comfort in the oppressive darkness. The walls down here were damp and spotted, giving off a fusty odor. The pervasive wetness was made worse by the icy chill. Isabelle's anxiety ballooned inside her, pressing against her lungs. She hoped Ansel had been given plenty of blankets, if he really was down here. *Someone* had to be down here, or why the torches, the candles?

Isabelle stood on tip-toe to take a candle from the candelabra, then ventured down the corridor. Trepidation tripped inside her, and it was only thought of Ansel that pushed her forward. By the small, uncertain light of her candle, she saw a row of prison cells lining the corridor, their bars rusted red and flaking like dried blood. But they were all open, all empty. "Ansel?" Isabelle called. She flinched at the sound of her own tinny voice. "Are you here? Ansel?"

There was no answer. Save for her words, echoing back as they bounced off the hollowed passages. *Ansel, Ansel, Ansel.*

She was on the verge of turning back when she spotted another corridor branching off to the right. As she lifted her candle, the tiny flame caught on something in the darkness, something that winked in the light. Isabelle stepped down the corridor and found another portcullis, smaller but otherwise very like the one in the courtyard. Not gilded in silver, Isabelle noted, as she ran a finger over the gate. It was painted bronze and not recently, she thought, feeling a rough spot where the paint had peeled away. The cold surface beneath was rough but durable. Solid iron.

The portcullis stretched from wall to wall, barring the way. Isabelle looked left and right. She spotted the lever quickly, down on the floor on her left. She was surprised to find the lever's system was built on clockwork gears. That sort of mechanism had only become common in the last century, and this castle had been abandoned longer than that.

She wound the lever round until she heard it *click*. The gears whirred to life, and Isabelle straightened, backing up, as the portcullis began to rise.

It was several seconds before it settled at the top with a heavy *clank*. Isabelle cringed, casting a glance behind her, but she heard no footsteps, no voices. She turned back as the gears slowed to a halt, their whirring dying away, and she stood before the open corridor, doused in silence and darkness.

For a moment, she did not move. The darkness was pitch black, the silence deep and beckoning. Silence broken only by Isabelle's skittering breaths, heavy in this moldering dungeon. Her stomach churned like a ship being tossed about in a storm. Still, she stepped forward, stretching an arm out into the black void.

She nearly dropped her candle when her fingers smashed into something solid, layered in sludge and grit. Her stomach clenched. But it was only a door, an iron door she hadn't seen by her candlelight. How odd that it was right here, not two paces from the portcullis.

Isabelle tried the latch and found it unlocked. Setting her candle on the floor, she pushed the heavy door with both hands, but it didn't budge. Turning, Isabelle leaned her whole body into the door, the cold of the iron seeping through her wool coat. She shoved with all her weight. With a jarring screech, the door opened slowly, inch by inch, the bottom scraping against the stone floor. Isabelle found herself holding her breath as the door gave way, her lips clamped shut and her chest tighter than ever.

But it was all for naught. On the other side of the door was only more corridor, more stone, thrown in shadow like the rest of the dungeon.

Isabelle's shoulders slumped. She felt weary with disappointment. Strangely, it wasn't so cold on this side of the door, but danker than ever, the air laden with a stench like wet dog.

Wiping a shaky hand over her brow, Isabelle bent to retrieve her candle. She couldn't understand it. Why all these locked doors and gates for nothing but dark, empty corridors? Raising her candle, she swept one last glance from corner to corner, surveying the darkness. But there was nothing.

She turned away, lowering her candle.

And out of the corner of her eye, something shifted at the end of the corridor.

Isabelle froze. Slowly, dread stealing her breath, she turned back.

Shadows rolled in the darkness. Isabelle caught another whiff of that ghastly stench. The shadows swelled, coalescing into something huge and hulking.

Something *alive*.

Isabelle watched with widening eyes as a hideous, terrifying, impossible *beast* emerged like a nightmare come to life.

It was enormous. Sort of wolf-like, but at the same time, *nothing* like a wolf. Nothing like any creature Isabelle had ever seen. It was entirely covered in fur like a wolf—black, knotted fur, tufts of it sprouting from between its pointed ears. But it stood upright on hind legs, its haunches as thick as tree trunks and corded with muscle. Its front legs hung unnaturally at its sides, jointed more like human arms than the legs of an animal. And where a wolf would have had paws, knobby fingers protruded instead, ending in razor-sharp claws.

Those claws *click-clacked* along the stone floor as the creature stalked towards her. The breadth of its shoulders was broad, sinew rippling and bunching as it came closer. Most terrifying of all was its long snout, lined with glistening, dripping, jagged teeth.

But it wasn't the teeth that drew Isabelle's gaze, nor its matted fur. It was its eyes. Yellow eyes like twin beacons, emanating with a predatory gleam. It wasn't hunger Isabelle glimpsed in those eyes. It was a visceral, *human* rage.

Fear crawled up Isabelle's airway, strangling her. She was so transfixed by the monstrous creature that it was within three paces of her before she thought to run. She stumbled back, grasping for the iron door.

The beast bared its teeth, let out a blood-curdling growl, and leapt at her.

3

IMPRISONED

ISABELLE THREW HERSELF PAST the iron door and spun, the sole of her boot skidding against the stone floor. She heaved her entire body into the door, her shoulder laid flat against it, all her muscles straining. But the heavy door squealed in protest, moving far too slowly.

She'd only gotten it halfway shut when the beast leapt for her. Its monstrous front paws crashed into the other side of the door, pushing it back into Isabelle, and its long snout burst through the opening.

Then its jaw clamped over her hand, and dripping canines pierced the back of her wrist.

Isabelle screamed. Out of pain, she supposed, though she didn't really feel pain. In that shocking, agonizingly long moment, Isabelle saw the beast's teeth puncture her skin. She watched them sink through her flesh like curved blades, but she felt...removed, as though it was happening to someone else, but no, *that was her hand* and *that was her skin.*

But she couldn't *feel* anything. And that disconnect, and the madness inherent in it, was the most horrifying thing she had ever experienced.

It seemed to last forever. Then the beast released her, ripping free, rearing its head back. Isabelle fell onto the floor in a daze. Her surroundings swam, tilting one way, then the other. The corners of her vision grew foggy.

The sight of the beast launching itself at the door again pierced through the fog. Its claws scraped at the door as it scrabbled to get through. By the guttering light of her fallen candle, Isabelle glimpsed its glinting teeth, stained red with her blood.

Sobbing for breath, Isabelle rolled and tried to climb to her feet. Behind her, the beast snarled, the sound echoing in her ears alongside her pounding heartbeat. With a ragged whimper, Isabelle summoned all the strength she had and lurched to her feet. She staggered, forcing herself to move, move, *move*. Slipping beneath the portcullis, she caught herself on the wall before she could fall again.

Whipping around, she fumbled for the gate's lever, but her hands shook so badly, she could barely grip it. Blood from the wound in her wrist dribbled down her hand, slickening her palm. She cast a feverish glance from the lever to the iron door, watching in mounting terror as the beast slammed the door open. It *banged* off the stone wall.

Isabelle's fear was so large, she could feel it burning up her throat. The taste of it was fetid in the back of her mouth. She had *become* it, this animalistic fear—a prey's frenetic desire to escape. Choking on another scream, Isabelle stumbled back, forgetting the portcullis, forgetting the lever. The beast's eyes fixed on her, and it dropped to all fours to run with full speed—

Isabelle turned to flee.

And a knife whistled past her head, so close she thought it nicked her ear.

Isabelle gaped at the man before her. It was the scarred hunter, the one who had escorted her into the castle. His arm was stretched out before him.

A resounding *crash* sounded out, and Isabelle jumped, her heart lurching into her throat. The iron portcullis had fallen, smashing into place, and when Isabelle glanced up, she saw the wire connecting it to the lever had been cut. The hunter's knife lay on the floor where it had fallen after slicing through the wire.

"I should have thought of that," Isabelle said dumbly, remembering the knife tucked down her boot. Her mind was still fogged with fear, her thoughts a jumble.

Another thundering *crash* startled her. The beast had slammed into the portcullis on the other side. It rattled beneath the weight of the monster but held fast.

Isabelle stared at the trapped beast. She felt ensnared by its yellow-eyed gaze, locked onto her with malice.

"What are you doing down here?"

Isabelle whirled to face the hunter. His dark eyes viewed her with as much hostility as the beast. His coat had been removed, revealing a rough-spun shirt and an ash gray vest over his breeches.

"Well?" he snapped.

Isabelle gulped a breath. Then another. As her chest began to loosen, she became aware of her thumping heart, her shuddering body, her *throbbing* hand. That fuzzy fog encroached on her again, and she blinked hard, fighting the woozy feeling. She wasn't sure how much time passed before she remembered how to speak.

"I'm...I was...I was looking for—" She broke off, the enormity of what had just happened sinking in. Flinging a hand at the snarling beast, she demanded, "What *is* that?"

"A beast," the hunter said.

"Oh, right." A breathy, hysterical noise escaped Isabelle's lips. "Of course. Why didn't I realize. A beast." Isabelle clasped her forearm above the bleeding wound. As much to keep from shaking as to staunch the pain. "*Why* is there a mutant *beast* in this castle!"

The hunter rolled his eyes. *Rolled his eyes.* As though she was a silly girl, as though she had asked a ridiculous question. Without answering, he stepped past her to retrieve his knife. Being in such proximity with the beast and its snapping teeth didn't seem to faze him.

But when he turned back, his brow was furrowed. "Did..." His eyes latched onto her injured hand. "You're bleeding." Far from sounding concerned, his tone was accusatory, as though she'd stuck her hand into the beast's jaw on purpose. He closed the distance between them in three swift steps, taking her arm in a rough grasp.

"The beast did this?" The hunter's gaze was harsh, made more so by the grisly scars crossing his face. "Did he bite you?"

"Yes." Isabelle tugged, trying to break free, but the hunter's grip was like iron. "Only a little." She peered at the wound, trying to gauge how bad it was. The blood was already drying, the flow staunched. The pain was persistent, but she'd suffered worse. "It doesn't look too bad. Good thing, too, there are lots of veins in the back of—"

"It definitely bit you?" the hunter interrupted. "It didn't claw at you, scratch you? It bit you?"

"*Yes.*" Isabelle gave another tug just as the man's grip went slack on her. She stumbled, barely catching herself.

The hunter's gaze was preoccupied. "Right, well. We should get it cleaned. Bandaged." Without another glance for the beast, the hunter took her by the shoulder, steering her away.

Isabelle did not appreciate this manhandling, but since her legs were turning to jelly and her vision still swimmy, she didn't protest. She didn't think she could walk in a straight line right now.

"You never said what you were doing down here," the hunter said curtly.

"I was looking for my brother." Isabelle cast an appraising look at the hunter. She did not understand how he could be so calm, but if he was, she would be too. "And if he's down here with that beast, then you're—"

"He's not down here," the hunter said, as though this should have been obvious. "He's being kept in the tower. We don't keep anyone down here."

"Well, I can see why. Your dungeons are reserved for ferocious beasts, apparently!"

"Beast. Singular. There's only one."

Isabelle jerked to a halt, forcing the hunter to stop too. She turned to stare at the beast through the portcullis. It had turned away from them, a lumbering shadow in the gloom. Now it paced on all fours, vibrating with agitation. Every bit the caged beast.

"Look." The hunter's tone was brusque. "Do you want to get that hand bandaged or not?"

Isabelle turned away. She didn't say a word as she followed the hunter down the corridor and up the narrow stairwell.

Isabelle tried not to squirm as the blond girl before her inspected her hand. "It's fairly shallow," the girl said. "Just broke the skin."

"Yes, I'm very lucky," Isabelle said in a droll tone.

The girl, Ellery, looked at her. She was around fourteen, Isabelle guessed, though her sober air made her seem older. She wore a dark, stiff skirt and matching blouse. Her wispy hair was pulled into a bun at the nape of her neck.

"I wouldn't say that," Ellery replied. "Luckier not to have been bitten at all." There was something unnerving about her unblinking blue eyes. "Anyway, you'll need a few stitches. I can root up some ether, if you like."

"Don't bother. I've had stitches without it."

Despite this, the needle piercing her skin still hurt like all the oldest fairy stones in the deepest pit of hell. Isabelle sat at the edge of her chair, lips clamped shut against the whimpers creeping up her throat.

The hunter had brought her to Ellery's room on the second floor of the castle. It was a nice room, for a servant—large and well-furnished. Given what she'd heard about this "lord," Isabelle was surprised he allowed his servants a room like this, with a featherbed covered in quilts and furs, and a gilded gold mirror over a chiffonier. The room smelled faintly of dried lavender.

Ellery finished her stitches. Isabelle slumped back, her body trembling with the imprint of pain.

"So." Isabelle expelled a breath as Ellery unwound a length of bandage. "Why is there a beast locked in your dungeons?"

Ellery's gaze flicked her way. For a moment, Isabelle thought the girl would not answer. But then she said, her voice toneless,

"The beast used to roam the forest around here. It was a bit of a problem. We managed to catch it."

"Hmm." A succinct explanation—with a few holes. "How, by the Gift, did you catch that monster?"

"Klaus caught it." Ellery noticed her puzzled expression. "Klaus is the man who brought you up here. He's our hunter. He grew up in the forest."

"So, he caught the beast?"

"He lured it back here." Ellery took Isabelle's hand in hers, her ministrations gentle and practiced. She lay the end of the bandage flat over Isabelle's palm and began to wind it around. "And he devised the portcullis in the dungeons to hold it."

"But why not just kill it?" Isabelle asked.

"It was Klaus's decision. He's a bit funny about killing wild things."

"I thought you said he was a hunter."

"He kills to eat. Not for sport."

"Nor, apparently, for self-preservation," Isabelle muttered. "So—the scars on Klaus's face. Are those from the beast?"

"Yes. *He* was lucky. He almost lost an eye."

And still decided not to kill it. Isabelle sent Ellery a sidelong glance. There was certainly more to that story, but Isabelle had other concerns right now. "You're the one who sent me the telegram. About my brother."

"Yes. He was a bit ill when he first arrived. I don't think he'd had any shelter or good food in a while."

"That must have been a month or more ago." Isabelle tried to moderate her tone. Whatever had happened to Ansel, it was not this girl's fault. There was no point taking her indignation out on her. "Is he better now? And why was he locked up?"

"He's...not sick anymore." Ellery evaded her gaze.

Before Isabelle could question her further, the hunter, Klaus, appeared in the doorway. He made a grim specter, his scarred face unsmiling. "I can take you to your brother now. The lord will meet us up there. Is she good to go?" he asked Ellery.

"Just about." Ellery secured the bandage around Isabelle's hand.

"And?" Klaus demanded.

Ellery looked at him. Isabelle could not tell what exchanged between them, but *something* did. Something significant. "And everything looks all right," was all Ellery said.

Klaus grunted. "Come on, then."

Isabelle followed Klaus down a maze of corridors. She matched the hunter's brisk pace, but her mind was racing. The haze of shock had seeped away, and now that she felt more like herself, she was beginning to process everything. Process it, but not understand it. Because nothing added up. None of it made sense.

Well, almost none of it. Out of the deep well of her subconscious, Klaus's first words to Isabelle floated back to her. What he'd said in the courtyard when she arrived. *It's only wolves. Regular wolves.*

Now she understood. Wolves seemed tame in comparison to that savage beast.

"Does this lord of yours have a name?" Isabelle asked. The floor beneath her feet was the same dark stone as the rest of the castle, as were the walls. Candelabras lined the corridors, but they were sparsely lit, adding little warmth to the gloomy castle.

"Not one he cares to share with most people," Klaus said. "He's a very private person."

I'm a private person too, Isabelle thought, *and I don't go around making people call me 'lord.'*

Despite the twisting corridors, it didn't take long to reach the tower. Climbing it, however, was another matter. The stairwell, dark save for Klaus's gear-bulb lantern, rounded up and up in an endless spiral. It was a good twenty minutes before they reached the top, where they faced a stout door. Isabelle heaved a breath, her legs quivering. Setting his lantern aside, Klaus reached for a set of keys at his waist and quickly got the door open.

Isabelle's trembling vanished in an instant. She rushed into the tower chamber. The air inside was glacial, the room plunged in darkness. There were two barred windows in the room, hardly more than slits, but night had fallen and the sky was overcast, so no light shone in. Klaus stepped in behind her with his lantern, and that was when Isabelle spotted the lump in the corner. *Ansel.*

Her brother barely stirred as she hurried towards him. He was wrapped in a thick, tan canvas from head to toe, only his face visible. Even still, he shivered. His eyes were squeezed shut as though he were sleeping, but he didn't look very restful. His brown face was tinged with gray, and his thick, dark hair, which had grown into tight curls, was matted with sweat. "Ansel?" Isabelle crouched down on the stone floor, reaching out to take his shoulder. "Can you hear me? It's Isabelle."

Ansel's eyes fluttered, but he didn't respond. Isabelle pushed the canvas back so she could feel for a pulse. His skin was cold and sticky. She noticed a white bandage peeking out beneath his wool shirt. Pushing the canvas back further, she pulled his collar down as far as she could. The entire right side of his chest had been wrapped, and recently, for the bandage was white and clean.

"What happened to him?" Isabelle turned to Klaus. "Ellery said he'd been ill. So why is he bandaged like this? Was he injured?"

Klaus folded his arms over his chest. He seemed as concerned about Ansel as he'd been about her in the dungeons—which was to say, not at all. "He was ill when he first got here. That was over a month ago. The lord let him stay, and Ellery tended him until he was better. That's when he decided to steal from us—the silverware, some candlesticks—and made off in the night."

Isabelle closed her eyes. Stupid, *stupid* Ansel, but she didn't expect any better. Still, that didn't explain the injury, nor excuse these appalling conditions. "If you're telling me your lord did this to him, or *you*—"

"We didn't touch him," Klaus said. "He ran into...some wolves. In the forest." Isabelle noticed his hesitation, but if it was because he was lying, she couldn't tell. "They attacked him. He managed to get back to the castle, but they mauled him pretty badly."

"And your lord *locked him up?* Even though he was injured—"

"Ellery tended his wound," Klaus interrupted, "and she changes the bandage every day. He's much better than he was."

"Yes, he looks fine!" Isabelle erupted. "That's why he's weak and shivering! It's bloody freezing in here, and he hasn't even been given a bed or proper blankets!"

Suddenly, the tower door *banged* open, so hard that it rebounded off the stone wall.

Isabelle jumped, startled, and was satisfied to see Klaus jump too. She hadn't heard footsteps on the stairs, but maybe that was because she'd been shouting. She glanced around.

A dark figure filled the doorway—literally *filled* it, the form tall and burly. The lord of the castle, Isabelle presumed. She found herself struck silent as he stepped into the tower. He was taller than Klaus and broad across the chest. He wore a long, thick overcoat; the black garment hung from his shoulders like bat wings. A hood, attached beneath the collar of his coat, covered his head, giving him the look of an executioner.

Isabelle could make out very little of the man's face beneath the hood—not a strand of hair, not a hint of eyes or nose. All she could see was the edge of a square jaw. He was like a wraith, some bringer of death and doom, cloaked and shrouded.

But that was ridiculous. He was just a man. His coming dressed like this was probably an attempt to scare her, making himself into a faceless monster. Unfortunately for him, Isabelle had dealt with *real* monsters. She stood to face him, squaring her shoulders.

"Are you the lord of this castle?" she asked, just as the hooded man said, "I am the lord of this castle."

A confused, awkward silence followed this exchange, as it does when two people accidentally speak at the same time.

"Right. Well..." Isabelle considered asking his name, then decided she didn't care. Better to get to the point. "Look, you have to let my brother go." She gestured towards Ansel. "He's not well; he needs a proper doctor. I know he stole from you, but—"

"I don't *have* to do anything," was the lord's reply. Isabelle was surprised by the smooth timbre of his voice. She had expected something harsher, uglier. "I am the lord of this castle."

"Yes. You said that already. So?"

Klaus, leaning against the wall, gave a soft snort.

"*So,*" the lord said, sounding irritated, "my word is law here. And I say your brother cannot leave."

"But—"

"I understand you saw the beast down in the dungeons." The lord turned from her, the edge of his coat whipping back.

"Yes. So?"

Without looking her way, he raised a hand to point at her. "He bit you?"

"Yes. But no need to worry. I'm fine."

"I wasn't worried."

"Of course you weren't," Isabelle said. If the lord wasn't worried about her ailing brother wasting away in this icy tower, she didn't expect for a second he would care about her. "Look, what does this have to do with Ansel? Will you let him go or not?"

The lord turned to face her—still hooded, still hidden. "I will not." He clasped his hands behind his back. "And you aren't going anywhere either."

"What?" Isabelle was sure she must have heard him wrong. "But—you can't keep me here! I haven't done anything! You can't just take me prisoner!"

"I didn't say you were a prisoner," the lord retorted.

"If I can't leave, then I'm a prisoner." Isabelle's words seeped through gritted teeth.

The lord waved a dismissive hand. "You don't have to stay locked up in here. You can have a room in the castle."

"I don't want a room!" Isabelle burst out, panic edging her words. She could not believe this. She could not *believe* this. The audacity of this *coward*, hiding behind his hood. He wouldn't even face her. Before she could consider what she was doing, she strode forward, coming to stand before the lord. "You can't keep me here. I've done nothing!"

"You saw the beast," the lord snapped. He stepped towards her too, closing the distance between them. Isabelle caught her breath as he towered over her, but she refused to back down. She only tilted her head to be sure the full force of her glare caught him. "I can't let you leave here to go spreading tales about him."

"Spreading tales?" Isabelle echoed, the pitch of her voice rising. "*Spreading tales?* Why would I do that? Who would I tell? I don't care about your stupid beast!"

The lord didn't respond right away. He let silence hang between them, broken only by Ansel's labored breathing, by the scuff of Klaus's boot against the floor. Then the lord said, "That beast has caused a lot of trouble for the people around here. For the villagers and those who live in the forest. Some of them would like *very much* to get their hands on it. So." He inhaled, his broad shoulders heaving. "I can't let you leave."

"But I *wouldn't tell anyone.* I swear by—"

"I don't care what promises you make. I trusted your brother and regretted it. I won't make the same mistake with you." Ignoring her gaping face, the lord turned and strode towards the door. "Stay in the tower with your brother or let Klaus give you a room. It makes no difference to me. But you are staying here. *Forever.*" And with that ominous pronouncement, he vanished into the darkness, slamming the door behind him.

4

TRANSIENT

G ARRETT PUSHED OPEN THE doors to Briar's quarters, bouncing with exuberance. "Briar!" he called, stepping into the parlor and sparing a wink for Briar's maid, Nell.

"Your Highness!" Nell protested. "She's not awake!"

"Of course she's not awake. It's not even noon. Briar!" Garrett called again, throwing open the door to Briar's bedroom. He stopped in the doorway, allowing his eyes to adjust to the darkness. Not a single gear-bulb lamp was lit, and heavy brocade curtains were pulled shut over the large window across the room.

Briar lay in the center of her massive four-poster bed. Presumably. All that was visible of her were a few strands of pale hair, sticking out from beneath a plush, burgundy coverlet and a mound of pillows, stacked around the princess like a barrier. Briar had trouble sleeping and used everything at her disposal to shut out as much light and sound as possible.

"Briar," Garrett said cheerfully. He crossed the room and yanked open the curtains. Pale sunlight spilled into the cold room, casting a thin sheen over everything. "I know you're awake." He lowered himself onto the broad bed. "I have some news!"

Some muffled grunting was the only reply. Then the mound of pillows began to shift, like a squirming snake disturbing a field of grass. The fat, velvet pillow on top of the pile tumbled to the side, and a second later, half of Briar's face appeared in the opening. Her gray eyes were narrowed to slits. "Are rotting corpses attacking the city?"

"No."

"Are you dying of your poisonous corpse wound?"

Garrett considered, absently resting a hand on his left shoulder—over the wound in question. "Not at the moment, no."

"Is the castle on fire?" Briar's eyes turned baleful in the shadow of her coverlet.

Garrett summoned his most devilish smile, knowing it would infuriate her. "No."

"Then go away," Briar groaned, "and leave me alone. For the next two hours."

"I didn't say it was *bad* news." Garrett pulled another pillow off her. "And I can't leave you alone, not unless you don't want me to say goodbye."

This caught Briar's attention. "You're leaving? For what? The hunting trip?"

"Yes, the hunting trip." Garrett nodded. "That's not the news I have though. This is much more exciting. So are you coming out of there, or must I drag you out of bed?"

Briar glowered. She pulled the last of the pillows away and sat up sluggishly. She looked terrible. Nobody really looked their best when they first woke up, but Briar looked especially terrible. The dark, purplish circles beneath her eyes were at their most prominent, like twin bruises taking up half of her face. The rest of her complexion—where she was not *actually* bruised, like the greenish mottling at her temple or the black imprints around her neck—was as pale as a fresh corpse.

Of course, that was not unusual for Briar. Given that she was, sort of, half a corpse. Or maybe one-third corpse. Thanks to the fairy curse that had plagued her and the rest of her kingdom.

Briar tilted her head, stretching out her neck. "I feel like a train ran over me," she mumbled. "I hate you. I hope you know that."

Garrett grinned, but he could not suppress a tiny twinge at her words. Not because she "hated" him; Garrett knew she did not. Or, well, if she hated him in this moment, it would pass. It was just that Garrett, hearing the words *I hate you*, could not help but think of the words *I love you*.

Words he was becoming more and more certain about when it came to Briar. Only, he hadn't said it yet. Neither had she. Garrett had no idea if she actually did. Love him.

Still, he wasn't about to bring that up now. He was leaving for his hunting trip today and would be gone for six weeks—longer, if the snows were bad in the Black Forest. Still grinning, Garrett reached into his pocket for his peace offering. "Don't hate me. I brought you breakfast." He opened his gloved palm to reveal what he'd brought.

A dead mouse.

Briar looked from him to the mouse, then back to him. Her expression was unamused. "You're hilarious."

"Thanks for saying so."

"You should have brought me a live one."

Garrett made a face. "You don't *really* eat live animals, do you?"

"Wouldn't you like to know?" Before Garrett could reply, Briar plucked the dead mouse from his hand. And before Garrett could protest, she opened her jaws wide and lowered the critter into her mouth by the tail.

"Agh!" Garrett leapt from the bed. "I was only joking! I didn't mean for you to actually eat it!"

Briar couldn't respond since she had a whole mouse in her mouth. She merely opened her eyes wide in an innocent expression and bit down with a *crunch*.

Garrett gaped. "Really? The whole mouse? What do you do with the *bones?*"

Briar twisted her lips and spat a tiny bone into the palm of her hand.

"Oh, stars." Garrett spun around to face the window. "I can't watch this."

Briar finished the mouse within a few seconds—*that quickly?* Garrett thought with a shudder—and at once looked the better for it, a bit of color coming into her cheeks. She also seemed in better spirits, for she beamed as he turned around.

"That was disgusting," Garrett told her. "I hope you know that."

"I'm a disgusting sort of person." Briar didn't seem a bit offended. "But then, as I recall, you decided you didn't much mind that."

Garrett smiled. Weird as it was, he didn't. Briar and the rest of her kingdom had been cursed to become rotting, living corpses. They'd put a stop to it before the curse could do much to Briar—or at least, Briar had put a stop to it, defeating the dark fairy who'd spun the curse. But there were lingering aftereffects, such as the bruising, the insomnia, and the need for raw flesh to keep her energy up.

"I don't mind." Garrett sat down on the bed, a little closer than he'd been before. "But don't expect me to kiss you after that."

Briar's eyes twinkled, and then she got serious. "So. What is your news, then?"

"Ah." Garrett leaned back. "Well, I haven't heard it from my father yet, but I heard from his secretary. He's agreed to authorize a commission for you to work on the steam-engineered vehicle."

This news elicited exactly the reaction Garrett had expected. Briar's eyes grew wide, her face shining with elation. Like she'd been lit up inside with ten gear-bulbs. "Are you serious? You aren't serious!" She clutched at Garrett's arm. "I get *my own* commission? *Really?*"

"Yes, really." Garrett winced—Briar's grip was quite strong—but he smiled too. "You're not the only one, of course. Some scientist is coming up from the Desert Kingdom with his own devices, and my father has a couple of others who have worked for him before—"

"I don't care!" Briar released him, and Garrett sucked in a silent breath of relief. "My design will be the most effective anyway."

"Of course."

"Although I'll have to get some idea what the man from the Desert Kingdom is cooking up—they've invented all sorts of things no one has even thought of anywhere else. The key is going to be in the navigation—without clockwork, or rather, with the added use of a steam-powered engine, cams won't be enough to direct the vehicle, but the idea is to move around freely off tracks or cables—"

"I don't see what's wrong with a self-propelled carriage."

"They're too slow, of course." Briar waved a dismissive hand. "These vehicles will be able to run as fast as a train!"

"They will? But how will you control it?"

Briar frowned at him. "That's what I was just talking about."

"Oh." Garrett spared her an affable smile. "Well, you can explain it all to my father later. I'm afraid I have to go—" He glanced out the window, where the sun sat high in the hazy sky. "It's nearly noon. We've got to be on our way if we're going to make it to Colne by nightfall." He rose to his feet, stretching his arms over his head.

"Well." Briar plucked at a stray thread in her coverlet. "I'll see you in a couple of months, then."

Garrett's throat tightened as he looked down at her. He hadn't spent more than a few days away from Briar since she'd come home to Glen Castle with him. Of course, she'd probably hardly notice he was gone, with all she had to occupy her. Briar was easily distracted by her work. Just as Garrett was easily distracted by adventure.

He had a feeling, though, that he would feel her absence keenly over the next several weeks.

He cleared his throat. "Well, I meant what I said. I'm not kissing you. You have mouse breath."

Briar threw a pillow at him, but she smiled. "Be careful. I'll miss you."

Garrett blinked. Maybe that shouldn't have surprised him, but it did. Briar was not one for spontaneous expressions of feeling. "I'll miss you too."

He left Briar's quarters with far less enthusiasm than when he'd entered, though the thought of being on the road cheered him. Remaining in the castle for nearly three months was a record for Garrett. But then, as much as he still enjoyed a little danger, it didn't drive his entire existence anymore.

He stepped out onto a balcony off the main corridor, over-looking the courtyard below. A glance over the stone railing showed him the five soldiers he'd picked to accompany him were ready and waiting, though redheaded Evans was struggling with a strap on his pack. Before he could head down to join them, however, someone appeared on his right and swept him a bow. "Pardon, Your Highness." It was his father's steward, Magan, a short, stout man with graying hair. "Your father the king would like to see you before you go. He's in his study."

"All right," Garrett said, hiding his surprise. He'd had break-fast with his father this morning and said his goodbyes then. What could he want now?

His father's study was in a square tower located off the central courtyard. It was a large room built from the same gleaming marble and warm mahogany much of the castle boasted, with a pale, vaulted ceiling above. A round window let in some daylight from the courtyard, filtered through paned glass, though on a cold, cloudy day like today, it was scant light. Two gear-bulb lamps and a crackling fire in the hearth were all that lit the rest of the room, leaving it dim. Still, Garrett had always found the room more cozy than ominous, the scent of mingled smoke and leather both familiar and comforting.

Garrett's father, Victor, King of the Glen Kingdom, stood behind his massive desk, studying some reports. He was a tall man of a height with Garrett, and his strong, widely set shoulders lent him a powerful demeanor, even with his flint gray hair. He had a stern face, though he bore laugh lines that spoke of the buoyant youth he had been. Garrett had known his father to laugh and enjoy himself, but he had a better sense of when to put the smiles away than Garrett did.

"Ah, Garrett." The king glanced up as Garrett shut the door. "Come in, son. I know you want to be on your way, but there's something I'd like to discuss before you go."

"All right." Garrett slipped into an opulent chair opposite his father, slouching a little.

His father remained standing, his face cast in shadow. He wore a dust-colored frock coat and matching waistcoat with a crimson necktie—formal day dress, as was expected of him in the castle. Garrett was more dressed down, but only because he was leaving for his trip. "I wasn't going to bring this up now," his father said. He didn't look at Garrett, frowning over his report. "I didn't want to trouble you before your trip. But perhaps it would be best if you have some time away from...the castle...to think on this matter."

"Sounds serious."

King Victor put his report down. "It's about Princess Briar."

Garrett placed a steadying hand on his knee, feeling jittery. "What about her? This isn't about her commission for the motor vehicle, is it, because Magan told me about that and—"

"No, no. I'm giving her the commission." The king lowered himself into his wingback chair. "Look, Garrett. This is hardly the first time you've brought someone into the castle needing a home or sanctuary. It's not unusual for you to go picking up strays, we both know that."

Garrett suppressed a smile. His father sounded vaguely exasperated, but "taking in strays" was something Garrett would never be ashamed of. He traveled a lot, and sometimes, he came across people who needed help—and what good was a prince if he couldn't help people? Though Briar was hardly a stray. She might have abdicated her right to her throne, but she was still a princess of the Mountain Kingdom.

"But it has not escaped my notice," his father went on, "that things are different this time. With regards to how you feel about this particular stray."

Garrett wrinkled his brow. He wasn't sure why his father was being so coy. Yes, Garrett had feelings for Briar, but his father was well aware of that. It wasn't as though they'd been hiding it.

Garrett asked delicately, "What's your point?"

His father asked, "Exactly how serious are you about Princess Briar?"

Garrett tried not to squirm. It wasn't that he was uncomfortable with these kinds of questions—well, he was, but he was used to them. He was the crown prince, and as such, his romantic interests could never be his own business. The trouble was, Garrett didn't know how to answer the question. Was he serious about Briar? Well, yes, there was no question about that. Did he see a future with her? That was more difficult to answer. He was serious about Briar. But he wasn't sure how serious she was about *him*.

"I'm—I mean—I *like* her," Garrett fumbled. "Obviously. You know that."

"Are you thinking of marrying her?"

Another expected question, given who he was. But still, it startled him. "I—not really. I don't mean I *don't* want to marry her. I just haven't really thought about it. I've only known her all of three months—"

"Yes, I know," his father interrupted. "I also have it on good authority that you often sneak into her quarters at all hours of the night."

Garrett's jaw dropped open. "That's not—it's not what you think."

"Then what is it?"

"Briar doesn't sleep well."

"I'm aware of that." His father's face gave a sour twist. "Never see the girl before noon."

"She doesn't sleep well, and—she has nightmares." Garrett was simplifying. Briar's troubles with sleep were due to her corpse condition. But she was also afraid to sleep during certain hours of the night. Because the djinn that had used her for eighty-two years—that had fed off her life force—could do so again. He'd pledged not to, but Briar didn't take him at his word any more than Garrett did. "Sometimes, I keep her company. And not *that* kind of company," he added hastily. "We just talk. That's all." Well, sometimes, they did a bit more than talk, but it never went further than a few kisses.

"I see," the king said.

"How did you know anyway?" Garrett prided himself on his sneaking skills. "You've had Magan spying on me, haven't you?"

"Garrett, please don't play the victim." His father rubbed a hand over his temple. "It's not my intention to police your private life. But who and when you marry is of great importance to the kingdom."

"Well, what if I do marry her? Is there a problem with that? Is it because her kingdom is a ruin? I know you agreed to a marriage with Snow because of the trade agreements we could get from the Mariner Kingdom—"

"Garrett," his father cut in, "I'm not opposed to a marriage between you and Briar because of her kingdom. In fact, capitalizing on an alliance with her people—now they're rejoining the world—would be a shrewd move. Don't think I haven't thought on that." His father's eyes gleamed with interest.

But Garrett wasn't fooled. He leaned forward. "Yet you *are* opposed to it?"

His father sighed. He clasped his hands atop his desk and looked Garrett in the eye. "I like the girl well enough," he said, in that blunt way of his. "She has a good head on her shoulders, and as independent as she may be, she doesn't go gallivanting around the countryside in riding leathers like Snow did."

Garrett stifled a snort. Briar wore gowns in the castle, but if his father thought she'd wear a dress to go "gallivanting" around the countryside, he had another think coming. "Then what's the problem?"

"The problem is her...condition."

Garrett frowned. He supposed that should have occurred to him, but then, he was so used to Briar's "condition" that he didn't consider it a problem. Still, he thought he knew what his father meant. Briar did what she could to cover up her mottled skin for social events, but she still drew some stares. Not that Briar cared—sometimes, Garrett thought she rather liked weirding people out.

"You're concerned what people will think of her," Garrett deduced.

"No, not really. I've no patience for idiots who judge a person based on their appearance. If people don't like her, they can deal with that on their own time."

"Well, at least we agree on that."

"Garrett." His father's voice turned sober. "I'm concerned what her condition means for her from a medical standpoint." When Garrett turned a confused look on him, the king went on, "I've spoken to the court physician. He seems to think, from what he's gathered about Princess Briar's condition, that she may not be able to have children."

Garrett stared at him. Well. Oh. "You spoke with the court physician about that."

"Yes."

Garrett had never thought to ask any physician anything of the sort. But then, it really wasn't his business. And it really wasn't his father's business either. "I don't suppose *Briar* has spoken with the physician about this." Garrett didn't bother to contain the ire in his tone. "Only, it would seem more her concern than yours, wouldn't it?"

"I am sure he will speak to her about it." The king sounded unrepentant. "And I'm sure he will refer her to a specialist who can give her a more determined diagnosis."

"And in the meantime," Garrett retorted, "why are we even discussing this?"

"You know very well why, Garrett," his father snapped. "You are the crown prince. You will be king one day, and you have to produce an heir!"

"I am *your* heir," Garrett pointed out, "and not by way of the woman who was your wife."

His father snorted. "I never planned for that, and you know it. Are you saying you could marry Briar and look elsewhere to produce an heir? You will forgive me, Garrett, if I don't think you capable of that." His tone softened. "I know you too well, son. You would not marry one woman and turn to another."

Garrett inhaled, turning away from his father. He stared out the window into the softening sun, the day made somber by a bank of clouds drifting in. He knew he couldn't do that either, but that wasn't what he meant. It just seemed so ridiculous, in this day and age, to think the kingdom could be in such peril because Briar couldn't have a child. One need only look to Garrett's own circumstances. His mother had been a commoner. He hadn't become a prince until she died and his father took him in. And were it not for his brother's problems, he would never have become crown prince. Life had a way of working itself out—Garrett knew that better than anyone.

"Garrett, I'm not trying to tell you who you can or cannot marry." His father's deep voice was as heavy as a stone. "You know I don't want to. But this could be a very real problem, and I just want you to think on it. Before things become more serious with Princess Briar."

Garrett bit back a dozen different replies. "If that's all?" he asked curtly, standing. His father nodded, and Garrett left before another word could pass between them.

He descended the stone stairs into the courtyard, his heart heavy. He wished his father had stuck to his first inclination not to "trouble" Garrett before he left for his trip. Of course, Garrett understood why he had. He wanted to give Garrett time to think about this away from the castle... away from Briar.

Well, it didn't matter how long he was away from Briar. Nothing was going to change how he felt about her. And he wouldn't be persuaded to give her up.

He'd already lost one love of his life. He was still amazed he'd been lucky enough to find a second.

"Pardon, sire, but your face is a storm cloud."

Garrett shook himself, focusing on the group before him. He'd been so lost in thought that he'd reached his hunting party without realizing it. The man who had spoken was one of his archers, Falcon, a broad-shouldered young man with dark brown skin and a perpetual grin on his round face.

Garrett forced a smile. "Just annoyed we haven't left yet." He pulled on his long, heavy overcoat. "It must be past noon already."

"Only just, Your Highness." Gemma, Garrett's best tracker, glanced at the sun overhead, shuttered by a thin layer of wispy clouds. Gemma had been his first pick for this trip; she was a necessity for any expedition into the forest. "But it'll be dark early."

"Then we'd best be on our way." As they walked towards the outer wall, Garrett tossed a grin in Spencer's direction. "Ready for another rout with this Black Forest beast, Spence?"

"I suppose," Spencer said heavily. Thin as a beanpole, he did not look much up to a rout with anything. "Though I'm not sure I've recovered from the corpses, sire."

Garrett laughed and was relieved to find it didn't feel forced. He shrugged off the last of the black humor his father had left him in and looked forward with excitement. "Well, I'm well recovered," he said. "Let's go catch a beast."

5

CONCEALED

I SABELLE WOKE AND DID not know where she was. Her eyes felt sticky, her body sore and heavy. She struggled to prop herself up, but she was bound in place.

Panic threatened until she realized the only thing binding her was a thick quilt twisted around her legs. A quilt. A bed. She was in a bed, and she must have tossed and turned so much that she'd become entangled in her blankets.

She tugged the quilt down and sat up. Her eyes *were* sticky, her vision blurred, and when she rubbed her face, she realized it was from dried tears.

That's when she remembered. Everything that happened last night—the forest, the wolves, the castle, the hunter, her brother, the *beast*—

With a gasp, Isabelle leapt out of bed.

Or at least, she tried to. She'd forgotten her legs were twisted in her quilt, so instead, she stumbled, falling flat on her face upon the floor. Groaning, she pushed herself into a seated position and rested her head against the side of the mattress.

The beast. Being chased and bitten by that beast. And then seeing her brother, Ansel, locked in that tower, and *then*, meeting...

The lord of the castle.

Isabelle scowled, shoving curly strands of hair from her face. The lord who had refused to let her brother go, who had condemned Isabelle to stay here too. Isabelle clung to the outrage bubbling inside her, because it felt better than fear. That this *lord* thought he had any kind of authority to keep her here—

After visiting Ansel last night, Klaus had shown Isabelle to a room in the castle. The hunter had conceded to bringing Ansel proper blankets, but he'd flat-out refused to move her brother somewhere more comfortable, saying it wasn't his call.

Isabelle knew very well whose call it was. And *he* had made it perfectly clear he didn't care how ill or injured Ansel was.

So Isabelle had been brought to this dreary room. It was a bit larger than the servant girl's room, with a massive four-poster bed and heaps of quilted blankets, thick furs, and lumpy pillows. While Ansel was stuck in a frigid, barren stone tower with no bed at all. Isabelle had stormed and paced the room for hours, her mind racing. She had sworn she would not sleep a single minute, but at some point in the early morning—after she'd succumbed to furious tears—she'd collapsed onto her (rather soft) bed and climbed beneath the blankets, if only, she'd told herself, to keep warm.

Evidently, she'd fallen asleep. And slept for hours, judging by the sunlight streaming through the high window above her bed.

She was still on the floor, cocooned in her quilt, when she heard the *click* of a latch on the door.

Someone was coming into her room.

Isabelle scrambled to her feet, shoving the quilt away and shooting straight up, but when the door opened, it was only the servant Ellery. The brief, mad thought of diving across the bed to make a run for it crossed Isabelle's mind, but before the thought had finished forming, Ellery shut the door behind her. The girl carried a large tray full of breakfast foods—more varied fare than Isabelle would have expected in this dark, dank castle. Sweetbreads, a bowl of berries, a large slab of fresh butter, two fried eggs, and a large helping of sliced ham. That was a bit much for Isabelle; she didn't usually eat meat first thing in the morning.

"Breakfast," Ellery said, her explanation laconic and yet unnecessary. There was also a pot of something steaming—tea, it smelled like. As Ellery set everything down on a round table, Isabelle inched forward. She eyed the distance between herself, Ellery, and the door, still weighing the possibility of making a run for it. The servant hadn't locked the door behind her.

But Ellery—though she'd scarcely looked at Isabelle—seemed to guess her intentions. "Stefan is just outside," she said in that neutral tone of hers. "If you need anything."

There was absolutely nothing pointed about the way she said it, but Isabelle could not help but think it was. "Stefan?"

"Another servant," said Ellery.

A servant. Not a guard. Not a hunter, like Klaus. Still, Isabelle had no idea how old this Stefan was—or more importantly, how large. And there was no way of asking without making it perfectly clear *why* she was asking. So Isabelle put aside thoughts of escaping and asked, "Did you check on my brother last night? Klaus said you would. How is he? He looked really ill."

Ellery nodded to all this as she finished setting out the breakfast fare, including a bowl of sugar and a cracked jug of cream.

"I checked on him. His bandages were replaced yesterday, and he didn't need new ones yet. He was a bit feverish—"

"Not surprising." Isabelle reminded herself it was not Ellery who insisted on keeping Ansel locked up, yet even so, she could not moderate her chilly tone. "Given the conditions he's being kept in."

"Klaus brought him some warm blankets." Ellery stepped back from the table, facing Isabelle head-on without meeting her gaze. Not being evasive, Isabelle thought. Just deferential, in the way servants were. She had experienced the same sort of thing from servants at Garrett's castle in the Glen Kingdom. It was ridiculous, really, because Isabelle was not a noble or even a merchant. She was a commoner like any servant. But she knew it was only their job, treating guests with respect.

Of course, that was at Glen Castle. Here in this old ruin, she was hardly a guest.

"I'll check on him again today," Ellery promised. "Make sure his fever isn't worse. But there were no other signs of infection. I'm sure he'll be all right."

Isabelle bit back a retort. If there were no signs of infection, then she had no doubt the damp, icy conditions in the tower were responsible for his fever. "Can I see him? I want to see him."

Ellery dithered. "That will be up to the lord."

"Then I want to talk to *him*."

"I'll ask," said Ellery, "but I think he's...out. With Klaus. They'll probably be out all day." She took a step back. "Stefan is just outside. You can knock if you need anything."

She was gone before Isabelle could ask anything else.

Isabelle stared at the door long after she'd gone. This time, she heard the turn of the key, the lock snapping into place. She wished she'd been closer to get a glimpse of the other servant, this Stefan. But she hadn't; she hadn't moved, and now she stood in the same spot, staring at the locked door. Dismay running through her in rivulets, like raindrops streaking down a window.

Eventually, the loud grumble of her stomach alerted her to her hunger. Hardly surprising—she hadn't had a proper supper last night. She took a reluctant seat at the round table and buttered a piece of bread. Within relatively little time, she consumed both fried eggs and two thick pieces of sweetbread.

Afterwards, she climbed back into bed, cupping her hands around a warm mug of tea. The room wasn't nearly as cold as the tower had been, but a chill hung in the air, bolstered by all the drab stone. The walls had likely once been hung with tapestries to ward off the chill, but now they were bare. Everything about the room was dark and doleful, from the faded, threadbare rug to the dark wooden furnishings. There was a fireplace on the far side of the room, but it was cold and empty. Isabelle wondered if she would be permitted a fire. Probably not, she thought glumly. She would just have to huddle beneath her quilts.

She eyed the window overhead. The ceiling arched high above her, and the window, though large, was set in the stone wall at its highest point. Even if she stacked all the furniture in the room and managed to climb it without falling, she didn't think it would reach. She suspected the window was bolted shut anyway.

Sipping her tea, Isabelle considered her options. It was much easier to do, rationally and carefully, now she'd had some sleep and something to eat. Her first move, she thought, should be to scour the room for anything of use—any way out, anything she could use to pick the lock or bear as a weapon. But the idea of escape disquieted her. Because she didn't want to leave Ansel.

She supposed, if it came to it, she could escape and go find help. But there was no help close by. Well, there were the villagers, some ten miles from here, but given how closemouthed they'd been about the castle, Isabelle was not sure they would aid her. She'd have to go further, perhaps back to the Glen Kingdom. And there was no telling what might happen to Ansel in that time.

So perhaps she should forget about escaping for now. At least until she got to see Ansel again. That would be her goal.

A goal that, it turned out, was easy to reach. Isabelle spent the rest of the day sleeping, eating, and exploring her room, though there wasn't much to explore—the room was furnished well enough but devoid of stray objects. In the evening, as the sun vanished from the window, the key *clicked* in the lock again, and Isabelle turned, expecting Ellery with supper.

But it wasn't Ellery. It was Klaus.

"Ready?" the hunter said, his eyes traveling the room with a chary air.

"Ready for what?" asked Isabelle, nonplussed.

"I heard you wanted to see your brother?"

Hope lurched through Isabelle, wild and ill-prepared. "I can see him?"

Klaus gave an impatient shrug.

Isabelle didn't need any other response. Hastily, she crossed the room and joined Klaus in the corridor.

Fifteen minutes later, they stood at the top of the tower stairwell again. Isabelle had tried to pay attention to her surroundings as Klaus led her through the twisting corridors, but she'd soon lost count of the turns they took. The castle, small as it was, seemed organized like a maze, and every corridor looked the same.

But Isabelle hardly cared about that now. As soon as Klaus had the tower door opened, she rushed inside, elbowing the hunter as she pushed past him.

The room was just as icy as before. But this time, when Isabelle spotted Ansel on the floor, she found him huddled beneath several heavy, quilted blankets, and another spread out beneath him. Isabelle's relief was a flood, but one quickly quenched by the flames of her displeasure. These blankets were the least of what he should have. He needed pillows, a proper bed, a *real* way to keep warm.

"Ansel?" Isabelle lowered herself to her knees beside her brother, ignoring Klaus, who hovered in the doorway. The floor was far too cold, the damp bleeding straight through her skirt. "Ansel, can you hear me?"

Her brother was sleeping. Less fitfully than before, she thought, which was something. Hopefully, the blankets had done him some good. She watched the steady rise and fall of his chest, took in the scrunched look on his face. He looked so small, sleeping like this. So young. Ansel *was* the younger of them, but only by two years. Still, it was easy to forget that, watching him now.

Isabelle reached out to him. She felt torn between letting him rest and her own desire for reassurance—to see him awake, to hear him speak. She swallowed her words, deciding not to rouse him, and laid a hand on his forehead.

But when she touched him, Ansel stirred, his eyes fluttering. Isabelle jerked her hand back, and Ansel reacted in kind, his eyes flying open. " 's that?" he mumbled. "Who—"

"It's all right, Ansel." Isabelle's voice was little more than a whisper. "It's me. It's Isabelle."

"Isabelle?" Far from being calmed by this, Ansel wrenched around. His feverish eyes fell on her. "No," he wheezed. "You can't be here."

"Ansel, it's all right—"

"No, *no.*" Ansel's voice was a pleading moan. He had never looked so like a little boy as he thrashed away from her. "You shouldn't—can't be here—"

"Ansel—" Isabelle reached for him again, unsettled by his agitation.

But Ansel recoiled. "I don't *want* you here."

Isabelle froze, her hand hovering in the air. Her brother's eyes were glassy with delirium; he wasn't well, she reminded herself.

But she still felt as though she'd been slapped.

I don't want you here.

Those were the same words he'd spoken to her three years ago. The last words he'd said to her. Until now.

Isabelle rose and backed away. On some level, she realized how calm her movements were, how measured and controlled, and was amazed. Because she didn't feel in control. Her face didn't feel like her own. It was a mask.

But Isabelle had become very good at this. Even before Ansel left, when she was still a small child. She had learned how to lock everything away, how to conceal it all. She'd had to.

She turned her back on Ansel and saw the doorway was empty.

Isabelle took a quick step, but her hope was short-lived. Klaus stood just outside the tower chamber, and he wasn't alone. He was talking with someone, their voices low and hushed. By the bright light of the lantern, hung inside the doorway, Isabelle caught a glimpse of a towering figure in a hood.

Klaus was talking to the lord.

"We'll know how bad he is soon," Klaus was saying. Isabelle took another slow, quiet step. She was hardly hidden from the doorway, but both hunter and lord stood slightly turned away. "Then maybe—"

"Maybe what?" The lord's voice was as Isabelle remembered, deep and rumbling. "Even if we let him go—" He broke off, as though hearing something. Even though Isabelle had not moved again.

He looked over his shoulder. And though his head was hooded, his face cloaked in shadow, Isabelle knew he had seen her. She expected a rebuke, but instead, the lord turned swiftly away. Without a word, he started down the winding staircase.

"Wait!" Isabelle hurried forward. She stopped, gripping the doorframe, for Klaus had raised an arm to block her from leaving. Isabelle stifled her indignation, her eyes fixed on the lord's hulking shoulders as he vanished around the bend in the stairwell. "I want to talk to you!"

For a moment, she thought the lord would ignore her. But he stopped on the stairs and said, without looking up, "If you need anything, speak to Klaus."

"I want to talk to *you*." Isabelle clenched her jaw. "Not your lackey."

Klaus made a noise that was half-snort, half-protest.

Isabelle arched an eyebrow. "Well, aren't you?"

Klaus answered in a voice so low, it was clearly meant for her ears only. "He may rule this castle. But I don't serve him."

"Klaus," the lord barked.

Mouth twisting, Klaus looked away. *Interesting*, Isabelle thought, as she looked from hunter to lord.

The lord sighed. Then Isabelle heard his boots thumping on the stairs and he appeared in full, coming up to face her. Isabelle was surprised. She hadn't expected him to give in that easily. She was even more surprised when the lord tossed a nod at Klaus, and the hunter turned to go, starting down the steps. A few seconds later, he was gone.

Leaving Isabelle alone with this *lord* of the castle.

"Well?" the lord demanded. He stood just out of the light of the lantern, swathed in shadow. "What do you want?"

Irritation surged through Isabelle. "Why must you wear that stupid hood?" she snapped. She was usually better at reigning in her temper, but something about this man *really* set her off. Had he no manners at all? "Is it meant to intimidate me?"

"*Does* it intimidate you?"

"No. Not in the least."

"Then it's not meant to."

"But why do you wear it, then?"

"None of your business!" he snarled. "Is *this* what you wanted to talk about?"

"No." Isabelle took a deep breath. "I wanted to talk about my brother."

The lord sighed, his broad shoulders heaving. "I told you, he's not leaving this castle. And neither—"

"—am I, I know." Isabelle rolled her eyes. *We'll see about that,* she thought, but all she said was, "Look, why does he have to stay in this tower? Couldn't he have a room? He can even have *my* room, and I'll stay up here, I'll switch with him—"

"*No.*" The lord made a sweeping, emphatic gesture. "He stays. Feel free to move in with him, if you like. But he stays in the tower."

Isabelle tried another tack, gritting her teeth. "A bed, then. Surely he can have a bed—"

"We brought him those blankets."

"It's not enough!" Isabelle shot back. "He's still sleeping on a cold floor in this horribly damp tower. He's never going to recover in these conditions! Or is that what you want? For him to waste away so you don't have to kill him yourself?"

"If I wanted him dead," the lord said coldly, "he would be dead."

Isabelle fell silent, but she did not back down. She glared at the lord, and though she could not see his face, she had a feeling he was glaring right back.

Isabelle won out. The lord said stiffly, "We can't move a bed up here. But...perhaps a mattress. I'll see what can be done."

"And perhaps some candles? I understand he can't have a fire, but—"

"Oh, yes, fine, candles." The lord's voice rang with sarcasm. "So he can burn the castle down around us."

Isabelle scoffed. "If he started a fire, he'd burn himself long before it would spread anywhere else."

"I notice you don't say he *wouldn't* do it."

Truthfully, Isabelle couldn't say that he wouldn't. But if he did start a fire, it would be out of sheer stupidity, not malice. "Look, I know he tried to steal from you. But my brother isn't a bad person. He—"

"Not a bad person?" The lord stalked past her. He stood in the doorway, gazing at the sleeping Ansel. The white glare of the lantern fell over the back of his hood. "He lied to me and stole from me. After we took him in, after we treated him—"

"He lied to you?" Isabelle echoed. "What did he lie about?"

The lord paused. It wasn't a long pause, but there was something weighted about it. Isabelle had a split-second's knowledge: She didn't want to hear the answer. But then—

"When I asked him about his family," said the lord, "he told me he had none."

Isabelle sucked in a breath. This time it was not a slap but a punch in the gut. Hammering her insides. Stealing the air from her lungs. It should not have surprised her; it certainly should not have hurt her. But it did. Isabelle wrapped her arms around herself.

"He denied your very existence." The lord's voice was oddly soft. Contemplative. "And yet you came all this way. You even volunteer to take his place in the tower."

Somehow, Isabelle pushed past the hurt. Somehow, she found her voice, though it shook when she spoke. "He's not perfect. But he's my brother."

"So?"

"*So.*" Isabelle dug her fingers into the scratchy wool of her coat. "He's my family. Don't *you* have any family?"

The lord whirled on her. Isabelle choked, taking a step back. Not because he had startled her, but because his sudden movement knocked back his hood.

For the first time, Isabelle looked upon the lord's face.

It was a young face. This lord was around Isabelle's age, she thought. And it was such a normal face. Rich umber skin and sharp cheekbones. Dark, thick eyebrows and shockingly full lips. Isabelle had expected to find the hood concealed some disfigurement. Scars like the hunter's, or some condition that distorted his features.

But there was nothing like that. Nothing strange except...his eyes.

"My family is none of your business." The lord's voice was low and seething. And though Isabelle had claimed the hood had not intimidated her, she found him less disconcerting without it. Less frightening, now she could see his face.

But his eyes...

There *was* something frightening about his eyes. They were a strange amber color, almost yellow. And perhaps it was a trick of the glaring lantern, but they seemed to gleam most unnaturally.

That was when Isabelle realized.

She had seen those eyes before. On someone else.

On some*thing* else.

"From now on, if you need something, talk to Klaus," the lord snapped. "Understand?"

"Yes." Isabelle gazed into his eyes, her voice distant and preoccupied. Preoccupied with other thoughts.

For something had just clicked into place.

"Yes," she repeated. "I understand."

6

ESCAPE

"I SABELLE, YOU CAN'T STAY here." Ansel grimaced, trying to sit up against the tower's concave wall. "You've got to leave. As soon as you can."

Isabelle pursed her lips, determined not to reach out to him. Determined not to help him. Three days had passed since she'd last seen Ansel. Three days since he had said to her, *I don't want you here.*

He was much better now. They'd brought him a mattress. It was thin and discolored with age, but at least he didn't have to sleep on the floor. They'd also allowed him a few candles. These improvements had done wonders for Ansel's health. He was awake and alert now, if still under the weather.

And if he remembered what he'd said to her that night, he made no mention of it. Given the state he'd been in, it was entirely possible he did *not* remember.

But Isabelle did. And now that he was on the mend, it was easier to hold back her concern for him. To pretend she didn't care. And though it was petty—even childish—Isabelle was determined to do just that. So she kept her hands to herself, arms

61

crossed over her chest, and watched her brother struggle to sit up on his own.

"I may not be locked in a tower," Isabelle said, aggrieved at his insistence that she leave him, "but I'm still a prisoner. I'm not free to walk out the front door whenever I like." Dropping her gaze, she adjusted her dark skirt on the floor around her. "And I came here for *you*, Ansel. Stones know why. I won't leave you here."

"I'll be fine." Ansel's pained voice belied his words. He slumped against the wall; he hadn't quite managed to right himself. Isabelle allowed herself some (definitely childish) satisfaction at that. *He doesn't want my help, after all.*

"I don't think he intends to keep me locked up forever," Ansel went on.

"The lord? I don't know what makes you think that. He was very clear we would stay here *forever*."

Ansel sneered. "First of all. He has a name."

"He does? I mean, what is it?"

"His name is Gryphon."

"Like...the mythical creature?" *How ironic*, she thought.

"Yes. Or at least, that's what he told me to call him," Ansel said. "As for keeping us here *forever*, well. I don't know if you've noticed, but he has a flair for the dramatic, Gryphon."

Well, that put it mildly. Strutting about as *lord of the castle.* Wearing that stupid hood to conceal his face. "Yes, but even so—"

"I heard him talking to Ellery once," Ansel interrupted. "When she was changing my bandage. And I swear she said something about quarantine."

"As in *you're* in quarantine?" Isabelle remembered the snippet of conversation she'd heard a few nights ago between Klaus and

the lord. Gryphon. *We'll know how bad he is soon*, Klaus had said.
"Were you *that* ill?" Isabelle resisted the urge to scoot back. A
quarantine would explain Gryphon's insistence that Ansel stay
in the tower. But then, why let Isabelle visit him and still allow
her to roam the castle?

Not that she was allowed to roam, exactly. She was still locked
in her room, and the few times she'd been out, Klaus accompanied her everywhere.

"I *was* quite ill when I got here," Ansel admitted. "Just a cold
that went bad, I suppose. I'd all but recovered by the time I left.
Tried to leave." He sighed. "Then I was attacked by those wolves,
and here I am again. Ill."

"By the time you left. By the time you tried to steal all their
silver, you mean," Isabelle said nastily.

"It isn't *his*. The *castle* isn't his. It's just an abandoned ruin.
He's a squatter."

Though this was hardly news to Isabelle, it did make her
consider the lord—*Gryphon*, she reminded herself—in a new
light. It made her wonder where he'd come from. Was he any
kind of lord or just pretending? Where had the servants come
from? For all Klaus might protest about "serving" him, it was
clear everyone here did.

Isabelle had met a few lords in her time, and if she had to guess,
she would say Gryphon *did* come from a lordly background.
His self-entitled air couldn't really be learned. But then, what
had happened to him that he found himself living in this ruined
castle? Especially one rumored to be cursed?

Admittedly, Isabelle didn't much believe those rumors; she'd
hardly given them a second thought. She knew very well curses
existed. But the few details she'd had from that trapper in the

woods hadn't made sense. Perhaps Gryphon was similarly disinclined to believe such nonsense.

Ansel was still talking. "...been weird. I just think there's more going on than they're telling us. That's why you need to leave, Belle. Forget me. Just get out."

Isabelle stiffened. "I told you. I can't just leave. When I'm not here, I'm locked in my room—"

"Oh, come on." Ansel gave her a knowing look. "You've gotten out of worse scrapes than this. We killed a witch, or have you forgotten? And you were only—what, ten years old—"

"I was thirteen," Isabelle corrected. "You were eleven. And I've dealt with worse than witches. A half-dead princess tried to eat me not four months ago." She exaggerated, of course. Briar might sound worse than a cannibalistic witch, but she wasn't, really. She was a perfectly lovely person.

Ansel looked puzzled. "A *princess* tried to eat you?"

"Never mind. It's a long story."

Shaking his head, Ansel said, "That's my point though. If anyone can escape this place, it's you, Belle. Don't worry about me. Just get out as soon as you find a way. I'll follow when I can."

Isabelle traced a finger along the grooves between the rugged stones in the floor. "Look, what do you care what happens to me? I thought you didn't need me anymore, or isn't that what you said? Back in the Mariner Kingdom?"

Her eyes were still glued to the floor, so she sensed, rather than saw, Ansel flinch. An awkward silence hung between them. Then Ansel said gruffly, "Well, that's my point. I don't need you. You shouldn't have come here in the first place, so leave when you can."

Isabelle woke early the next morning, a good hour before the sun was up. The air in the room was crisp with cold. She lay in bed, reluctant to leave the warmth of her coarse quilts. Tilting her head back, she could see straight out the window, set so high on the wall. The sky outside was clear and black, and Isabelle caught a glimpse of the full moon, winking as it soaked in the last of the night.

The yellow light of the moon made her think of the lord of the castle. Gryphon. She hadn't seen him since they'd spoken in the tower a few days ago. She'd gleaned from the servants that he kept odd hours, up late into the night. Which might be considered strange, Isabelle thought. But what was stranger was that, evidently, he spent some of his odd hours as a beast.

She didn't know it for certain. That was part of the reason she hadn't said anything to Ansel. She didn't think Ansel even knew about the beast, in which case, best not to give the lord another reason to keep him locked up. But she had suspected it ever since she'd seen Gryphon's eyes—his strange, yellow eyes. Eyes that seemed to *glow*.

They were the same eyes she'd seen on the beast.

She'd asked Ansel if Gryphon had worn a hood around him, and Ansel said no. His eyes were a bit strange, Ansel conceded, but Gryphon had told him he'd inherited his yellow eyes from "his mother's side of the family."

Which only made Isabelle more certain of her suspicion. Gryphon had worn the hood around *her* because she'd seen the beast. Perhaps he had feared she would recognize his eyes and make the connection.

It seemed mad, but then, as Isabelle had discussed with Ansel, she was all too familiar with impossible things. So the idea that Gryphon might turn into a raging beast didn't seem so weird.

For all she knew, he elected to turn into a beast. Even that didn't seem weird, given what an unpleasant fellow he was. Perhaps it was some bizarre way of expressing his anger. A sort of unconventional emotional therapy.

No, that was very unlikely, she had to admit. But she did think he might have been cursed to turn into a beast. It was even possible that Gryphon's...condition...had something to do with the rumored curse on the castle, though Isabelle couldn't see how. The story she had from the woman in the woods alluded to a curse cast over a hundred years ago.

It was a puzzle, certainly. And there was nothing Isabelle loved more than a puzzle.

Unfortunately, she couldn't afford to stay and solve this one. Ansel—much as she hated to admit it—was right. Whatever was going on in this castle was too dangerous. She still didn't like the idea of leaving her brother, not when she'd come all this way for him. But she couldn't see how to get him out of the tower, and he was not well enough to travel. It would be best to escape on her own and go for help. Even if she had to go as far as the Glen Kingdom.

She had a good idea how to escape too. She'd finally caught a glimpse of the servant Stefan, the one Ellery had mentioned. Fortunately, he was not large. He was a boy, twelve or thirteen at most, and short and weedy.

Easy enough to overcome.

And today would be her best opportunity. She'd heard Klaus tell Ellery he would be hunting today—and that he'd set out early. So if Klaus was not around, the task of guarding Isabelle would fall to someone else. Someone like Stefan.

When Isabelle rose and knocked on her door, however, it was Ellery who entered. Ellery waited outside her door every morning, usually with a breakfast tray. This time, Ellery entered with several gowns strewn over her arms. Since Gryphon had declared Isabelle would be here "forever," and Isabelle, of course, had not brought enough clothing to last "forever," Ellery had scoured the castle for anything she could find.

Most of the gowns she'd found were fancier garb than Isabelle was used to. They were also old, from periods past, Isabelle noted, sorting through the dresses without much enthusiasm. Not only were they impractical for traveling, but they were not to her style. Most of the gowns favored huge bell sleeves and heavy fabrics, or else dripped with lace. Isabelle preferred a more sensible look.

Fortunately, there was one dress—a deep violet gown—in a slightly more modern style. The sleeves were long and snug, and the dress lacked lace or other frippery. But most *un*fortunately, the skirt was massive—made up of so much fabric, Isabelle thought she would drown in it.

"It's meant to be worn with a bustle," said Ellery. "I think I saw one upstairs. If you want me to have a look?"

Isabelle considered. Tempting. It would get Ellery out of the room, give Isabelle a chance to escape. But. Isabelle wouldn't have time to undress—stones, even with all the time in the world, she'd never manage to get out of this dress on her own. There had been about a million buttons up the back.

"I never bother with bustles," she said. "Perhaps we can pin it?"

Ellery did just so, draping the skirt up in the back and pinning it in an elegant fashion that would leave Isabelle free to move around. When they were done, Isabelle surveyed herself in the dusty mirror. She put on a frown, as though unsatisfied with the look. "You know," she said, trying to sound casual, "I think I will try that bustle after all."

Ellery gave her a speculative look. There was far too much knowing in that look, but all she said was, "All right. Stefan is outside if you need anything."

Then she was gone. Leaving Isabelle alone.

Isabelle wasted no time. There was no telling how quickly Ellery would find that bustle. She immediately began throwing everything into her pack. It didn't take long—some of her belongings had been taken from her. But she had provisions, enough to get to the nearby village; she had snuck some tinned herring and a few apples off her breakfast tray yesterday. She didn't much fancy going into the Black Forest without her pistol, but that was the first thing Klaus had taken from her, as well as her hunting knife.

As soon as everything was packed, she tugged on her fitted coat, securing the top button across her chest and leaving the rest open over her gown's bulky skirt. Then she picked up her pack, crossed the room, and rapped on the door three times.

She heard a key turn in the lock. Isabelle stepped back so that, when Stefan pushed open the door with a soft *creak*, she was concealed behind it.

"Hello?" said Stefan, his tone uncertain. Isabelle waited until he ventured into the room. He was not *so* young, she thought waveringly, as she stood behind him and raised her pack—weighted with books—high above her head. Thirteen, maybe. He was not *so* young, she thought with a twinge of guilt.

She swung her pack as he turned towards her.

The weighted pack smashed into the side of his head with a solid *thunk*. Stefan crumpled to the ground.

Cringing, Isabelle bent down to the boy's motionless form, checking for a pulse. It was there, steady, and he was breathing just fine. Only unconscious. Letting loose a sigh of relief, Isabelle sat back. Even better—the boy had a pistol holstered to his waist.

Isabelle took the pistol, stepped over the poor boy—he was only doing his job; it was not *his* fault his lord was a surly maniac—and hurried out into the corridor, shutting the door behind her.

She had been more attentive the last time Klaus escorted her to the tower, so she crept down the castle corridors, sure of where she was going. The infrequent candelabras cast cavorting shadows over Isabelle as she darted by, and she found herself shuddering away from the light, feeling safer in the stretches of darkness between sconces.

When she reached the grand stairwell above the entrance hall, she peered over the railing, then hurried down the stairs. She'd just reached the bottom when a side door banged open across the hall.

Breath seizing in her chest, Isabelle threw herself behind the stairwell. Caught in a snare of cobwebs, she crouched down to blend into the shadows, stifling a sneeze. She watched through twitching eyes as two people appeared in the hall, their footsteps ringing against the stone floor.

Klaus. And Gryphon.

"...out tonight," Gryphon was saying. He wore a dark waistcoat and matching frock coat, having dispensed with his hood. His hair, which Isabelle hadn't noticed before, was thick and black, longer than the current fashion, curling at his jaw line. Isabelle had to admit, grudgingly, that the unusual style suited him, emphasizing the strong lines of his face. He was—Isabelle admitted even more grudgingly—not unattractive. In fact, without that stupid hood, he cut a rather impressive figure. "So make sure you're back before dark."

"Of course," Klaus said. "I might cut it a bit close though."

"Klaus." Gryphon's tone was a warning.

"You know I'll be careful."

"You'd better be." For a moment, Isabelle was afraid they were going to walk right towards her, but Gryphon turned for the front door. "Ellery said she'll keep an eye on the thief today. I suppose we'll know soon enough how bad it is."

"I'm telling you," Klaus said, raising the bar on the door, "I don't think it was..."

But whatever Klaus didn't think, Isabelle didn't hear. His voice faded as he and Gryphon stepped outside, leaving the door open behind them. The temperature in the room plummeted as frigid air invaded the hall.

Isabelle bit her lip. This was what she wanted—the door right there, wide open. Though Gryphon would probably be back any minute.

This was her window. And it was closing fast.

But...but.

It had occurred to Isabelle that if Gryphon *was* the beast, then the beast wasn't in the dungeons all the time. And the best way to get to the bottom of that particular mystery—to solve the puzzle—was to explore the dungeons. And now was as good a chance as any, since she *knew* Gryphon wasn't down there.

Isabelle turned her options over in her mind. She could sneak down to the dungeons now, take a quick look around, then come straight back. She only wanted to see if the beast was there.

She peered around the staircase. Gryphon had yet to return. This was her only chance. Hefting her pack, she scurried across the hall and slipped through the door that led to the dungeons.

She felt a nasty burning in her chest as she hurried down the narrow stairwell, her breath loud in her ears. It was a moment before she realized the burning was fear, clawing through her as she descended into the dungeon—the same place where she'd been attacked by the beast. Isabelle reminded herself that even if she was wrong and the beast was down here, it would be secure behind the portcullis.

But when Isabelle reached the portcullis, she found it open. Excitement outweighed fear now; surely, if the beast were down here, the gate would be closed. Driven by curiosity, Isabelle crossed beneath the portcullis towards the iron door. It was hard to see in the dim light, but it looked like it stood ajar—

"*What are you doing down here?*"

Isabelle whirled around. For a moment, she was transported back to her first day here, when she'd found herself with the beast on her heels. The memory of that fear was so palpable, her heart began to race. She was actually relieved to see it was only Gryphon behind her and not the beast.

Then she remembered that Gryphon *was* the beast.

He certainly looked beastly now, shaking with rage. Disheveled tufts of hair rose from his head. He'd discarded his coat and waistcoat, and the white linen shirt he wore was half-unbuttoned, the sleeves rolled up to his elbows. He looked so different down in this dank dungeon, candlelight casting spectral shadows over him. She'd seen him not five minutes ago upstairs, and now he was so *different*.

So menacing. A threat.

"I'm...I was just..." Isabelle stuttered. "I was looking—"

"You have to get *out* of here!" A violent shudder rippled through him, and Isabelle realized he was not shaking with rage—he was shaking uncontrollably, his body gripped with spasms. "*Now!*"

"But...are you..." Dimly, in the recesses of her mind, Isabelle realized what was happening. But confronted with it, right in front of her, it was too terrible to understand. She couldn't move. "What are you—"

Gryphon threw his head back and let out a roar—an actual roar, the sound resounding through the yawning reaches of the dungeon. He gripped her by the arms and swung her around, throwing her from him. Isabelle nearly smacked into the bars of an empty cell. She slid down the opposite wall, trying to get her bearings. The sleeve of her coat bore a long, thin rent in the fabric. Where Gryphon had grabbed her.

Where his claw had sliced through her sleeve.

She looked around, real terror piercing through the haze clouding her mind. Ellery—she hadn't even seen the girl come down—was lowering the portcullis. It slammed shut with a heavy *clank*, and as Ellery bent to secure it, Isabelle realized Gryphon was gone. She didn't understand where until she heard another beastly roar echo down the corridor. On the other side of the portcullis.

He really is the beast, Isabelle thought, trying to accept it. *Gryphon is the beast.*

"Miss Isabelle." With the portcullis secured, Ellery turned towards her. "Are you all right? Miss Isabelle?"

Isabelle had thought she understood. It hadn't seemed so impossible. But now that she'd seen it—seen him in the grip of this monstrous transformation—now that she'd felt the brutal strength in his grip—

I have to get out of here.

Isabelle scrabbled at the wall to push herself up. The stone scraped her palms, leaving damp grit beneath her fingernails. She broke into a run, ignoring Ellery's calls as she fled up the stairs.

Gryphon is the beast.

She couldn't accept it. She could accept that it was real—she had seen it with her own eyes. But she couldn't accept that it was all right. It was *not* all right.

She skidded into the entrance hall, catching herself before she tripped. She ran at the front doors so hard, she slammed into them. They were not locked—only latched by a long, silver bar. Isabelle did not stop to consider the oddity of the silver as she hoisted the bar up and flung open the door.

The sun was creeping over the horizon, chasing away the deep aubergine of the night sky.

"Miss Isabelle!" Ellery appeared behind her, running across the hall. "You can't leave! Miss Isabelle, *wait!*"

Isabelle ignored her. She dashed outside, slipping and sliding over the frosted courtyard.

"Miss Isabelle! Please, you can't go out there!" Ellery's calls turned desperate, filled with more emotion than Isabelle had ever heard from her. "It's not safe—the *wolves!*"

I can handle wolves, Isabelle thought, sprinting for the courtyard gate. *I can't handle your beast.*

7

RESCUE

ISABELLE RAN AS LONG as she could. Her boots sank into slushy snow, and her heavy pack banged against her hips, bruising the bone. She switched it from arm to arm, her shoulders burning.

When she could run no more, she slowed to a walk, trudging through the woods. She had no idea how far she'd run or for how long. Her mind was a tangle of impressions, reason blotted out by fear. Her pulse skittered, and she wondered blindly how long it would be before someone came after her—but, she reminded herself, Klaus had gone for the day, and Gryphon—Gryphon—

Best not to think of Gryphon.

But as she tramped through the snow, as her racing heartbeat slowed, Isabelle's head cleared too. Thoughts became easier to face. Still, everything that had happened—just a couple of hours ago—seemed a blur. From the moment she'd donned that violet gown until she'd run out of the castle—all the moments in between ran together.

Knocking Stefan over the head. Sneaking through the corridors. Hiding from Klaus and Gryphon in the entrance hall. Slipping down into the dungeons.

Gryphon in his beastly rage. Gryphon—with claws instead of fingers—throwing her from him. Gryphon bellowing that inhuman roar.

She glanced down, eyes trailing over herself. She still wore the violet gown. She'd forgotten. Like some damsel princess out of an old tale. It was a shock, even though she'd made the conscious decision not to waste time changing. Perhaps it was just, were it not for the dress, she could have convinced herself none of it had been real. That it had all been a mad dream. A *nightmare*.

She fingered the tear in the sleeve of her wool coat. Where Gryphon had grabbed her.

No, it had not been a nightmare. It was all real.

As Isabelle's nerves settled, the bitter cold pierced her. She was suddenly aware of her chattering teeth, her raw nose. She took a moment to draw her coat more tightly across her chest, securing more buttons. Then she cupped a hand over her face, breathing warm air into it. She cursed as she waded through the snow. When she'd come to the castle a few days ago, snow had been sparsely scattered over the forest floor, icy clumps here and there. Now it covered everything two feet deep. She had covered the distance between the village and the castle in a single, short winter day. But with the snow this deep, Isabelle didn't think she'd make it this time.

She'd just have to get as far as she could. That's all there was to it.

She could not go back.

Still, when the gloaming darkness descended over the forest, Isabelle felt heavy with despair. She was tempted to go on through the night, but she had no lantern, and it was hard enough slogging through the snow when she *could* see. And besides, she was dead on her feet. She needed sleep.

She decided to camp beneath a stout spruce tree, its thick, prickly branches providing some shelter. She set up her tent and immediately crawled into it, not bothering to undress before scooting into her sleeping rug. She would have loved a fire to heat some tea, but it was possible Klaus was after her by now, and smoke would be a dead giveaway to a tracker. So after a cold dinner of tinned herring, Isabelle huddled down into her rug.

Sleep came quickly, weariness chasing away her fears of being found.

When she woke later, she woke to howling.

Isabelle shot upright. The howling cut through the black and the silence. Isabelle's shallow breaths misted the air in the tent, but all she could hear were those baleful cries, coming from all directions at once.

As though she was surrounded.

Isabelle shook off the last of her sleep. *Wolves.* Vaguely, she remembered Ellery shouting about wolves as she'd run from the castle, and she remembered, too, hearing them in the woods the day she'd arrived. How she'd feared they'd been chasing her.

They seemed less frightening now. Quite a prosaic threat compared to what she'd faced since then. But still a threat.

Isabelle hustled out of her tent, clutching the pistol she'd taken from Stefan. The baying of the wolves continued. Her pulse quickening, Isabelle tucked the pistol inside her coat, then reached for a low-hanging branch on the spruce tree, hoisting herself up. If she could get high enough, she could wait until the wolves had gone. The moon peered down at her as she climbed, the full light of it piercing the treetops to light her way.

Heaving a breath, Isabelle glanced over her shoulder. To her dismay, she hadn't climbed as much as she thought she had. Perhaps eight feet. Then a low growl came from the shadows below, and Isabelle's dismay gave way to dread, prickling at the back of her neck.

A wolf slithered out of the foliage, stalking towards her spruce tree. Its yellow-eyed gaze was malevolent and familiar, and she didn't know if it reminded her of Gryphon or of...itself. Of the wolf she'd glimpsed on her way to the castle.

Then the full shape of the wolf emerged as it stepped into a beam of moonlight, and Isabelle forgot about its eyes.

The wolf was *huge*.

Isabelle's breath stuck in her throat. It was not so big as Gryphon's beast but still enormous, too big for a normal wolf. Much too big to be dismissed as *prosaic*. On all fours, it was nearly as tall as Isabelle, and its lean, muscled body had to be six feet long. Its broad back was a good three spans across, its haunches as stout as the branch she perched on.

If that wolf reared back...if it jumped at her.... She was barely ten feet from the ground. Isabelle threw a desperate glance up, but she couldn't go farther. The branches above were crooked and thin; they'd never hold her weight. Dropping her gaze, she saw the monstrous wolf advance, a snarl twisting its jaws. Isabelle reached wildly for another branch, her eyes still glued to the wolf—

The wolf dove for the tree, reaching it in three, loping strides. Then it leapt *up*.

A scream wrenched from Isabelle, for just as her fingers closed around a thin branch, she felt herself yanked backwards, the wolf's jaws clamping around the hem of her gown. Isabelle's feet slipped from under her, and then she was falling, falling, weightless and terrified—

She hit the ground hard, landing with a breath-stealing, rib-bruising *thud* in the snow. Her chin banged against the ground, her teeth clacking together. She didn't lose consciousness, but for a second, everything went black.

Her terror returned as soon as her breath did. Isabelle blinked watery eyes, gulping. Her entire body felt battered; her hands and face burned with cold and fresh scrapes. She knew she needed to *get up*, but she couldn't move, couldn't even see—

Her vision cleared. Painstakingly, Isabelle lifted her head.

And found herself staring into the yellow eyes of the giant wolf, face to face with its maw of glinting teeth.

"Oh, *stones*," Isabelle whispered. "Please, please—"

The wolf let out a growl that stopped her heart in her chest.

Then a shadow hurtled out of the darkness, tackling the wolf to the ground.

Isabelle's heartbeat returned with a stutter. Heedless of her beaten body, she pushed herself up to look.

The shadow was *Gryphon*.

Gryphon. His thick arms were wrapped around the wolf's massive flank, his own teeth bared in a snarl. They were human teeth; *he* was human, and yet there was something beastly about him as he wrestled with the wolf, forcing it onto its back. The wolf growled, twisting its head to bite Gryphon, but Gryphon evaded, rolling away. He snapped into a crouch, and by the light of the plump moon, Isabelle saw his tousled, tufted hair and glowing yellow eyes.

"You have *got* to be kidding me," Isabelle muttered.

The wolf rolled upright too, shaking snow from its fur as it rounded on Gryphon. It had forgotten Isabelle, bent on its attacker. Then another shape coalesced from the dense wood, like a demon forming from the darkness, dashing forward with impossible speed.

"Look out!" Isabelle cried, lurching to her feet.

Gryphon whirled as the second wolf lunged at him. They both tumbled back, growling, scratching, snapping. Isabelle watched with wide eyes, then realized the first wolf had turned, stalking towards her.

Isabelle fumbled for her pistol. "No, you don't." She tried to force some resolve into her voice as she yanked the pistol out and cocked it. "Don't even think about it."

The wolf leapt.

Isabelle fired, letting off two rapid shots.

The bullets took the wolf in its flank. It collapsed at her feet, a dying whine escaping its shuddering body. Then it lay still.

A great knot loosened in Isabelle's chest. She looked for Gryphon and saw him throw the second wolf from him with incredible strength. It rolled, tumbling through the snow.

Then two more wolves appeared, creeping through the woods. Their yellow eyes were bent on Gryphon, full of malice. Malice that was entirely too *human*.

Gryphon's shoulders slumped, but the rest of him tensed like a coiled wire. He jerked around as Isabelle lurched forward, coming to stand beside him. Her hand shook as she raised her pistol, but she cocked it back with surety, finger on the trigger, ready to fire. Fear was a distant thing, buried beneath a haze of adrenaline and bizarre confidence. Her eyes locked on the wolves, and she lifted her chin. A challenge.

One of the wolves snarled, but it was a quiet, defeated sound. And then—unlikely as it seemed—it looked around, its gaze seeking the fallen wolf. The wolf Isabelle had killed.

With one last growl, the two wolves turned, racing into the night. The last wolf rolled to its feet—cast a look full of hatred at Gryphon—and followed its brethren, vanishing into the forest.

Isabelle didn't lower her pistol. She didn't think she could. She felt frozen solid, like a beetle caught in the sap of a pine tree. She didn't even think she could breathe. Her hair, tangled and loose around her face, flitted as a soft wind picked at it, but it was the only part of her that moved.

Gryphon, too, was utterly still. Staring after the wolves. Then—slowly, as though not to startle her—he turned, placed a hand over her pistol, and gently urged it down, lowering her arm.

Shoulders heaving, panting for breath, he said, "You—should never—have left."

Isabelle stared at him. He wore only trousers, tucked into thick boots, and a wrinkled linen shirt. His dark waistcoat was unbuttoned, his shirt open at the neck, exposing several inches of bare brown skin. Isabelle's gaze traveled down his chest, where she spotted two long tears in his shirt. Dark blood glistered through those tears.

"You're bleeding." Isabelle half-reached for him, but he twisted away.

"So are you." He raised an arm to point.

Isabelle felt her face. Her fingers came away spotted with blood. Perhaps from a branch, scraping her as she'd fallen from the tree. "It's fine."

Gryphon dropped his hand, turning his back on her. He staggered away.

Isabelle hurried after him. "You must be freezing!"

"I left my coat back there." He jerked his thumb over his shoulder, into the woods. "I heard you scream. I couldn't move fast enough." He turned as though to face her but didn't quite manage it, standing in profile. The white light of the moon beamed over him. "I know you don't want to come back with me," he said, his voice gruff. "But—"

"Are you joking?" Isabelle swallowed. "I want to go back. I want to go back *now*."

Gryphon looked at her, stupefied. Isabelle understood how he felt. But it was the truth. As the lingering adrenaline seeped away, her knees buckled, exhaustion sweeping over her. She suddenly wanted nothing more than to be back in the castle, surrounded by stone walls, huddled and warm beneath the scratchy quilts on her bed. For some reason, that option felt far more comforting than the unfriendly villagers in the other direction.

Maybe that was weak of her. And maybe she still should have been wary of Gryphon. She remembered thinking the wolves were nothing compared to his beast.

But not these wolves. And not this Gryphon. This Gryphon had come after her. This Gryphon had saved her life.

Everything was different. Everything was changed. She wanted to go back. Get out of these woods.

"Well, good." Gryphon sounded almost gratified. "Then let's go."

Isabelle scrambled into her tent, throwing everything in her pack. When she emerged a few minutes later, Gryphon was gazing overhead, his expression plainly anxious. "Don't worry about the tent," he told Isabelle. "Klaus can retrieve it later. Or we'll get you a new one." His tone was distracted, rambling. "It must be near midnight. We have to get back by first light."

He turned to lead her through the woods. Isabelle hastened after him. "Why do we have to be back by first light?" she asked.

Gryphon cast her a sidelong glance. His yellow eyes were unfathomable. "We just do."

They trekked through the tangled trees, coming upon Gryphon's abandoned overcoat within a few minutes. He didn't even stop, slinging it on without breaking stride. They trudged through the snow in silence, shafts of broken moonlight cutting through the trees.

Despite their relentless pace, Isabelle shivered. The adrenaline that had coursed through her during the wolves' attack had gone, leaving her cold and stiff. She could feel all her bruises and scratches, every place a branch had caught her skin, all the tender spots in her body. Stinging, throbbing, quivering, she followed Gryphon as he wove through the forest, her wooden gaze fixed upon his rolling shoulders.

Less than twenty-four hours ago, she had fled the castle, driven by her terror of Gryphon. Now she followed him to that same castle. She wondered if she was mad to return. If she shouldn't turn back now and run from him. But even if she could have convinced her tired, bruised body to run, she wouldn't have.

Because he had come for her.

Maybe he'd only done it to keep her from "spreading tales" about the beast. (About *him*, she realized.) But he could have left her to the wolves, and he hadn't. He had *fought* them. Seeing him wrestle that monstrous wolf with his bare hands had been…impressive. In a way that made Isabelle feel rather flushed.

She didn't know what to make of that. But she was curious enough that she wanted to find out. And afraid enough of those wolves. And exhausted enough, desirous of a safe, warm bed.

But first, they had to make it back. The hike seemed endless. Isabelle had caught only a few hours of sleep. Gryphon, she presumed, had none. Yet he soldiered through the snow, moving forward, forward. As an hour passed, and then another, Isabelle fought to keep up with him. Her feet ached with every step. Her eyelids grew heavy. She struggled with her pack, switching it from one shoulder to the other every few minutes. The distance between her and Gryphon began to widen as she fell behind.

Gryphon noticed. Glancing over his shoulder, he stopped, turning to watch her slog after him. "Here." He held out a hand. "Give me your pack."

"I've got it," Isabelle panted. "You're injured—"

"Give it to me," he repeated, a trace impatient.

Isabelle didn't have it in her to argue. She handed over the pack, her arm trembling, and he took it with a grunt. Isabelle had no trouble keeping up after that, but she could not help but notice Gryphon's pace slowed considerably. She watched as he switched the pack from one arm to the other, wincing as it banged against his wounded flank.

"Oh, look, just—give it back." She held her arm out.

"I've got it—"

"No, just for a minute—look—" She tugged at the pack so he was forced to let her take it. Isabelle threw it open, dug out a heavy tome, and tossed it into the snow. Then a second book. And a third. Each one she tossed aside with a small *pang* for their loss.

Gryphon looked incredulous. "Really? All this time—"

"Not a word," said Isabelle, handing the (much lighter) pack to him. "Not. One. Word."

It was good advice. They had hours to go. Hours that passed in a cold, white blur. The snowy landscape blinding in the darkness. The wind baying through the trees and cutting through their coats. Fatigue settled into Isabelle like poison. Her boots and stockings were soaked through, her toes numb with cold.

The hem of her gown dragged in the muck, made heavy with damp and dirt. Her vision began to swim, the trees blurring together. She shook her head, fixing her gaze on Gryphon's increasingly hunched shoulders.

The moon began to sink, but the sky didn't seem any darker. *We have to be close*, Isabelle thought in a daze, *we must be nearly there*, but she had no idea where they were, no sense of how much time had passed.

Suddenly, she tripped over something in the snow, jutting up like a boulder. She grabbed at the thing to steady herself and looked down.

It wasn't a boulder. It was Gryphon. She hadn't seen him fall, but there he was, sunk to his knees in the snow. He was still upright, but barely, swaying back and forth. Isabelle came around to face him.

"Gryphon." Isabelle bent a little—afraid to get too close to the ground, afraid she, too, would fall and not get up. "Gryphon, we have to keep going."

Gryphon looked drawn. His eyes were glazed and unseeing. Isabelle took his face in her hands and found his skin surprisingly warm to the touch. "Gryphon." She raised her voice. "You have to get up. We're almost there."

She had no idea if that was true.

Still, he seemed to latch onto her words. "We're almost there," he repeated, his voice slurring.

"Yes." She glanced up, glimpsing a patch of lightening sky through the trees. "But it's almost dawn. And you said—"

This seemed to reach him. His amber eyes focused, and he lurched to his feet so suddenly that Isabelle stumbled.

"Yes," he said in a ragged voice. "We have to—get back. Let's go."

They continued on. The sky faded from the inky black of night to the deep blue of early morning. Then into the rusty violet of the coming dawn. Isabelle was afraid to look up, afraid she might see the sun peeking over the horizon. She kept going. Her left ankle throbbed, making her limp, and a stray thread inside her gown chafed at her, rubbing her skin raw. But she kept going. She kept going—

They staggered out of the woods. Into a clearing. The clearing before the gully, stretching between them and the castle. Isabelle's gaze alighted on the bridge with relief.

But beside her, Gryphon said, "*No.*"

Isabelle looked at him. His terrified gaze was fixed on the horizon. Where the first of the sun's rays crept over the trees.

"Gryphon." Isabelle didn't really understand. She didn't know the significance of the dawn, why they'd had to get back in that time. But on a basic level, she understood his urgency. "We're almost there. We just have to cross the bridge."

But Gryphon's whole body shuddered. With cold, Isabelle thought, befuddled, her exhausted mind trying to make sense of it. But then she remembered. Gryphon, down in the dungeons, twenty-four hours ago. At dawn. Wracked with violent spasms just as he was now.

As the beast overtook him.

It's the sunrise, Isabelle thought with dawning horror. *He can't control it.*

Seized with panic, Isabelle tugged at one of his brawny arms. "Come on. Come *on.*" He shook so vehemently, she could barely hold onto him. "We're nearly there, just move—come *on,* Gryphon! We're nearly there!"

But his body gave a tempestuous spasm, so great that Isabelle fell back. Gryphon fell too, onto hands and knees. He managed

ELIZABETH KING

to lift his head, locking eyes with Isabelle. "Go—r-run." His words came through gritted teeth. "*Run.*"

"You're almost there!" Isabelle screamed. She felt unhinged with fear and pain and cold. They were *steps* away from the bridge. "Get up! Keep going!"

Gryphon opened his mouth and let out a bellowing roar. Just as he had in the dungeons. It was a howl more chilling and piercing than the wolves', an unearthly cry that touched some buried instinct in Isabelle, waking a fear more dark and dread than any she'd ever felt.

But this time, Isabelle detected something else in that cry. She heard *pain*, indescribable pain. And as she looked on, she realized why.

Gryphon hunched over, bowing his head. His fingers fanned across the ground, clenching into the snow. Then the joints in his hands *snapped* and *cracked* as they curved inward, forming claws. Isabelle lifted a hand to her mouth, all the air trapped in her lungs, as bones broke all over Gryphon's body. He arched back, contorting, his spine popping again and again. His twisting body tore free of his clothes. His ribcage expanded, swelling until it looked like his skin would burst. The breadth of his shoulders broadened, bones shattering with a terrible *crunch*. His jaw stretched, lengthening into a snout, making room for the fangs sprouting from his gums. And lastly—finally—black fur sprouted all over his body, growing thick and fast.

And all the while, Gryphon's yellow eyes bulged in a silent, agonizing scream.

Then—ripping free of the last of his clothes—Gryphon fell to all fours, snapping and snarling. The beast once again, fully transformed.

And Isabelle realized she had not followed his last command. She had forgotten to run.

8

INHERITANCE

G RYPHON BECAME THE BEAST.

The world around him changed. Colors shifted, fading into single hues. Fine lines and distinct shapes blurred, blending into a scape of impressions and shadows. It was a muted world. A stark world.

It was a world of absolutes. A harsh world. A world that would hurt him if it could.

But not if he hurt it first.

He had the power to hurt. Even as his vision dimmed, sounds and scents sharpened to a near infinite degree. He could hear the fluttering wings of a hummingbird in the woods behind him. He could hear the soft, sighing gurgle of a mostly frozen creek in the gorge below, only a trickle of water sluicing through the ravine. He could smell the damp of dead leaves and the spicy sap of fir trees and a very specific breed of moss, growing rampant on the walls across the gully.

The scent of that moss, earthy and lush, was familiar to him. As was the scent of the creature facing him.

Human.

He didn't like humans. He couldn't pinpoint why, but he understood them to be a source of pain and misery. But his was the power to hurt. His was the power to *kill*. His body burst with strength and speed. His muscles were taut and primed, his fangs thirsting for blood. He *was* power. He was strength.

The human creature before him stood still. Fear rolled off it in waves. He could hear the tinny patter of its pathetic, thudding heart. It made sounds at him, pitiful, mewling sounds.

It was weak. His for the taking. His to kill.

The human backed onto the wood stretching across the gully. He advanced, crouching low, preparing to spring.

Other human noises caught his attention. There was movement across the gully. More humans. He could smell them too.

The human before him turned and ran down the length of wood. Her strides were slow and clumsy, a worthless attempt to escape. Still, he relished the chase. Snarling, he tore after her, paws thundering against the wood. He was close—his teeth snapped at the human's heels—another step and he would have it—

Then a small, stabbing pain took him in the shoulder. He growled, twisting. It was nothing, a pinprick—but it had distracted him from his prey—

Everything was going dark. Shadows closed in around him, narrowing his line of sight. His senses dulled. His body felt weak and heavy. He could not remain upright.

He collapsed, and all he knew was darkness.

—◆—

When Gryphon came to, he was human. And he was in bed.

Everything hurt. Muscles stiff and sore, joints creaking. That wasn't unusual. He turned into the beast every day, and the transformation took a toll. The change broke and reformed every bone in his body, but simply *being* the beast was not easy either. Trapped in the dungeons, the beast grew agitated. He clawed and beat at the walls; he bit and scratched himself. He ran himself ragged in circles, trying to get free.

What *was* unusual was that Gryphon was in a bed. He often fell asleep as the beast in the late hours of the day. But the change into human form always woke him, and he came back to himself in the dark, on the stone floor in the dungeons.

Why wasn't he in the dungeons?

A familiar smell filled his nostrils, warm and caustic. Oil lamps. He was in his own bed, lying beneath two thick, embroidered quilts and a peacock blue coverlet. That would explain why he was so feverishly warm; he never slept under so many blankets. The heavy curtains on his bed were pulled back, giving him a view of his chamber. The oil lamps doused the room in a low, somber light, one placed at his bedside and one on the mahogany chest across the room.

Someone had put him in his own bed. Who, and why?

He tried to sit up and regretted it, pain flaring all over him. His calves were so tight, they felt about to pop, and his ribs burned as though he'd been beaten. Weirdly, sorest of all were his feet; he winced at the pang in his soles as he flexed them beneath the covers.

No—the sorest was his shoulder. He glanced down and saw it was bandaged, with a pillow placed beneath his arm to cushion it. That tender spot around his ribs was bandaged too. Ellery's work, if he was not mistaken.

"Good, you're awake."

Gryphon looked around. A lean figure lounged in the corner, blending into the shadows so neatly, Gryphon didn't think he would have seen him if he had not spoken. Though if he hadn't been so preoccupied, he would have recognized the human scent.

Klaus materialized, stepping away from the stone wall. His arms were folded over his chest in a familiar pose. "Thought you'd want to know," he said, "the thief did all right last night. Looks like he's in the clear."

"What?"

"Ansel," Klaus clarified. "The full moon?"

"Oh. Right." Gritting his teeth against a groan, Gryphon forced himself upright. Klaus made no move to help as Gryphon awkwardly reached around to bunch up his pillows, creating a plush platform to support himself. "It's the full—wait. It's already passed?" Gryphon frowned, trying to get his bearings. "Klaus, what happened? What am I doing in here?"

Klaus cocked an eyebrow. "You don't remember? You went to get the girl back."

The girl.

Isabelle.

Gryphon's eyes began to widen, but he checked himself, reigning his expression in. His memories slid into place. The girl, Isabelle, had escaped the castle at the worst possible time; he had gone after her as soon as he'd changed back. He'd barely gotten to her before the wolves did, and then—

"You almost got back in time," Klaus went on. "You were still outside the walls when you changed. Isabelle lured you across the gate, and I shot you there—" He indicated Gryphon's shoulder "—with an arrow shaft. Laced it in sedative. Sorry about that."

"A sedative? That worked?"

"I thought of it after the last time you got out." Klaus slouched against one of the deep gray bedposts. "It was the strongest sedative we have. It knocked you out, but only for a few minutes. Your shoulder was a right mess when you turned back. Ellery said the arrowhead broke off in your arm. She had a time getting it out. You don't remember?"

Gryphon cast his mind back. He never remembered being the beast. Though sometimes, he dreamed of it...but he had no idea if those were real memories. He vaguely remembered a sense of cold and wet—he thought he'd been lying in the snow. But Ellery working on his shoulder—he didn't remember that at all.

"Well, she knocked you out for most of it," Klaus explained. "Ether." He straightened, running a hand over his rumpled hair. "Anyway, you should rest. Just wanted to let you know about Ansel."

He turned to go. The flickering light of an oil lamp fell over him, throwing his face into sharp relief. In that moment, the hunter's jagged red scars seemed starker than ever.

Gryphon balled his hands into fists in his lap. He never remembered being the beast. He never remembered anything he *did* as the beast. He wasn't in control.

He didn't remember nearly killing Klaus. He didn't remember mauling him. But he had.

Gryphon glanced up, realizing Klaus had said something else. "What?"

"Ansel," Klaus repeated. "What do you want to do about him?"

Gryphon was quiet for a moment. Then he said, "I'll let you know."

Klaus took his leave, shutting the door behind him.

Gryphon slumped back. He had to decide what to do about Ansel. Keeping him locked up until the full moon had been inevitable, of course, but Gryphon would have been content to let him rot in the tower after that. When Ansel had first arrived at the castle—weak, hungry, battling a cold—Gryphon had been loathe to take him in. There was the beast to consider, his secret to conceal. But it was not the first time a traveler had turned up needing help, and they always gave it, if reluctantly. What else could they do?

But Ansel had proved surprisingly friendly. In a way. Gryphon had never been one for socializing, but he'd found Ansel easy to get along with. Not that they spent much time chatting—Gryphon mostly left his care to Ellery and Klaus—but the few times he had stopped in to see how Ansel was doing, it had been...not unpleasant. And slowly, in their care, Ansel recovered.

Then he stole from them and made off in the night. And Gryphon realized he'd been stupid to think the thief had been a friend. All his talk about having no family—like Gryphon—hadn't even been true. He'd only wanted a place to rest and someone to steal from. Gryphon should have known.

It was the mistake he always made, trusting where he shouldn't.

Still, he didn't want to be responsible for the boy's death. He hadn't realized the conditions in the tower had made him so ill. He hadn't looked in on Ansel until the other night. When he went to speak with the sister.

Isabelle.

Gryphon shuddered, thinking what a close call last night had been. He could recall the terror that had swooped over him when he'd changed at dusk, only to be told Isabelle had run off—on the eve of a full moon. He'd felt the same terror when he'd found her inches from the wolves.

A knock on his door startled Gryphon. "What?" he barked.

Klaus's head appeared. "Sorry," he said in that way of his; he never really sounded *sorry*, "but the girl is here. Isabelle. She's been wanting to talk to you." His tone was sour. "Ambushed me in the corridor."

Gryphon furrowed his brow. She'd been waiting to talk to him? A hot, unpleasant sensation kindled inside him. He didn't want to see her. She knew what he was now—she'd seen him change. He didn't want to talk about it, didn't want to face her questions. But...

"Shall I let her in?" Klaus pressed.

But even if he let her brother go...*she* would have to stay here. Maybe it was best to answer her questions now. Get it over with.

"Let her in," Gryphon groused.

A moment later, she appeared. Isabelle. She peeked her head around the door, then stepped inside. Her dark, curly hair flared around her face, and she wore a wool pajama set—baggy bottoms and a button-up top. And no dressing gown. Most people would not have found that "strictly proper," but then, neither was it proper for Gryphon to talk to a girl he barely knew in his bedchamber, in the middle of the night, bare-chested. Gryphon had never cared much what people thought was *proper*, anyway.

Isabelle seemed to have the same disregard. She approached him without hesitation or embarrassment, coming up to his bedside. She eyed him openly, her gaze sweeping over him. As though he was a specimen for study.

Gryphon stiffened. Well, many *would* find him a subject for study if they knew what he was. Suddenly, he felt uncomfortable beneath her gaze.

She had seen him *change*.

"Well, now you know," Gryphon said. "What I am. What happens to me."

Isabelle cocked her head to one side. "You mean that you change into a beast? I already knew that. Or I suspected."

Gryphon felt like he'd been punched in the gut. "*What?*"

"Well, you know, your eyes are the same regardless of what form you're in." Her tone was matter-of-fact, as though they were discussing what had been served for tea. "And unfortunately, I got a rather close-up look at the beast's eyes the first day I was here. So. It wasn't difficult to parse out."

Gryphon goggled at her. His eyes. His damned *eyes*. True, he had donned that hood just in case...but he'd never really thought she might figure it out. He felt more naked than ever, sitting there, as she casually explained away his deepest, darkest secret.

"But." Isabelle shook her head, her brushed-out curls flouncing around her. "I *don't* know why this happens to you, and considering I helped get you back into the castle, I think I deserve an explanation. Don't you agree?"

Gryphon was still speechless. Her eyes, he noticed, were a most peculiar shade. Her brother's eyes were the same color as his hair, a dark umber. But Isabelle's eyes were several shades lighter. Rusty brown, like leaves changing color in the fall. Rich and round and fierce.

"Well?" Isabelle prompted.

Gryphon jerked his gaze away. "There is no explanation. I turn into a beast. The end."

"There has to be more to it than that."

"Maybe there is," Gryphon said in a harsh voice, "but it's none of your business. Did that ever occur to you? I suppose not, since you were sneaking around my dungeons. You realize, had you never been down there, you wouldn't be stuck here? *I wouldn't be stuck with you?*"

He half-hoped this reprimand would scare her off, but it had the opposite effect. Isabelle squared her shoulders. "Maybe I shouldn't have gone into your dungeons. But I did, and that's done now. So let's learn from that particular mistake and move on, shall we?"

Learn from that mistake. Gryphon had never been good at that.

"As for your condition being none of my business, I disagree," she continued. "I'm stuck here, as you pointed out, so what is the *point* of keeping me in the dark? I can't tell anyone. Don't you think it's better I know what's going on so I don't do anything else to put myself in danger?"

"Well..." Gryphon tried to find some hole in this argument, but all he could come up with was *I don't want to tell you anything, so there.* And he had to admit that was rather childish. He gave her his best glare, which was small consolation. "You already know I turn into the beast. With the sunrise."

"And turn back when the sun sets, yes." Isabelle nodded. "And Klaus told me you have to be on the castle grounds to turn back, or else you won't. He said you've gotten free twice before, including when you first changed."

"Well, if Klaus told you all that—" Who was Klaus, to go telling her everything? "—what else could you possibly want to know?"

"You must be joking." The look she turned on him was incredulous. "I want to know how this *happened* to you. What caused it?"

Gryphon shifted. "I don't know."

"What do you mean, you don't know?"

"I mean, *I don't know.*"

"So, what...you just woke up one day and turned into a beast?"

"Approximately."

Isabelle shot him a suspicious look. Gryphon held her gaze, though this was more difficult to do than he might have thought.

The truth was, Gryphon found Isabelle perplexing. It was her direct way of speaking—no, it was more than that. It was how plainly *unafraid* she was. Gryphon had never asked people to fear him; contrary to what most thought, he'd never liked that. And yet they always had, ever since he'd begun to grow out of boyhood. Perhaps even before that.

It was just one more thing that set him apart from the world.

But Isabelle was not afraid of him. Or if she was, she didn't show it. Even now, knowing what he was—stones, she'd confronted the beast on her own *twice* now, and still she was not afraid. She hadn't been afraid in the woods either. The way she'd faced down those wolves beside him...

As though hearing his thoughts, Isabelle said, "Well, what about the wolves, then? The ones that attacked me in the forest?"

Gryphon snapped out of his thoughts. "What about them?"

"Well, they weren't normal wolves."

"Weren't they?"

Isabelle gave him a look of deepest exasperation. "Am I going to have to wring every detail out of you? Look, I came back, didn't I? You have to explain."

Gryphon bit back an oath. "You're going to think I'm mad."

"Don't worry," Isabelle said dryly. "My opinion of you is not that high to begin with." Her brow wrinkled. "Does this have something to do with the supposed curse on this castle? Or rather, on the royals who used to live here?"

Gryphon's whole body tensed. "What do you know about *that?*"

Isabelle's gaze sharpened. "So it's true?"

"I don't know. That depends on what you've heard."

Isabelle waved a vague hand. "Nothing specific. The last Forest king crossed a witch, who, in turn, hexed him and his whole family. Whatever she did plunged the entire kingdom into ruin. Oh, and some blather about his descendants haunting the forest."

"Well, they sort of do." When Isabelle raised an eyebrow, Gryphon said, "You met some of them. Last night."

"Who? Wait...you mean the *wolves?*"

Gryphon nodded.

Isabelle seemed to consider this. Then she turned and hoisted herself onto the foot of his bed, folding her legs beneath her. "So there really is a curse? Cast by some witch?"

For a moment, Gryphon was too indignant to register her questions. That was *his* bed she'd just climbed onto without invitation—and nearly sat on his foot in the process. Then he realized Isabelle was watching him, waiting for an answer. He searched her face for any sign of skepticism. Perched on the foot of his bed, she was further away than she had been before, but somehow, the space between them felt smaller. The low lamplight cast an intimate glow, ensconcing them together. Creating a sense of...something like trust.

Gryphon shifted beneath his quilts, ignoring the twinge in his shoulder. Trust was a dangerous thing. "Look...I don't know everything, and some of it is only a guess. But..." He clasped his hands together before him. "The last Forest king *did* cross a witch. And in retaliation—on the night of a full moon—she cursed the king and his family. Though legend says one princess escaped—one of the king's daughters. Supposedly, she fled the castle before the curse was cast."

"But how did she get out?" Isabelle interrupted.

"No one knows. Though some say the witch let the princess escape."

"But why? And how was she free of the curse just because she wasn't in the castle? I mean, if the bloodline was cursed—"

"Will you let me finish? If you ask a million questions, I'll never get through it all." Gryphon huffed a breath, continuing only when Isabelle remained silent, her lips pursed. "You just have to remember that princess. Because she's important. Anyway. The hex was this: that—"

"—the entire family would turn into wolves on the full moon?" Isabelle cut in. She ducked her head when Gryphon shot her a glare. "Sorry. But if those wolves that attacked me are the descendants—"

"You're partly right. The witch cursed them to turn. But not into wolves." Gryphon paused. "Into beasts."

Isabelle's eyes flew to his face, startled. "Beasts? You mean like *you?*"

"So it would seem." Gryphon sagged back against his pillows. This tale was already taking a lot out of him. Or maybe that was just the day he'd had. "The royal family were cursed to turn into beasts. They transformed every day and only turned back if they were on the castle grounds. Sound familiar?"

"But the wolves—the descendants—"

"As I understand it, the curse has...diluted, over the years," Gryphon explained. "Through the passing generations, the descendants of the royals became less like beasts and more like wolves. They also turned with less frequency. Now they only turn on the night of a full moon."

"But how are there descendants at all?" Isabelle asked. "If they couldn't leave the castle—no, perhaps I don't want to know—"

"Again, there are only rumors. Some say the eldest princess was carrying a child when the curse took hold—and that child was the first descendant, not bound to the castle like the others. Another rumor is the family learned how to control their turning." Gryphon highly doubted this. *He* had lived with this curse for over two years now and never come close to controlling it. "But the wolves that attacked you—they are the descendants. A pack of siblings mostly."

"Hmm. And how do you know all this?"

Gryphon's gut gave a nasty twist. "I've had some dealings with those wolves. The eldest sibling—Viveca—became rather interested in me when she found out I was living here. And that I'd become the beast."

"Yes." Isabelle—who had also begun to slump, looking drowsy—sat up straight. "About that. It sounds like you suffer from this same curse. Care to explain?"

Gryphon spread his hands. "What I told you before was true. I don't know for sure what caused my curse. And I *did* wake up one morning and turn into a beast—"

"Oh, please," Isabelle scoffed.

"—twenty days after I arrived in this castle," Gryphon finished. "The morning after the first full moon I spent here." He flexed a hand, unwilling to relive those memories. "You see, the moment I stepped into this castle, something *struck* me. Something that laid me out for over a week. It was the magic, I suppose. The curse." He gave a bleak shrug. "You asked how that princess escaped the curse if it was tied to the bloodline. I think it *is* tied to the bloodline, but it's also tied to the castle. That's what happened when I stepped foot in here. I activated the curse."

Isabelle's eyes lit with dawning understanding. "That princess—the one who escaped—"

"I have no proof," said Gryphon, "but it *does* make sense with what I know of my family. I believe the princess who escaped was my ancestor. I'm *her* descendant. So when I stepped into this castle...I activated the original curse. And brought it down on me."

9

HUNTED

G ARRETT HAD SOME EXPERIENCE in the Black Forest,
hunting the same beast they were after now. He had no
idea if the beast was even real—though he thought they'd caught
a glimpse of it the last time he was here, a little over a year ago.

There had always been tales of beasts and evil creatures in the
Black Forest, but Garrett had a knack for following *particular*
stories, collecting those legends that were based in real truth. It
wasn't until about two years ago that tales of a mutant beast in
the Black Forest—particularly in the northern reaches—began
to coalesce into something with a ring of truth.

He'd been intrigued by the prospect of hunting a monster
beast from the start, but he hadn't had the chance straightaway.
For one thing, his father hadn't been so keen to let him run
off wherever he wanted back then, considering he'd been only
sixteen. And for another thing, right around the time he'd begun
planning the venture, Snow died. After that, he'd avoided the
hunting trip until about a year ago. They didn't catch the beast,
and there was some dispute among his soldiers as to whether

they'd actually seen it, but it had been a fun trip nonetheless. Garrett had always wanted to come back.

"We're bound to get it in our sights this time," Garrett said enthusiastically, shrugging off his pack. They were still in the southern reaches of the Black Forest; they'd just reached the woods a few days ago. The sun rose and set so early this time of year that it cut into their traveling time—even now, in the early evening, it was already full dark. Since they were in no particular rush, this was no real problem. "In fact, I'll wager we have a much better chance this time around."

"What makes you say that?" Spencer asked.

Garrett grinned. "We have Gemma."

Gemma was not only Garrett's best tracker, she was an excellent sharpshooter—his second best after Kinsley. And she was a hunter, born and raised in the Black Forest. As a child, she'd lived in one of the villages here, and after her mother died, her father had taken her on the move. They'd lived off the forest, foraging, hunting, and selling pelts. She'd only joined Garrett's company a few months after his last expedition to hunt the beast.

"Aw, she's not so special, sire." This jibe came from Falcon. "I reckon it'll be one of our arrows that brings the beast down, don't you think, Roy?"

"Definitely." Roy flashed a smile. He was a square-jawed young man, the eldest in the group at twenty-three. He had a compact build that made it easy for him to stay hidden.

Gemma eyed them both, clearly unconcerned by this teasing. Gemma was a quiet girl, around Garrett's age. She had tawny skin and keen eyes. Like the rest of the soldiers, she wasn't in uniform—as it was only a hunting expedition, they'd dressed casually. Gemma wore baggy trousers tucked into her boots and a forest green coat. Her dark, wavy hair was piled and pinned behind her head. "I think it'll be Prince Garrett that brings the beast down," she said, "since that's what he ordered."

"Well, I'd like to do it myself," Garrett said affably. "But if any of you have a shot, you should take it. We don't want the beast getting away like last time, do we, Spencer?"

Spencer sent him an injured look. "That wasn't my fault, sire!"

Garrett laughed. "I know. I'm only teasing." Spencer was the only one here who'd been on the last trip into the Black Forest. Garrett had chosen him for that reason, and because he was the only one in his company proficient with Garrett's new repeater rifle—given that he'd had firsthand experience with it in the Mountain Kingdom against a horde of corpse creatures.

Young Evans rounded out the last of their party. He was the youngest at sixteen. He had tomato red hair and a scrawny build. He was often unsure of himself, but he'd proven his courage against the corpses. Garrett had lost quite a few soldiers on that venture. Evans was one of the few who'd survived.

They set up camp between the trees, pitching tents and preparing an evening meal. Gear-bulb lanterns hung on pitched poles gave them light, as did the full moon in the sky. It shone through the wintered treetops like a beacon.

Spencer wrinkled his nose as he stepped into a deep patch of snow, his boot sinking ankle-deep. "Wet, this," he remarked, "isn't it?"

"Usually," Garrett agreed in good humor. Their last trip had been early enough that they had avoided much snow. "I thought we might have more of it."

"There will be more further north." Gemma raised her head from hammering a stake into the ground. "I thought we might get some today. The air smelled of it, but—" She shook her head. "I think it stayed north of us."

Falcon looked incredulous. "You can't *smell* snow."

"Of course you can." Unruffled, Gemma turned back to staking her tent.

Falcon exchanged a skeptical glance with Roy, then looked to Garrett. "Fire tonight, sire?"

"Definitely," said Garrett. Once they were deeper into the forest, they'd have to forgo fires—the deeper the woods, the more dangerous it became, harboring threats of beast and man alike. Bandits weren't unheard of. Better they enjoyed their fires now while they could.

Falcon tossed a sly look in Gemma's direction. "Fancy helping me find some firewood, Gemma?"

"Sure." Gemma hammered in her last stake, then rose. The look she directed at Falcon was noncommittal. "You go that way—" She indicated towards the east "—and I'll go this way." She pointed west. Ignoring Falcon's crestfallen expression, she headed into the woods alone, her rifle in hand.

Roy chuckled as he passed Falcon, clapping a hand on his shoulder. "Better luck next time, mate."

"Clueless," Falcon grumbled. "Utterly clueless." He stomped off east, disappearing into the darkness.

Garrett kept his grin to himself. He was pretty sure Gemma wasn't clueless. Just disinterested.

He and the remaining soldiers continued, finishing with their tents and laying out cooking supplies. Despite their lanterns and the moonlight, the night hung heavy, as though a cloak of shadows had dropped over their camp. There was something *thick* about the night in the Black Forest, something impenetrable; perhaps, Garrett thought, that was what had earned the forest its name.

The resinous woods scented the brisk air, sharpening the cold. That cold sent a shiver through Garrett. The wind had been fierce today, whipping through the trees from the south. It had settled now, and fog began to form, stealing over them like a thief.

Garrett shivered again, rubbing his hands together. Everything was prepped for supper except— "Where are Gemma and Falcon with that wood?"

As though in answer, a piercing *crack* split the night air. A gunshot exploding into the quiet.

"What the hell?" Spencer, reclining against his pack, jumped up.

Garrett spun around, listening intently. But in the wake of that single shot, there was only silence. And a dreadful stillness.

"Gemma?" Garrett called, trying to repress an uncertain note in his voice. "Falcon?"

"Falcon didn't have a gun," Evans fretted. "Had to be Gemma."

Garrett spun into action. "Evans, stay here," he ordered, rooting his second pistol out of his pack. "Spence, with me. Roy, see if you can find Falcon, but don't stray far."

He and Spencer hurried through the trees at a wary jog, Garrett in the lead with his pistol in one hand and a lantern in the other. Spencer stayed close, watching their rear. The light of their lantern bobbed in the darkness, creating a white halo four feet deep ahead. Everything else was concealed in darkness, the bare trees indistinct in the black. A snarl of bramble *snapped* beneath Garrett's boot, the sound unnaturally loud.

"Gemma?" Garrett called again. "Gemma?"

When there was still no answer, he slowed to a halt. Spencer followed his lead. They stood for a moment, motionless, listening. The forest was mistier than ever, silvery fog snaking through the trees and wrapping around their ankles. There was something *off* about the forest, Garrett thought, something wrong about how still it was. No wind sloughing through the evergreens, no creatures scurrying along the forest floor. As though everything alive in the forest had abandoned it. Everything except them.

Garrett opened his mouth, preparing to call for Gemma again. Before he could, another shot rang out—this one from behind, back towards their camp.

"Curse it," Garrett muttered. "What the hell is going on?"

"Bandits?" Spencer said in a low voice. "This far south?"

"Maybe." Garrett gnawed his lip as he started back, motioning for Spencer to follow. "Or wolves. Though I don't remember having trouble from them the first time around."

"We saw some signs of them deeper in the forest, I recall," Spencer said. "But not this far south. I think—" He broke off with a high-pitched yelp as a dark shadow descended before them, dropping from an oak tree.

Garrett stumbled back as the shadow landed, lithe as a cat. But as the figure unfolded, Garrett saw it was not a cat or creature of any kind. It was a person.

"Your Highness?"

"Gemma." Garrett released a breath, raising his lantern. The halo of light fell over the figure, revealing Gemma's face. She still carried her rifle, hefting it in both hands.

"What happened?" Spencer asked. "We heard shots."

"I'm not sure," Gemma's dark eyes narrowed. "I was heading back to camp when something knocked into me from behind. Knocked me down."

"What was it?"

"I didn't get a good look. But I think it scratched me—is my coat torn?" She turned, giving him a look at her back.

Garrett squinted. "Yes, it's all ripped. Are you all right?"

"It must have just grazed me, sire." She turned back to face him. "It didn't get through my clothes. It must have been some kind of animal." She shook her head. "But I didn't hear it coming. Once I got back to my feet, I looked around, but..."

"But what?" Spencer prompted.

"I thought I saw—" Her jaw tightened. "*Something*. Just a shadow, really. Running north." She pointed. "But I don't know—maybe I hit my head when I fell—it was *big*, sire. Whatever it was."

Garrett chewed his lip, considering. "Wolf?"

"It moved like one," Gemma admitted, "but the size...more bear-like."

Garrett and Spencer exchanged a quick look. "It can't be the beast, Highness," Spencer protested. "Not this far south. Surely not."

"Well, it's been a year." Garrett turned, heading back to camp. He set a rapid pace, weaving through the trees, and Gemma and Spencer hastened to keep up with his long strides. "Who knows what might've happened? Maybe food's gotten scarce up north, maybe the villagers drove it off—"

"I heard another shot." Gemma skipped every other step to keep up. "That second one—it wasn't me."

"I know," Garrett said grimly. "It sounded like it was back at camp."

When they reached the camp, they found everything in ruins. Their tents had been torn down, bits left in tatters, and their food and supplies were scattered across the ground—though the food was largely untouched, Garrett noticed. He would have thought an animal would have been after food. He picked through the wreckage, raising his lantern to inspect it, looking for some clue of what had happened.

Then a dark figure caught his eye, lingering behind the nearby trees. Gemma must have seen it too, for she raised her rifle in a flash, cocking the trigger back.

"Whoa!" The figure stepped into the light, revealing a familiar brown face and dopey ears. It was Roy. "It's me."

"What happened here?" Garrett asked. "Where's Falcon?"

"I never found him, sire. I came back when I heard another shot. Thought it must be Evans, but—well, he's gone too."

Gritting his teeth, Garrett swept another glance around, surveying the destruction. There was no telling where Falcon and Evans had gone, if they were together or separated, and no telling what had drawn them off.

No telling if it was the beast.

"Someone ran this way." Garrett spun around and found Gemma crouched near a cluster of barren birch trees. Her gaze was bent as she studied the earth, tilting her head back and forth. "Someone with a light step. Evans, probably. He was running fast."

Garrett pinched his forehead, trying to get a grip on himself. Gemma, of course. Hadn't he just been boasting what a brilliant tracker she was? "Running after something or away from it?"

"Not sure." Gemma pursed her lips. White fog crept over her, masking her face. She took a few shuffling steps forward, the mist dispelling around her. "He was definitely in a hurry. Broke up all this bramble here. I think maybe—ah. Here we go." Gemma straightened. "I'd say he was the one doing the chasing." Her expression was grave.

"Then why do you look like—that?" Roy asked bluntly, indicating the look on her face.

Gemma pointed. "Because that's what he was chasing."

Garrett stepped forward, bending to peer at the ground.

It was an animal track. A paw print, like that of a wolf, embedded in a thin layer of icy, muddy snow. And it was *enormous*. At least twice the size of a normal wolf's print. Maybe even three times the size.

Garrett gawped. "Wolf?"

"Or something," Gemma replied.

"I don't know, sire." Spencer shifted to one side as he studied the print. "Oh, I'm sure it's wolf," he added hastily, catching Gemma's dark look. "If you say it is. I'm a city boy. I don't know much about tracks except what I've learned from Prince Garrett here."

"I don't know anything about tracks, Spencer," Garrett said.

"That was sort of my point, sire."

"What do you mean, then?" Roy flicked an impatient glance into the shadow of the woods.

"Well, I know we didn't see more than a glimpse of that beast last time, sire," Spencer went on, "but it wasn't exactly a wolf, was it? Kelley swore he saw the thing walk on two legs, and a wolf can't do that. I'm just saying, perhaps this isn't the beast."

"No, it's just a giant wolf," Gemma said flatly. "How is that better?"

"Well, it's not, really. I just thought I'd mention it."

Bam. Bam. Bam. Three more gunshots, cracking like a whip.

"Curse me." Roy whipped an arrow from his quiver.

Gemma pointed. "Came from that way."

"You don't have to be a tracker to know that," Roy said. "Sire?"

"Let's go. And stick together." Garrett took off at a careful run, trying not to slip over the frosted ground. "Whatever this thing is, it took advantage of splitting us up. Let's see how it handles us all at once."

Spencer ran ahead, taking point, while Gemma dropped back to the rear. Roy flanked Garrett on the right, an arrow loosely nocked to his bow. They ran as fast as they could, ducking beneath low-hanging branches and dodging clusters of shrubs.

More shots rang out. Then a howl rose through the air, swelling in an eerie crescendo around them. The cry echoed, bouncing from tree to tree so that Garrett couldn't tell what direction it came from.

"Creepy!" Spencer called. "That was creepy, right?"

No one answered. They only ran. Garrett tried to pick up his pace, but the ground grew icier and more sludgy. His muscles grew tense as he tried not to slip, and then he *did* slip, his boot sliding over a damp stone embedded in the ground. Garrett glanced down, catching his balance before he could fall.

He looked up just in time to see a dark, impossibly fast shape hurtle through the trees ahead. It was there one second and gone the next, vaporizing like smoke. Garrett's breath tangled in his throat; he stumbled to a halt, half-raising his pistol. Out of the corner of his eye, he saw another shape dart forward, but it was only Spencer, rounding a thick oak tree.

Then Spencer let out a bodiless shout.

Garrett didn't falter; he spun, pistol in hand and ready to fire. Then Spencer shouted, "It's us, it's us!" and a moment later, *Falcon* materialized from the shadows, an arrow nocked to his bow.

"Falcon." Garrett drew his arm back at the elbow, raising his pistol to the sky. Evans was there too, his red hair evident in the darkness. Relief flared through Garrett like a sputtering flame, not strong enough to douse the adrenaline coursing through him.

Falcon lowered his bow. His eyes were bright and cagey. "Sorry, sire," he said, out of breath, "but that thing is toying with us! It lured Evans out here, and we can't get a clear shot, the way it's darting about—"

"What is it?" Gemma asked. "Did you get a clear look?"

"No. But I think it's—"

Something zipped through the trees behind Falcon. A shadow, darting past so quickly, Garrett didn't have time to shout a warning. Then it was gone again, and Garrett whirled around, wondering if he'd imagined the whole thing.

Then Evans screamed.

Garrett spun again. Evans, still screaming, was on the ground, pinned by—by something massive, something covered in dark fur. Even over the boy's screams, Garrett heard the menacing growls, the jagged, awful *tearing* of teeth. Someone was shouting; Garrett aimed his pistol in the dark, wary of hitting Evans as he flailed—

A shot burst into the air, so loud that Garrett felt his right ear go deaf.

It was over in a second. The creature spasmed. Then it collapsed, utterly still, atop Evans.

Garrett ran forward. Together with Roy, they heaved the gargantuan beast off their companion. Garrett barely spared it a glance, his attention all for Evans. The boy's screams died away to ragged, mewling breaths as his head rolled away from his savaged shoulder. The sleeve of his shirt was shredded, and so was his skin. His collarbone was a mess of punctured flesh and gummy blood.

"Evans, can you hear me?" Garrett took the young man's head in his hands. "Evans? You're going to be fine, all right? Evans?"

"Didn't puncture any major arteries, sire," said Roy, his voice clinical as he examined the grisly wound. He was their medic on this trip. "But we need to get him back to camp and get him stitched up. Watch for infection."

Garrett motioned Falcon to help Roy, then rose to join Gemma, who stood over the carcass of the dead beast. It was her shot that had felled the creature, and she stood with her smoking rifle over her shoulder, a grim expression on her face.

"Was Spencer right?" she asked Garrett. "Could this be your beast, Highness?"

Garrett stared at the dead animal. "No. I don't think so." This creature was, quite clearly, a wolf. It had the shape of a wolf—the limbs, the snout, the ears, and the paws of a wolf. It was at once recognizable in form.

But it was *massive*. Three times the size of a normal wolf. Garrett had never heard of one so big.

"Spencer was right," he said slowly. "The beast we saw last time was shaped differently. And I reckon Kelley was right about it walking on two legs. Also..." Garrett hesitated, glancing at Gemma. "It was a bit bigger than this."

Gemma looked at him incredulously. "Bigger than *this?*"

"Yes." Garrett ran a hand over his mouth. "Bigger."

10

ARMISTICE

G RYPHON CLIMBED THE STAIRS from the dungeon more
slowly than usual. The wounds he'd suffered two nights
ago had already healed; it was one benefit of his...condition. But
the change took its toll on his body. He let out a ponderous
sigh as he mounted the last few steps, pushing a steadying hand
against the pitted stone wall. Sometimes, he felt like all he did in
this castle was climb stairs.

When he reached the top and emerged into the entrance hall,
he found Klaus waiting. That was not unusual, but what he said
next was. "Isabelle wants to talk to you."

"About what?"

"She didn't say, but I'd wager everything I own it's about her
brother."

"Do you actually own anything, Klaus?"

"The clothes on my back," Klaus replied. "She's up in her
room. She demanded I bring her to you, but Ellery won't hear
of it. Says she needs to stay in bed."

"Why?"

"She's ill," said Klaus. "Taken a chill, Ellery says."

Gryphon looked at him sharply. Klaus had spoken in the same toneless voice he always did, and studying his face now, Gryphon couldn't detect any hint that Klaus meant more than he was saying.

Klaus seemed to intuit Gryphon's concern. "Just a chill. Bit of a fever. She *was* out all day and night in knee-deep snow, after all. With hardly any sleep. It's not so weird she'd fall ill."

Gryphon nodded, leaving Klaus behind to climb the grand staircase. His eyes ran blindly over the network of wispy cobwebs stretching betwixt each banister. *Klaus is right*, he told himself. It was not so weird that Isabelle was ill.

When Ellery let him into Isabelle's room, however, she didn't look particularly ill. He'd expected to find her tucked in bed, buried beneath too many quilts. Instead, Isabelle was pacing her room, wrapped in a mauve dressing gown. The folds of crushed velvet rippled and deepened with each step she took. "*There* you are," she said. A rather churlish greeting. Gryphon was not sure why her lack of social graces bothered him when he himself had scorned such things for years. "I told Klaus I wanted to talk to you an hour ago."

"The sun only just went down." Gryphon made an aggravated gesture towards the window in the far wall.

Isabelle glanced up at it. "Oh." She did not sound particularly abashed.

"Ellery said you were ill," he said. "Too ill to leave your room."

Isabelle waved a hand. "It's just a cold. You can't make me stay in bed."

Gryphon raised his eyes heavenward. For the Gift's sake, he didn't care if she stayed in bed or not. He was too tired to argue, so he said, "What did you want to talk to me about? Only, given how I spend my days, this is usually the time *I* go to bed."

The look Isabelle gave him was peculiar. "It's dusk. This is the time most people go to bed."

"Yes, well..." He supposed that was true. The difference was, he only slept for a few hours, waking before midnight so he had *some* time to himself. "Look, if this is about your brother—he can go as soon as he's well enough to travel."

He didn't know when he'd made the decision. The words left his mouth before he'd thought them, but he meant it. Isabelle had to stay here; there was no question about that. She would be trouble enough on her own—better to take Ansel out of the equation. At the very least, he wouldn't have to listen to Isabelle harangue him about her brother anymore.

"You'll really let him go?" Isabelle asked. "Just like that?"

"I was always going to let him go," Gryphon muttered. That was twisting the truth. "I just wanted to...teach him a lesson first." That sounded like something his father would say. Gryphon regretted the words at once.

But Isabelle barely seemed to have heard him. "Yes, well, that's the issue." She leaned back against her small dining table, gripping it on either side of her. "He's not going to want to leave without me."

Gryphon forced himself to hold her gaze. "Well, he'll just have to."

"Will he?" There was a jagged edge to Isabelle's words. "I still have to stay?"

Gryphon set his face like flint. Klaus's words floated back to him. *It's not so weird she'd fall ill.* "I told you before. You've seen the beast. I can't let you leave."

"The beast is *you*!"

"Even more reason you need to stay. I can't risk you'll go telling the first villagers you see—"

"Do you *really* think I'd do that?"

"I don't know, Isabelle," he said tightly. "I don't know you at all."

"What aren't you telling me?" Isabelle crossed her arms over her chest. "This is about more than just keeping your secret." She studied him a moment. Then, "The wolves. You said my brother was attacked by wolves. He was attacked by *these* wolves, wasn't he? By this Viveca and her siblings?"

Gryphon guarded himself. They were skirting close to some dangerous topics. But this—he couldn't keep this from her. He would have to explain. "Yes. That's why we had him locked in the tower."

Isabelle's gaze was still trained on his face, but she seemed to be looking through him. Her forehead wrinkled in preoccupation. "Quarantine," she murmured.

Gryphon's stomach flipped. "What?"

"Ansel told me he heard Ellery say something about quarantine." Isabelle refocused on him. "I thought it had something to do with him being ill, but..."

Gryphon gave a reluctant sigh. "We didn't know if he'd been bitten. *He* didn't know. The wolves had injured him, but it wasn't clear if it was a bite or not." He gauged Isabelle for a reaction, but her face was inscrutable. "Anyone bitten by those wolves—they become ill. *Very* ill. And if the victim lives long enough...they eventually go mad. Just before the end."

"The end?"

"Before they die," Gryphon admitted. "It can get bad. Usually, the victim becomes violent. And there is no cure. Nothing that can be done." At the aghast look on Isabelle's face, he was quick to add, "But your brother is fine. We know that now. The victims always die before the next full moon. Ansel made it through, so he couldn't have been bitten. He should recover."

None of this seemed to reassure Isabelle. "And what about me?" she asked, her voice strained. "*You* bit me."

Gryphon hesitated. "I'm not one of them."

"But something's going to happen to me?" Isabelle's voice was hushed. "Am *I* going to go mad? Am I going to...die?"

"I don't think so."

"You don't *think* so?"

"I've never bitten anyone before. Viveca once told me that it's another mutation in the curse, the madness. She said the original curse didn't do that. But—" Gryphon spread his hands. "We can't know for sure. Viveca knows a lot about the curse, yes, but all from stories passed down through her family. Stories that are over a hundred years old. There's just no way to be sure."

Isabelle stared at him a moment longer. Then she expelled a long breath and sank back, collapsing into the chair behind her.

"I really think you'll be fine," Gryphon lied. Lied, not because he thought she *wouldn't* be fine. But because...he just didn't know. He *did not know.*

"I'm ill now." Isabelle wiped a tremulous hand over her brow.

"A cold," Gryphon dismissed. "Just a cold."

"You said the madness sets in by the following full moon." Isabelle frowned. "But that's already happened—you bit me, what, five days?—before the full moon."

"Another reason to think you're probably fine. It's just...given that it was so close to the full moon, I think it's best if you stay until the next one. Just to make sure."

Isabelle's eyes fell shut. She looked very tired and very fragile, her slender shoulders sagging. "How many people have these wolves killed over the years? I mean, why don't they lock themselves up like you do? They'd only have to do it once a month. They attacked Ansel, they attacked me—"

Gryphon grimaced. "Viveca and her family...you have to understand what they're like."

"Evil?" Isabelle guessed.

Gryphon shrugged. It was as good a word as any. "They don't view themselves as human. In their eyes, they're set apart...a different species. They don't value *human* life. To them, humans are just prey." He rubbed a hand over his eyes. "Viveca, in particular, sees herself as a superior being. Not just because of the curse, but because she's descended from the Forest kings. The way she sees it, this is *her* land, her forest."

Isabelle's gaze turned shrewd. "No wonder she took an interest in you. You've met her?" When Gryphon nodded, she asked, "And what did she want from you?"

Another tricky question. "An alliance," he hedged. "In her mind, I belong with them. After all, we're distantly related. But I made it clear I want nothing to do with her, and now—well, she leaves me alone."

Isabelle went silent. She traced a finger over a fresh scab on her cheek. A wound she'd taken in the confrontation with the wolves. She was quiet for so long that Gryphon began to wonder if he should leave, but then she said, "So, all this time...when you had Ansel locked up. You thought he was going to go mad and die?"

"We didn't know," Gryphon repeated. "We had to be sure."

She looked at him, her eyes flashing. "So it wasn't about him stealing the silver at all!"

For some reason, this rebuke stung. "I wouldn't say *that*," Gryphon said icily.

"But you could have told him!" Isabelle's wrath returned in full force. "He'd been attacked and injured. He might've been dying, but instead of warning him, you just *locked him up?*"

"What good would warning him have done? And what do you care, anyway?"

"What do I *care?* Ansel is my *family.* Don't you understand what that means?"

Gryphon's chest clenched. A torrent of unwanted emotions flooded through him, too deep and complicated to parse out. Too shaded in darkness to *want* to parse out. "You know, your brother told me he had no family, Isabelle," Gryphon snapped. "Why would he say that? Did you abandon him?"

Isabelle recoiled, her whole body tensing. The look that flared across her face was enough to make Gryphon regret his words. Because he *recognized* that look. It mirrored the same darkness that had just swept over him. Without meaning to, he'd hurt her, ripping into some old wound. Digging beneath the scar tissue. And he knew then, in a flash of clarity.

Isabelle hadn't abandoned anyone. She had *been* abandoned.

"You know," Isabelle said, sounding as though she'd developed a sore throat as well as a cold, "my past is none of your business." Arms wrapped around herself, she turned away from him. "I'd like you to leave now. I need to rest."

Gryphon stared at her for a long moment, chagrined. Then he turned and quit the room.

Although he was tired, Gryphon didn't go back to his room to sleep. Instead, he went out into the courtyard. The shock of the cold air was a relief, cooling his nerves. He rounded the castle, making for the back of the courtyard. There sat a round, squat turret on the corner of the ramparts.

That little tower was Gryphon's destination.

It was cold in the tower too. Gryphon didn't mind, but he needed light. So the first thing he did was start a fire in the grate, and then he lit the large gear-bulb lamp on his pine worktable.

The tower was his workshop, where Gryphon spent most of his free time. Two long, rustic shelves held many of his past creations: clay and wood figures, his smaller sculptures, hand-crafted urns. He had a few paintings propped up in the far corner next to a gear-operated potter's wheel. His worktable was littered with half-done charcoal sketches and clay jars of paint. He'd recently acquired a large chunk of white marble, which sat at the foot of his small bed. (He had his bedroom in the castle, of course—but he kept a bed here in case he wanted a nap while working on a project.)

Gryphon looked around. A large canvas painting sat partway done on an easel, but Gryphon left it there, his eyes going to the chunk of marble.

Gryphon worked in different mediums, but more often than not, he sculpted. There was something appealing about forming art out of a hunk of rock. Finding the life inside, chipping away piece by piece until it revealed itself. The process calmed and exhilarated him at the same time. It was a feeling he had never been able to capture anywhere else, doing anything else.

He had taken even more refuge in his art after the beast's curse fell upon him. The change terrified Gryphon. Seven-hundred and sixty-nine days of it hadn't changed that. It wasn't the pain he feared, not anymore. What scared him was losing himself. The beast was savage and graceless, with no desire but to dominate and kill. When he was the beast, he lost his freedom, his expression. Every time he turned, the beast chipped away at his soul.

Chipping away at his block of marble seemed to help restore it.

Gryphon sat, one hand on the plaster and the other gripping his chisel. Something was itching to get out of him, but he couldn't piece it together. He tapped a restless foot against the leg of his wooden stool.

Unfortunately, he left his tower an hour later, glummer than ever. Neither sculpting nor painting had proved a worthwhile distraction from his troubles, and, frustrated, he'd given up. He thought perhaps he should just find something to eat and get a few hours' sleep.

When he stepped out into the courtyard, packed snow crunching beneath his boots, he caught a whiff of something un-expected—a smoky, greasy residue, cutting through the glacial air. The smell of something burning.

Gryphon stepped around the corner and ran straight into Klaus.

Gryphon blinked. "What are you doing out here?" Klaus's scent was familiar to him; he could usually sense when he was near. But that smoky odor had masked the hunter.

In answer, Klaus tipped his chin upwards.

Gryphon turned to look. An old-fashioned torch sat atop the back corner of the castle ramparts, set in an old, dented metal brazier. The torch's flames blazed, its iron gray smoke barely visible as it rushed into the night sky.

Beside the torch was Isabelle. Standing atop the ramparts, gazing out at the wintry landscape.

"What is she doing up there?" Gryphon flung a hand at the wall. "She's supposed to be resting!"

Klaus arched an eyebrow. The hunter had no fiery torch of his own, only a single gear-bulb lantern. "Aren't you concerned?"

"I'm *concerned* that you left her up there where she can—she can—I don't know, get the lay of the land—"

"The lay of the land," Klaus scoffed. "I doubt she can see much of anything in the dark, even with that torch. Anyway, I thought she agreed to stay?"

"Did *she* tell you that?"

"Well, not exactly, come to think of it."

Gryphon snorted. Even after explaining about the bite, he had no doubt the girl was still entertaining thoughts of leaving. Especially considering the way they'd left things.

As though reading his mind, Klaus said, "Look, she was going stir-crazy. I gather you two had words earlier, and not of the friendly sort?"

"Not my fault," Gryphon shot back. "She's not the easiest person to be *friendly* with."

"Right. Because you're normally so friendly with everyone."

Gryphon decided to ignore that. "You could have at least gone up there with her. Make sure she doesn't try to escape."

"How could she escape from up there? Fly off the wall?" Klaus only sounded more amused. "It's bloody freezing out here, thank you very much. I don't fancy going up there in the wind."

All the more reason Isabelle shouldn't be up there either, Gryphon thought, given the cold she was nursing. *If that's really what it is*, an unwanted voice said inside his head. He banished the thought.

"About the wolf pack," Klaus said. A swift glance showed the mirth had gone from his face. "About Viveca. Do you think she'll make a move against you? Because of Isabelle?"

Gryphon pressed his tongue against his teeth. "I suppose it depends how much she *knows* about Isabelle."

"What could she know?"

"There's no telling." Gryphon's gaze wandered, fixing on Isabelle's slender form. "What the wolves can sniff out." He cast Klaus a sidelong glance. "Better recheck the entry points just in case. Be sure we've got silver everywhere."

"Sure. And about Isabelle..." Klaus trailed off. Not hesitating, Gryphon thought. More asking for permission to continue.

He gave it reluctantly. "What about her?"

"Well, if she really *does* have to stay forever—"

"She doesn't have to stay *forever*," Gryphon snapped. "I don't think."

"—maybe it would be easier for...everyone...who lives here...if you tried to be a little more...well, if not *friendly*, then...civil. To her."

"Klaus," Gryphon warned.

"I'm just saying." Klaus gave an innocent little sigh. "You could start now. Go up there. Talk to her. Apologize..."

"Apologize?" Gryphon spluttered. "I didn't do anything."

"Hmm."

"What does that mean?"

"What does what mean?"

"You said, 'hmm.'"

"It doesn't mean anything," Klaus said neutrally.

"But you were thinking something."

"Well, just that...I know apologizing doesn't come easy to you..."

"I can apologize easily enough if I want to," Gryphon retorted.

"Can you? Well, all right, then."

"I can do it right now, in fact."

"Well, good."

"Good." Gryphon spared him a waspish look. "Just to be clear, I'm doing this because *I* want to. Not because you said I should."

"Of course, of course."

Muttering beneath his breath, Gryphon stomped up the stairs built into the side of the ramparts. Klaus had been right; when he emerged at the top, he found the wind bracing. Gryphon had always "run hot" since he was a boy; the cold didn't bother him like it did others. The beast's curse had only enhanced that. But the wind wasn't just cold; it stung, nipping at Gryphon's face.

"You really shouldn't be out in this," he said.

With a choked sound, Isabelle spun around. She moved so quickly, her foot slid right out from under her—probably on a patch of ice—and she teetered, arms windmilling as she slowly toppled backwards—

Gryphon was there in a flash. Closing the distance in two strides, he caught her by both hands, pulling her upright.

"Stones," she swore, breathless. "Don't *do* that."

"Keep you from falling?" Gryphon asked. He thought, belatedly, that he'd meant to inject more hostility into his words. But he was distracted by the feel of her hands in his. They were bare and *freezing*; he could feel the icy touch of her skin through his gloves.

"Don't *lurk* in the shadows like that." Isabelle shifted, trying to regain her balance.

"I wasn't lurking. I spoke as soon as I got up here." Without meaning to, Gryphon squeezed her hands. He wanted to rub them between his gloved palms. "Your hands are like ice," he said crossly. "What are you doing up here? It's freezing."

"I didn't know you cared."

Gryphon had yet to let go of her hands. She wobbled again, and thinking she must still be on a slick spot, he stepped back to give her space—

—and slipped as he stepped right onto a patch of ice himself.

Gryphon cursed. Isabelle gasped. They were still holding hands, so Gryphon had no way to catch himself. He fell flat on his rear, landing with a *thump* against the cold, damp stone. Isabelle, caught in his grip, tumbled with him, a yelp escaping her as she pitched into him.

Into the awkward silence that followed, Gryphon cursed again. Isabelle's head was buried against him; she gave a little groan as she sat up, gripping his arm to steady herself.

Gryphon's rear smarted. *That's going to bruise*, he thought. "Are you...all right?"

"I will be," Isabelle groaned. Then, amazingly, she gave a weak laugh.

"There's nothing funny about this," Gryphon grumbled. "Now I'm wet as well as cold."

"Oh, come on. You want to laugh. Everyone laughs when someone falls, it's like a—a biological imperative."

"I don't laugh when *I* fall."

"Stars." Isabelle slumped, touching her fingers to her forehead. She was practically sitting in his lap, Gryphon noticed, her hand braced against his chest. "My head feels stuffed full of wool. I really do need to rest."

"I told you," Gryphon said gruffly. "Come on—" Grasping each other, they managed to climb to their feet without slipping. "Can you walk?" Gryphon asked.

"Yes, I'm fine." Isabelle looked up with an imprint of amusement on her face. But it faded when she met his gaze, her expression turning complicated. Gryphon was distracted by her eyes again, drawn to their coppery richness. He found himself trying to memorize their hue, the warmth of that brown…wondering what paints he could mix to form that exact shade—

"Is something wrong?" Isabelle asked.

"What?" Gryphon felt a tug in the pit of his stomach. He'd been staring at her. "No. It's just…" He cast around for something to say besides, *I was just realizing how beautiful your eyes are.* "Look," he said abruptly, "if Klaus asks, tell him I apologized."

Isabelle looked nonplussed. "Apologized for what?"

"Exactly."

"Maybe for lying to me about why I had to stay here?"

"I'm not sorry for that," he said, and Isabelle glowered. Eager to stave off another argument, Gryphon hastened, "Look, if I *were* to apologize for something…I suppose it would be for, well. For upsetting you."

Isabelle's eyes softened. "You want me to tell Klaus that?"

"Well. If he asks."

"What, did you two make a wager?"

"Not exactly."

Isabelle said, her voice arch, "You'll owe me a favor, you know. If I tell Klaus you apologized."

Gryphon's stomach gave another tug. Clearing his throat, he asked "What kind of favor?"

Isabelle swept past him, starting down the stairs. "That's for me to know, and you to find out."

11

BARGAIN

I SABELLE DREAMT SHE HAD fallen into a shadow world.

There was no other way to describe it. Everything turned to shades of gray, blurry and indistinct. Isabelle's sight shifted, tapering as darkness encroached on the edge of her vision. As though she was losing consciousness.

But she wasn't. No, something inside her was very awake, very *alert*. Her heart raced, pumping blood through her body with alarming speed. She burned with it. Her blood wasn't blood; it was lightning, arcing through her again and again.

She felt *alive* in a way she never had before.

She was outside. In the castle courtyard. A layer of fresh snow covered the flagstones. Isabelle stood barefoot in it, immune to the cold. A torrent of wind whirled past her, but all she felt was the crisp whisper of it on her skin, the way it teased through her hair.

She wanted more. She wanted to feel the wind.

She wanted to run.

She tore across the courtyard. Her feet ghosted over the snow, too light and fast to slip or slide. She ran like she never had before, driven by some deep-seated desire, sprinting and bounding, her strides massive leaps from one patch of snow to the next—

Then she slammed into the silver portcullis barring the exit. It jangled beneath her but would not budge.

She was trapped. Captive. A prisoner.

Caged.

No, she thought, and the fear fueling that thought was crazed, violent, untamed. She threw the full weight of herself against the metal bars. *No, no, no, let me out—LET ME OUT—*

The dream dissolved.

When Isabelle woke, she was soaked in sweat, even though she lay atop her quilted blankets, her face smashed into a pillow. Her wool pajama top stuck to her clammy skin. Rolling onto her back, she wiped damp strands of hair from her face and gazed up at the ceiling. Slowly, the heat seeped out of her, leaving her shivering.

Isabelle tugged at a blanket, draping it over herself. Judging by the muted daylight streaming through the window, it was well past dawn. She'd slept late. That was unusual for her, but everyone else in this castle kept odd hours—everyone else in this castle was practically nocturnal. Isabelle had begun to adjust to that. And besides, she needed the sleep. She'd spent the past couple of days resting, fighting off that blasted cold.

Thankfully, she had improved. Her pounding headache and sniffles were gone. This was more reassuring than it ought to be; it was a sign that Gryphon's bite did not carry the same infection as that of the wolves.

But Isabelle was still worried—not for herself but for her brother. Ansel. Yes, he was in the clear, Gryphon said; he had not been bitten by the wolves. But he was still unwell. Too much time languishing in that cold tower, she was sure. Even Ellery thought Ansel needed a proper doctor. It was time for him to leave this castle and get better care.

A tentative knock on the door announced Ellery waiting with the breakfast try. Isabelle was loathe to leave the warmth of her blankets, but she was also starving—stars, she felt like she hadn't eaten in days. With a noise halfway between a sigh and a groan, she pushed herself out of bed.

Her hand gave a *twinge* of pain. Isabelle frowned. The base of her hand felt strangely sore. She pressed her thumb into a tender spot near her wrist. Perhaps she'd fallen asleep on her arm? She'd done that before.

As Isabelle approached the round table with her breakfast laid out, Ellery asked, "Was there anything wrong last night, Miss?"

"Wrong?" Isabelle looked up. "Wrong how?"

"I don't know." Ellery's gaze was fixed on the tea kettle as she set it nearby. "Stefan said he heard...a banging noise. Like you were banging at the door. But when he called to you, there was no answer. He was wary about entering on his own after..." She faltered.

"After I hit him on the head last time?"

"Yes, that." Ellery's tone was as neutral as ever. "So he came and fetched me. But when we entered the room, you were sound asleep."

"Hmm," Isabelle mused. "Perhaps Stefan fell asleep too. He might have been dreaming."

Ellery didn't answer. She only dipped her head. It seemed a likely explanation to Isabelle, but Ellery probably didn't want to admit such a weakness in Stefan. After all, he was supposed to be guarding her.

Once Ellery left, Isabelle pulled back her chair at the table—and winced, her sore wrist giving another twinge. Lifting the hand, she noticed a faint bruise forming at the heel of her palm, marring her brown skin. Where had *that* come from?

In a sudden, flooding instant, she remembered her dream. She remembered throwing herself at the portcullis. Heaving her whole body against the gate—banging at it—

A chill touched Isabelle. What had Ellery said? *Stefan heard a banging noise. Like you were banging at the door.*

Isabelle looked from the purpling bruise on her hand to the solid oak door. Had she—had she climbed from her bed in the middle of the night and banged at the door? Just as in her dream? No, surely not. That would mean she had *sleepwalked*, and she'd never done that before. Not once.

It was a deeply troubling thought. One that made Isabelle grateful for the lock on her door. She took her seat at the table, trying to think calmly as she lifted her teacup. But her hand trembled, sloshing tea over the side.

If she had sleepwalked...if she had banged at the door...this wasn't a sign of madness, was it? Clutching her cup between both hands, she tried to remember what Gryphon had said of the illness inflicted by the wolves' bite. *If the victim lives long enough, they eventually go mad. Just before the end.*

Isabelle took a soothing sip of her tea, inhaling the cinnamon-scented steam. The madness took hold at the end of the illness just before the victim died. Well, her illness had ended, Isabelle thought, with a sliver of unease. But she didn't think that was what Gryphon had meant. It didn't sound like the victims *recovered* from their illness and then went mad.

Then again, she hadn't been bitten by the wolves. She'd been bitten by Gryphon. And there was no precedent for that. Which meant there was no real way of knowing what might happen to her. What might be happening even now.

Isabelle took another sip of her tea. *Stop it*, she told herself. She could drive *herself* mad, fearing every little thing that happened to her, wondering every minute if she was going to die. *There's no use worrying over it.* Perhaps if she ran into Gryphon, she could ask him about the sleepwalking. It was a strangely comforting thought, going to him for help. Of course, that was foolish too.

Gryphon had risked a lot coming to save her from the wolves on the night of the full moon. And that meant a lot to her. But she still didn't know if she could trust him. She still wasn't sure he'd told her everything. He had been awfully cagey when explaining about the bite; every word had looked like it was being torn from him. But was it just reluctance to share his secrets or something more?

She would ask him about the sleepwalking. But in the meantime, she couldn't rely on him. She needed to know that—if it came to it—she could leave this castle on her own. Though Isabelle had listened to his reasons for wanting her to stay, Gryphon seemed to have realized she hadn't actually agreed to do so. She was still under guard. But Isabelle had already escaped this castle once. She would do so again if she needed to. And this time, she would be more prepared.

Which was why—the first chance she got outside her room, later that day—she gave Klaus the slip and found her way out into the courtyard.

It was nearly dusk. The sun wasn't visible beyond the walls, the last of its light blanched beneath layers of pewter gray clouds. But it hadn't set yet. Gryphon was down in the dungeons, not yet human, and with any luck, Klaus would be searching for her on the top floor of the castle for a while.

Isabelle wrapped her cold hands together as she peered towards the back of the courtyard. She wasn't going to escape, not yet. She wouldn't risk it before Ansel was free. But she wanted to know if there were other ways out of the castle and where they led.

She felt a small, remorseful pang at the thought of leaving. But the fact was—between Gryphon's curse and the pack of mutant wolves prowling the woods—this castle was dangerous. And even if she *did* fall prey to illness and madness, that didn't mean she had to stay. She could go mad and die anywhere. It wasn't as though anyone here could do anything to help her.

And yet—and yet. Isabelle could not help the way it made her stomach turn. When she thought about leaving this place. Leaving Gryphon. That night on the ramparts, he had been almost...not *kind*. Less beastly, perhaps. Squeezing her cold hands in his to warm them, apologizing for upsetting her...asking if she was all right when they slipped and fell. Isabelle swallowed, remembering how firm his chest had been beneath her hand. How she'd felt the rhythmic beat of his heart through his shirt, and the slow rise and fall of his breath—

That really was just foolishness. So he was a nice-looking, well-formed man. But who was Gryphon to her? She barely knew him. There was certainly no trust between them. She suspected he was still hiding something, and he clearly thought she might escape again. So it was ridiculous to feel she was betraying him if she decided to leave. He was no one to her. No one except her captor, for the Gift's sake.

But she could not banish it. That pang of regret.

Still, it wasn't going to stop her. She crossed the courtyard to the corner she'd seen Gryphon emerge from a few nights ago. There was a back gate there, solid wood, honey-colored oak striated with black veins. A sturdy beam barred the gate, and as Isabelle fiddled with the lock and latch, she noted that all—lock, latch, and bar—were gilded in silver just like the other gates and doors.

Isabelle slid the bar up, pushed open the gate, and slipped outside the castle walls.

And gasped.

The ground nearly gave way right in front of her. She knew the castle was built upon a crag, jutting up out of the vast gulch below, but she hadn't realized how steep and sudden the drop was at the back of the castle. There didn't seem to be any way out from here. Wallowing in disappointment, Isabelle turned, looking for a path—

She nearly missed it. There *was* a path, hidden beneath snarls of dead ivy and an overgrown hawthorn, its knobby trunk growing right out of the base of the castle. Isabelle ducked beneath its thorny branches, flinching where they snagged at her.

Beyond the tangle of ivy and hawthorn was a narrow, rocky path, wending a treacherous slope down the crag. Someone had attempted to smooth out stony steps, but even still, Isabelle found herself clinging to the castle wall, then to the cliffside as the wall gave way. At the bottom, she half-slipped, half-scurried the last few steps, emerging into the valley below.

This close to nightfall, the gully was dark. Only a ghost of daylight remained, casting a pallor over the glistening landscape. Isabelle let out a low breath, watching it mist the air in front of her. Fir trees rimmed the edge of the gully, creating a crescent-shaped glade here in the shadow of the castle. It was probably quite lush and green in the warmer months, but now, the dead, stubby grass was frosted over with packed sleet. In the distance, the colossal stone pillars supporting the castle bridge loomed like the legs of some giant creature, vanishing into the thick gray fog overhead.

There was an odd...smell...down here. It prickled at Isabelle's nose. There was something that didn't belong...a leathery, almost peppery scent—

Something *snapped* in the icy stillness. Deep in the fir trees, just beyond her line of sight.

Isabelle went rigid. She drew the closest weapon she had, a little knife tucked into her belt. She had a pistol as well but didn't want to fire it if she didn't have to. For all she knew, there wasn't anything out there but a startled rabbit.

Then a figure emerged from the woods, prowling into the gully.

It was not a rabbit. It was a woman.

Isabelle stared. It was a woman she recognized. The trapper, the woman she'd met on her way to the castle—the one who'd told her about the curse. She had the same thick, red hair that Isabelle remembered, though it had been braided before. Now she wore it loose around her shoulders, a fiery mane framing a sharp face.

But if the woman remembered Isabelle, she didn't say so. All she said was, "That little blade wouldn't do you much good. Not unless it's pure silver."

"What?" For a moment, Isabelle was too confused to be frightened. She had the distinct impression that she was supposed to be frightened—that these words were a threat—but that was buried beneath a flurry of other thoughts: *Who is this woman? Does she remember me? What is she doing here? Of course my knife isn't silver.* It was the last thought that stuck. "Why would it be silver?"

"It's our one weakness." The woman weaved forward, closing in on Isabelle. "One nick of a silver blade would kill me in minutes. It's like poison to our blood. We can't touch it. Can't even cross it."

Isabelle processed this information too slowly. *The silver on the entry points...they can't cross...of course, of course*—

"But if your blade isn't silver, as I suspect," the woman continued, "you would need a good thrust to kill me." A slow smile spread over her face. "And you would never get close enough."

Isabelle stared a moment longer, still saddled with confusion. Then the pieces fell into place.

Our weakness. Our blood.

"You're one of the wolves," Isabelle breathed. "But...you helped me get here. You gave me directions. Why?"

The woman shrugged. It was a casual gesture, but the way her eyes never left Isabelle's face was distinctly *not* casual. "You needed help. I gave it. Isn't that enough of a reason?"

Isabelle suspected not. But she decided not to pursue it. Because the woman had just taken another step towards her.

"That's far enough." Isabelle lifted her blade higher.

The woman let out a low laugh. The sound unfurled through the gully like the creeping fog overhead. "I already told you. That knife won't do you any good."

"And this?" Isabelle reached beneath her coat and pulled out her pistol, leveling it at the woman. "Will this hurt you? Or do the bullets need to be silver?" Even now, Isabelle was fascinated by the possibilities. "That would be interesting to see, really. It's too bad I don't have my shotgun. Would it just blast a hole in you, and you'd skip off home, or—"

"It doesn't take silver bullets to kill me," the woman drawled. Isabelle couldn't tell if she was bored or annoyed by this conversation. "Regular ones do the trick. As you well know." The woman tilted her head to one side. "I could almost like you, girl, if not for that."

"If not for what?"

"You killed one of mine." The words were even and deadly. "Or have you forgotten?"

Oh. *Oh.* She was talking about the wolf. The mutant wolf Isabelle shot in the woods that night she'd escaped from the castle. Four wolves had come after them. Three had gotten away.

One, Isabelle had killed.

Isabelle's pistol suddenly felt warm and heavy in her hand. She resisted the urge to cock back the trigger. "He was going to kill me."

"Oh, he was only following his instincts." The woman flashed a smile. It was as menacing as it was unexpected, that flash of teeth. A wolf baring its fangs. "During the full moon, we are *wolves* in every sense of the word. Driven by appetites no human could understand. But there's no malice in it. Just pure, predatory instinct. It's the most natural thing in the world." Her words dripped like honey from her lips. "It certainly wasn't personal."

A slow shiver crawled up Isabelle's spine. "Well, I followed my instincts too. I defended myself. It wasn't personal."

The woman laughed. A very human laugh. Not so chilling as before. But far from putting Isabelle at ease, it made all the hair on the back of her neck stand up. This woman, she thought, was mad. And she knew now. She knew exactly who she was.

"You said he was one of yours," Isabelle said. "The wolf I killed. You're her, aren't you? The leader of the pack. You're Viveca."

"Oh, you've heard of me? Only good things, I hope."

"I heard you're descended from that last Forest king." Isabelle selected her words carefully. It began to dawn on her that she might not make it out of this gully alive. Though it was not a full moon, Isabelle had a sense that this woman was lethal—in any form. "You told me the rumors say the descendants haunt these woods. I guess the rumors are true."

"Well. Some are."

"And the others in your pack are, what? Your siblings?"

"Siblings. A few cousins. My family."

It occurred to Isabelle she had an opportunity here. To glean some information. Overcome by curiosity, she ventured, "And Gryphon? He's your family too, isn't he?"

Viveca's answer was rueful. "He's blood, maybe. Not family. Though he could be."

"If he joined you, you mean?"

Viveca was unamused. "I know what you're doing, girl."

"My name is Isabelle."

"Isabelle." Viveca began to move again, stalking along the tree line. "What exactly are you doing in that castle? You came looking for your brother, right? But you leave without him on the night of a full moon. Making easy prey of yourself." She tossed a nod at the specter of the castle. "Now you're sneaking out even though it meant nearly breaking your neck coming down that cliff. And trying to get information about Gryphon out of *me* rather than asking him."

Isabelle bit her cheek. Not only had Viveca guessed what she was doing, but she knew her movements—she'd watched her leave through the back of the castle, seen her escape last week—

She was keeping an eye on Isabelle. Or, perhaps, on the castle.

"He's holding you against your will, isn't he?" Viveca deduced. "But why? Your brother I understand—Gryphon probably thought he'd been bitten. But you suffered no bite. So why? Why is he keeping you?"

Isabelle considered this question. She was on the verge of answering truthfully when something stopped her—an ominous fluttering in her chest. Just like she'd experienced the day she arrived at the castle.

She said instead, "Gryphon doesn't want me telling tales about him turning into a beast. I told him I won't, but he doesn't believe me."

"Hmm." Viveca sounded almost disappointed. "Sounds like Gryphon."

"Yes."

"So you're running away again?"

"No," Isabelle said. "Just getting to know my escape routes."

"Smart. I *do* like you, girl." Viveca circled closer. She really did move like a predator, sinuous, her muscles rippling beneath the leathers she wore.

Isabelle tightened her grip on her pistol. "I said it before. That's close enough."

Viveca stopped in her tracks. "Gryphon is your captor. Yet it's *me* you're afraid of? Not him? Not even knowing what he is?"

"I'm not afraid of you *or* him. I just don't trust either of you."

"No?" Viveca placed her hands on her hips. "And there isn't anything I could do to earn your trust? Not even if I...helped you and your brother escape? Granted you safe passage through the Black Forest? Made sure Gryphon didn't send anyone after you?"

Isabelle did not bother to hide her incredulity. "You would just let us go. For nothing."

"I didn't say that. You'd have to get out of the castle on your own. Gryphon has every entry point gilded with silver. But if you were to leave a door open on your way out..."

Isabelle bit the inside of her cheek. Bracing herself, she said, "Sorry. No. I won't do that."

Viveca's face hardened. She didn't move, but there was a predatory stillness about her that made Isabelle's heart falter.

"You're very loyal to him," Viveca said after a long, tense moment. "Even though you've just met. Even though he's your captor." She didn't sound displeased. She sounded curious. "What did he do to earn that loyalty?"

Isabelle wanted to deny it. But she thought about that regret she harbored at the thought of leaving the castle. How much it felt like betrayal. And somewhere, deep down inside her, a small voice spoke.

He came for me.

That was the truth of it. He'd come for her. He could have left her to the wolves; that would have solved all the problems she'd caused for him.

But he hadn't left her. He had come for her.

And she was so very used to everyone in her life doing the opposite.

Maybe it didn't mean anything, Isabelle thought. It probably didn't mean anything. But some part of her...the raw, wounded part of her...wanted it to.

"I'm not loyal to him," Isabelle said. "But there are innocent people in that castle. I'm not letting you in to attack them."

"Who said I wanted to attack them?" Viveca looked darkly amused. Amused, but not pleased. "He really hasn't told you anything, has he? I bet he hasn't even told you the real reason he's holding you there."

"What reason?"

"I don't know. But I'd wager everything it's more than just keeping you from spreading tales." Viveca shook her head. "He didn't tell you about us—not at first. You wouldn't have been so foolish to leave on the full moon if he had. He didn't tell you about the silver. He didn't even tell you what it is I want from him. So how much more is he keeping from you?"

Isabelle wavered.

"Stay if you want," Viveca said. "But my offer stands." She jerked her head, lifting it to the air. Like a dog catching a scent. Her eyes fixed on the steep, craggy path behind Isabelle. "Klaus is coming. I suppose he discovered you missing."

Isabelle didn't want to turn her back on Viveca. But her eyes flashed sideways.

Viveca noticed. "He's still inside the walls. But probably not for long."

"You can *smell* him?"

Viveca smiled. "I know his scent." She dug into a pocket on her vest, and Isabelle tensed, but all she withdrew was a small, gold coin. "Here." She tossed the coin to Isabelle, who didn't try to catch it. Her pistol was still trained on Viveca.

The coin landed at Isabelle's feet. "What is that?"

"The coin is enchanted. I have a very useful friend, you see. A *witchy* friend." Viveca stepped back, retreating into the forest. "If you want to meet me, just turn the coin over three times in the palm of your hand. I'll meet you in this clearing." Viveca held both hands up. "I have no reason to harm you, Isabelle. But I'm not so sure Gryphon can say the same."

Isabelle didn't move. She didn't drop her pistol or turn away, not even when Viveca melted into the shadows beyond the line of trees. She waited several long seconds before taking a step back and tossing a glance over her shoulder.

Isabelle wasn't stupid. She knew Viveca didn't really want to help her. And the wolf hadn't told her anything she didn't already suspect. But Isabelle knew now. Gryphon *had* lied to her. He'd told her Viveca had offered him an alliance and—when he turned her down—she'd decided to leave him alone.

Yet for some reason, Viveca wanted inside that castle. She wanted something from Gryphon. And Gryphon knew it...because every entry into the castle was gilded in silver. Which meant Gryphon was actively keeping the wolves out and had been for a while.

By the time Isabelle clambered up the sloped path to the castle, she felt dizzy, her body tired and trembling. She should probably get some more rest, she thought, trudging back into the courtyard. Especially if she was going to escape after Ansel.

But, she thought, quietly sliding the bar across the gate, *maybe I shouldn't escape just yet.*

Maybe she needed to stay and figure out what Gryphon was keeping from her...and why. Because his secrets could put her in even more danger.

And she didn't need danger following her anywhere.

12

RECONNAISSANCE

I SABELLE SAW ANSEL OFF from the castle two days later. It had taken some convincing to get him to go. In the end, even Ansel had been forced to admit he needed a doctor's care. Isabelle had whispered to him that she would escape once he left, assuring him she'd found a way out of the castle. She promised to meet him in the village of Spalding, the closest town with a proper physician.

It was not *really* a lie. She *had* found a way out of the castle, and she did intend to escape. Just...not right away, as Ansel likely assumed.

So Ansel agreed to go, setting off in a self-propelled carriage Klaus dug out of the bowels of the castle. Isabelle saw him off from the courtyard. The wind was fierce that day, winnowing across the gorge. Isabelle flinched every time it cut past her. It was so loud, she almost didn't hear Ansel when he called after her from the carriage.

Wrapping her arms around herself, Isabelle turned back. "What is it?" she asked, tilting her head towards her brother.

"Isabelle." Ansel sat slumped in the carriage seat, holding the door open. "I have to tell you—in case something happens to me—"

"Nothing is going to happen, Ansel." Isabelle frowned. "You'll be fine—"

"But I have to tell you, Belle—I'm sorry."

"Sorry for what?" It was not that she couldn't think of anything he might be sorry for. Rather, she could think of a whole *host* of things he might be sorry for, and she wondered which he meant.

Ansel's grip on the door tightened as another gust of wind hammered at them, threatening to slam the door shut. "Isabelle. You have to know. I never meant any of it. I only..." He trailed off, looking helpless. "I'm *sorry*. For everything. I—"

But he was interrupted by Klaus rapping on the side of the carriage. "This weather's only going to get worse," the hunter told Isabelle. "He needs to be off, or he'll be caught in a storm. He'll barely reach the road today as is."

So Isabelle said a last farewell and backed away from the carriage. She watched it trundle off, carrying Ansel away, and wondered what he'd meant when he said, *I never meant any of it.*

She spent the rest of the day locked in her room, pacing back and forth, gazing at the ceiling from her bed, and wondering if she was going mad. Her mind reeled from abject boredom to bouts of anxiety to sudden, piercing loneliness.

It was that last feeling that was so strange. Isabelle lived in seclusion and had never minded the solitude. But she usually had plenty to keep herself occupied. Her big house to tend to, and her books and research. Which was why she needed to get to work *here*. To figure out what was going on between Gryphon and the wolf pack, and how she might have been drawn into it.

She just needed a way to dig up information. If only she had an excuse to leave her room...and perhaps an excuse to spend more time with the servants who might have some answers...

The next day, Isabelle offered to help Ellery with her chores around the castle. The girl seemed bemused at the request, but Isabelle was quick to point out she had nothing better to do. And—much to Isabelle's delight—Ellery acquiesced.

They spent the day dusting the grand staircase, polishing cookware in the kitchen, and lastly, washing linens and laundry. That task was not so difficult as Isabelle had feared, for Ellery had a small washing machine instead of just a scrub board.

"Well, of course there weren't any machines in the castle," Ellery said as she stuffed Gryphon's shirts into the machine. "But Klaus traded one off a peddler."

It was after dusk. They were in a large chamber on the ground floor where Ellery kept her cleaning supplies. The room was dark stone and dim, sparsely lit by two small oil lamps and one gear-bulb lantern Ellery had brought down with her. The glaring white light of the gear-bulb felt harsh against the warm glow of the oil lamps. Neither light filled the room, leaving patches of darkness around them while they worked.

As Ellery sorted through more garments, Isabelle wound up the washing machine. She turned the lever round just as the door opened and Gryphon walked in. "Ellery," he said, "do you know where my—" He broke off when he saw Isabelle, goggling at her as though she'd grown horns.

"What," he said, "are you *doing?*"

Nonplussed, Isabelle round the lever a couple more times. "Your laundry, apparently."

Gryphon looked aghast. Isabelle had to suppress a laugh.

"*Why?*" he demanded.

"Well. I don't have much else to do."

"But—you're not a servant," Gryphon spluttered.

"No, I'm a prisoner. What's the difference?"

"I can leave if I want to," Ellery said, as monotone as ever. "That's the difference."

Isabelle choked back a laugh.

Gryphon looked strangely troubled. "What do you usually do?"

"What, at home?" Isabelle tried to hide her surprise. There was no trace of Gryphon's usual ill temper on his face. He seemed...genuine. "Well, I'm a scholar. Of history."

"So...what do you *do?*" Gryphon repeated.

As he appeared sincere, Isabelle struggled not to roll her eyes. "I research," she said. "You know, with books? I write dissertations. Occasionally, I get in touch with other scholars, but not often. I prefer to keep to myself." She shrugged. "But as you don't actually *have* books here, I can't do any of that." It was true. She'd lost the books she'd brought with her the night she'd escaped. Ellery had scrounged the castle and found all of five books, none of which interested Isabelle—four were lurid romances and the fifth a book on genealogy (which *would* have been interesting if half the pages hadn't fallen out).

Gryphon seemed to mull this over. But all he said was, "Huh." Then he left the room.

Isabelle raised an eyebrow as she turned to help sort the laundry. "How did you come to work for him, Ellery? Did he recruit you?"

"Sort of." Ellery set a full basket aside and turned her attention to a pile of linens. "I left my village after my sister died. I went looking for work. I ran into Klaus one day in the woods, and he brought me here."

Though this was a succinct explanation, Isabelle thought it might have been the most she'd ever heard Ellery say at once. "And you weren't—er—put off by working here?" she asked. "I mean...considering?" *Considering your lord is a grumpy bugger who turns into a monster every morning?*

Ellery didn't answer right away. Isabelle glanced at her. The lamp closest to the servant had grown dimmer as the oil burned, and the small, guttering light cast eerie shadows over the girl's face.

Ellery said, "Lord Gryphon is good. He can't help his curse."

Isabelle considered this. She wasn't sure "good" was the word she would have used. For some reason, Viveca's words floated back to her. *What did he do to earn your loyalty?*

She found herself curious to know Ellery's answer to that too.

"What about the other servants?" Isabelle asked. She knew now there were only two: Stefan and Tilda, the cook. "Were they recruited too?"

"Tilda was. Stefan came with Lord Gryphon. He was his personal servant before."

"Before..."

"Before he came here." As always, Ellery's tone was carefully neutral. Neither unfriendly nor inviting of questions.

"Hmm. So, what about Klaus? How did he and Gryphon meet?"

"They met in the forest somewhere. Before Lord Gryphon moved in here," Ellery said. "I think they met Viveca and her wolves around that time too."

Isabelle pricked up at that. "What makes you say that?"

"Well. I just know Viveca was after Klaus."

"After him? She attacked him, you mean?"

Ellery shook her head. "Not after him like *that*. She was...interested in him."

Isabelle frowned. Then she understood. "Interested in, as in...*interested in?*"

Ellery glanced at her, her face impassive in the dying lamplight. "Interested in."

Once again, Isabelle remembered Viveca in the gully. How she'd smelled Klaus coming from so far off. *I know his scent.* Now she wondered how *well* she knew his scent...and why. "Weird," said Isabelle. "I guess there's no accounting for taste."

"Well, this was before Klaus was scarred."

"I wasn't talking about his scars, Ellery." Isabelle shook out a clean bathing towel and folded it. What had Viveca said? *He didn't tell you about the silver. He didn't even tell you what it is I want from him. So how much more is he keeping from you?*

Could *Klaus* be the thing Viveca wanted? No, it had to be more than that. For one thing, Klaus went into the woods all the time, and though he likely armed himself with silver, he alone would never be a match for the whole pack. No, it was clear that—whatever Viveca felt about Klaus—she left him alone. Besides, it sounded like what Viveca wanted was specific *to Gryphon.*

Adopting a casual tone, Isabelle said, "So I suppose that's why Viveca and her wolves leave Gryphon alone. Because she's *interested* in Klaus?"

Again, Ellery didn't answer right away. Isabelle waited, resisting the urge to look at the girl. She folded another towel, disguising her impatience. Wondering if Ellery would uphold the lie Gryphon had told her—or share some truth with Isabelle.

But Isabelle was disappointed. "Yes," Ellery said. Belatedly. "That's why they leave us alone."

A few nights later found Isabelle retiring to the parlor with a cup of tea and a tray of biscuits. The parlor was a spacious room adjoining the dining hall, with lofty ceilings and long bay windows overlooking the gully below. It was far more welcoming than the rest of the castle, the walls dusty but ornately gilded, the floor paneled wood instead of stone. Mahogany tables, upholstered armchairs, and long chaises littered the room. A huge, marble fireplace took up half of one wall, and another wall was lined with bookcases, cabinets, and even a long desk.

When Isabelle first discovered the parlor, it had harbored the same stale air of neglect that so much of the castle did. She didn't think Gryphon or anyone else had used this room before. But Isabelle had looked over it with a strange feeling climbing inside her. Homesickness.

It *was* a strange feeling. Because Isabelle didn't know what it was to have a home. She didn't really think of her manor, out in the middle of nowhere, as *home*. But in the manor was her library...and she loved her library. She missed the mismatched bookshelves, overflowing with historical tomes, leatherbound volumes, and even some well-worn novels. She missed her cozy, rustic furniture. And she missed the windows—three floor-to-ceiling windows lining the eastern wall. Just like the windows here in the parlor.

Yes, it reminded her of her library. And she ached for missing it.

Ellery had kindly helped her clean the room out, and now here she was, setting her tea and biscuits down on a stained end table beside a sumptuous chaise. She was just about to sit when she noticed her *escort* was still in the room, hovering nearby. Though he blended into the shadows well, his presence was still a nuisance.

"Klaus," Isabelle said primly, "you don't have to stay in the room." She rapped on the window behind the chaise. "They don't open. And even if they did, it looks like a steep drop down."

Klaus turned to her, hands clasped behind his back. "Funny," he remarked, "that's very similar to what you told me last week. You remember. When I left you perusing a set of rooms upstairs and found you an hour later, out in the courtyard?"

Isabelle ignored this, seating herself in the chaise. Unfolding a newspaper—Klaus often brought them back from the nearby village—she said in the sweetest tone she could manage, "You know, Ellery told me something about you, Klaus."

Klaus was unfazed. "Something fascinating, I'm sure."

"Indeed. She told me Viveca was *interested* in you."

"Yes, well, plenty of women are interested in me. I'm hard to resist."

"If you say so." Isabelle shot the hunter a surreptitious glance. She'd only been hoping the jibe would make Klaus uncomfortable enough to leave the room. Unfortunately, nothing made Klaus uncomfortable—but perhaps she had another opportunity here.

Rustling her newspaper, Isabelle asked, "What about Gryphon?"

"Gryphon has never been interested in me."

Isabelle shot him a vexed look. "I meant, was *Viveca* ever interested in Gryphon?"

"Why do you care?"

"No reason." Isabelle flipped a page in her newspaper. Wondering if she'd made Klaus suspicious, she chanced another glance at him—and found him smirking at her, his dark eyes amused. *Oh, stones,* she thought in dismay, *he thinks I'm asking out of jealousy.* Well, that was ridiculous. As though she cared who fancied Gryphon, *or* who he fancied.

"Well?" she snapped, flipping another page.

Klaus's smirk deepened. "No. Viveca has never been *interested* in Gryphon. Nor's he interested in her, by the way."

"I didn't ask if he was interested in her."

"Right."

"Right." Isabelle pursed her lips. This conversation was not going the way she'd hoped. "You know, going out into the forest as you do, you must run into Viveca from time to time."

Klaus didn't answer right away. His silence was oddly tense. When he spoke, his tone bristled. "And if I do?"

Isabelle looked up, startled. *That* comment had bothered him. "Well, it's just," Isabelle said lamely, "she must really have a liking for you. To let you travel the forest safely."

"She doesn't *let* me do anything," Klaus retorted. He moved suddenly, his steps soundless as he crossed the room. "I'll be outside if you need anything."

Isabelle blinked as the door swung shut behind him. *Finally,* she thought, settling back into the chaise. The room was more relaxing without Klaus's watchful presence.

Isabelle sipped her tea, gazing through the long window. The world outside was black and unknowable; there was nothing to see in the darkness save for the shifting clouds, lit through by the stars they shrouded. But it was enough. Enough to remind Isabelle there *was* a world outside this old ruin. Enough to reassure her she would return to that world soon.

She spent the next half hour there, sinking into the comfortable chaise, perusing the newspaper by the winking candlelight, and inhaling the lingering aroma of her cinnamon tea, the dregs scenting the room.

Then the parlor door *banged* open. Isabelle nearly choked on a ginger biscuit as Gryphon walked in.

"Don't you ever knock?" she sputtered.

"Why should I knock in my own castle?" was his reply. If he was surprised to find her here, he didn't show it. Instead, he disappeared through the doorway. Before Isabelle had time to wonder where he'd gone, he reappeared—this time with a teetering stack of books in his arms.

Isabelle gawked. She probably should have gotten up to help, but she was so shocked by the sight of *the lord of the castle* lugging around a pile of books, she didn't move. He plunked the stack down on the table nearest her with a *thud*, and a great cloud of dust burst into the air. Isabelle sneezed.

"Here," Gryphon said laconically.

"Here what?" Isabelle waved a hand to dispel the dust. "What are these?"

Gryphon looked at her as though she was an idiot. "Books."

"No, really?" Isabelle craned her neck to look at the titles. "What books? I mean, where did you get these? Ellery searched the whole castle and barely found any."

"Most of these were in some back rooms on the top floor. Those rooms are all locked. Anyway—" Gryphon began unstacking the books, sparing cursory glances for their covers. "I didn't really see what they were, but maybe there are some you—hmm." His yellow eyes sharpened as he picked up a square-shaped book.

Isabelle was curious against her better judgment. "What is it?"

"Book on art technique. Drawing." Gryphon's expression was preoccupied as he flipped the book open and rifled through it. He looked as though he'd forgotten Isabelle was there. Slowly, he lowered himself into a chair at the table, propping the book open before him.

Isabelle raised a quizzical eyebrow. "And you're interested in art?"

"You could say that." Gryphon didn't look at her as he slouched back.

With a bemused glance for him, Isabelle looked through the books. She was pleased to find three historical volumes—including one she had back home and was quite fond of. There was also a book on old religions in the Forest Kingdom, an explorer's account of his travels to the Desert Kingdom, and a comparative volume of various philosophies. Taking the book she'd read before—*A Brief History of the Settlement of the Five Kingdoms*—Isabelle slid into her seat, pushed aside the newspaper, and began reading.

She and Gryphon sat in silence for close to an hour. Perhaps it should have been awkward, but truthfully, Isabelle was so engrossed in her book, she forgot he was there. The room grew chilly as the night deepened, but Isabelle was warmed by a fresh cup of tea and her velvet dressing gown, wrapped snugly around her. She hadn't felt so relaxed in a long time.

Near midnight, Ellery came to see if Isabelle wanted anything else.

"No, thank you," Isabelle said absently.

"Ellery," Gryphon said. Isabelle started, having truly forgotten him. "Bring me a pencil and some paper."

Ellery curtsied and left the room. "You could say 'please,'" Isabelle noted.

"What?" Gryphon looked startled, the expression leaving his face open in a way that was almost...endearing. Then his features fell into their usual truculence. "Oh." He turned a page in his book. "I don't need to say please. I'm lord of the castle."

His expression didn't twitch, but Isabelle eyed him suspiciously, wondering if he was making fun of her.

As soon as Ellery returned with paper and pencil, Gryphon set his book aside and leaned forward. He began to sketch, his hand flying across the paper. His head was bent so low, it nearly touched the table.

Isabelle watched him, fascinated. This intensity was both like and *un*like him. He always had a sort of *harsh* intensity about him. But the way he looked now, sketching...the passion in his movement, the pensive furrow in his brow...this was a gentler, deeper intensity. One that made Isabelle's heart flip.

She watched him a few seconds longer, then returned to her reading.

Nearly two hours later, Isabelle closed her book and stood, stretching her arms over her head. She was beginning to adjust to the odd hours here, but she didn't stay up until dawn. It was time for bed.

Gryphon still sat at the nearby table, sketching. As Isabelle passed him, she caught a glimpse of a discarded sketch. "*Oh.*" She picked up the drawing, a depiction of a castle, her eyes roving over it. "This is really good."

"What?" Gryphon glanced up, brow wrinkled. "Oh. It's all right. I mucked up the turrets." He turned back to his current sketch.

Isabelle watched him, perplexed. She could not reconcile this person sitting here, as engrossed in his art as she was in her book, with the snarling lord she had come to know.

She left the room without another word.

She spent the next several nights in the parlor, reading and taking notes. To her surprise, Gryphon often joined her. The first night, he slunk in with his usual surliness, as though he expected Isabelle to kick him out or make a smart remark. But Isabelle only murmured hello and returned to her reading, while Gryphon sat at the same table to flip through his drawing book and sketch. She couldn't help but notice he chose that same table—the table closest to her—rather than any of the others scattered throughout the room.

Night after night, he came in to sketch while she read. They did not speak. But just as before, Isabelle found the silence neither awkward nor uncomfortable.

One night—perhaps the fifth night they'd spent together—Isabelle found her attention wandering from her book. Perhaps it was the book itself (a rather dry genealogy of the first Forest kings), or perhaps she was more tired than usual. Whatever the reason, she found herself gazing out the window, lost in thought.

Then she turned her gaze on Gryphon.

His head was bent over another sketch, his rich black curls hiding his face. That long hairstyle really suited him. Not only because it was unconventional, but because he had such thick, beautiful hair. She couldn't help but wonder what it would feel like to run her hands through it.

She watched him for a long time, her eyes following his hand as it glided over his paper. He had such large hands; she remembered how they had engulfed her own when he'd caught her on the ramparts. And yet there was grace in the way he held his sketching charcoal, in the slight flicks of his wrist. Her gaze traveled up his arm to the set of his shoulders, hunched inward over the table. She found herself dwelling on that night on the ramparts, when she'd fallen into him. She remembered leaning into his broad chest, how warm he'd been...

Gryphon looked up from his sketch and locked eyes with her.

Startled, Isabelle dropped her gaze, slumping down to hide behind her thick tome.

When she plucked up the courage to chance another glance at him, he had returned his attention to his drawing. Isabelle relaxed, slumping further into the chaise, this time for comfort rather than embarrassment. She leaned her head back, trailing her fingers up and down the filmy page of her book.

She was getting sleepy. Her eyelids growing heavy. Drowsy, she glanced up.

Gryphon was staring at her from his seat at the table. When she blinked at him, he jerked his gaze away, returning to his sketch.

Isabelle stifled a laugh. Really, how silly this was. They were behaving like children. Isabelle could not abide awkwardness between people. It was a construct, really. Built from society's inane obsession with the rules of engagement. She watched Gryphon openly, waiting for him to look at her again. When he didn't, she shut her book forcefully.

"Isn't drawing one of the feminine arts?" she asked.

If Gryphon was startled, he didn't show it. Which was a little disappointing. Without looking up, he said, "You'd know better than I."

Isabelle narrowed her eyes, wondering if she should be affronted. Now Gryphon *did* look up, and he added hastily, "Not because you're...especially feminine."

Isabelle narrowed her eyes further.

"I just mean, you're a...you know." He gestured vaguely. "Girl. Er—woman. A lady—"

"Yes, I understand. I have anatomical parts usually assigned to a female," she said acidly, and was disappointed again when Gryphon did not blush. All he did was give her a droll look. Goodness, he really was as irreverent as she was. "Anyway, I'm no lady."

"I didn't think so," Gryphon murmured, "given your brother is a thief."

Isabelle sighed. "He's not *usually* a thief."

"Then again," Gryphon mused, "I have known some noblemen to turn to thieving. Ones who have fallen on hard times."

"Like you, you mean?" Isabelle asked astutely.

Gryphon frowned at her.

"Not the thieving part." Isabelle waved a hand. "The...fallen on hard times part. Or isn't that what happened to you?"

Gryphon eyed her cannily. "You could say that."

"So you *are* a nobleman."

"I was."

"A nobleman versed in the feminine arts."

"Well, I was never a very good nobleman."

"Clearly." When Gryphon scowled, Isabelle pointed out, "Well, I'm sorry, but you've been far from gentlemanly. You never even introduced yourself when we met. I had to learn your name from my brother. Not very lordly, wouldn't you say?"

"How would you know?" Gryphon didn't look offended. The twist of his mouth was amused. "Not being a lady, I mean."

"I do have *some* noble friends, I'll have you know."

"Really." Gryphon didn't sound the least bit interested. He returned to his sketch, but he didn't seem as closed off as before. This was a chance, Isabelle thought, to get some information out of him. But she had to be careful. Go slow. Make it seem like only conversation.

"So how *did* you become interested in drawing?" Isabelle asked. "Being a nobleman."

Gryphon did not answer right away. His shoulders tensed, and Isabelle wondered if she had been mistaken, thinking he would talk to her. But then he said, "My mother. She was an artist." He looked up. "So I suppose you are right that it's a feminine art. My father certainly never thought much of my interest."

"And your mother...she's—"

"She's dead," Gryphon said, guessing correctly what she had been thinking.

"Oh. I'm sorry." Isabelle fidgeted with her sleeve. "My parents are dead too. Well—" She broke off, her mouth going dry. She had been on the verge of confessing something she never told anyone.

My father isn't dead. But he may as well be.

She swallowed, glanced up, and found Gryphon looking at her. She felt suddenly naked beneath his gaze. She wanted to look away, but she couldn't.

He said, "I'm sorry. About your parents," and returned to his drawing.

Isabelle felt oddly shaken. This was not how she had expected this conversation to go. She just wanted to know more *about* him. Gryphon. Who he was. Why he'd come here. What Viveca wanted from him. But she no longer felt up to sleuthing. She couldn't believe she had nearly shared something with him she had never shared with anyone, not even Prince Garrett. How stupid that would have been.

And yet, a part of her still wanted to say it. To confide in him.

Isabelle rubbed a hand over her eyes. Her weariness had returned like a bolt of lightning, swift and unexpected. "I'm sorry." She climbed to her feet, sweeping past him. "I'm rather tired, Gryphon. I'll see you tomorrow night."

"Will you?"

Isabelle stopped. Slowly, she turned to look at him.

His expression was expectant, waiting for her answer. His eyes smoldered with that deep intensity she'd glimpsed while he was sketching.

Isabelle forced herself to breathe. "Well. I'll be here anyway. So I suppose that's up to you."

She quit the room, feeling far too warm, for some reason, despite the chill in the room.

13

EXILE

G RYPHON DREAMED OF ISABELLE.

He was in the forest. There was no snow on the ground, no bitter chill in the air. The woods were washed in a hazy gray-green, like the moss spidering up the sides of the trees, like the lichen coating the boulders on the ground. He stood in the muffled stillness and breathed it in. Breathed it out.

The breath he exhaled lingered, shifting into a dense fog. It ghosted over the forest floor, curling around his ankles until he couldn't see his feet.

Not his feet. His paws.

A *snap* of a branch cut through the stillness. A fleeting movement caught his eye. A flash of deep, dark red. Something running through the woods.

With a growl deep in his throat, Gryphon leapt after it.

The fog remained, disguising his surroundings, darting through the trees. Teasing him with flashes of his prey. He caught a snatch of windswept brown curls, scented like roses. A flicker of dainty leather boots, crunching over bramble. Another flash of deep crimson, a long garment streaming back.

Gryphon burst through a stand of fir trees. Evergreen needles sprayed the air.

He skidded to a stop.

His prey stood before him. Serene. Unafraid.

It was Isabelle.

She stood garbed in a deep red gown. The gown bared her collarbone, showing off an expanse of dark, coppery skin. Her curly hair hung down her back, the wind stirring it ever so slightly.

Gryphon bared his teeth. Everything in him was screaming to jump, attack, *kill.*

But Isabelle did not run. She circled towards him. Gryphon felt a deep whine building in his chest.

He lowered himself to the mossy, muddy ground. Bending his head. Docile.

And Isabelle reached out, laying her hand atop his head. Her fingers curled into his fur—

And Gryphon woke with a start, fully human, in his quarters. For some reason, the bed felt cold, his blankets rumpled beneath him. He was *never* cold. The oil-lamps had all been doused, the room awash in darkness. It was strangely disorienting. Gryphon felt as though he had been snatched from sleep. From whatever he'd been dreaming.

Then he realized what had awoken him. Someone was knocking on his door.

"What?" he barked.

The door *creaked* open, and Stefan peeked his head in. "You wanted me to wake you," the boy said in his reedy voice. "It's a quarter 'til ten."

"I'm awake," Gryphon said. Then, recalling something, he added, "Thank you."

Stefan gave a quick nod and shut the door.

Gryphon rubbed a hand over his eyes as he sat up. At this time of year, with the blessing of longer nights, he usually slept for a good six hours after dusk. But for the past week, he'd cut into his sleeping schedule to wake earlier than usual.

So he could spend time in the parlor. With Isabelle.

It was stupid. *He* was stupid. Or at least, that's what he felt when he dwelled on his motives for too long. Which was why he preferred not to examine them. That parlor was a nice place to spend a few quiet hours. That was all.

It had nothing to do with Isabelle being in the parlor. Nothing at all.

For the most part, they didn't even speak, whittling the hours away on their solitary pursuits. But there was something about just being with another person in companionable silence...

Gryphon was so very starved for company.

He was not, by nature, a social person. He could go days by himself and be just fine. He preferred it that way. But even the most reclusive person could not go for*ever* without human contact. And he'd had precious little of that. Oh, there were the servants, but it was not the same. Even Klaus was not really an equal.

Isabelle, somehow, was.

Once he was dressed, he found his way to the parlor. Isabelle was already there. As usual, Gryphon seated himself and began sketching without a word. Isabelle murmured her usual "Hello" but did not look up, her attention bent on her book.

Yet she seemed restive tonight. Though he looked wholly engaged in his artwork night after night, Gryphon paid Isabelle a lot more heed than she noticed. Most nights, she was engrossed in her reading and her notes, but other nights, she was distracted and dreamy. Looking up to gaze out the long, dark window or contemplating some invisible spot on the wall.

Tonight was one of those nights. She seemed...discontented. Frowning at nothing. Shifting around as though she couldn't get comfortable. Drumming her fingers against the pages of her book.

"Something wrong?" Gryphon asked.

The words were out before he could stop them. Before he could remind himself he was supposed to be sketching, not watching her.

But they were said. Isabelle looked around. "Hmm?"

"Nothing." Gryphon ducked his head, glad for the reprieve. But then—

"It's the fairy blood," Isabelle said. "I just don't understand it."

Gryphon blinked. "*Excuse* me?" He wondered if he'd misheard her, or—barring that possibility—perhaps Isabelle was indeed going mad, thanks to his bite.

Isabelle looked at him, still preoccupied. Then she shook herself and smiled. "Sorry." She turned to face him more fully. "I suppose that came out of nowhere."

"You could say that."

She tapped a finger on the pages of her book, splayed open in her lap. "I was reading this passage about the Gift, the pact between fairies and humans. Apparently, it was sealed by an actual *gift* of fairy blood to the five royal families. A friend of mine heard this *from* a fairy who claimed the blood was bestowed in some kind of ritual, but beyond that, they were frustratingly vague. And I've been thinking—what is the difference between the Gift and witch magic? Because *they* apparently use fairy blood to access magic; I think they actually imbibe it, and, well, this fairy my friend spoke to *did* specify that the royals didn't drink the fairy blood, but even so—if fairy blood gives witches access to magic, then why didn't it for the royals? Obviously there's some difference in the manner it was given and how witches take it, but *what* difference?" She shook her head.

Gryphon gaped at her. He waited a moment to be sure she had finished. Then he said, "Are you all right?"

Isabelle looked startled. "What?"

"Do you need a glass of water?"

"No." Isabelle cocked her head. "I've still got my tea here. Why?"

"I just don't think I've ever heard anyone say that much at once."

Isabelle glared. "I'm fine, thank you."

Unless Gryphon was mistaken, Isabelle's cheeks had grown rosy in the shaded glare of the gear-bulb lamps. He'd embarrassed her, he realized. Once, he might have found this amusing—and still did, if he was honest—but he also knew what it was like to feel self-conscious about his interests. So he cleared his throat and said, "Why the interest in magic and fairy blood?"

"Well, why not?" Isabelle asked with a note of defensiveness.

"I just thought you were a historian."

"Oh. Well." Isabelle perked up at that, looking pleased. "I'm not *terribly* interested in magic as a field of study, no," she admitted. "But magic is a big part of our history, isn't it? It's influenced a lot in the Five Kingdoms and still does today, even though society has shifted its focus to technological advances. I know a lot of people see magic as, well, medieval and the stuff of myth, but that's really not so. Fairies are still casting curses. And witches—well, I don't have to tell *you* about witches."

Gryphon gave a start. "What makes you say that?"

Isabelle turned a wide-eyed gaze on him. "Your curse. It was originally cast by a witch, wasn't it? Or so the story goes. Why, what did you think I meant?"

"Oh—nothing." Gryphon let out a silent breath. "Right, my curse."

Isabelle looked half-amused, half-concerned. "Did you forget about it?"

"Well, it's part of my everyday life." Gryphon tapped his pencil against the table. He didn't want to talk about his curse. "How do you know all that about witches and their magic? From a book?" He was looking for a change in subject, but he was also genuinely interested. Most people knew very little about witches and their ways; it was a rather taboo subject.

"Some from books," Isabelle admitted, "but also..." She cast Gryphon a rather serious glance from beneath her lashes, as though she was sizing him up. Wondering if he would make fun of her again, Gryphon wondered? Or wondering if she could trust him?

Whatever the reason, he found himself wanting to meet her approval. He returned her studious gaze with one of his own, afraid to blink.

Finally, Isabelle gave a little nod and said, "Some friends of mine...er, ran afoul of a fairy curse a while back. I'm not being intentionally vague." She gave a toss of her head. "It's just a long story. Anyway, while trying to break the curse, they interviewed a witch to find out more about magic. They told me what she said, most of which was rather horrific—" Isabelle gave a shudder "—including the bit about drinking fairy blood. Actually, she mentioned *eating* fairies, but I'm hoping she was just being facetious."

"Yes, that sounds like the sort of thing a witch would find funny," Gryphon said with a straight face.

"She also mentioned that witches make *deals* with...some sort of dark force...in order to access magic through fairies," Isabelle went on. "I've been researching that. Trying to figure out what these dark forces *are*. But—" She sighed. "Most of the relevant volumes are in my library at home. I doubt I'll find anything on the subject here."

Gryphon's stomach gave a bitter twist. "I suppose not."

Isabelle's eyes flicked his way. "Not that I'm not grateful," she said quickly, "for the books, I mean. That is...you didn't have to go looking for them."

Gryphon shrugged, but the bitterness inside him dispelled. "They weren't hard to find." He hesitated, then added, "Perhaps Klaus can see if he can get more. The next time he's out trading."

"That would be nice." Isabelle's voice was tentative. "Thank you."

Gryphon gave a noncommittal grunt. He watched Isabelle a moment longer. She'd gone to some faraway place in her head again, judging by the distant look in her eyes. Her forehead sort of...*scrunched*...when she was thinking very hard, and Gryphon noticed it now as he gazed at her. He couldn't help the smile that tugged at his lips.

Unfortunately, Isabelle noticed. "What?" she asked.

"Nothing." Gryphon wiped the smile from his face.

Isabelle looked suspicious. "Have I got something in my teeth?"

"Don't be stupid." Gryphon gave a cough. "I was just thinking that...er...well, that you're one to talk."

"Excuse me?"

Gryphon gestured towards her. "You were talking the other day about my interest in a *feminine art*. But there can't be many female historians."

Isabelle's face relaxed. "True, no. It is a male-dominated field."

"And? How did you become involved in it? Or were you always scholarly?"

"Stars, no. I didn't even know how to read until I was...eleven or so."

Gryphon's jaw dropped open.

"I know." Isabelle smiled. "But my father was a woodcutter. Well, he did some hunting too. He raised Ansel and me on the road. I had quite the rural upbringing." She ran a hand over the crinkled page of her book. "It wasn't until we spent some time in a village in the Glen Kingdom that I learned to read. From an old spinster who lived there. After that, I read whatever I could, whenever I could. Mostly penny press papers, and what few books I could get my hands on."

Gryphon propped his chin in his hand. "So why the interest in history?"

"That came later. When I was fifteen, Ansel took a job as a castle guard in the Mariner Kingdom. I had a chance to spend some time in the castle library until—" Isabelle broke off.

"Until..." Gryphon prompted.

Isabelle shook her head. Too late, Gryphon noticed the strangled look on her face. "Until I left." Her tone turned curt. "I went to the Glen Kingdom then, and I visited every library and college I could find." She tried to smile again, but it was a weak attempt, fading quickly from her face.

Gryphon studied her, frowning. Something he had said—or something she'd thought of—had bothered her. Something about living in the Mariner Kingdom? No—something about Ansel. Her brother.

He remembered, then, with a swooping feeling, how he'd accused her of abandoning her brother. He remembered the look of devastation on her face, and how he'd realized—in that moment—that it had been the other way around. That Ansel had abandoned her.

Gryphon felt a lump form in his throat. He wanted to tell her that her brother was a fool—plainly because he *was*; Gryphon had experienced that for himself—but he didn't know how to get the words out. Besides, she hadn't actually told him anything, and it wasn't his business to dredge it up.

Blinking, he realized Isabelle was watching him, her brown eyes uncertain. Gryphon returned to his sketching, and silence fell over them again, the rustle of pages and the whisper of his pencil the only sounds in the room.

———◦◦———

The next night, Isabelle was restless again. Rather than asking after her thoughts, Gryphon pretended not to notice, focusing on his sketch. A part of him was a little afraid of what wounds their words might open tonight. Though another part of him was curious to see if she would strike up a conversation with him.

His patience was rewarded. After a time, Isabelle said, "We could do something else, you know."

Gryphon jerked his head up. "What, right now?"

"No, not tonight. I'm hardly dressed." She was garbed, as she usually was at this time, in her velvet dressing gown, her curls pulled back at the nape of her neck. "No, just...sometime. We could do something different besides sitting in here."

Gryphon eyed her. It was true they had spent this time together every night for over a week. It was true they had become more civil with each other. But making actual *plans* to spend time together sounded beyond their relationship. It was not that the idea did not appeal to him. But he was suspicious of her motives.

And rightfully so, as it turned out. "Something different like...?"

Isabelle gave an innocent shrug. "We could take a walk outside."

"You mean, around the courtyard? It's not that big."

"Or outside the castle walls..."

Ah. There it was. "No," he said at once.

"Not far beyond the castle," Isabelle protested. "I mean, it would be dark out, so—just along the ravine—"

"*No*," Gryphon repeated. "I don't go beyond the castle walls."

"Not *ever?*"

Gryphon shook his head.

Isabelle looked perplexed. Gryphon could not understand why. She knew about his curse. Crossly, Gryphon returned to his sketching. He felt disappointed, for some reason. Like a child who had been offered a treat he could not eat.

"I know you have to be careful," Isabelle said, "because of your curse. I know you have to be back by dawn. But surely a short trip outside—"

"And if something happens?" Gryphon looked up. "If I got stuck out there—injured or unconscious—" *Or if Viveca got her hands on me*, he thought darkly. That was the real concern. "No. I don't take the chance. Not ever."

Isabelle was quiet for a moment. Gryphon returned to his sketch.

Then she said, very softly, "But you left before. To come after me."

Gryphon's hand stilled. "That was different. I had to."

"And before that?" Incredulity colored her voice. "You've never left since you arrived here?"

"Well, I got out a couple of times. Before we perfected our system in the dungeons. But the last time was over a year ago." That had been enough of a disaster to convince them they needed a better way to confine him. Gryphon had escaped for days and wandered quite far, and Klaus...Klaus had ended up with those scars. He was lucky to be alive.

In that same soft voice, Isabelle repeated, "But you came for me."

With a stroke of annoyance, Gryphon put his pencil down and looked at her. Her expression banished his ire. She sat up straight on her chaise, hands in her lap. She struck him as strangely childlike. In her confusion. In her vulnerability.

Gryphon swallowed. "Like I said. I had to. You would have died if I hadn't."

"You could have sent Klaus."

Gryphon had considered it. Ellery had pleaded with him to wait for Klaus. But he'd known he had no time. And— "I'm stronger than Klaus. Even he wouldn't have been a match for four wolves."

Isabelle kicked her heel against the base of the chaise, looking thoughtful.

She said, "You could have left me to die."

This irked him. The simplicity in it.

"Is that the kind of person you think I am?" he asked acidly.

"I don't know what kind of a person you are." Her big eyes watched him. "Ellery says you're...to use her word...'good.' She says I've nothing to fear from you."

Gryphon's heart pounded like a drum. He wasn't sure *that* was true.

After all. Look what he'd done to her the first day she was here.

"I don't know anything about you," Isabelle said, earnest. "I know your mother was an artist. I know you didn't always live here. That's all, though. I don't know why you left your home. Why you came here."

Gryphon sucked in a breath. It was true. They were not friends, after all. Yes, they'd made some small talk, but they had not exchanged life stories.

But...Isabelle *had* told him a little about herself. She'd told him about her studies, her life on the road growing up. How she'd learned to read.

Gryphon drummed his fingers against the table. He felt...worried, almost panicked. He wanted to tell her about his past. He wanted to trust her, to forge a connection.

But he was afraid. Afraid of her judgment. After all, no one had ever taken his side. Why should she?

"I..." His voice came out hoarse. "I left home because I had no choice. I was exiled. By my father."

He looked at the table as he said it. He could not bring himself to look at her. But she said, "Your own *father* exiled you? Why?"

Gryphon said bitterly, "Don't you mean, 'what did I do?'"

"I mean *why*. What happened?"

Gryphon chanced a glance at her. He tried to make his tone dismissive. "There was a woman."

Isabelle's eyebrow twitched. "Oh?"

"We were...involved," he added reluctantly.

Isabelle looked amused. "Like, *involved*, involved?"

"Can we be mature about this?"

"You're the one who said *involved*."

"I don't mean—not like that," he clarified. "I was only four-teen. She was older. It was fairly innocent." *Not to mention, one-sided*, Gryphon thought sullenly. "As it turned out, she was up to no good. Just using me. To get to my father and our...prop-erty. Our lands." He shook his head. "She didn't get what she wanted, but. Our actions—*my* actions—caused a lot of trou-ble and embarrassment for my family. Then she disappeared, and—well, I was the only one left to blame. I was banished."

Isabelle said, "But this woman—she was the one in the wrong."

"I let her manipulate me."

"You were fourteen!"

"I had responsibilities," Gryphon said sharply. And in those words, he heard his father's voice. And he hated it. Running a hand over his face, he said, "In all fairness, my father—I don't think he was only trying to punish me. There were people he had to answer to. He had to save face. Someone had to take the blame."

"And that person had to be you."

"There was no one else," he said, but the words felt hollow.

Silence fell between them. Gryphon stared at the tabletop, his eyes fixed on a scratch in the table. He ran his pinky over the groove, back and forth, until a sliver of wood broke off in his skin. Cursing silently, Gryphon put his finger to his mouth to suck out the splinter.

"I'm sorry, Gryphon."

Gryphon snapped his head up. "You're what?"

"I'm sorry that happened to you." Isabelle nestled down in her chaise. "It doesn't seem fair, really."

Gryphon stared. She had already pulled her book into her lap, turning her attention from him. Everything went still and quiet again in the parlor. Peaceful.

But on the inside, Gryphon was not at peace. His heart racketed around in his chest.

No one had ever said they were sorry for him. No one had ever said he'd been treated unfairly. Gryphon had never allowed *himself* to believe it.

Gryphon sketched into the silence, but he scarcely knew what he was drawing. Inside, he was a tempest.

A little while later, Isabelle closed her book and stood. Gryphon's gaze flicked to the clock on the mantel; yes, it was about the time she retired. He should say good night, he thought, but he felt strange and raw after his confession. So he said nothing, intent on his sketch.

Isabelle started past him. He was all too aware of her warm body passing by his table, of the whisper of her dressing gown against the floor. Of the flowery scent of her long, curly hair.

And then she stopped. Just past his table.

"My father," Isabelle said.

Gryphon tensed, raising his head.

"I told you he was dead." Isabelle's voice sounded strange. Rusty, as though she hadn't spoken in years. As though it was not *her* speaking, here and now, but the Isabelle of years' past. The child Isabelle, reaching forward in time to speak. "But that's not true. At least, I don't know if it is." She inhaled a shaky breath. "He left us. Me and Ansel. A long time ago."

Gryphon sat stock-still. He was afraid to move. Afraid he would break this spell of truth.

"I've never told anyone that before," she said. "Not a soul."

Then she turned and swept away, leaving him alone in the parlor.

14

WRECKED

GARRETT DUCKED INTO THE tent Evans and Spencer shared. It was dark inside, save for the bright white light of a gear-bulb lantern, illuminating the redheaded young man inside. "Hey, Evans," Garrett said, his voice more cheerful than he felt. "How're you feeling?"

It was clear Evans was not well. He lay swathed in his sleeping rug, two blankets stuffed around him. His face was pasty white, his freckles starker than usual. He peeked his eyes open when Garrett spoke. "I'm...all right. Sire." He turned his head and gave a weak cough. "Just tired."

Garrett's smile felt frozen on his face. "Well, it was a long day," he said lamely. "I'm sure we'll all feel better in the morning."

It had been nearly three weeks since the giant wolf attacked their camp and bit Evans. The boy's wound had improved visibly. The stitches had come out a few days ago, and while his collarbone was scarred and bruised, the area looked clean and uninfected.

But this morning, Evans woke feeling unwell. Garrett hadn't realized *how* unwell until the soldier nearly collapsed when they stopped to set up camp. They'd put Evans to bed straightaway.

"Just let me know if you need anything," Garrett said. "All right?"

Evans lifted his chin. "I'm supposed to do that for you, sire."

Garrett forced another smile, though his heart clenched. "And you do a right good job of it. Better than most. So let me take care of you for now."

He left the tent with gnawing worry. Outside, a ring of gear-bulb lanterns lit their small camp of four tents, pitched in the center of a copse of barren trees. In this part of the forest, evergreens were scarce, the wood populated with ash and hickory trees. The spindly branches on the ash trees stretched straight towards the sky as though in supplication, while the crooked branches of the hickory trees meandered and tangled like crossing streams.

Roy sat perched on a small boulder, looking through his medical supplies. "What do you think?" Garrett asked. "About Evans?"

Roy squinted at the label on a blue bottle. "Could be the wound's infected, Your Highness. It did look a bit swollen, and he's got a low fever—we'll keep an eye on him tonight."

Garrett cursed under his breath. "I wish Thatcher were here." Then he glanced up. "Sorry, Roy. I didn't mean—"

"It's all right, sire." Roy sounded glum. "I wish he was here, too."

"You're more than capable of helping Evans," Garrett assured him. "It's just Thatch has some experience with..." He trailed off, clapping a hand to his own shoulder.

"Speaking of." Roy slipped a syringe and a small, dark bottle out of his supplies, holding them up in either hand.

"Oh, right." It was that time again. Garrett removed his overcoat and tan sack coat, then tugged up his shirt sleeve, rolling it behind his elbow. "Hurry up, will you." He shivered, the frigid cold piercing through him. "It's freezing."

"Is it? I hadn't noticed."

"Just do it, Roy." Garrett glanced at his shoulder. Beneath his shirt were the faint white scars left by the teeth of a rotting corpse creature. Otherwise, there was nothing to show that poison lurked inside him, kept at bay by a transfusion of corpse creature blood every three weeks.

"I'm just saying, sire." Roy placed the tip of the syringe in the crook of Garrett's elbow "You're the one who wanted to go hunting in the dead of winter."

"Yes, well, the Black Forest will be swarming with hunters come new spring." Garrett stifled a flinch as the needle pierced his skin. "Just wanted to beat the crowd."

"A crowd which you started, I believe."

It was true the number of hunters in the forest had risen dramatically after Garrett's first expedition here. His trip had been the subject of much media attention when he'd returned; his adventures often were. It was King Victor's policy they not talk to reporters, as royals. But some of the soldiers did, and the story spread from there. Even some of the penny press papers in the Mariner Kingdom had covered it.

"All done," Roy announced. The syringe in his hand was empty, the tube splattered with dark, purplish corpse blood. "You'll live for the next three weeks."

"Thanks." Garrett hastily pulled on his coats, expelling a breath of relief.

"You'd probably live for another month," Roy said in a jovial tone, packing up his medical supplies. "You wouldn't feel well at all, though. You remember. More of the fever and weakness and general pain."

"I remember, Roy."

Spencer appeared, weaving his way through the trees to join them. "Does anyone else smell that," he asked, "or am I imagining things?"

"Smell what?" said Roy.

"Woodsmoke," Spencer answered.

Garrett breathed in deep, turning in a slow circle. At first, he didn't smell anything, but then, as the wind rustled past—

"Yes," Garrett said. "I smell it too. Coming from..."

"That way." Roy pointed into the black of the woods. "Couldn't tell you how far off. Maybe Gemma could."

"Where is Gemma?" Garrett asked.

Spencer said, "She and Falcon are out collecting firewood."

Roy raised his eyebrows. "Out collecting firewood, or *out* collecting firewood?"

"Aren't they the same thing?" Spencer furrowed his brow.

Garrett rubbed a hand over his chin. Roy was right; whoever was burning something—most likely a fire—could be a ways off. But if they were close by.... Well, perhaps it was just a hunter or traveler. Perhaps it was a woodsman, someone who lived around here. But they were well into the depths of the Black Forest, and it was rough territory. Some of the people in these parts were not exactly friendly. In fact, some were downright predatory.

"Roy, stay with Evans," Garrett ordered. "Spencer, with me. Let's scout out in that direction and see what—who—we might be dealing with."

He and Spencer set out into the darkness. Spencer carried the repeater rifle, while Garrett carried a pistol and one of their lanterns. He raised the lantern as high as he could. It was still early, but the last of the daylight had vanished on the horizon. They could see quite a bit of sky through the trees' bare branches, but it was a deep, dark sky with little light shining through. A cloudy haze drifted overhead. The same haze that had drizzled sleet on them all day.

"What did he mean, sire," Spencer asked, as they picked through the woods, "*out* collecting firewood?"

Garrett squinted through two hickory trees up ahead. The dense fragrance of the woodsmoke was stronger now; the source had to be close. "It's a euphemism, Spence."

"What's a euphemism?" Before Garrett could answer, Spencer tripped and stumbled, catching himself at the last minute. "Oh. You mean when you say one thing, but mean another?"

"Something like that."

"Well, what is 'out collecting firewood' a euphemism for, sire?"

Garrett glanced aside. "Do I really have to explain this to you?"

"I thought Gemma didn't like Falcon," Spencer observed.

"That's what I thought. But I'm hardly an expert."

"More than me, you are."

Garrett slowed as he spotted something ahead, looming from the shadows—an immense, round shape that seemed out of place in the woods. "Why do you care anyway?"

"About what?"

"About who Gemma likes."

"I don't," Spencer said defensively. "Sire."

"Right."

"I don't!"

"Shh," Garrett whispered. Spencer went on alert, hefting his rifle. The heady woodsmoke was stronger than ever here, filling Garrett's nostrils, though he couldn't see any firelight in the gloom—only the glare of his own lantern.

They crept through the darkness, pushing aside frosted branches and ducking around clumps of bramble. As they closed in on the rotund shape—was it just a massive boulder?—a smaller shadow darted past, disappearing behind a tree.

Garrett and Spencer went still. Then a voice called, "Who's there?"

"Falcon?" Garrett said.

"Prince Garrett?"

"Yes, and Spencer," Garrett said, relieved. He started forward, Spencer at his heels. "Is Gemma with you?"

"Right here, sire." Gemma stepped out of the trees on their left, a rifle in her hands. Her thick, dark hair was braided back. Falcon materialized from the darkness, coming up beside the large shadow. As Garrett neared him, he saw the object was a carriage—a carriage that had crashed into a thick oak tree. The model was self-propelled, Garrett thought, though it was hard to tell as it had turned on its side. A large wheel stuck up in the air, two of the spokes broken, and part of the door was also smashed in.

"Where did this come from?" Garrett asked in amazement.

"No idea," said Gemma. "It's a bit fancy for the villages around here."

"There is a castle in these woods," said Falcon, "isn't there?"

"At least there was." Garrett was dubious. "Seat of the old Forest kings. Might just be ruins by now. Though if it's not..." He rubbed a hand over his chin "...there could be someone living there."

"So maybe that's where the carriage came from."

"You haven't seen anyone?" Garrett raised his lantern high to survey their surroundings.

"No." Gemma dug her foot into the earth, and Garrett realized she was toeing the cold, ashy remnants of a fire—the source of the woodsmoke. The peaty smell was very strong. "Though someone was here."

"Recently? It smells recent."

"Not really." Gemma bent to examine the charred logs and gray ash. "Woodsmoke can linger for a while. I'd say this fire's about a day old. Burnt this morning at the latest." She glanced up at Garrett. "I did find some signs of someone heading that way—" She pointed west "But it's too dark to follow the trail now."

"Well, there's no need to follow it, is there?" Spencer reasoned.

"Unless whoever was here was injured in this crash," said Garrett.

"Yes," said Gemma, "and I think he might have been, judging by his tracks. There were indications that he—or she—might be limping."

Garrett dithered. "But you didn't see anyone? And you don't think we can go further tonight?"

Gemma shook her head. "Tomorrow, maybe."

Garrett hated the idea that there might be someone close by, injured and suffering. As thick and dark as the forest was, someone could be quite close, just out of sight, and they'd never know it. "All right. Tomorrow." He turned to head back. "Anyone know what's in that direction? I'd have to check a map."

"There's a town, isn't there?" Falcon looked to Gemma.

"Spalding," she said. "I'm not sure, but I think it's quite close."

"Well, if our friend here was injured, hopefully he headed that way," said Garrett. "And if it is close, it might be a good idea to head that way ourselves. Evans could see a doctor, get some rest in a proper bed."

The night passed slowly for Garrett, who lay awake for a long while. When morning dawned, it came with more gray clouds and wintry winds, though thankfully, no sleet. After a quick breakfast, they spent a good half hour scouting around to be sure there was no one in the area, while Gemma studied the trail she'd spotted last night.

"Definitely seems like they headed for Spalding," Gemma confirmed.

"Then we'll head that way too," Garrett decided.

Evans was a little better today, after a long night's rest. He still looked a bit weak and pale for Garrett's liking, but his fever had subsided. He was well enough to travel. Still, Garrett thought, a night or two of rest in an inn would do him some good.

Spalding, it turned out, was only half a day's journey to the west. They arrived in town just short of supper time. It was one of the larger villages in the Black Forest. Most of its streets were paved with stone, and the main square boasted a large inn, a long, timbered building in good condition. They booked a few rooms straightaway. Evans insisted he didn't need a doctor, which Roy and Garrett accepted so long as he took to bed.

"I'd still like to know where the physician's house is," Roy told Garrett. "Just in case he worsens overnight."

"Good idea. And we can ask after our mystery carriage rider. See if anyone injured came through in the last day or two."

"We did have a young man arrive yesterday," the physician said. He was a tall, thin man with a dimpled chin. "He stumbled in a few hours after dark. He didn't say anything about a carriage, but he wasn't too coherent. Had a broken wrist and a couple of bruised ribs, so I suppose he could have been in a carriage crash." The doctor shook his head. "You don't see many carriages out here. We don't have fancy folk, and there aren't proper roads to travel them anyway."

"Yes, we thought it was strange," Garrett agreed. He cast a quick glance around the front room, noting the warm wood furnishings, the shaded gear-bulb lamps. The house bore the faintest scent of something sharp and herbal—eucalyptus, he thought. "So will he be all right? The young man?"

"I think so. Though he's quite feverish—seems like it's been a while since he's had proper care. You can look in on him, if you like." The physician seemed to take kindly to Garrett's interest in the stranger.

The physician's wife led them to a room down the main corridor. Inside, a young man lay tucked away in a neat bed. He was sleeping, but the physician's wife woke him for his evening meal. She bustled out of the room to fetch the food, and Roy hung back as Garrett stepped forward.

"Where 'm I?" the young man asked, blinking groggy eyes. His black, curly hair was damp with sweat, plastered to his forehead. He looked around Garrett's age, perhaps a bit younger. He was so thin and frail, it was difficult to guess.

"It's all right," Garrett told him. The boy focused his bleary gaze on him. "We think your carriage crashed, and you've been injured. But you're in Spalding now. In a doctor's house. We—" Garrett broke off, gazing into the boy's large, dark eyes. There was something very familiar there... "Do I—er, know you?"

"You..." The boy's voice was faint. "You're...Prince Garrett."

Garrett stared a moment longer. It came to him, not all at once, but slowly. A white castle capped with blue spires. A marshy woodland. The briny scent of the sea drifting over pale green grass. Memories of a place he hadn't thought of in a while. Memories of this boy in that place. "You were a guard. In the Mariner Kingdom."

He remembered now, though it had been over two years ago. He'd seen this boy quite often in the Mariner Kingdom the summer he'd visited to court Snow. The summer he'd fallen in love with her. How bittersweet those memories were, even now.

Garrett certainly didn't remember every member of the queen's guard, but he remembered this young man because he'd been so young, even younger than Garrett. He thought they'd even exchanged a few words, though he couldn't recall a specific conversation. "You *did* work in the castle, didn't you? One of the guard?"

The boy nodded. "My name is...Ansel." Ansel coughed weakly. "I don't know—if you know, but I—helped your princess. Princess Snow. I..."

"Ansel." It came to him in a flash. "Of course! Snow told me about you. You're the one that helped her escape the kingdom."

Ansel's face was ashen. "Only because I couldn't—kill her."

Garrett remembered the story. Snow's stepmother—the witch, Delphine—had framed Snow for the king's death. When Snow fled the castle, Delphine sent a young guard to murder her—this boy, Ansel. But Ansel had helped Snow instead, sneaking her out of the kingdom.

"Well, you were only doing as commanded." Garrett put on a reassuring smile. "And it was very brave of you to betray the queen and help Snow."

"Didn't—do any good." Ansel squeezed his eyes shut. "In the end."

Garrett felt his smile slip. "No. I suppose it didn't."

"I'm sorry," Ansel said. "I didn't mean—"

"It's all right." Garrett clapped a gentle hand to the boy's shoulder. "You don't have to say anything else. You need to eat and get some rest."

"Wait." Ansel reached up, grasping Garrett around the wrist. His eyes were hazy with pain. "Please. I have to—tell you." He cleared his throat. "It's important. My sister."

"Your sister? She wasn't with you, was she? In the carriage?"

"No." Ansel gave a sluggish shake of his head. "No, I had to—they made me—I left her." The worry on his face was plain. "At the castle."

"Castle? What castle?"

"The old—forest kings," Ansel choked. "Been abandoned—or it was. Now...*he's* there."

"Who?" Garrett was bewildered. Ansel wasn't making much sense; he seemed to be growing weaker. Garrett wondered if he really knew what he was saying.

"He's a tyrant. A m-monster." Ansel let out a hacking cough. "Kept me prisoner—now my sister.... He's got her. Is—Isabelle."

Garrett, on the verge of interrupting, went still. "Isabelle?"

"Please," Ansel begged. "Help her. Please."

"Your sister Isabelle." Garrett licked his lips, staring down at the boy. Taking in every part of his face—the curve of his cheekbones, the high forehead, the heart-shaped chin. The same wide eyes—just a few shades darker than he was used to.

There was another reason Ansel looked so familiar, Garrett realized. Because he looked like his sister.

He looked like Isabelle.

The physician's wife returned with Ansel's supper, and Garrett stepped back to give her room. Roy sidled up beside him.

"I heard what he said, sire," Roy said. "About his sister. You don't think—"

"I do," Garrett said. His brain was having trouble reconciling these two stories—the guard who'd helped Snow escape, and the boy who was Isabelle's brother. But the more he thought about it, the more it fell into place. He'd first met Isabelle on the road between their two kingdoms. She'd been robbed by bandits and lost all her things, and she'd been doubly distraught because she'd just had a row with her brother, who'd taken on a new job.

Then a few weeks later, he'd arrived in the Mariner Kingdom. Where Ansel worked as a new member of the guard.

"Isabelle's not an uncommon name," Roy pointed out.

"It's her, Roy," Garrett said tightly. "I know it is. I don't know how—" Stones, the last time he'd seen Isabelle, she'd been heading back to her house in the northern reaches of the Glen Kingdom. "But it is."

"Then what do we do?"

"The only thing we can do." If Isabelle really *was* being kept prisoner in the old castle, then Garrett wasn't going to leave her to rot. "We're going after her."

15

INTERESTS

G RYPHON STOOD ON THE front steps of the castle, gazing across the courtyard. It was just past dusk. Darkness hung over the castle, but for once, it wasn't a gloomy or oppressive darkness. The night was clear and crisp, the air thick with promise.

Gryphon had only just changed back. He'd found Stefan waiting to let him out of his cell, strangely. (Klaus should have been around, Gryphon thought.) But rather than go to his bedroom for some sleep, Gryphon had come out here, heading for his workshop. He felt restless tonight, wide awake. He wanted to work on his sculpture before he met Isabelle in the parlor later. Over the past couple of days, he'd been alight with inspiration, his waking thoughts often drifting to his sculpture, his hands itching to work.

But on his way down the front steps, he'd caught a whiff of a familiar, rosy scent and heard the murmur of voices in the far corner of the courtyard.

It was Isabelle. With Ellery.

He'd spotted them even in the dark of the gloaming, blessed with supernatural senses as he was. Well, and it was a clear night, the moon pouring its light into the courtyard. The two young women strolled the perimeter as though patrolling—though he was sure they were just walking for their own enjoyment. Getting some fresh air, he supposed. It *was* a nice evening for it. The low hum of their voices reached his ears, though not their actual words. Perhaps that was for the best, he thought, his stomach plummeting. What if they were talking about *him?*

No, that was ridiculous. Of course they weren't talking about him. Why would they? Ellery knew better than to run her mouth about his affairs. For that matter, Ellery hardly ever spoke. No, it was likely Isabelle doing all the talking, horrifying Ellery with tales of witches eating fairies, or else boring her by reciting genealogies of all the nobles in the Mariner Kingdom.

"What are you smiling about?"

Gryphon whipped around. Klaus, a shadow in the darkness, sauntered out from the back of the courtyard. He smelled of cold and cracked leather, and as he stepped up onto the stairs, Gryphon saw his cheeks were flushed.

"I'm not smiling," Gryphon snapped. *Had* he been smiling? Of course not. He hadn't been doing anything but standing here and...

...thinking of Isabelle.

"If you say so." Klaus folded his arms over his chest. "What were you doing, then?"

"Nothing." Gryphon mirrored Klaus's posture, feeling edgy. He hoped Klaus couldn't hear or see the women from here. "Where have you been? I didn't know you were going out today. You just came back from the village yesterday." And their stores of game were well-stocked too.

Klaus shrugged, but his expression belied the casual gesture. He looked as edgy as Gryphon, his arms tightening around himself. "I just wanted some space, is all. Feeling restless."

Hmm. Well. Gryphon was, too. That's why he was out here. "Right, well." Gryphon turned. "I'll be in my tower for the next few hours. If you're looking for me."

A sudden burst of girlish laughter echoed into the night, carrying across the courtyard. The sound was as pleasant as it was unexpected; Gryphon recognized the laugh at once.

Then he remembered Klaus. The hunter craned his neck to look around Gryphon. "Isabelle's out here?" he asked.

"With Ellery," Gryphon said shortly. "If you're not too tired, perhaps you could keep an eye on them. Until they head back inside."

"Is that what you were doing?"

"Of course." Gryphon kept a neutral tone.

"Right." The sarcasm in Klaus's tone was blatant.

Gryphon rounded on him. "If you have something to say..."

Klaus levelled his gaze at him. "Look, if you want to know—she asked about you. Isabelle."

"Asked about me?" Gryphon was bemused. "What do you mean?"

"She asked if Viveca was *interested* in you. As in...romantically."

"What?" This conversation was taking a very strange turn. Gryphon latched onto the part he could make sense of. "Viveca loathes me. She'd like to get her hands on me, yes, but not because of any..." He shook his head wildly. "Why would Isabelle ask *that?* Are you sure you understood her?"

Klaus muttered something under his breath. Gryphon caught the word *idiot*. "She asked," the hunter said slowly, "because she's...what was that word?...*interested*. In you."

Gryphon felt dumbfounded. "Huh?"

"Isn't it obvious?"

"Er...no. Definitely not." Gryphon ran a hand over his face. "Klaus, this is absurd. Even if she did ask you that, why would she be..." He could barely say the words "...*interested* in me?"

"Hell if I know. Can't see the appeal myself."

Gryphon shot the hunter a glower. "And why are you telling me this?"

"Why do you think?" Klaus retorted. Then he sidled down the steps and across the courtyard, his form growing hazy in the darkness as he joined the women.

Gryphon stared after him for a long while. It wasn't until he heard the murmur of their voices, growing in volume as they started back this way, that he shook himself out of his stupor and hurried into his tower.

He tried to shrug off Klaus's words. Tried to forget that very weird conversation. But as he lit the lamp and started a fire in the grate, as he lowered himself onto his stool in front of his sculpture, his thoughts swirled around and around.

Klaus was the idiot. Gryphon was sure that—even *if*, by some strange twist in reality, Isabelle was *interested* in him—she would never talk to Klaus about it. She would never have asked after his *prospects*. Klaus must have misunderstood. That, he could easily believe. Isabelle and Klaus did not seem like two people on the same page, so to speak.

But that wasn't the part he couldn't forget. That wasn't the part stuck in his mind, echoing over and over.

Why are you telling me this?

Why do you think?

Klaus's meaning was plain. He'd told Gryphon because he thought Gryphon would want to know. And the only reason Gryphon might want to know was if Klaus thought that he, Gryphon, was also *interested*...in Isabelle.

"Stupid," Gryphon muttered. "Why would he think that?"

Why indeed.

Gryphon buried his face in his hand. He knew why. Because Klaus had caught him *smiling* when he'd come into the courtyard, smiling as he thought about Isabelle and her penchant for rambling on about all the strange and random things she read. Because Gryphon had asked the hunter to make an extra trip to the village to see if he could find more books. Because Gryphon had spent every night for the last ten days in that damned parlor, in Isabelle's company...and not because the parlor was pleasant and quiet.

It was because he knew Isabelle would be there. And because being in her company made him feel light and content and *whole*—

By the Gift, he thought miserably, *I'm a damn fool.*

Because though Klaus might have correctly guessed his own feelings, he was quite sure the hunter was wrong about Isabelle. She didn't fancy him; how could she? *I don't know you at all*, she'd said. Yes, he'd confided in her about Malina and his father and his banishment, and she hadn't blamed him—but that was a far cry from feeling anything romantic towards him.

She'd thought him the sort of person who might leave her to die. And why not? He'd locked her brother up, he thought bitterly. Worse, he'd ignored Ansel's failing health because of his rancorous feelings towards the boy. He could have *died* in that tower, all thanks to his own selfishness.

But she told you about her father, a small, stupid, hopeful voice inside him said. *She confided in you...something she'd never told anyone...*

And so what? Gryphon thought. She'd seen what a wretch he was and shared her own wretchedness in return. That was hardly the basis for any kind of relationship.

Gryphon ran his hand back, tugging at his hair. And that was to say nothing of what he had done to *her*. What she didn't even know he had done...

No. There was absolutely no future for him with Isabelle. None at all.

That did not stop him from returning to the parlor that night as he always did. Perhaps it would have been better to break with that tradition, but no, he was too pathetic for that. He went to the parlor at the usual time.

But when he entered the parlor, Isabelle was not there. The room was empty, save for the stack of books and his drawing supplies sitting on his table.

Gryphon looked around, nonplussed. He came down about this time every night, and Isabelle was always here, ensconced in their corner. Trying to ignore the sinking feeling inside him, he turned back to the door.

And nearly ran straight into Isabelle.

"Oh," she said, startled. She held a steaming cup of tea in both hands, her grip tightening as the liquid inside sloshed a little. "Hello."

"You're late," Gryphon accused.

He wanted to take the words back straightaway. What a stupid thing to say. It was not as though they had a prearranged meeting time. This was no assignation; he had no reason to expect her here at all.

But if Isabelle thought his words strange or amusing, she made no comment. She only said, sounding distracted, "Am I?" and moved past him, heading for her chaise by the windows.

"Well." Gryphon coughed, following her. "I mean—"

"I fell asleep." Isabelle flopped onto the chaise. "I took a walk out in the courtyard with Ellery earlier. I suppose it took a bit more from me than I realized. I fell asleep as soon as I got back to my room."

Gryphon frowned. As he seated himself at his table, he studied her, thinking she *did* look tired. Her face was drawn, her eyes glassy. She opened her book and took out her notes as usual, but as the time passed, Gryphon noticed she wasn't really reading. And not because she was distracted. When she looked up from her notes to gaze out the window, she didn't look like she was caught up in contemplation. She looked like she was trying to stay awake. At one point, Gryphon saw her lean her head into one hand, rubbing her forehead.

"Are you all right?" he asked.

"Hmm?" Isabelle blinked at him, as though taking a moment to process his words. "I'm fine." She slumped down, leaning against the side of the chaise. "I just have a headache."

Gryphon kept his face carefully blank. People got headaches all the time. "Do you get them often?"

"Hmm. Not really. Though it's not unusual when my sleep is disrupted," she said. "And I've had some weird dreams lately. I blame this depressing castle."

Gryphon nodded, disguising his discomfiture. *It's just a headache.*

They fell silent, returning to their respective pastimes. An hour passed, the minutes ticking away on the ornately carved clock on the mantel. Gryphon became absorbed, barely noticing the passing time.

When next he looked up, he found Isabelle had fallen asleep. She lay on her side, facing him, her head pillowed against the arm of the chaise. One of her delicate hands was curled beneath her chin, as though even in sleep, she pondered some historical event.

Gryphon watched her for a long moment. He watched the steady rise and fall of her chest. His gaze lingered on her dark curls, tumbling over her shoulder and across her neck, and on the little crease in her forehead. He longed to smooth a finger over that crease, knead it away, and all her grief with it.

Then—hesitantly—he rose to his feet. Slowly, he crossed towards her. Stones, but it was freezing here by the windows. He wondered why Isabelle had never said anything; there was a massive fireplace beneath the mantel. He would ask Ellery to build a fire tomorrow night.

A thin coverlet was folded at the foot of the chaise. Trying not to disturb her, Gryphon tugged at it, unfolding it in one, swift motion. He draped it over her, pulling it up to her chin. His throat tightened as he lingered there, his hand resting on her shoulder. Inside, his heart was a shambles. Inside, he ached with desire and misery.

To be this close to her was heaven.

To be this close to her was torment.

A silent sigh rumbled through his chest. He turned away from her, his hand slipping off her shoulder.

But Isabelle caught his hand before he could go.

Startled, Gryphon looked down. Isabelle's eyes were still closed, her breathing deep and steady. He might have thought her still asleep but for the way she clutched his hand.

"Isabelle?" Gryphon prompted. His voice felt like gravel, deep in his throat.

She did not open her eyes. But she spoke, her voice a scratchy whisper. "I want to trust you." Her fingers tightened around his. "I want to believe I'm safe here. With you."

Her words struck a dark, discordant note. Gryphon crouched before her, enclosing her hand between his. His first instinct was to comfort her, but...he could not find the words.

To say, *You're safe here* would be a lie.

He ran his tongue over his teeth and said, "I would never hurt you."

That felt like a lie too. He had *already* hurt her. It would have been truer to say, *I don't want to hurt you.* And he thought, as he gazed into her troubled face, that he would do whatever he must to keep her from being hurt.

But there was only so much he could do about what he had already done.

Isabelle did not respond. She did not squeeze his hand. After a moment, Gryphon ventured, "Isabelle?" Her name was a ghost on his lips.

Still, she said nothing. She must have fallen back asleep, he realized. Gently, he laid her hand against her chest and stood, turning away.

Klaus stood in the doorway.

Gryphon gave a start. "Something wrong?" He crossed the room to join the hunter. He didn't want to wake Isabelle.

"I'm gonna get some sleep." Klaus's eyes flickered past Gryphon. "Just wanted to check you didn't need me to stand guard."

Gryphon shook his head. "We're fine here."

Klaus looked at him a moment longer. Gryphon forced him-self to hold Klaus's gaze, their earlier exchange hanging between them. He expected Klaus to make another needling comment about Isabelle's *interests* or Gryphon's feelings.

But what Klaus said was, "When are you going to tell her the truth?"

Gryphon recoiled. He should have expected that, he sup-posed. It wasn't like he didn't know what Klaus was talking about. It was just—to say it like that—

It made it sound like Gryphon was lying to her.

Aren't you? said a snide little voice inside his head.

Gryphon balled a hand into a fist. "What's the point of telling her anything?"

"I don't know." Klaus rolled his eyes. "Maybe to keep her from getting into trouble? You know I found her out in the courtyard last week on her own. It wouldn't have been too difficult for her to get beyond the walls."

"*You're* supposed to make sure that doesn't happen, Klaus," Gryphon said icily.

"She slipped by me somehow. Look, she's not some helpless princess, Gryphon. Her skills are nowhere near my level, but she knows how to move quickly and quietly."

Gryphon bit the inside of his cheek.

"I mean, why *not* tell her?" Klaus asked.

"Why?" Gryphon echoed. "*Why?* Why do you think, Klaus? You have no idea—" He didn't want to scare her. He knew what it was like, living with that fear, the knowing but *not* know-ing—and drumming up every horrible thing you could imagine, all the worst possible scenarios... "I don't want her to be afraid."

Because she wasn't. She might not have any romantic interest in him, but she was so wonderfully, beautifully, inexplicably unafraid. Of *him*.

And that was the truth of it. He didn't want her to look at him differently. With judgment. With fear. He couldn't *bear* that.

"And if something happens?" Klaus asked. "And she has no idea what's going on? Is that *better*? And how long do we wait? If nothing happens, you have to let her go. At some point, you have to say *something*. Because she can't stay here forever."

Why not? Gryphon wanted to ask, but he bit back those pitiful, loathsome words. He felt irrationally angry towards Klaus in that moment, as though this was all the hunter's fault. Well, wasn't it? Why all that talk earlier about Isabelle's *interests*? Why poke at Gryphon about his own feelings, only to dash any hope for those feelings to the ground?

Because he knows there was never any hope, Gryphon told himself. *Just like you know.*

"Just let me think about it." Gryphon couldn't keep the bitter note out of his voice. "All right?"

Klaus tipped his head. Then he left the room.

Gryphon sighed, turning back to Isabelle. As he did, he thought he caught a flicker of movement from her. A twitch of her hand, perhaps, or something in her face...?

No. She looked the same as before. Lying in the same position, eyes shut, breathing deeply. Undisturbed. So blissfully unaware of the danger she was in.

Let her stay that way a little longer, Gryphon thought.

But deep down, he knew the longer he waited, the worse it would be. Because the longer he waited, the more he would come to care for her.

And the more it would hurt when she turned her back on him.

16

BITTEN

I SABELLE EYED HER REFLECTION in the dusty mirror without really seeing it. Ellery had altered more dresses for her, and—in an attempt to distract herself—Isabelle had begun to try them on. Currently, she wore a gown of deep burgundy, the style even older than the others Ellery had found. In some ways, this style was preferable—the long torso trailed a free skirt that was easy to move in. The bodice, however, scooped low, nearly baring her shoulders. Which was unnerving, not to mention, hardly appropriate for the weather.

Still, she barely noticed. She turned from the mirror and began to pace, frustrated by her room's confines. It was past twilight. A gibbous moon beamed through the window, its light muffled by wispy clouds drifting in.

She still had a headache, though it had dulled to a nearly imperceptible throbbing. For the last two days, it had shifted around her head, varying in feeling and intensity. At times, it was a vice-like pain clamped around the back of her skull, other times, an incessant pounding behind her eye.

She was not used to headaches. That was more worrisome than it should have been, with the threat of impending madness and death hanging over her like a headsman's axe. For the last two nights, Isabelle had lain in bed and watched the moon outside her window, noting its growing form with growing anxiety. Well, Gryphon had not seemed concerned when she'd mentioned the headache.

Isabelle grimaced. Gryphon. *He* was the reason she was so distracted right now. She could not stop going over the snatch of conversation she'd heard between Gryphon and Klaus two nights ago.

I don't want her to be afraid.

And if something happens? And she has no idea what's going on? Is that better? At some point, you have to say something.

She'd been half-asleep when she'd heard it, and across the room. She'd tried to convince herself she'd misheard or dreamt it all. But she knew it was real. And perhaps it shouldn't have upset her so. After all, she knew Gryphon was keeping something from her. It was the reason she'd stayed, wasn't it?

But... he'd told her about his past. She'd confided in him about her father. She thought he'd begun to trust her. Yet his only response to Klaus's plea for the truth was: *Let me think about it.*

Two days had passed since then. Isabelle spent last evening in the parlor with him despite her blasted headache. She'd wanted to see what he might say. What he might *tell* her.

But he'd said nothing.

After that, she couldn't bring herself to spend another evening with him. Instead, she had Stefan tell him she was going to bed early because of her headache.

Perhaps she should have simply asked Gryphon. Confronted him about what she'd heard. That would have been the sensible thing, *that* was what Isabelle usually would have done. She didn't play games or beat around the bush. She'd always found being direct was the best way. But strange and infuriating as it was...she wanted Gryphon to tell her on his own. She wanted him to show some trust in her.

But he hadn't.

Isabelle flopped down on the foot of her bed, closing her hands into fists. Enmity towards Gryphon burned inside her; she hadn't felt this incensed about him since she'd first arrived and he'd banned her from leaving. She held onto that anger, because not far beneath it lurked something far worse.

Pain. Of the most wretched kind.

Isabelle squeezed her eyes shut. Stones. She'd told him about her *father*. She'd exposed the most shameful part of herself. Aside from Ansel, there was not a person in the world who knew her father had deserted her. Only Gryphon.

To know now, of a certainty, that he'd been keeping something from her, something that *affected* her...that was a hurt graver than a bite from any beast.

Isabelle shuddered a breath. The burning inside her calmed to a smolder. Gryphon wasn't going to tell her the truth. And for all that the servants had grown fond of her, she knew they wouldn't either. Not without Gryphon's permission.

That left only one avenue for Isabelle. One other person who might have information, who might could tell her something. Someone who didn't live in the castle.

Isabelle propelled herself from the bed and yanked open her wardrobe. She rooted through her pack, tossing garments and toiletries and trinkets aside as she searched for what she needed. The item in question was buried at the bottom of the pack.

She pulled it out.

It was an old, gold coin.

She placed it in the palm of her hand and turned it over three times.

———◦———

By the time Isabelle made it out of the castle—first pulling on her coat and boots, then convincing Stefan to accompany her into the courtyard for a stroll, then giving him the slip as they headed inside—a good hour had passed since she'd used the enchanted coin to summon Viveca. But when she reached the gully below the castle, Viveca was not yet there.

Isabelle crossed her arms against the cold. A glacial chill had invaded the clearing, deepening the black of the night. Isabelle had thought the gully dark before, but now, well after dusk, the dark was impenetrable. She couldn't make out the stone pillars in the distance, nor the fir trees rimming the other end of the glade. Her single lantern, though bright, was too small to be much help.

But blind as she was, Isabelle could still hear. The quiet *snap* of bramble caught her ear, the gentle crush of dead leaves beneath a pair of boots. Isabelle frowned, listening intently. Was it only one pair of boots...?

"I knew you would be back."

Viveca's voice came from the right, somewhere ahead. Isabelle turned her gear-bulb lantern in that direction. And she saw that she'd heard right.

Viveca had not come alone. There was another woman with her.

"Who's this?" Isabelle asked as the two women approached. Neither carried any light, so Isabelle couldn't see them properly until they came within the ring of her lantern's glow. Viveca, her red hair unbound, her green eyes gleaming. And her companion, tall and willowy. Though Viveca wore no overcoat, this woman was garbed in an old-fashioned cloak, the dark hood pulled over her head.

"One of your wolves?" Isabelle asked. She did not pull her pistol, but she was prepared to.

"Not a wolf." Viveca's voice was roguish. "This is Adela."

Adela pulled back her hood. The face she revealed was long and pale, save for two rosy spots in her cheeks. From the cold, perhaps.

Viveca said, "It's thanks to Adela we could meet tonight."

Isabelle heard these words with foreboding, but before she could put the pieces together, Adela smiled and cupped her hands before her.

A ball of flame burst to life, hovering over her cupped hands.

Isabelle's heart stilled. "You're a witch."

"I told you I had a witch friend," said Viveca. "Don't worry. You've nothing to fear from her."

"Yes, don't fret." Adela's high, girlish voice was somehow far from reassuring. "Viveca says you're not to be harmed, so you won't be."

Isabelle ignored her. Eyes trained on Viveca, she said tightly, "You trust a witch?"

"This witch," Viveca replied, "raised me. She raised my mother. And my grandfather. In fact, if it weren't for her, my bloodline would have vanished long ago."

Isabelle turned a dubious gaze on Adela. "You're older than you look, then."

"Oh, yes." Adela's eyes were small and black in the light of Isabelle's lantern. "I was at the castle that night—the night of the full moon. When the last Forest royals were cursed and turned into beasts."

"You were *there?* Was—were you the one—"

"—who hexed them? No." Adela shook her head. "That was my sister." Her eyes hardened "Or someone I thought was my sister. No, I didn't curse the royals. I served as advisor to the king. And while he was not a perfect or easy man, he didn't deserve the fate that befell him. Nor did his family, his children."

Viveca cut in, sounding bored. "Yes, but what that sister of yours didn't know is she did us all a favor. In the end." She looked Isabelle over. "Let's not waste time. I'm sure it wasn't easy for you to get away, girl. Unless Gryphon allowed you to leave?"

Isabelle stared at Adela. She was itching to ask more questions of the witch, even though her proximity was unsettling. But here was someone who had the answers Isabelle sought, about witches and their magic and the deals they made for it. And if she had lived a hundred and fifty years ago...the things she'd seen, the things she *knew*—including what really happened to the last Forest king. *Why* had a witch cursed him to begin with? What had he been up to?

But Viveca's impatience was palpable, like any hungry wolf. Reluctantly, Isabelle turned her gaze from the witch. "No," she answered. "I'm still not allowed to leave."

"And?" Viveca's gaze heightened. Sinister shadows, created by Adela's flames, capered over her face. "You're dressed for the weather, but I don't see you've brought any supplies. Are you ready to accept my offer? Escape from this place?"

"I—" Isabelle faltered. "That's not why I've—"

"I know your brother left," Viveca confided. "I let him leave. Perhaps you will take that as a token of my goodwill."

"I didn't come to escape," Isabelle said. The wind picked up, billowing with savage fierceness. "But—thank you for letting my brother go." She forced the words through her teeth. She had nothing to lose by them, but they were galling. As though Viveca owned the woods. "I hoped you could give me some information. I've been here for a month, and—I'm still not sure why Gryphon has made me stay."

Viveca let out a short laugh. "Well, I don't know the reason. I don't know anything about you, girl."

"But there's something else he hasn't told me," Isabelle persisted. "Something you *do* know." She braced herself as another blustering wind hurtled past them. Though Adela's magical flame didn't gutter, the darkness seemed to intensify with each gust. "You said you didn't want to get into the castle to hurt people. So what *do* you want? What do you want from Gryphon?"

Viveca and Adela exchanged a look, Viveca frowning. But the witch's black eyes burned in the light of her flames like two smoldering coals. She wore a knowing expression. For a moment, the two seemed to communicate in silence, and then Viveca smiled. She turned to Isabelle.

"I want Gryphon to grant me what's rightfully mine," Viveca said.

Isabelle was bemused. "You mean...the castle?"

"Oh, no. He can keep that dreadful ruin. I prefer the woods. No, there is only one thing I ever wanted from that castle—and it failed to give it to me. Instead, it gave it to *him.*"

"I don't understand," Isabelle confessed.

Adela said, "It would be easier to show you."

"Show me? Show me how?"

"Like this," said Adela, and without warning, she flung her arms wide. The ball of flame vanished, and in its place, a bright, violent light exploded, flashing out to engulf them all. Isabelle cried out, recoiling, but the light washed over her harmlessly with no sensation. When she dared open her eyes, she found herself transported.

The light that had burst from Adela remained, hovering over the gully like a giant, crackling dome. Isabelle somehow stood at one end of this dome, and Adela and Viveca at the other, even though that was a good twenty paces away and she would have sworn they had not moved. Isabelle wanted to call out to them, but before she could, shapes coalesced before her, enclosed in the dome.

A long, vast room materialized. The walls were dark stone, hung with floor-to-ceiling tapestries in every color: emerald green, peacock blue, and blood red. Sconces bearing gleaming brass candelabras lit the room, and a thick, plum-colored rug blanketed the floor. Gilded chairs filled the space, as well as a long table covered in a rich, gold-tasseled cloth. The table was so laden with glittering platters of food and vats of wine, it was a miracle it hadn't collapsed.

Isabelle frowned. There was a door open at the far end of the room, and through it, she glimpsed a familiar sight—long windows set over a wood-paneled floor. The parlor?

That's when she realized. She'd seen this room before, this long hall with all the food. She walked through it every night on her way to the parlor.

It was the dining hall in the castle. Lit so brightly, glimmering with such opulence, she hadn't recognized it. The hall she knew was dim, bare, and dusty; no one used it for anything. Certainly not for eating.

And now Isabelle understood. *It would be easier to show you.*

This was a vision. A vision from the past.

More shapes appeared, materializing from nothing. People. People dressed lavishly. Women in gowns so layered with lace and jewels, it was a wonder they did not fall off, and men in jackets of stiff, embroidered brocade. They mingled through the hall, picking at food, clustering in small groups. A buzz of chit-chat filled the air, but muted, as though Isabelle was listening through a pane of glass.

She looked again through the open parlor door. The long windows looked as they always did, except they were hung with heavy rose curtains. The curtains were pulled aside to give a view of the clear night sky.

And the plump full moon, overlooking everything.

Isabelle's hand flew to her mouth. She knew what night this was.

The muffled noise in the hall was broken by a bloodcurdling scream. Isabelle looked around. She heard more screams and shattering glass, but all she saw was a huddle of people in the corner, gathering around something on the floor. It wasn't until that huddle broke apart, everyone fleeing in different directions, that Isabelle saw what they'd been gawping at.

It was a girl. Perhaps twelve years old. She knelt on the floor, her pastel gown spilling around her. Isabelle noticed the dress first, as though some part of her knew she didn't want to see the girl's face.

When she did, it wasn't a girl's face anymore.

It was the snout of a beast.

Screams filled the hall. Everyone ran, tripping over themselves and trampling each other to get away. The door to the parlor had been shut. Someone must have barricaded it, for a mass of people banged at it, shouting for it to be opened.

Isabelle looked back for the cursed girl, but she was gone. There were too many people in her line of sight, shrieking, fighting, fleeing.

Then a familiar snarl filled the room. Isabelle looked and saw someone else turning, a woman. As she completed the change, the beast ripped free of her embroidered gown. Bits of silk and a mountain of jewels scattered in every direction, sapphires and opals raining down. Isabelle watched, heart in her throat, as the beast lunged for the nearest person, pinning them to the floor and tearing into them with claws and teeth—

"*No,*" Isabelle cried. But no one could hear her. She couldn't stop anything. This had already happened.

It was still devastating to watch.

"Stop it," she said, her words a thin whisper. Raising her voice, she shouted, "Stop it! I've seen enough!"

Adela must have heard her. The dome of light gave one last, crackling *burst*, and then it was gone, et up by the night.

Isabelle gasped. She felt like she had been doused in black, icy water. The darkness of the gully and the frigid air returned in full force; the dome had shielded her from the elements, she realized. Not only that, but it had begun to snow—light, slurry snow, falling fast and dampening Isabelle's hair.

Adela and Viveca stood before her again, three paces away. As Isabelle sucked in another breath, Adela cupped her hands together, summoning her flame.

"What—what *was* that?" Isabelle's voice shook.

"That was my own memory," Adela said. "Of a sort. Plucking the vision from my mind alters the perception. But that was what I witnessed that night. The night the royals fell to the curse."

"But there were *other people* there." Isabelle gave a frantic shake of her head. She couldn't be calm, not after seeing that. "So many people—"

"For what it's worth—" Adela sounded unconcerned "—my sister warned the king a curse was coming for him that night. But there was, as you saw, a grand dinner planned. He went right ahead with it."

"Most of the people there—the ones who couldn't escape—were killed." Viveca also sounded unconcerned. Stars and stones, she sounded *bored*. This talk of innocent people being mauled to death bored her. "But a few survived. A few suffered a bite from a beast—and lived."

"Lived?" Isabelle shivered. "But your bite kills people. Drives them mad."

"*My* bite does." Viveca's tone dripped with rancor. "It's part of the weakness in my diluted blood. Perhaps you noticed, Isabelle. Those royals who were cursed became something more than just wolves, turning one night a month. They became beasts like Gryphon.

"I want to be that something *more*. Something stronger and faster. A creature that can turn any time. I want to be *powerful*. A force to be reckoned with." Contempt carved Viveca's face into an ugly mask. "They call it a curse. It's a *gift*. My ancestors were cowed by it. They allowed themselves to be culled until the bloodline nearly went extinct. When they should have *used* it to create an army—a kingdom—greater than any other." Her eyes flared, wild and ardent. "And with Gryphon's help, I can do that. I can achieve what none of my ancestors could."

Isabelle gaped at her. She remembered what Gryphon had told her about this woman: *Viveca sees herself as a superior being...set apart, a different species. The way she sees it, this is her land, her forest...*

Isabelle could see it now, in this creature standing before her. And it made for a horrific vision. "So the beast Gryphon turns into...that's what you want to become?"

"Yes," Viveca breathed. "Once, I hoped the castle might grant me my wish. Especially once I heard about Gryphon. He's descended from the same bloodline, and walking into the castle activated the curse in him. I hoped it might do the same for me—but it didn't. The castle didn't alter me one bit."

Adela clucked her tongue. "The original spell was too powerful. And you've already been touched by it, however lightly."

"But I don't understand," Isabelle said. "What is it you want from Gryphon?"

Viveca said, "His bite, of course."

Isabelle stared.

"I told you." Viveca's smile was victorious. "There were a few people bitten that night in the castle. When the curse first fell. Bitten—but not killed—by the beasts."

Bitten but not killed. Isabelle felt like she couldn't breathe. The back of her left wrist seemed to pulse, even though the wound there was healed now, nothing left but a slightly raised scar. With some difficulty, she asked, "And what happened to them? The ones who were bitten?"

"They were infected," Adela said. "Not with the illness that drives victims mad. With the curse itself."

"They *became* beasts, Isabelle," Viveca said. "Just like the royals themselves."

Isabelle felt like she was in Adela's dome again, listening through glass, everything muffled. Viveca's words caught in her brain, blocking everything else out.

They became beasts.

"They became *something*," Adela interjected. "I had to flee the castle that night, so it's not as though I conducted a case study. But I heard the stories from the royals once they were free of the castle. Their bite transformed the bitten."

Transformed the bitten.

They became beasts.

This cold reality spread through Isabelle like a poison. It crystallized her veins, turning her insides to ice. "So if Gryphon bites someone?" Miraculously, Isabelle's voice was calm. Because her voice was not her own. She heard it as though someone else was speaking. "They would turn like he does? Every morning and night?"

"Eventually." Viveca waved a hand. "I don't think Gryphon turned until a full moon. The curse takes a while to settle in. As for changing every morning, well..." A grim smile came over her face "I'm sure I can control it better than he does."

Adela gave a toss of her head. "Undoubtedly. The original royals controlled it. Whether that would apply to someone he bites—"

"We don't know anything for sure," Viveca admitted. "It's not as though he'll bite anyone and let us know. But if we could get our hands on him..."

Isabelle did not immediately react to this. She still felt shielded, numb to her surroundings. To the snow falling from the sky. To the wind gusting through the glade. To the darkness thickening around them. To Viveca and Adela.

She heard Viveca's words belatedly. Then she jerked her head up.

Viveca and Adela watched her with equal expressions of hunger and malice. In the harsh light of the witch's flames, they both looked like wolves, ready to devour their prey.

Isabelle fumbled for her pistol, but her fingers were stiff with cold. Viveca laughed when Isabelle finally drew it out, and when she raised it, the wolf slapped the gun from her hand, sending it skittering into the snow. Isabelle gaped, flooded with fear and foreboding. She suddenly realized what a stupid position she had put herself in. Outside the castle walls, alone, in the middle of the night, cornered—and no one knew where she was—

A shot rang out.

Viveca cursed and jumped back as a bullet ricocheted off the ground near her foot. Flecks of snow flew into the air. Perhaps it had ricocheted *off* Viveca's foot, because, still cursing, she half-stumbled, half-hopped away. Adela backed up too.

Klaus emerged from the shadow of the castle, a rifle in hand. Staggering relief washed over Isabelle.

"Now you're *shooting* at me?" Viveca spat.

"That was a warning shot," Klaus drawled. "You know I don't miss." He sounded completely unruffled. But as he came closer, Isabelle saw his eyes blazed. "This next one will take you in the head if you and your pet witch don't leave this place. Now."

"You wouldn't." Viveca's tone was venomous, but a slow smile spread across her face. "You *couldn't*."

"You sure about that?"

Viveca watched him a moment longer. Her smile faded as he stared her down.

"Come on," Viveca said to Adela, turning away. With a spiteful look for Klaus, Adela followed, the two of them vanishing across the glade.

Klaus waited a long moment after they'd gone, tense and motionless, his rifle pointed into the darkness. Then, finally, he lowered the gun and looked at Isabelle.

"What the hell are you *doing* out here?" Klaus's tone was furious.

Isabelle did not care. She stood clutching her lantern, her teeth chattering. Somehow in all this insanity, she had never let it go. Her frozen fingers felt welded around the handle.

Every part of her was frozen, from her chapped cheeks to her numb toes. But the cold seeping into her was a different kind, not born from the sleet wetting her hair, nor from the wintry wind cutting through her. This was the cold of shock, stealing through her like a sickness. It coated her brain with icy fog, it froze her heart solid. She felt weak, exhausted, trembling from head to toe.

Something of it must have shown, for Klaus frowned at her. "Are you all right? Did they hurt you?"

She tried to make sense of these words. *Did they hurt you.*

"Gryphon hurt me," she said.

"What?" Klaus stepped towards her.

"Gryphon hurt me," she repeated. "Gryphon bit me."

She met Klaus's gaze. Klaus gazed back, silent and grim.

"He bit me," Isabelle said. "And his bite—" She couldn't find the words she wanted. "Am I...going to be like him?"

"What did they say to you?"

"Just tell me!" Isabelle snapped. "Am I going to turn like him? Become...what he is?"

Klaus let out a long breath. "Isabelle—"

"Where is he?" Isabelle realized she sounded mad, out of control, but she didn't care. "Where is he right now?"

"He's in his tower, I think, but—Isabelle—wait!"

But Isabelle did not wait. She tore past Klaus, stumbling and sliding in the rising snow, and scrambled up the path back to the castle, while Klaus cursed and called after her, following in her wrathful wake.

17

BEREFT

G RYPHON WAS WORKING THROUGH the curve of the chin
when Isabelle burst in.

He nearly fell off his stool. He had never told Isabelle about
this place—his workshop, his sanctuary. But here she stood in
the doorway, letting in the sleety chill.

She was rife with fury. Gryphon wasn't sure how he
knew—physically, she looked *cold* more than anything else. But
there was an energy about her, a violent pulse. She quivered with
it from head to toe.

Gryphon met her eyes. He had never seen a look like that on
her face.

"What are you doing here?" he asked. He checked his sculpture—he thought he'd nicked it—then stood, dusting off his
hands on his trousers.

Isabelle didn't answer. She just stared at him with that crazed
look. As though she'd forgotten how to speak.

Unsure whether to feel concerned or vexed—he was a bit of
both—Gryphon tried to peer through the open door behind
her. The damp cold rushed into the tower like a tidal wave,

carrying the sharp scent of snow. "Is Klaus with you? Or Stefan? I thought you weren't feeling well, Stefan said—"

"Why—" Isabelle finally spoke, her voice dreadful. "Why didn't—you—*tell* me?"

Gryphon was sure his heart stopped beating.

"What?" His voice came out strangled.

Isabelle's wild gaze fixed on him. Gryphon saw her hands clench and unclench.

"Why didn't you tell me?" she rasped.

"Tell you about wha—"

"*Don't*. Don't do that. Don't pretend you don't know what I'm talking about."

Oh, stones. *Stones.* She couldn't really know...how could she have found out...

"Who told you?" he asked flatly.

"*No.*" Isabelle marched into the tower, leaving the door wide open. "You don't get to do that either. You don't get to be angry—just look me in the eye and—" She heaved a breath. "Just tell me why you lied to me. Why you didn't t-tell me." Her voice cracked, but she barreled on. "All those times, all that piffle about not trusting me, and then thinking I might go mad—when that wasn't it at *all*—"

Gryphon bit back a retort. He tried to keep a stony expression, but inside, he felt like he was plummeting down a dark hole.

"Why didn't you tell me?" Isabelle burst out. "Why didn't you tell me I'm going to become—that I'm going to be like—"

"Like me?" Gryphon said evenly.

Isabelle gulped in another breath. And it was that—that ragged sound—that made him realize. He looked at her and saw the unshed tears in her furious eyes. She wasn't shaking because she was in a temper, or because she was cold.

She was not all right. Very much not all right.

Gryphon felt the ridiculous urge to either laugh or scream. What a heartless idiot he was. Of *course* she wasn't all right. Wasn't that the whole reason he hadn't wanted to tell her?

He let loose a long exhale. "Isabelle." Crossing behind her, he shut the door against the flurries swirling outside, coating the courtyard in snow. Then he turned back to her. She wore her black coat, which was snug but not terribly long. Not warm enough for such wintry weather, Gryphon thought. It was soaked through, her shoulders and hair damp.

"You're freezing." Gryphon reached for her. "Come sit over here, I just built up the fire—"

But Isabelle flinched away, jumping like a skittish deer. She looked at him with fear in her big, brown eyes. It was fleeting, there and gone, but Gryphon saw it. He saw and took it like a bullet in the gut.

He clenched his jaw, keeping the hurt to himself. "Please." He made a miserable gesture towards the fire on the far wall. There were no chairs in the room—only stools—no proper furniture except for the narrow bed by the grate. "Sit. You're cold and wet. Take off your coat and get warm."

As though reminded of her sorry state, Isabelle shook even more. But she didn't move.

"Please." She closed her eyes. "Why didn't you tell me?"

Gryphon made a hollow sound. It might have been a laugh, if that would have been at all appropriate. "Because of this," he said, helpless. "Because I didn't want to...upset you. I didn't want you to be afraid."

Eyes squeezed shut, Isabelle nodded. As though she had expected this. "But you would have told me eventually? Wouldn't you?"

"I—"

"I mean, you would have to, wouldn't you?" Isabelle's eyes flew open. "When I start to—ch-change—but why—" Her voice rose. "Why *haven't* I changed? It's been nearly a month—"

Gryphon tried to make his voice calm. "I didn't change right away. I told you before. It wasn't until after the full moon. The first full moon I was here in the castle." He rubbed a hand over his forehead. "I know there's been a full moon since I bit you, but it was so soon. I've been afraid maybe...that it might take longer to settle in. Like it did with me."

"That's right. They said that," Isabelle murmured. She sounded a little more like herself, a little steadier, though her eyes were still glazed. "And then you began to change every day. But she said that wasn't right, that it could be controlled..."

"Who said?"

"Adela." Isabelle's voice was absent.

"*Adela?* The *witch?* You spoke to her? Wait—she got inside the castle?"

"No, no." Isabelle sniffled, taking a step towards the fire. "This was outside. I left."

"You *left*?"

"Just for a bit." She took another few steps, then turned to face him. It was like she was melting. Like her fury had been doused by the damp cold soaking through her, sizzling off her in spiraling steam. Revealing a softer, more vulnerable Isabelle—not exactly the Isabelle he knew, not quite. She was calmer, but raw. Sensible, but dazed.

"So I might not turn at all?" she asked in a small voice.

"Maybe not," Gryphon said quietly. "There's no way to know. I think if you get through this next full moon...then maybe..."

217

"Would you have told me then?" she asked. "At the full moon?"

He had to be honest. "I don't know. I didn't really have a plan, Isabelle."

"Of course you didn't." She made her own rueful not-a-laugh, wiping her sleeve across her face. "You don't make plans, do you?"

"I'm not very good at them," he confessed.

Isabelle's face twitched. He realized she had tried to smile but not quite managed it.

"What will happen to me?" she asked. "When—if I change. What will happen?"

He looked at her, confused. "You've seen me change."

"But what will *happen?*" Her voice was infused with fearful need. "What—what *happens*, what does it—"

Something broke inside Gryphon. A heartstring snapping, leaving him untethered. "We don't need to talk about that right now."

"No, I have to know. I n-*need* to know. What will happen, what will I—"

"We don't even know it *will* happen." Gryphon tried to sound gentle. He wasn't sure he pulled it off. *Gentle* wasn't his strong suit. He probably just sounded weird.

Isabelle wrapped her arms around herself. "I need to know."

"You need to take that coat off," Gryphon disagreed. "It's soaked through, it's not keeping you warm. Come on—please—" And this time, he managed to guide her back into the corner, where the fire crackled warmly. She shrugged out of her coat and handed it to him, then bent to remove her sodden boots.

Gryphon turned to toss her coat over an empty easel. When he turned back, he caught his breath.

Isabelle perched on the foot of the bed. She wore a gown of dark crimson. It fell freely from her waist, draping over the delicate angles of her body. The bodice was cut wide, exposing her collarbone. With her head turned towards the fire, the graceful arch of her neck was accentuated, her rich brown skin gleaming in the light of the flames.

He could not say why the sight of her in that dress struck him so. Probably because it was a ridiculous choice for this weather, he groused to himself. That was why.

Gryphon stepped forward. Isabelle looked around, her eyes traveling the room. "What is this place? I've seen you come here before—"

"It's my workshop. Where I work on my art." He managed half a smile. "When I'm not sketching in the parlor, anyway."

Her eyes lingered on a dark still life, not quite finished, in the corner behind him. The painting featured a vase of haphazardly strewn roses, giving the flowers an untamed look. The burgundy of the roses nearly matched Isabelle's gown.

"You're very good," she said simply. "I've seen your sketches, but I had no idea.... I suspect your mother would be proud."

She would be the only one, Gryphon thought, but he couldn't summon the usual rancor for his father. He didn't even want to think about his father. "Are you warm enough?" Gryphon asked. "I—maybe you should go back to the castle."

"I don't want to," she said in that same simple tone. "Not yet."

Gryphon looked at her for a long moment. Then he made a vague gesture towards the bed. "Can I...?"

She shifted around to make room for him, facing the fire. Gryphon lowered himself onto the empty space beside her, slowly, as though she was a frightened rabbit who might skitter off. But she didn't flinch away this time. She only let out a breath, tension seeping out of her body.

"Why didn't you tell me, Gryphon?" she asked. For what must have been the tenth time. Her voice was soft and resigned. She gazed into the fire, the dancing flames reflected in her eyes. "You say you didn't want to frighten me. But...was that the only reason?"

Gryphon closed his eyes. Perhaps, before, he would have denied it. Perhaps if he wasn't so tired, he would have. Instead, he opened his mouth and spoke the truest words he had. "Why do you think?" He looked at her, feeling more powerless than ever. "I told you, didn't I? What happened to me. Why I was banished—how my father perceived me. A poor excuse for a lord, spending my time painting instead of hunting. A liability who fell for the wrong woman and embarrassed him."

He ducked his head. "That's all I ever was—a disappointment. Or someone to be feared. The servants were always afraid of me." Perhaps that was his fault. He had never been good at engaging with others. He knew how he seemed to most people. And he'd learned to just give into it. There was no other point.

But Isabelle...*Isabelle*. She didn't see him that way. She wasn't afraid of him. *Unless she is now.* He cupped his hands over his knees, squeezing them tight.

His eyes were still fixed on the floor when Isabelle placed a hand over his. Startled, Gryphon looked at her. She gazed back, squeezing his hand.

"I'm not afraid of you," she said.

"You *weren't*." Gryphon tried to draw his hand away, but she held fast. "That's why I didn't want to tell you." His voice turned hoarse. "I didn't want it to change." He didn't even know what *it* was. What was between them. Was there anything between them? Was it all in his foolish, lonely head?

Isabelle reached across to cover his hand with both of hers. "I'm not afraid of *you*, Gryphon."

"You should be," he said unsteadily.

"No." She said it as though it were simple fact. As true as any historical data in one of her books. "I am afraid," she admitted. "Of what might happen to me. What I might...become." She let out a shaky breath. "I'm sorry. I—"

"We don't have to talk about it." Gryphon suddenly realized how close she was, leaning into him. About ready to topple over, by the look of it. "Isabelle. You're exhausted. Are you sure you don't want to go back to the castle, to your room?"

She shook her head. "I don't think I'd make it up all those stairs."

Gryphon considered. "You can...sleep here, if you want?"

"Can I?" Isabelle's eyes were weary, hopeful, fragile. "Is that all right?"

"Of course. I'll wake you before I go down to the dungeons." But when he shifted, preparing to stand, she leaned into him even more.

"What you said before," she told him, her voice low. "About being a disappointment. I...know what that is. To feel that way."

Oh. Yes. "I know you do."

"Because of what I told you about my father?"

"Your father. And...your brother too. Right?"

Isabelle trembled. He could *feel* it, her trembling. He wanted to help her. To hold her.

"Yes. My brother too." Her voice was choked with suppressed tears. "He didn't leave me. But he told me to leave him. He told me he didn't need me. That I was a bother, a nuisance—even though he was the one always getting in trouble—"

"He said that?" Gryphon reached for her, taking her elbow in a gentle, steadying grip.

"Yes. He said that." Isabelle lifted her head. Her face was inches from him. So close, he could see the tears glistening in her eyes. As he watched, one spilled down her cheek.

"Then he's a fool," Gryphon said, his voice rough. He felt...unspooled. He had never been so close to anyone. Not like this. He had never said so many true things, so many deep and raw things. Now he was coming apart at the seams, bits of him spilling about. A part of him wanted it to stop, but he didn't know how to stop it. He didn't know how to put everything back in place.

Isabelle lifted her hands, but she didn't draw away. Gryphon turned to face her head-on. He drew one knee onto the bed. Brushing her hip.

She still leaned into him. As he turned, and his shoulder slipped from beneath her, she fell towards him. Not in an uncontrolled way. More...deliberate.

A choice.

Gryphon was frozen. Her mouth hovered close to his. He didn't move a muscle. He wasn't sure he was even breathing.

Isabelle placed a hand on his chest. Slowly, she pressed the tips of her fingers into him, exerting *just* a little pressure.

"Isabelle," Gryphon whispered.

Isabelle flicked her eyes up. Met his gaze.

Then she kissed him.

Gryphon felt a rumble deep in his chest. Waves of shock rolled through him. Waves of...something else, too. Something he hadn't felt in a long time. No, something he had *never* felt, not like this. Not with such deep, blazing wanting—

Isabelle's lips parted beneath his. Gryphon slid his hand up her arm. He had not realized that kissing someone could feel so *right*. Like the curves and edges of a sculpture emerging from a hunk of rock. Revealing what had always been there, buried inside the stone.

Showing what it was meant to be.

A minute later—warm, breathless, mussed—Isabelle pulled back. Just far enough to speak. "You said I could stay here tonight," she whispered, her words caressing his lips.

"Yes." His voice was ragged with desire. Tinged with disbelief that this was even happening.

Her hand ghosted along his waist. "Will you stay with me?"

"Yes." He did not hesitate, giving his answer before she'd finished the question. "Yes."

He didn't know who moved first. But then they were kissing again. Hands exploring. Hearts racing. Pressing into each other, closer, deeper. Desperate to banish their fears for this one night.

———◆———

Several hours later, Gryphon woke, a violent shudder racking his body.

His eyes flew open. He was utterly disoriented. Exposed to the cold air, his skin prickled with goosebumps. But his arm was draped over something warm.

Another shudder rocked him, and he bolted upright, doubling over. He had no idea where he was, *when* he was. His eyes ran over his surroundings—a long pine table, a block of marble, tools and brushes and paints. His workshop. He was in his tower.

Gryphon glanced aside. He was in his bed, in his tower. With Isabelle. She was asleep, though she stirred, curling towards him. A light quilt lay strewn over her, and as Gryphon watched, she reached for it, wrapping it tightly about herself. The fire in the grate was long dead, the air around them frosting with cold.

It was the cold that drew his attention. The fire. It was out, but he had added more wood just before Isabelle came in. When had she come in?

As the full events of last night came rushing back to him, his body was enveloped in another shudder.

Panic seized him. He glanced at the small window. It was shuttered, but he could see light straining in through the cracks between the wooden boards.

Morning light. Sunlight.

Daylight.

"Gryphon," Isabelle mumbled. "What is—"

"*No.*" Gryphon trembled from the tips of his fingers down to his bare toes. He tripped in his haste to scramble from the bed, swearing loudly as he stubbed his foot. "Isabelle, wake up! *Wake up!*"

"What...why?" Out of the corner of his eye, he saw Isabelle sit up. Gryphon cast around for his shirt before he realized what a waste of time that was.

"What's going on?" Isabelle's voice was laced with sleep.

Gryphon tried to answer, but pain shattered through him, stealing his breath. It started deep at his center, a match striking against a stone. The match caught, flames of agony erupting through him, flooding every bone in his body.

"Oh, stones—*Gryphon.*" Isabelle awoke at last. "It's sunrise, it's morning—oh, stones, *stones.* Gryphon, you have to get down to the dungeons!"

He tried. He tried to move. But his muscles were as rigid as stone. The part of his brain that wasn't consumed with pain screamed in fear. *Isabelle, Isabelle—*

Somehow, he turned away. Somehow, he staggered across the tower, toppling into his stool and knocking over an easel. He yanked open the door with such a surge of unbridled strength, he pulled it off its hinges. Then he stumbled out into the cold.

Facing the sun, rising over the castle walls.

He heard Isabelle behind him. "Gryphon, run!" she cried. "You have to get down to the dungeons! *Run!*"

He tried. He took a lurching step. Then another.

He managed one more. And then his bones began to break.

18

UNFETTERED

ISABELLE WATCHED IN HELPLESS horror as Gryphon fell to his knees, his back arching, his spine snapping. She knew she should run or try to barricade herself in the tower, but she was rooted to the spot, clutching the doorframe. The bitter cold of the dawn rolled over her, but Isabelle didn't feel it.

Just like the last time she'd witnessed this, Isabelle felt hours pass in the space of a few minutes, while every bone in Gryphon's body reformed. As he fell to all fours, she stepped out into the courtyard, hardly aware she was moving. She felt weirdly drawn to Gryphon, transfixed by the sight before her. The sight of him changing.

This was what was going to happen to her.

Then Gryphon looked at her, and he wasn't Gryphon anymore. His yellow eyes were the same, but set in the gnarled face of the beast.

Isabelle stopped dead. Her heart beat a million times a minute as the danger finally sank in. The last time this happened, she'd barely escaped. The last time this happened, Klaus had instructed her to run as fast as she could across the bridge, luring the beast inside, where Klaus shot him with a sedative.

Klaus wasn't here now. No one was.

But the seconds ticked by, and the beast didn't move. He didn't bare his teeth or snap at her. A flock of small birds gathered on the wall, trilling and flitting about. A brisk wind whorled through the courtyard, rustling past. And the beast simply stared at Isabelle, unblinking.

Isabelle held her breath. She didn't dare move. But she said quietly, "Gryphon?"

The beast let out a huff, startling her.

Then he turned and bounded away, making for the back gate.

"Oh, no," Isabelle breathed. She scrambled after the beast. "Oh, no, oh, no, oh, wait—"

She reached the corner of the courtyard just in time to see the beast smash through the back gate. The gate exploded in a *crash* of squealing metal and splintering wood, and then the beast was gone—outside the castle walls.

"No, no, no, wait!" Isabelle picked her way through the debris to peer around the back of the castle.

The beast was tearing through the steep, overgrown path down the crag, spanning the distance with massive leaps and strides. As Isabelle watched, he made one final leap into the gully, then vanished into the trees.

"Oh, damn," Isabelle cursed.

———◦◦◦———

"He smashed through the gate?" Klaus looked dumbstruck. "Are you joking? But how did he get down the cliff?"

"He took the path, of course." Isabelle tugged on her boots, hastily tying the laces. "In about two minutes."

They were in Gryphon's workshop. As soon as she'd seen Gryphon run into the woods, Isabelle had gone for help. Luckily, she didn't have to go far. She met Klaus in the courtyard as he returned from some early hunting in the forest. Once she'd outlined the situation—with much frantic waving of her arms—Klaus located Stefan and sent him to bring supplies from the castle, while Isabelle went back to the tower to dress.

With boots and coat on, Isabelle headed out into the courtyard. She didn't wait for Klaus, who, she thought, was taking far too long to digest what had happened. "Where is Stef—Stefan!" she called, spotting the boy as he hurried out of the castle. He met them halfway across the courtyard, arms laden with supplies. He handed a crossbow to Klaus, and a satchel lined with bottles of sedative. He also had a short bow and a quiver of arrows, which he handed to Isabelle.

Klaus stared as Isabelle strapped the quiver to her waist, over her fitted coat. "What do you think you're doing?"

"I'm coming with you, of course," she said. "After Gryphon."

"Uh, no." Klaus was nonplussed. "No, you're not."

"*Yes,* I am. We don't have time to argue. We both know I'm not going to run away, and I'll be safe enough from the wolves with you."

Klaus stared some more. Isabelle thought his jaw had been hanging open for the last ten minutes.

"Let's get going." Isabelle gestured for Stefan to raise the portcullis. "We will find him together and come back here. Me, you, and him. I'm not going anywhere, and neither is he. All right?"

"All right, all right," Klaus muttered. "Let's go. We're wasting time."

As though I didn't just make that same point, Isabelle thought, stalking across the bridge.

The sun was still low in the sky; it was just past dawn. Isabelle hadn't been awake at this time of day in weeks. There were few clouds in the sky, and the sun shone bright and cold—pretty, but providing scant warmth. The sleet had turned to snow overnight, a thick layer covering the forest floor.

"Don't worry," Klaus said of the snow. "Should make it easy to track him."

He wasn't wrong. As they traveled north along the ridge, Klaus pointed out Gryphon's tracks in the snowy gulch below, visible here and there through the trees. They were not so much tracks as a wide, deep swathe, cut through the snow like a scar.

But Isabelle could not be as calm as Klaus was. Anxiety nibbled at her, and she was sure it would not stop until Gryphon was back in the castle. If anything happened to Gryphon out here—if anything happened to anyone else *because* of Gryphon—she would be partly to blame.

"It is dangerous out here, you know," Klaus said, keeping an eye on Gryphon's tracks as they tramped through the snow. "I'm flattered you're so confident in my abilities to hold off the entire wolf pack on my own, but—"

"You're out here all the time," Isabelle pointed out.

"Yes, well, they don't want anything from me," Klaus murmured. "Or rather, they know they won't get anything from me. You, on the other hand—"

"All Viveca wants from me is a way into the castle. And I'm not about to give her that."

"If Viveca knew you'd been bitten by Gryphon, she'd want a hell of a lot more from you. In fact, she'd probably be happy to settle for you and forget about getting into the castle." He paused. "Although, I think only Gryphon can turn others with his bite. Because he was affected by the original curse. As I understand it."

"But I haven't turned. Or shown any sign of it."

Klaus squinted at her. "Nothing at all? You're sure?"

"Well." Isabelle evaded his gaze, surveying the gangling birch trees along the ravine. "I don't think so. I'm not exactly sure what might indicate I'm turning into a monster."

Klaus didn't respond at first, and Isabelle thought he'd dropped the matter. But then he said, "Gryphon was laid up for a full week when he first entered the castle. The curse hit him hard. Even after that, he was out of sorts. Ill, most of the time—"

"I was ill," Isabelle said, troubled.

"You had a cold. You recovered. Gryphon had bouts of illness on and off, and it was more than just the sniffles. He had weakness, fever, heavy fatigue. Pain in his joints, in his chest."

Isabelle glanced at him. "Headaches?"

"A few, yes. But he'd ache all over. Some days, he couldn't get out of bed. Then he'd go days without sleeping at all." Klaus shrugged. "Like I said. Out of sorts."

Isabelle listened to this, not entirely comforted. She'd had that blasted headache, which was not usual for her. Though it was gone now, Isabelle realized, entirely gone.

Klaus cast her a sidelong look. He pushed aside a stray branch hanging from a spruce tree. "For what it's worth, I don't think you've had anything near as bad he did. I'm not trying to give you false hope—it just doesn't seem the same."

Isabelle supposed he might be right. But then, as Klaus had pointed out, Gryphon's curse was not quite the same.

"Doesn't mean Viveca would leave you be, though," Klaus added. "If she knew you'd been bitten."

"On the off chance she could use me? To create her kingdom of monster beasts?"

"She told you that, huh?" Klaus said grimly.

"She told me everything." Isabelle heaved a breath. "Honestly, I'm not sure why. She had to know the one thing that would keep me from helping her was showing me just how mad she really is."

Klaus slowed, peering through a tangle of branches on a soaring oak tree. "Thing is, Viveca doesn't see it that way," he murmured. "She sees herself as perfectly rational. Might be she thought she'd get you on her side, showing how Gryphon lied to you."

Isabelle wrinkled her forehead. Yes, of course she was angry Gryphon had kept the truth from her. But to think she'd take Viveca's side... "Right. Because it's perfectly rational to go around attacking people."

"Think about it." Klaus picked up his pace, satisfied whatever he'd seen was harmless "It's not like she can live among other people. Her ancestors tried, and it didn't go well. Add to that, she was raised by a mad witch, and, well. She never really had a chance."

Isabelle looked at him. There was an odd softness in his voice she had never heard from him before. Klaus had been prepared to kill Viveca last night; she was sure of it. But she remembered what Ellery said too: *Viveca was after Klaus. She was interested in him.*

Was it possible, Isabelle wondered, that Klaus had been...interested back?

"Maybe she didn't have a chance," Isabelle admitted, "but she *could* keep herself from killing innocents. Gryphon does, and he turns more often than the wolves."

Klaus was silent for a moment. Then he said, "I don't disagree."

Isabelle watched her steps, careful as she picked her way over a pebbly patch in the ground. "How do you know that, anyway? About Viveca's ancestors?"

"She told me," Klaus said simply.

Isabelle raised an eyebrow. It was odd to think of Klaus having a casual chat with Viveca. It didn't fit with what she'd seen pass between them last night.

"Anyway," said Klaus. "The wolves aren't the only reason it's dangerous out here. We may be after Gryphon, but he isn't Gryphon right now. He's the beast."

Isabelle hummed in agreement, but she wasn't so sure—she wasn't sure what that meant. *He's the beast.* The first time she'd seen Gryphon change, he'd chased her, intent on hunting her down. But this morning had been different. He'd stood fifteen paces from her. And he hadn't even tried to attack her.

Why was that?

She clicked her tongue. "This is all my fault."

"Don't give yourself too much credit," Klaus said. "Just because you and Gryphon got snuggly last night—"

Isabelle spluttered. "Got *what?*"

"—doesn't mean it was your fault." Klaus stepped over a large boulder, then turned to give Isabelle a hand up. "For one thing, Gryphon's been doing this for a while now, and he knows better than to be so careless, sleeping past sunrise. He usually sets up an alarm. Also, I wasn't there," he admitted. "I would've gone looking for him."

"Well, you're not always there at dawn," Isabelle pointed out. "Someone else must meet him in the dungeons in your absence."

"Usually Stefan does. But I wasn't meant to be out this morning, I..." Klaus shook his head, a muscle working in his jaw. "I thought I told Stefan. No, I'm *sure* I did. But by the time he realized Gryphon wasn't coming, it might have been too late. Especially if he had to look for him first."

An hour later, Isabelle's frustration had mounted beyond what she could reasonably control. "How will we ever catch up with him?" she lamented. "Not only did he have a half hour's head start, but he's faster than us. If we had horses—"

"If we had horses, he would eat our horses," Klaus said. "As it is, he might eat us. He won't run forever. We'll catch up."

The sun climbed higher as the day wore on, but by noon, slate gray clouds had settled over the sky like a mantle. A smattering of icy sleet misted over them. Isabelle shivered, tucking as much of her hair beneath her hat as she could.

"I don't believe it," Klaus said. Isabelle started. It was the first time either of them had spoken in over an hour, and she'd grown so tired and numb with cold, she'd half-forgotten Klaus was there.

"What's wrong?" she asked.

"Stay here. I need a closer look at his tracks."

Isabelle waited as Klaus half-jogged, half-slid down the slope of the ravine, vanishing into the white landscape of snow and birch trees. She gripped the ends of her coat's thick, high collar and pulled them tight, wishing Klaus would hurry up.

The hunter returned a few minutes later, panting as he trudged up the slope. "Come on." He waved an arm. "He cut across the creek down in the gorge. Took a turn northeast."

Isabelle didn't bother to hide her dismay as she started after him, stumbling in the slushy snow. "How do we cross the creek?"

"It's pretty frozen and not very wide. If he crossed it, we should be fine."

The bottom of the gorge was lined with silver birch trees on the southern side, but covered thickly in dark firs to the north. Gryphon's tracks were still easy to follow, but, Klaus warned, they would need to keep a closer eye out to be sure they didn't stumble upon him unknowingly.

The good news was, the further they went, the more easterly Gryphon's tracks turned—which would take them back to the castle, Klaus said. But the clouds in the sky grew darker, the air colder and gustier. The sleet had stopped, but Isabelle wasn't sure how much longer she could keep going. Fatigue tugged at her, turning her resolve to defeat and misery. *We have to find him soon*, she thought, trying to keep her spirits up, *we just have to—*

The afternoon wore on. Eventually, Gryphon's tracks led them back across the creek and up the ravine. To their consternation, his path turned south into the forest. Isabelle's gaze worried at the horizon as they stepped beneath the dark, twisted eave of trees. She didn't know how much time was left until dusk. She didn't want to ask.

"Hang on." Klaus flung an arm up, nearly taking Isabelle's head off. He crouched behind a stocky fir, and Isabelle followed suit. "Something moved there, through the trees."

"Gryphon?"

"Don't know." Klaus glanced at her. "Hope so. We're actually quite close to the castle." He looked at the bow she carried. "You can actually use that?"

"I grew up in the woods too," Isabelle said tightly.

Klaus gave a swift nod. "All right. I'm going to double around, see if I can get behind whatever's up there. You stay here. Shoot anything that moves."

He snuck off, deft and silent as he disappeared around the gnarled trunk of a huge yew. Isabelle watched until he was gone, then took an arrow from her quiver, nocking it loosely to her bow.

Then she waited. For a quarter of an hour, she waited. She was just wondering if she shouldn't go look for Klaus when something *snapped* behind the trees on her left.

Isabelle whirled around. That could have been anything in the forest—a prowling fox or badger—but something had every hair on the back of her neck prickling. Something was not right, something was out of place...

A strange smell. Isabelle wrinkled her nose. It wasn't a bad smell, but it didn't belong. Oiled leather and acrid powder and something...familiar—

Another *snap* pulled her from her reverie. She raised her bow, pulling it taut. "Who's there?" she called in a harsh voice. "I know you're there. Come out slowly. I'm armed." This little speech wouldn't do her any good if it was Gryphon hiding behind those trees, but then, nothing would do her any good if Gryphon was behind those trees.

Abruptly, someone stepped into view, not ten paces from her. Isabelle was startled even though she'd known *something* was there. She wiped her expression clean, taking in the young man before her. He was tall, his double-breasted coat engulfing his lanky frame. His black hair was wiry and shorn close to the head, in the style her brother usually wore his hair.

He also carried a rifle in his hands.

"It's all right." The young man sounded nervous, as though she was the one with the gun, and he the bow. As Isabelle watched, he slowly lowered himself into a crouch, placing the rifle on the ground. "I won't hurt you."

"But I might hurt you," Isabelle said coolly. "Who are you? What are you doing in this forest?"

"I'm part of a hunting expedition." He held his hands up in an expression of surrender. "From the Glen Kingdom. There's a small party of us."

"You're hunting in this weather? That's brave of you."

"Yes, well, the man I serve is rather—" He broke off, cocking his head to one side. Something dawned in his eyes, as though he had only just seen her. "Sorry," he said, "but—are you Isabelle?"

Isabelle gave a start. But before she could answer, an unearthly howl sounded out, filling the air around them. Isabelle went cold, but something inside her *twisted*. It was an odd feeling—as though that cry had touched some part of her she didn't know existed.

Then her brain caught up with her body. "Gryphon. That's Gryphon."

"What did you say?" the young man asked.

"I have to go!" she called, and, heedless of any danger the man might possess, she turned and ran through the snow. Her stockings quickly dampened inside her boots, her dress grew sodden at the hem, but she didn't slow her pace. That howl had penetrated the entire forest; it could have come from anywhere, and yet, Isabelle knew where to go. She didn't question the instinct as she scrambled up a rise in the woodland, skidding to a halt as she crested the top.

Before her was a small clearing in the woods, a glade on the edge of a thicket of spruce trees.

In the middle of the glade—face to face with Isabelle—was the beast.

And beyond the beast, some twenty paces back, was Prince Garrett.

For a ridiculous moment, Isabelle was far more stunned to see him than she was to see the beast. Garrett. *Garrett.* She couldn't make sense of it. He was here in the Black Forest, not two miles from the castle. He wore a heavy, brown overcoat, and he held a long rifle in his hands.

A long rifle, raised, in his hands. Pointed straight at the beast.

Pointed at Gryphon.

19

BROTHERLY

G ARRETT'S HEART TURNED TO ice when Isabelle appeared on top of the hill, less than ten paces from the monstrous beast. Any shock at seeing her *there, now* was swept away by fear of her proximity to the beast. They'd stopped for a quick lunch break when Gemma, who'd gone to relieve herself, marched back into camp with a rangy, dark-eyed hunter held hostage at the point of her rifle. The hunter, it turned out, was looking for the same beast they were—and had tracked it to a small rise half a mile away. The hunter made some noise about capturing the beast, but Garrett hadn't paid him much heed. They left Falcon and Evans guarding the hunter, while he, Gemma, and Roy went after the beast. They'd managed to surround it in the glade atop the rise, and Garrett had been poised to bring it down before it brought *them* down.

And then Isabelle appeared, and Garrett's brain disintegrated in a rush of panic.

Isabelle spoke before he himself had the wits to say anything. "Garrett." She didn't shout, but her voice carried across the rise. *"Don't."*

Garrett's mouth went dry with fear. The beast had pricked up at the sound of Isabelle's voice, looking around for her. It was a monster of a creature, even bigger than Garrett remembered. Standing on its hind legs, it was several feet taller than Garrett. It *was* strangely wolf-like—if a wolf could have walked on two legs—with dark, thick fur, tufted ears, and a long snout lined with jagged teeth.

As the beast turned in half a circle to face Isabelle, Garrett found his voice. "Isabelle." He wondered if she could hear him; he was afraid to speak too loudly. "Isabelle, don't—move."

Several paces to his left, in the shade of an oak tree, Roy shifted, an arrow nocked to his bow. Gemma was on his right, crouched within a clump of wild holly. The point of her rifle protruded from her hiding place. Garrett, carrying his own rifle, sighted a perfect shot as the beast turned its back on him. He took aim.

"Garrett!" Isabelle hastened forward, the distance between her and the monster growing smaller. "Please, don't—*don't shoot.*"

Garrett lowered his rifle by a hair. "Isabelle—"

"Please," she repeated. She wasn't looking at him, Garrett realized, but at the beast. She craned her neck up as though trying to lock eyes with the creature. "Garrett." Isabelle's voice was halfway between calm and pleading. "You don't know what's going on here. You can't shoot him."

"Isabelle," Garrett said, "have you lost your mind?"

Isabelle took another step forward. Garrett knew he should take the shot while he had the chance, but Isabelle stood so close now, and the beast hadn't moved to attack. In fact, it had gone silent. It stared at Isabelle, utterly still.

Isabelle, her gaze latched on the beast, said, "We're going home now." Her voice trembled, but her tone was firm. It took Garrett a second to realize she was addressing the beast. "All right?"

239

And as Garrett watched, his chest tight, the beast bent, folding itself in half, and settled on all fours.

With measured, wary steps, Isabelle circled the beast, still drawing its gaze. Garrett held his breath. She was a blood red beacon in the white landscape, her crimson skirt like a rose planted in the snow. As she turned, the beast turned with her, its yellow eyes as intent upon her as she was on it. Garrett had gone so still, he thought even his heart had stopped beating. He'd heard of snake charmers in tales from far-off lands, people who controlled serpents in a hypnotic trance. He felt like that was happening before him now. Isabelle the charmer, and the beast the snake.

Isabelle spoke in a low voice. "Garrett." Her tone was soothing, as though she meant to charm him too. "I'm going to walk away from here. Back to the castle. And this beast is going to follow me."

Garrett took a deep breath. "Isabelle—"

"You can follow us," she went on, "but at a distance." She didn't break eye contact with the beast. "No shooting. No chasing. No talking—just follow us. It's about two miles from here—we should make it before sunset. All right?" She took another breath. "Garrett, I know it seems insane, but—you have to trust me."

Garrett swallowed. He looked between Roy and Gemma. Roy was wide-eyed, Gemma profoundly skeptical.

Garrett tossed a nod to Gemma, indicating she should retrieve the others. "All right," he told Isabelle, then cringed. He was afraid his voice would break the silent spell Isabelle had wrapped the creature in. But the beast never looked at him. "We'll follow."

The trek through the snowy woods was less than an hour, but to Garrett, it felt much longer. By the time the castle came into view, he was stiff with tension, his muscles aching from the strain. The castle was a dark, gothic thing, overgrown with dead ivy, but Garrett hardly noticed the details. His eyes were trained on Isabelle and the beast, fifty paces ahead, as they crossed a long wooden bridge over the gully below. He and his soldiers followed, passing beneath a grimy stone arch and into the castle's small courtyard.

But Garrett lost sight of Isabelle as she and the beast disappeared into the castle. He hurried across the courtyard to close the distance between them, mounting the broad steps two at a time. By the time he got inside, Isabelle and the beast were gone.

"Where did they go?" He looked around wildly. He stood in a dark, cavernous stone hall, empty save for the grand staircase centered at the back. A young girl stood at the bottom of the stairs, but she only looked at him, unblinking. As his soldiers entered the hall through the double doors, Garrett whirled around. The dark-eyed hunter entered with them; Garrett had forgotten all about him. "Do you know where they've gone?"

"Probably down to the dungeons," the hunter drawled. He was a tall man, as tall as Garrett. Three crooked scars ran across his face, impossible not to notice. The scarred hunter tore his arm free from Falcon and pointed towards a door that stood ajar across the hall. "But you can't go down there—"

"Of course I'm going down there." Garrett hurried towards the door.

The hunter jogged after him. "Look, I don't know how she's controlling him, but if you go charging down there, you might break her hold." The man reached for Garrett's arm. "It's nearly sunset, just wait—"

"If you don't know how she's controlling him, then that beast could be devouring her as we speak." Garrett rolled his shoulder, dodging the hunter's grasp. He ducked through the open door.

He was in such a rush, he nearly toppled down the dimly lit stairwell on the other side. Catching himself at the last minute, he started down the stairs at a trot. He stumbled once or twice in the darkness, the torches on the wall too sparsely placed to give enough light. He reached out to the wall to steady himself, shuddering at the dampness of the stone. This stairwell was so narrow, it was a wonder that beast had fit inside.

The dingy staircase opened into an equally dingy corridor lined with rusty cells. The moldy dank in the air filled Garrett's senses most unpleasantly. He reached back to take one of the torches from the stairs; he hadn't thought to bring a lantern down, and there was no lighting beyond the stairwell.

He ventured down the corridor, past the empty cells. It was a moment before he found a second corridor with a raised, iron portcullis. What lay beyond the portcullis was concealed in darkness. Garrett cursed quietly, raising his torch.

There was a door ahead. A thick, iron door, standing ajar. Garrett peered around it, wondering if he'd come the wrong way. But then a bright, wavering light appeared in the darkness. Squinting, his eyes adjusting, Garrett saw Isabelle, half-hidden in shadow. She was the source of the light, carrying a torch like him. She trudged out into the corridor from some kind of cell, stretching up to set her torch in a sconce on the wall.

Garrett edged around the door, concerned by Isabelle's faltering steps. If that beast had harmed her.... But as he drew closer, he realized she was simply exhausted. Her shoulders slumped, her face drawn.

When she saw Garrett, her tired eyes went wide. "Garrett." She threw a quick glance over her shoulder. "You shouldn't be down here—"

"Are you all right?" Garrett asked. "Where is the beast?" He peered into the open cell she'd just left, squeezing past her and raising his torch for a better look.

"Garrett, wait, don't—"

But her words were drowned out in a rush of shock, flooding through Garrett. For inside the dark cell was the beast—only, it wasn't the beast anymore. Not entirely.

As Garrett watched, captivated with horror, the beast hunched in on itself. There was a sickening *crunch*, like bone grinding into dust, as the beast's long torso contorted and shrunk. The black, matted fur covering the creature's body retreated into its flesh, revealing deep brown skin. At the last second, the beast fell forward onto all four paws. Only they weren't paws anymore, but hands and feet—*human* hands and feet.

The beast had become a human, bent forward on its knees.

Then it looked up, and it wasn't just a human.

It was Garrett's brother.

Gryphon.

Garrett couldn't understand what he was seeing. He'd had one too many shocks in the last hour—finding the beast in the forest, Isabelle taming the beast, the beast becoming human, the human being his *brother*. That last bit was too much. Garrett couldn't process it. A terrible, mirthless laugh escaped his lips.

"Garrett?" Isabelle ducked beneath his arm, coming into the cell. He could feel her eyes on him, but she didn't really register.

Gryphon—stones and stars, it was *Gryphon*, and he looked just like Garrett remembered, only fiercer and more vulnerable, naked on the floor—stared at Garrett with equal incomprehension. He blinked several times. His eyes were different, Garrett realized. Not brown like he remembered, but the burning yellow eyes of the beast.

Then, in a voice like a ghost from Garrett's past, his brother snarled, "What are *you* doing here?"

"What am—" This time, Garrett felt the totally inappropriate laughter bubbling up his throat, but he still couldn't stop it. "What am I—what am *I*—you just—you were just a beast!"

"Do you two *know* each other?" Isabelle asked. She sounded confused, though Garrett was sure she could not be as confused as he was.

Gryphon, still on his knees, squeezed his eyes shut. When he opened them again, they mirrored Garrett's disbelief. A shadow passed over his brother's face, a warning of the anger he was about to unleash, and for a second, Garrett felt like a scared little boy again, cowering from his terrifying big brother.

"*You.*" Gryphon's voice was guttural and enraged. "*You* shouldn't be here. You *can't* be here. Get out of my castle!"

"*Your* castle?" For the first time, Garrett looked at Isabelle. He was beginning to feel calmer, but only because he felt weirdly outside of himself. "This is *his* castle?"

"Garrett—" Isabelle began.

"Yes, it's my castle!" Scowling and wincing, Gryphon rose to his feet, also looking at Isabelle. "What is he doing here? What the hell *happened?*"

Isabelle drew a deep breath. "Gryphon—"

"What happened," Garrett retorted, "is you were just a *beast.* And now you're you. Somehow."

"No, really?" Gryphon's voice rang with sarcasm. He looked a terrible sight, his dark, thick hair mussed, his eyes bright with malice. "I'm so glad you told me. Otherwise, I might not have noticed!"

"Excuse me," Isabelle cut in, "but *how* do you two know each other?"

"He's my brother," Garrett and Gryphon said simultaneously.

A dreadful silence followed this pronouncement. Garrett could feel the shock radiating off Isabelle. After a beat, Gryphon muttered, "Well, my half-brother."

"I'm sorry." Isabelle sounded shaken. "You're—you—" She turned to Gryphon. "You're *Garrett's brother?*"

Gryphon's brow wrinkled. "Do *you* know him? I still haven't heard what he's doing here—"

"Isabelle—" Garrett rounded on her. "What are *you* doing here?" He gestured frantically with his flaming torch, indicating Gryphon. "He's completely naked!"

"Stones." Gryphon rolled his eyes. "Garrett, brilliant as always. Did he hit his head or something?"

"He just saw you change." Isabelle's voice was faint, but there was a trace of impatience there too. "Have a little compassion? And yes—" She reached out and took Garrett's torch from him, perhaps so he wouldn't set anything on fire in his bewildered state "—he is naked." She eyed Garrett pointedly. "Perhaps you could give him your coat?"

Garrett's confusion was beginning to give way to something entirely different. Gryphon was here—Gryphon, his half-brother, his surly, menacing brother, who had tormented and possibly tried to kill him. Gryphon, who had been exiled, there one day and gone the next. "I'm not giving him anything," he said.

"Of course not," Gryphon spat. "Garrett's never given *me* anything. He just comes and takes what's rightfully mine!"

"Oh, yes." Garrett rounded on him, taken aback by the mess of resentment and hostility boiling inside him. "Because I *chose* for my mother to die, I *made* you attack me in the middle of the night—"

"You don't know *anything*." Gryphon stepped forward, closing the distance between them, and Garrett was pleased to see that he was of a height with Gryphon now. "You're just a stupid little boy—"

"Not so little anymore," Garrett shot back, facing Gryphon down. "I don't know about the stupid part, but I'm not little anymore. You can't bully me, Gryphon, you can't send me off crying to hide in my room—"

"Want to bet?" Gryphon asked, his voice low and threatening.

"Right, well, okay." The next thing Garrett knew, Isabelle had come between them, though there was very little space to do so. Garrett had forgotten she was there. She waved the torch in Gryphon's face, forcing him back a few steps, and placed her other hand on Garrett's chest, firmly pushing him away. "I'm still trying to get my head around the fact that you two are related, and on top of that, I spent the day hiking in the snow—"

"You did?" Gryphon frowned.

"Well, so did I," Garrett grumbled.

"—so I don't have the energy for this very manly drama right now," Isabelle finished. "We're all going to find some space and calm down. Garrett." She turned to him. "Go upstairs and wait in the entrance hall. I'll be up in a minute, once I've filled your...your brother in on what happened today."

Garrett inhaled, sparing half a glance for Gryphon. Isabelle seemed perfectly at ease around him—even though he'd just been a beast, even though his face was a storm cloud, and even though he was, really, completely naked. "But—"

"*Now.*" The look in Isabelle's eyes brooked no room for argument. Garrett had seen that look on her face before. With a venomous glance for his brother, which Gryphon returned, Garrett left the cell and made his way back down the corridor. He passed a boy on the way, carrying a bundle of clothes. The boy hurried by without a word, but Garrett recognized him—Stefan, Gryphon's pageboy.

A crowd of people waited in the entrance hall—all five of Garrett's soldiers, the scarred hunter, and the silent blond girl. Garrett looked at them all blankly.

Gemma watched him with an astute glint in her eye. "Are you all right, sire?"

Garrett traipsed over to the staircase. "No." He collapsed onto the bottom stair. "I'm really not."

No one made a reply. Garrett buried his face in one hand. The tightness in his shoulders had crept up the back of his neck; he was going to have a throbbing headache later. Guilt for ignoring his soldiers tugged at him, but it was fleeting. He knew he should put on a good face and assure them everything was fine, but. He simply didn't have it in him right now.

Gryphon. Gryphon was here. He'd never known the exact circumstances surrounding Gryphon's exile. He never thought he'd see his brother again. To find him in this Black Forest ruin—with Isabelle—to realize he was the same beast Garrett had been *hunting*—likely the same beast he'd seen in these woods a year ago…. It boggled the mind.

Isabelle appeared a few minutes later, alone. Unlike Garrett, she'd regained her composure, unperturbed as usual. She took one look at Garrett and said to the blond girl, "Ellery? Could you take Prince Garrett's people up to the parlor? And see if Tilda can cook some dinner for everyone."

The blond girl, Ellery, gestured for the soldiers to follow her. They all looked at Garrett, who gave a weary flick of his hand. They left reluctantly, heading up the stairs, leaving him alone with Isabelle.

Isabelle stood before him, her forehead creased. "Are you all right?"

"Are *you* all right?" Garrett asked. He took a moment to study her. Looking for any injury he might have overlooked, any signs she'd been mistreated. He had forgotten Isabelle was the reason he was here. They had come to find her for Ansel, to *rescue* her. But she didn't seem to need rescuing.

"I'm fine." Isabelle actually smiled. "You're the one who looks like he's seen a ghost."

Garrett ran his hands over his face. "I feel like I have. Isabelle—what is going on here? We found your brother in a town five days from here—"

"Ansel?" Isabelle made a strange, jerky movement with her arm. "Is he all right?"

"He will be. He was ill and injured, but under the care of a doctor. They said he'll be fine with some rest and recuperation." Garrett scrubbed a hand through his hair. "Ansel wasn't too clear, but—Isabelle, he said you were being held prisoner."

Isabelle sighed. Slowly, as though too sore to move, she lowered herself onto the step beside him. "It's a little more complicated than that. Even more complicated than *I* realized."

"Clearly," Garrett retorted. "Ansel didn't say anything about your captor turning into a beast."

Isabelle opened her mouth to respond, but before she could, there was an odd scraping sound behind them. It was a small noise, but the way it echoed in the vast hall made it startling. Garrett and Isabelle twisted around.

At first, Garrett didn't see anything. The stairs stretching before them were bathed in shadow, the top landing unlit. It was like gazing into an abyss. But as Garrett stared, the darkness seemed to *move*.

Then he realized it wasn't the darkness moving. It was a person.

"Evans?" Garrett rose to his feet. Relief washed over him, but it didn't last, a spike of concern shorting it out. It *was* Evans; Garrett could just make out his pasty face in the dark. But he couldn't shake the sense that something was wrong. Foreboding prickled down Garrett's spine.

"Are you all right, Evans?" Garrett climbed to his feet and started up the stairs. His footsteps resounded through the hall like the funereal toll of a bell. "Is something wrong? Where are the others?"

Evans didn't answer. He stood at the top of the stairs, gazing down. He was too far away and too shrouded in shadow for Garrett to see where his eyes were focused—if they were focused at all. His concern growing, Garrett hurried up the stairs. Evans had seemed much better over the last few days, but perhaps all the traveling had been too much for him—

"Evans?" Garrett called again, nearing the top of the stairs.

"Garrett." This was not Evans but Isabelle; she had inched up the stairs behind him. Her voice carried an edge. Garrett paused a few steps from the top, turning to look at her. "I think you'd better—"

Wham.

Garrett's breath seized in his throat as something tackled him on the stairs, shoving him back into the railing. He slammed into the stone with a bruising *thunk*, all the air rushing out of his lungs.

"Garrett!" Isabelle screamed.

Everything that happened next happened very fast. Garrett, his back smarting, his vision swimming, wrestled with a body pinning him to the railing. He struggled to keep his footing, the sole of one boot teetering on the edge of the stair. It was a few breathless, panicked seconds before he realized he was wrestling with *Evans*. The boy's pale hands scrabbled at Garrett's throat, trying to get a hold of him. Trying to *choke* him.

"Evans!" Garrett fought to get Evans by the arms, trying to push him away. But his hands slipped over the boy's clammy skin. "Evans, stop!"

Isabelle was still screaming; she sounded closer than before, but Garrett couldn't see her. All he could see was Evans, his eyes bulging with a crazed light.

Then Evans was gone. His hands were gone, the weight of him gone. Garrett nearly toppled over. Clutching at the railing, he saw Falcon and Spencer drag Evans up the last few stairs to the landing.

"What happened?" Roy cried.

"I—don't know." Garrett took in a shaky, bewildered breath. "He just—"

"He attacked him!" Isabelle sputtered. She was trembling like mad, but she wrapped a hand around Garrett's arm. Her eyes were huge. "Are you all right?"

Garrett gaped at her. "I don't understand—"

"Is he ill?" Gemma looked from Garrett to Roy. "Could his wound be causing this?"

"I don't—" Roy began, but Isabelle interrupted him.

"What wound?" Her voice was low. "What happened to him?"

"He was mauled—bitten." Garrett ran a hand over the base of his neck, feeling wobbly. "In the forest, a few weeks ago. He was attacked by a wolf—"

"A massive wolf," Gemma corrected.

Isabelle's hands flew to her mouth. She had gone terribly gray. Somehow, in all the madness—Evans raging, Spencer and Falcon holding him back, Roy struggling to examine him—in all this awful din, Garrett saw Isabelle. He saw the look on her face.

"What?" he asked. Something told him he didn't want to hear the answer. "What is it? Isabelle?"

Isabelle's eyes filled with dread. Slowly, she lowered her hands from her face. "I think I know what's wrong with him, Garrett," she said. "I know what this is."

"*What?*" Garrett pressed.

"It's why your brother had Ansel locked up," she said. "It's what I was afraid was going to happen to me." Isabelle's face was bleak. "Your soldier is ill, Garrett. And...I'm afraid there's no cure."

20

CASUALTY

G RYPHON EASED THE DOOR shut behind him as he entered the dining hall. The room was engulfed in shadow,
lit only by a few candles. But Gryphon hardly noticed. It was
difficult to pay attention to anything in the room beyond the
overpowering stench of death.

The young man in question—one of Garrett's soldiers—lay
on the floor in front of the empty fireplace. Ellery had given him
a sedative and done what she could to make him comfortable.
But there wasn't much anyone could do beyond wrapping him
in a quilt and laying his head on a pillow.

Ellery said nothing as Gryphon joined her on the floor, kneeling beside the young man. Evans, they'd said his name was. He
had bright red hair and a freckled face that was shining with
sweat. Gryphon had heard his agitated moans out in the corridor, but under Ellery's administrations, he'd quieted, his gangly
body going slack.

Gravely, Ellery drew back the young man's collar.

Gryphon released a silent sigh. The wound—the *bite*—was
red and oozing, even though Garrett said it had been healed a

few days ago. He had taken the bite at the full moon, Garrett told him, though Gryphon had already figured that out.

The next full moon was a few nights away. By then—if what Gryphon knew held true—Evans would be dead.

Truthfully, Gryphon thought he would go much sooner than that.

There was nothing to do. Nothing that could be done.

"Go tell Isabelle and...his companions...tell them he hasn't got long," Gryphon told Ellery. Perhaps it was cowardly of him, but he didn't want to be the one to do it. He liked to think it was not cowardly so much as kindly. He wasn't the sort of person people wanted in times of grief. "I'll stay with him."

Ellery left the room. Gryphon shifted, folding one leg beneath him. He was not the sort of person to comfort the dying either, but the young man was quickly losing consciousness.

He fought it, though. His eyes fluttered, his head jerking from side to side. His hands spasmed, and without thinking, Gryphon took one of them.

The boy's eyes flew open. His body gave a shudder. Startled, Gryphon nearly pulled his hand away, but Evans clutched it tight. His back arched, every muscle in his body straining. Gryphon was on the verge of shouting for Ellery when the boy's glazed eyes fixed on his face.

Gryphon could not look away.

"Out—" Evans croaked. "Get—out—"

Gryphon frowned. Was he telling Gryphon to leave? But Evans gripped his hand tighter than ever.

"—m-*me*." The boy's feet scrabbled at the floor. "Get—out—me. Want—out—want it—*g-gone*."

Gryphon ran a hand over his mouth. Evans wasn't talking about Gryphon. He was talking about the sickness. The poison coursing through him. Shriveling his insides, rotting his mind. Eating him whole.

The boy's jerky motions began to slow. His thrashing limbs stilled, his labored breathing evened out. His hand went limp, but Gryphon held fast to him.

"Protect..." Evans murmured. "Have to...protect..." His unfocused gaze found Gryphon's face. "Protect...Garrett..."

Gryphon tried not to flinch.

"Protect—please..." Evans gave one last shudder. His eyes fluttered shut.

They did not open again.

When Gryphon stepped out of the dining hall, all heads turned his way—Ellery, Isabelle, Garrett, the soldiers, even Klaus. Much as he didn't want to, Gryphon found Garrett's face in the crowd.

"I'm sorry," Gryphon said. "He's gone."

The numb devastation on Garrett's face was plain. He looked bloodless in the white glare of the gear-bulb lanterns clustered around them.

"There has to be something," Garrett begged. "Gryphon, there has to be *something* we can do—"

"There wasn't anything to be done," Gryphon cut in. "He's gone. Not everyone can be saved, Garrett. Sometimes, you have to let a person go."

He hadn't meant to sound so harsh. But he couldn't seem to be anything else. Ignoring the stares of everyone in the corridor, he swept past them, hurrying down the grand staircase.

Gryphon lay in the narrow bed in his workshop, beside the empty fireplace. He had retreated here as soon as he'd left the others. He could not sleep. His body was leaden with exhaustion, but his mind felt wide awake. He stared up into the gray, hazy heights of the tower, the darkness veiling the ceiling.

He could not stop hearing the boy's last words. *Protect Garrett. Have to protect Garrett*. He went over it again and again, but he could not puzzle it out. He didn't know if the boy had been saying he, Evans, needed to protect Garrett—or if he had been asking Gryphon to protect him.

Gryphon could not protect Garrett. Well, he didn't look like he needed much protection these days. Surrounded by soldiers, all unwaveringly loyal to him. One glance at them had told him that. It was clear in the way they hovered near him, the way they looked to him for everything. No, Garrett was well protected. That was not to mention he had grown about two feet since Gryphon last saw him.

There was a quiet knock on the tower door. It creaked open before Gryphon could answer. He lifted his head and saw Isabelle standing in the entrance.

"Can I come in?" she asked, her voice low.

"Of course." Gryphon rubbed a hand over his chest. The tower felt so different this evening than it had last night. Last night, the tower had been warm with the blazing fire. Warm with their shared desire. Crackling with life and *feeling*. Now it felt cold and barren, the events of the day looming unhappily.

Perhaps Isabelle could chase away the gloom.

"The door is fixed," Isabelle noted.

Gryphon laid his head back, resuming his study of the ceiling he could not see. "Stefan or Ellery must have done it. I suppose they had plenty of time today."

He did not look at Isabelle, but he could hear her moving towards him, her russet skirt rustling over the floor. When she slipped into the bed beside him, he didn't know if he was surprised or not. Trying to disguise his apprehension—even from himself—he shifted, making room for her. She lay alongside him, molding into him with such sweet perfection, it made him ache inside. He felt like he was missing her, even though she was right there.

It was because—though it had been less than twenty-four hours since they'd shared this bed—everything had changed.

And he was afraid of what that meant.

When Isabelle said nothing, Gryphon asked, "Are you all right? After...everything. Coming after me, I mean—"

Isabelle turned her face into his arm. "I'm tired. *So* tired. But I'm not hurt." She laid light fingers on his chest. "You never hurt me. When you turned this morning, you didn't hurt me. And then all the way back to the castle...you don't remember it?"

"No more than usual." Vague, distorted impressions, nothing else. Gryphon's stomach clenched at the thought that he could have hurt her.

"It makes me wonder if you could learn to control it." Even half-asleep, Isabelle's voice was laced with curiosity. "Viveca seemed to think it's possible."

"I've never managed it." Gryphon had long given up on the idea. It was a depressing topic; he didn't want to discuss it. He said, "So you know my brother."

There was rancor in his voice he couldn't suppress. Perhaps *this* was not a topic they should discuss either.

Isabelle sucked in a breath. "I had *no idea* he was your brother."

But she knew him. Garrett. "You two seemed friendly."

Isabelle sat up at once. Gryphon evaded her gaze.

"Yes, we're friends." She placed no special emphasis on the word *friends*. "I've known him for years. Ever since...well, since I left Ansel. Since he told me to go." She paused. "After I left, I was robbed on the road to the Glen Kingdom. I met Garrett there. He helped me, and. We've been friends ever since."

Of course that was how they'd met. Of course Garrett had rescued her.

"And what," he said more softly, "has he told you about me?"

"Nothing at all. I didn't even know your name, did I?"

Gryphon slanted his gaze sideways, looking her in the eye.

She was not cowed. "He doesn't talk about you. Ever. I knew there was an elder prince who'd been exiled, but no one knows why. There are rumors, of course." Isabelle ran a hand over her forehead, then slid it back over her hair. "Stones. You're a *prince*."

Not really, thought Gryphon. His title had been stripped from him. "And what are these rumors about me?"

Isabelle eyed him cannily. "I'd rather know the truth than talk about rumors." Her voice was as quiet as a guttering candle. "I'd rather hear it from you. *All* of it."

There was no note of accusation in her voice, but it was implied. *All the truth.* Because he'd told her the truth before, but only in vague half-phrases.

Gryphon's gaze flickered up towards the shadows swarming above him. He didn't want to look at her while he spoke. "I told you the cause of my exile was an association with an...unsuitable woman. What I didn't tell you was she was unsuitable because she was a witch."

He heard an indrawn breath from Isabelle. "You were involved with a witch?"

"She wasn't a bad sort," he said dully. "She didn't seem to be. At first." He laced his fingers behind his head, pressing them into his skull. "She wanted to do a spell. She said the Glen Kingdom was facing a terrible threat, and she needed to seal the land with a spell of protection."

"What sort of threat?" Isabelle asked.

"She wasn't specific. An otherworldly threat." He could feel the skepticism radiating from Isabelle—or perhaps that was only his own projection. Because he knew now how naïve he'd been. "It was stupid to believe her. But—"

"You were fourteen," said Isabelle. "And she was, I suppose, quite beautiful."

There was no envy in her voice. Gryphon glanced her way, trying to gauge her expression. But in the muted light, he could barely see her face.

"You suppose right," was all he said. "She needed royal blood for the spell. My blood, which I gave freely." He hesitated. "But she said it wasn't enough. She said we needed Garrett's blood too." This time, Gryphon did not wait for a reaction. He wanted this tale over. "So we snuck into his room late at night. Malina said she would make sure he didn't wake."

"Malina. That was her name?"

"Yes." Gryphon felt a lump in his throat. "Anyway. Whatever she meant to do, something went wrong. Because I'd barely nicked Garrett's arm when he woke screaming. Then—" He rubbed a hand over his eyes. "Everything happened so fast. Malina used magic to throw Garrett back. I shouted at her—guards ran in—they had guns and blades drawn, and I grabbed Garrett—I was just trying to get him away from—well, all of it."

Isabelle was quiet. Gryphon closed his eyes.

"They thought I was attacking him," he said. "And when it was done—once the chaos was over—Malina was gone. And it was just me. Holding a bloody knife."

Isabelle let out a slow exhale. "She left you there?"

"Yes."

"And for that, your father banished you."

Gryphon gave a humorless snort. "I told him everything. I don't know how much he believed. It didn't matter, in the end. He was trying to make an alliance with the Mariner Kingdom, and they're dogmatically opposed to witchcraft and magic. Rumors were already spreading about what I'd been up to—at least, within the court." Gryphon could hear his voice going hollow. "He had to distance himself from me. There was no choice but exile."

Isabelle shook her head. "I told you before I was sorry, Gryphon. I still am. You didn't deserve this fate. I know your father is a hard man, but I didn't think he was...so unreasonable."

Gryphon's gaze flew to her. "You know my *father?*"

"Well, we've met."

Gryphon sat up. "And? What does my father think of you?"

"Well, he likes me well enough, or so Garrett says. We're not fast friends, Gryphon. I've stayed at the castle a time or two—"

"Perhaps even in my old rooms," he said sarcastically.

"I rather doubt it." Isabelle's voice turned sharp.

Gryphon bit back a retort. He didn't know why he was so irate all of a sudden. He had told her the truth, and she had not blamed him. But then *this*, this reminder that she knew his family, his brother and his father.... It was like she was no longer the Isabelle he knew. The Isabelle he'd come to know *intimately*. She belonged to another world now, a world that had once been his—a world that had cast him out.

That wasn't her fault. But it stung even so.

These bitter thoughts must have shown on his face because Isabelle drew back. She seemed so far away, and he felt cold without her at his side. "You should talk to your brother," she said. "Tell him what you've told me. Because I don't think he knows why you were exiled, not your *side* of it—"

"I don't think he'll care, Isabelle."

"You say that because you don't know him." Now she stood, pushing herself off the bed. "You don't know each other at all. You told him some people can't be saved. Garrett knows that better than anyone, Gryphon. He's not the same boy you knew, and I suspect *he* has never known you at all. So talk to him. He'll have to stay a few nights anyway, until after the full moon. That gives you plenty of time."

With that ultimatum, she swept from the tower, letting in an icy blast of air as she left.

Hours later, Gryphon dragged himself back into the castle. Dawn was an hour away, and he wanted to eat before heading to the dungeons. But when he reached the kitchens, Tilda, the cook, was not there.

But Garrett was.

He was alone. None of his soldiers were in sight. He sat at the rustic wooden table Tilda kept, his head in his hands. The kitchen was dim, the lamps from the stove casting a low glow over the brick walls and stone floor. But even in the near-darkness, Gryphon could see that Garrett looked a mess. His gray waistcoat was unbuttoned, revealing a dark, rumpled shirt beneath, and he smelled vaguely of alcohol.

For a moment, Gryphon stood in the entry and looked at him. He felt a stab of unwanted pity. Gryphon could not stop seeing that young man, Evans, in his final moments, nor could he forget his last words. All those years ago, when he and Garrett had lived in Glen Castle, it had often been *him*, Gryphon, making his brother this miserable. There was a part of him that knew how wrong he'd been, that understood those actions had been born of resentment for a little brother who hadn't been to blame for any of Gryphon's problems.

But even now, that was hard to admit.

Garrett looked up. His gaze fell on Gryphon. There was nothing sudden about it, and yet Gryphon felt caught out, standing there, staring.

"Oh," was all Garrett said. His voice was unsteady. "It's you."

"You were expecting someone else?" Gryphon shifted. "One of your soldiers?"

"I was expecting Stefan," Garrett said bluntly. "I told him to find me a drink."

"Seems you already found one."

"Yes, well. It seemed the thing to do, since we're stuck here." Garrett rubbed his bloodshot eyes.

Gryphon wasn't sure what to say. Eyeing Garrett the way he might unstable dynamite, he slunk into the kitchen. Tilda usually left some food if she wasn't around. Sure enough, he found a basket of meat pies near the stove, wrapped in a cloth and still warm. They smelled of thyme and gravy and fresh, yeasty crust. He took two for himself, then turned and found Garrett watching him.

Feeling rather stupid, he held up a meat pie. "Want one?"

Garrett turned his back on him. "Not hungry."

"Kitchen's a strange place to be then."

"Isabelle told me to come eat something," Garrett admitted.

"But you figured another drink would be better."

"What do you care?" Garrett sounded more defeated than cross.

Gryphon continued to watch him as he bit into a meat pie. Isabelle's words floated back to him, unbidden. *He's not the same boy you knew. So talk to him.*

Gryphon cleared his throat. "Look, I'm sorry...what happened to your man. Evans." He tried to think of something comforting to say. He had no idea what *comforting* was supposed to sound like. "It only would have gotten worse."

"So it's better he died now? In this awful place, so far from home?"

Gryphon gritted his teeth. "I didn't say that."

"Look." Garrett shifted around, swinging his legs over the bench to look at Gryphon. "Once this full moon is over, I'm leaving. And I think Isabelle should come with me."

"She can't leave here." There was no heat in Gryphon's words, the response rote. She *could* leave here, Gryphon realized. Whether she turned or not—she could leave if she wanted. The thought made the food in his mouth taste like ashes.

"Why not?" Garrett asked hotly. "Because *you* say so?"

Gryphon narrowed his eyes. "How is it possible you've gotten more annoying since I left home?"

"You just don't like me standing up to you for once."

"Look," Gryphon said, trying to contain his temper, "I don't know how much Isabelle has told you, but she must have said something. Did she tell you I was her captor? Did she tell you she *wants* to leave?"

Garrett's expression was a picture of Gryphon's usual truculence. "No. But given everything that's going on here with—you..." He gestured at Gryphon "...it seems like she would be safer elsewhere."

"Well, talk to her about it," Gryphon shot back. "Because it's not that simple, Garrett. Did it ever occur to you she's staying here *because* it's safe? No, of course not. Because how could she be safe with me, right?"

Garrett's gaze was direct. "Is it really so weird for me to think that? Considering what you tried to do to *me* the last time I saw you?"

The words were a punch in the gut. This, Gryphon thought, this was why he couldn't talk to Garrett. Why he could never *explain*. Garrett had made up his mind about him. He would never understand.

"You don't know anything," Gryphon muttered, and he strode from the room, clutching his meat pie so hard, it crumbled in his hand.

21

OVERTURE

GARRETT BROODED BEFORE THE crackling fire, watching
the flames dance in the hearth. He sat on the floor, a
threadbare rug beneath him. He'd had his overcoat draped over
him like a blanket when he first sat down, but now, half an hour
later, the fire had warmed him, and he set it aside.

Half an hour. About the time it had taken Isabelle to fill him
in on everything going on here in the castle, everything about
Gryphon and his curse and the wolf pack, and everything about
Isabelle, and how she'd been caught in this mess.

"So that's the long and short of it, then," he said glumly.

"More or less." Isabelle sat above him, ensconced in a deep,
upholstered armchair. She held a cup of tea in both hands,
though she must have finished it by now. Garrett's tea had gone
cold; he'd set it aside when he sat down and forgotten about it.
The pungent ginger odor of it scented the air.

Garrett cast a glance around the parlor. It was the nicest
room he had seen in this castle, with its gleaming mahogany
furnishings and paneled floor. But it was not enough to raise
Garrett's spirits. They had been here for two days, and Garrett

was growing mad with cabin fever. Perhaps it was the specter of Evans hanging over him, but all the dark, cold stone and somber lighting had buried Garrett in misery. Glen Castle was always warm and bright, even in winter.

"Well." Garrett stretched his legs towards the fire. "I've never been so glad Gryphon and I are half-brothers."

"What do you mean?"

He tilted his head back to look at Isabelle. "Else I'd have been doomed the moment I stepped inside this castle."

"*Oh.* That's right, isn't it? But you have different mothers."

"I'd always heard Gryphon's mother—the last queen—was old nobility. I thought she came from one of the high houses in the Glen Kingdom, going back to Demetri's time. From what I understand, her origins are a mystery."

"Until now." Isabelle paused. "Did you know her? Gryphon's mother?"

Garrett shook his head. "She died before I was born. Not long after Gryphon was born, in fact."

They both went quiet. Isabelle sipped the last of her tea, and Garrett cocked his head, transfixed by the fire.

"So," he mused, "Gryphon thinks you're going to turn into a beast like him?"

"He doesn't know what's going to happen."

Garrett curled his legs in towards him. "Well. Perhaps you won't turn at all."

"Perhaps." Isabelle sounded...not afraid, but. Dubious. "Klaus says I haven't exhibited as many symptoms as Gryphon did. Gryphon seems to think we'll know if I make it through the full moon. That was when he started turning."

Garrett nodded absently.

Isabelle shot him a vexed look. "You're taking this all in stride."

ELIZABETH KING

Garrett shrugged. "Briar's a half-dead corpse. The wolf that killed Evans was a person. I saw my brother turn into a beast. Not to mention all the other things I've seen." He didn't want to make light of what Isabelle was going through, but it was starting to feel rather par for the course. "Your brother didn't mention any of this."

"He didn't *know* any of it." Isabelle leaned back to set her cup on the nearest table.

"He's worried about you."

Isabelle's gaze hardened. "He made it clear a long time ago that he didn't care about me."

"*I'm* worried about you," Garrett said quietly.

Isabelle looked at him, her expression gratified.

"You must be frightened." He kept his tone soft, easy. "About what might happen."

"Yes. Of course. But there's no use dwelling on it when nothing might happen."

Garrett couldn't repress a smile.

"What?" she asked.

"You and Briar. You're so alike."

"Practical, you mean?" Isabelle asked primly. "Unpretentious? Clever? Forthright?"

"Yes. All those things," Garrett murmured. "Far less emotional than me, at any rate."

"And than your brother," Isabelle said. "I would say it runs in your family, but the parent you have in common—your father—isn't emotional at all."

"You don't have to tell me that," Garrett said darkly. When Isabelle looked curious, he explained, "We had an...unpleasant conversation before I left. And according to you, there are some

266

important details he's never told me about Gryphon's exile." He cast Isabelle a sidelong glance. "If that's true, anyway."

She shook her head. "You're not getting anything out of me. This is between you and Gryphon. The two of you need to *talk* to each other."

As though summoned by her will, the door to the parlor opened, and Gryphon walked in. He was dressed down in a white shirt and dark waistcoat, his sleeves rolled up to his elbows. He looked as sullen as ever. Even more so when he saw Garrett.

"Oh," he said stupidly. His gaze flickered between Isabelle and Garrett. "I'll just—"

"Oh, do come join us, Gryphon." Isabelle sounded half-exasperated, half-amused. "You two are stuck in this castle for another two days at least. You can't just avoid each other that entire time."

"I don't know about that," Garrett said, a streak of resentment flashing through him.

Gryphon crossed his arms. "It's a big castle."

"It's a small castle," Garrett disagreed. "But it is a *castle*. So...yes. Lots of space."

"Fine." Isabelle unfolded from her armchair, rising to her feet. "But so long as you continue to avoid each other, *I'm* not talking to either of you. So if you will excuse me..."

Garrett protested. Gryphon sulked. Finally, after more hemming and hawing, Gryphon joined them in front of the fireplace. Isabelle resumed her seat in the armchair.

"So." Garrett eyed his feet and not his brother. "Isabelle's told me about your situation here. With these were-wolves."

"With these *what?*"

"Were-wolves." Garrett looked between Isabelle and Gryphon. "You haven't heard the stories? There have always been tales of men turning into beasts and wolves. Mostly you hear about them in the far north. They're called were-wolves."

Gryphon scoffed at this. Isabelle said, "Hmm. Well. *Were* is an ancient word for man, so...I suppose it makes sense."

"Yes. Sure." Garrett waved a hand. "Whatever you call them. Isabelle filled me in."

"And?" Gryphon scowled as he leaned over the back of Isabelle's chair, hands clasped above her head. "I suppose you have an opinion."

"My opinion is, why haven't you *done* something about them?"

"Like what?" Gryphon threw up his hands. "I can't leave this castle. So what do you propose I do? Send Klaus to kill the whole pack?"

"You have got more men now." Garrett summoned his most cordial smile. "Let's see. There's me. Spencer. Gemma, Falcon—"

"I get it," Gryphon said flatly.

"They are *people*," Isabelle pointed out. "The wolves."

"People who are happy to murder innocents," Garrett said. His voice felt dangerous, deep in his throat. The memory of Evans pierced him, stoking his desire to do *something*.

But Isabelle objected. "*Viveca* is happy to murder innocents. Her family may feel they have no choice but to follow her. At least, some of them might."

Garrett conceded this. "Then it sounds like the best option is to depose her."

"Good luck with that," Gryphon said. "I'm sure if you ask nicely enough, she'll back off. Let someone else lead her pack. Or just move up north where there are no people."

"Well," Garrett said, "it's a start."

Gryphon stared at him.

Isabelle said, "You really want to try and negotiate with her?"

"Why not?" Garrett sat up straight, clasping his hands before him. "It's usually the best thing to do before opening hostilities. As far-fetched as it might seem, you never know when you can avoid bloodshed by just having a frank conversation."

"I've had a few conversations with Viveca." Isabelle shifted in her chair, mistrust plain on her face. "I doubt she'll agree to leave Gryphon alone."

"Even still," Garrett persisted, keeping his tone light and pleasant. Partly because it came naturally to him. Partly because he knew it would infuriate his surly brother. "*I've* never talked to her. I think it's best I do."

"And how—" Gryphon sounded predictably exasperated "—do you propose to do so?"

Garrett blinked at him. "I'll set up a meeting with her, I suppose. Meet under a flag of truce. Either of you know how to get in touch with her?"

Isabelle hesitated. "I might have a way."

———◄○►———

It was nearly dawn, and Garrett couldn't believe he was awake. Of course, he was usually an early riser. But everyone in this castle kept odd hours, and even after a couple of days, Garrett had begun to do the same, sleeping in late.

Today, though, he wanted plenty of time to prepare for his meeting with Viveca.

Isabelle had used her enchanted coin to contact Viveca. This, Isabelle said, would summon the wolf to the gully below the castle. Only, instead of Isabelle setting out to meet her, Klaus went in her stead. He'd returned a short while later with confirmation that Viveca had agreed to meet.

That was yesterday. Since the full moon was tonight, they were meeting as early as they could, just after sunrise. Gryphon had grumbled that they should have waited another day—citing something about the wolves being weaker after they turned—but the meeting was set, and Garrett didn't want to put it off.

He began to dress by the dim light of a single gear-bulb lantern. There was no window in his room—he was sure Gryphon had given him the smallest, dingiest room in the castle—but he knew it was still dark out. Secretly, Garrett enjoyed being up so early. The world was quiet and dark in a way the late night was not. Quiet with unshed potential. Dark with hope and anticipation.

He'd just pulled on a clean pair of trousers when there was a knock on his door. Spencer poked his head in. "Your brother wants to talk to you."

Garrett was surprised but gave his assent. A few seconds later, Gryphon walked in. He spared Garrett no pleasantries. "Where are you meeting Viveca?" he asked.

"Good morning to you too." Garrett shrugged into his shirt. "Speaking of, shouldn't you be locking yourself up?"

"I have a little time," Gryphon said curtly. "But only a little. So answer my question."

"The clearing past the bridge." Garrett tucked his shirt in. He couldn't quite see Gryphon's face in the low light, but his brother's silence was dubious. "Don't worry. We won't let them get far past the tree line. I'm taking all my soldiers with me—"

"All four of them," Gryphon noted. His sarcasm was as subtle as ever. "Great. There are seven or eight wolves, so it's not like you'll be outnumbered."

"We've got some silver bullets from Klaus," Garrett went on, unperturbed, "and we've fashioned some silver arrowheads for my archers. Besides, they won't *be* wolves. They'll be human."

"Well, just in case, I've told Klaus to stay with Isabelle in her room." Gryphon slouched against a bedpost. "Viveca might think to use this meeting as a diversion. I've got all entry points sealed in silver, but..."

"What about you? You're the one the wolves actually want."

"As you pointed out, I'll be locked up in my own dungeon," Gryphon replied. "And unlike the wolves, I won't be human. I'd like to see them take me like that."

Garrett eyed his brother surreptitiously. He spoke casually of his enchantment, as though it were little bother to him. At first, Garrett had assumed that was so. After all, this was the same brother who'd attacked him in the middle of the night. But then, Isabelle said he didn't know the whole of that story, and though it pained him to admit it, a couple of days with his brother had been enough to make Garrett see him differently—not as the shadowy, enigmatic figure who'd haunted his childhood, but more as...just a person. A person who, maybe, did not find it a simple thing to become a raging beast every day.

"Look, be careful with Viveca," Gryphon said grudgingly. He shifted in the darkness, still leaning against the bedpost. "She's a piece of work."

Garrett grinned as he buttoned up his waistcoat. He'd chosen navy blue today. "Gryphon, I didn't know you cared."

"I care if this is all some trap to get into the castle."

"It's all right," Garrett said airily. "I won't tell anyone you're worried about me."

"Will you be serious for one minute?" Gryphon exploded. He straightened, his yellow eyes flashing. "You're putting us all in actual danger, but you act like it's a summer stroll. You do realize what could happen if this goes wrong, don't you? Sometimes, Garrett, the worst actually happens. Maybe you should consider that!"

Garrett felt the grin slip off his face. "I know perfectly well the worst can happen."

"Do you?"

"Yes." Garrett turned his back on his brother and opened the wardrobe. He pulled out his sack coat and slipped it on. "I learned that the worst can happen a long time ago. In the worst possible way." He cleared his throat. "So just because I *hope* for the best doesn't mean I don't plan for the worst."

"What do you mean, you learned in the worst way?"

Garrett strapped on the low-slung belt for his pistols, his jaw tightening. His past was none of Gryphon's business. Certainly not one of his most painful experiences. He didn't owe Gryphon an explanation. But then.... *This is between you and Gryphon,* Isabelle had said. *The two of you need to talk to each other.*

Garrett let out a silent sigh. Without looking at his brother, he asked, "Did you know Princess Snow?"

"From the Mariner Kingdom?" Gryphon sounded as though he had expected Garrett to say anything else. "I met her once when we were children. But I was five—I don't really remember her." He paused. "I heard she died. I heard they all died—her father and sister too. The queen poisoned them or something?"

Garrett nodded tensely. He didn't know why he felt so unstable. In the past few months, he'd found it easier to talk about Snow. He didn't know if that was because of Briar, or because time made the grief more manageable—a bit of both, he supposed. But for some reason, speaking of her now—with Gryphon, who had always made him feel as small as possible.

"Yes, they died," Garrett said. He cast around for his boots. "But not before Father and King Laurent set up a betrothal between Snow and I. Father sent me to court her the summer before the king died. After that, the queen banished Snow, so she lived with us at Glen Castle for a while. Before the queen lured her back and killed her, anyway." Garrett said all this very quickly.

"You were engaged to Princess Snow?" Gryphon said.

"Yes." Garrett spotted his boots at the foot of the bed and reached for one, tugging it on. He focused on this simple task, avoiding his brother's gaze.

"Did you know her well?" Gryphon asked, his tone neutral.

"Yes." Garrett tugged on his second boot. "I loved her." He stood and turned to face Gryphon, grateful for the darkness that obscured his brother's expression. "But I couldn't save her." He shrugged, as though feigned nonchalance could bring on the real thing. "So, yes. I know the worst can happen. But that doesn't mean I'm going to walk around with a storm cloud over my head like you do."

Gryphon sulked. "I do *not*—"

"You mope more than any person I've met," Garrett said lightly. "Anyway, shouldn't you be off? It must be close to dawn, and I'd rather you don't turn into a beast in here. And don't worry," he added, when Gryphon opened his mouth to speak, "I'm not going to let these wolves get past me."

Gryphon sighed. "All right." He turned to go, then paused. "I was just going to say…" His head turned slightly towards Garrett. "I'm sorry. About Princess Snow."

He left before Garrett could register his surprise.

A short time later, Garrett assembled in the entrance hall with his soldiers. His chest ached as he looked over each of them: Gemma, Spencer, Falcon, and Roy. There seemed an empty place where Evans should have been. Still, a few days' rest had done them all some good. The mood was cautiously optimistic, grimly determined. Garrett was no stranger to losing soldiers, and neither were the others. But they were setting out to meet these monsters, kin to the one who had killed Evans.

"Everyone ready?" Garrett asked as they followed him into the courtyard. The sun shone overhead in a clear sky, reflecting off the snow so strongly that Garrett winced. Still, a weight seemed to lift from his shoulders as he left the dark castle behind. The fresh air bolstered him.

"We're ready, sire," Falcon said. He and Roy carried silver-capped arrows in their quivers, while Gemma and Spencer carried rifles loaded with silver bullets.

"If they make a move," Garrett said, "I want the archers to shoot first."

"Why?" Spencer asked.

"Because we're better shots," Falcon said.

Gemma spared him a condescending look. "You're adorable."

"Why, thank you." Falcon grinned. "I knew you'd come around eventually."

"I want the archers to shoot first to see if we can get them to back off," Garrett interrupted. "Only if they move to attack us, mind." He glanced at Ellery, Isabelle's maid, who stood ready to raise the portcullis. As the silvery gate began to rise, *clank-clank-clanking* all the way to the top, he turned to face the soldiers. "I know they killed Evans," he said, "but we don't *want* a war with these creatures. We want them to back off. So unless they come at us, we don't hurt them. All right?"

"Understood, sire," Roy said. The other three murmured their assent.

Per Garrett's instructions, Ellery lowered the portcullis behind them as they started down the long bridge across the gully. Garrett was on alert, but he didn't see any sign of the were-wolves yet. He squinted at the sun, glimmering over the tops of the trees.

They spread out in a pre-planned formation once they reached the clearing. Garrett stood dead center, Falcon and Gemma on his right, Roy and Spencer on his left.

"They're late," Roy noted.

"No, they're not." Falcon's keen eyes were bright. "They're here. Look."

Sure enough, Garrett spotted movement along the tree line, the foliage surging. Then one of them emerged into the clearing, slinking into view. It was a young man, early twenties perhaps, with sleek golden hair and an aquiline nose. He was garbed in worn breeches and a heavy coat. A brown scarf was tucked into his shirt, but he wore no gloves or hat. He eyed Garrett's soldiers with dark eyes, then smiled lazily.

More of them emerged from the trees. They were all dressed similarly in rumpled trousers and breeches, patched vests, light coats, all in shades of brown and gray and tan. Contrary to what Gryphon had said, there were only six of them. Garrett hoped that didn't mean one of them was somewhere else, trying to get into the castle.

"Which one of you is Prince Garrett?"

Garrett looked at the woman who'd spoken. She stood in the center of the pack, a few paces ahead of the others. Before Garrett could speak, her eyes fixed on him and she answered her own question. "It must be you. The one dressed like a prince."

"And you must be Viveca," Garrett returned.

Viveca smiled in a predatory fashion, as though Garrett was a rabbit she might take in her jaws. She was older than he was, tall and leanly muscled. She wore no coat, only a brown corset fitted over her shirt, with a thick leather strap belted across the chest. "Gryphon's brother." Viveca's smile widened. "Here in the Black Forest. But this isn't your first time here, is it, Your Highness? You've been here before. On a hunting trip, I believe."

"Yes." Garrett assumed a casual pose, tucking his hands into his pockets. "I like hunting."

"So I hear." Viveca's smile vanished. "You've brought all manner of hunters on us since then, Prince Garrett."

"I'd be happy to bring more." This was getting right to the point, but maybe it was better that way. "More hunters. A whole army of them, even, outfitted from my father the king."

Some of the wolves, arrayed behind Viveca, shifted at that. Nervous predators, eager to go on attack. But Viveca was dauntless. "Funny you should mention your father," she replied. "Only, as I understand it, he was the one who exiled Gryphon in the first place. So why send aid now?" Her gaze ran over Garrett's soldiers. "And so little aid, at that?"

"I'm not here for my brother," Garrett said. "We're not exactly close. I'm here for a friend of mine. Her name is Isabelle."

"Isabelle." Viveca's gaze sharpened, a wolf pricking up its ears. "Well. I told her she could leave this forest unmolested. And I'll make you the same deal. Help us get into the castle, and you can *all* go—Isabelle too. You say you're not close to your brother. So why not?"

Garrett squinted, openly displaying his dislike of these terms. "I had another deal in mind. We leave here with Isabelle—with*out* letting you in the castle—and we won't come back to annihilate your pack."

"You can't annihilate anyone if you're already dead."

"You think my father won't stop at nothing to hunt down the person who kills me?" Garrett asked mildly. "You think he won't send his entire army into this forest if I don't return? Besides, I wonder how you propose to kill us when we've got an arsenal of silver weapons—and you have nothing except your teeth, one night out of the month."

Viveca's eyes slanted. "Tonight is one of those nights."

"Yes, but seeing as we're holed up in a castle you can't penetrate, I'm not sure that means much."

"Are you that certain of your defenses?" Viveca placed her hands on her hips, and Garrett tensed before remembering she wasn't armed. She had no blades or pistols to reach for at her waist. "Are you really so sure there aren't any weak points?"

"I'm assured silver covers every entry."

"Who assured you?" Viveca asked. "Was it Klaus, perhaps?"

Garrett stifled a frown. Viveca brimmed with smug confidence, and something about it disquieted him.

"And you're sure you can trust Klaus, are you?" Viveca asked.

"I barely know him," Garrett said with impatience, "but—"

"I don't suppose he told you," Viveca interrupted, "that I saw him recently?"

"When he came to arrange the meeting? Yes, I'm aware."

"No, before that. A few days ago, early in the morning. Before the sun was up." Viveca's eyes glittered as the sun rose higher overhead, shedding light over the clearing. "I believe it was...the day you arrived here. The morning Gryphon escaped the castle." She cocked her head to one side. "Funny, isn't it? That instead of making sure Gryphon was locked up tight, Klaus was sneaking out to meet me? Now what do you suppose we had to talk about so very early, where no one could hear us?"

Garrett tensed. "I don't know what you're implying—"

"Funnier still," Viveca went on, "that wasn't the first time the beast escaped the castle. It happened twice before. Oh, the first time was an accident, of course—when Gryphon first turned. But the second time—" Viveca released a mocking sigh. "Whose fault do you think it was the second time he escaped?"

Garrett went stock-still. Viveca was talking about the time Garrett and his last hunting crew had been in the forest—a year ago, when he'd first caught sight of the beast. Isabelle had confirmed that Gryphon had escaped then, though she didn't know the details. Only that Gryphon and his people hadn't yet "perfected their system" in the dungeons.

"I'll answer that for you." A wicked smile stole over Viveca's face. "It was Klaus's fault. And it wasn't an accident."

"You're lying," Garrett scoffed.

Viveca shrugged. "Ask Klaus, then. Ask him whose fault it was. Ask him who *let* Gryphon out of the castle that day—and hear his answer for yourself."

22

BECOMING

I SABELLE'S HEADACHE RETURNED WITH a vengeance. She felt it even in her sleep, throbbing behind her eye as she tossed and turned. That was why she woke only a few hours after turning in. Pale daylight slanted through the window overhead. Either the day was overcast, or it was so early, the sun hadn't properly risen yet.

Isabelle felt like she hadn't slept at all. The stabbing ache behind her eye had migrated downward. Her cheekbones pulsated with pain. Reaching up, she pressed two fingers into the side of her face. Then she froze.

A strange scent prickled her nose. A combination of smells—sweat and leather and the faintest hint of soap.

A very *human* smell. Which was why it was strange. Because it was here in her room.

Isabelle sat up slowly.

Klaus sat at her round table.

Isabelle gave a start. "What are you doing in here?"

The look Klaus slanted her way was amused. Probably because she'd clutched at her quilt, pulling it up to her chin in a misguid-

279

ed attempt to protect her modesty. Misguided, because she slept in full pajamas. She was hardly indecent.

"Gryphon told me to guard you, remember?" Klaus reminded her. "While your prince friend is meeting Viveca."

Isabelle squinted through the high window. So it was still early, then. Unless Garrett's meeting with the were-wolves was taking a long time, which seemed unlikely.

"Yes, well, you can guard me from out in the corridor," Isabelle said. "Like you always do."

"Gryphon said he wanted me in your room."

"He might have told *me* that," Isabelle grumbled.

"Wouldn't you have just told him I didn't need to be here?"

"Well. Yes. I suppose so."

"Probably why he didn't tell you, then."

Isabelle rubbed her fingers into her temples. "Why don't you make yourself useful, then," she said, dragging her hands down her face, "and get me some tea?"

"I'm not to leave," Klaus said brusquely. "But I'll see if Stefan can fetch some."

He went to the door and stuck his head out, speaking to someone outside. Stefan, presumably. Isabelle pushed herself out of bed. The cold in the air was impossible to ignore, and yet, Isabelle didn't *feel* cold. She felt flushed from the inside, exerted by her headache. She staggered over to the porcelain wash basin in the corner of the room. There was a jug of fresh water beside it; Ellery refilled it every night before Isabelle retired. She poured it out to splash some water onto her face, rubbing at her eyes. Then she blinked, leaning over the basin, the water dripping into it with a *plink-plink-plink*.

She turned around and choked on a gasp.

Klaus stood right behind her.

"Will you stop doing that?" Isabelle snapped.

"Stefan's fetching some tea," he said, unapologetic as ever. "I told him to make it willow bark."

Isabelle gave him a dry look as she stalked past. "Do I look that awful?"

"Moderately, yes. I know you've been having headaches."

Disgruntled, Isabelle wrenched open her wardrobe, looking for something to wear. Truthfully, she wanted to stay in her pajamas, but if she was going to be up, she might as well dress. The thought of donning another gown was literally painful. She skipped over them—Ellery had altered a few more—and chose garments she'd brought with her: a stiff, sensible skirt and a blouse with sleeves that cuffed around her wrists.

"I suppose you won't leave long enough for me to dress?" Isabelle snapped.

"You have a dressing screen," Klaus pointed out.

Isabelle shot him a nasty look. Perhaps it was unfair—really, she'd felt much more kindly towards Klaus since he'd accompanied her to retrieve Gryphon. And he was only doing what he'd been told. But she had a bloody headache, and she wasn't in a kindly mood.

For his part, Klaus paid her no heed as he resumed his seat, propping his scuffed boots up on the table. Which only made her feel *less* kindly towards him. She ate on that table.

Isabelle pulled the tri-fold dressing screen around in the corner, enclosing the wash basin and the long, spotted mirror. The screen was black and opaque, intricately painted in gold and garnet.

"What time is it, anyway?" Isabelle asked through the screen. "Has Garrett been gone long?"

"He set out about twenty minutes ago," said Klaus. A peek around her screen showed Isabelle he was not facing her. He sat with a rumpled newspaper in his lap, flicking through it. "Should be back any minute."

"So you don't have much faith in this meeting either."

"Do *you?*"

"No," she confessed. "But I see the logic in it."

Klaus snorted. "I don't."

"The logic," Isabelle said, "is that Garrett intends to do something about Viveca and her pack. Something more direct than anything Gryphon has done. And if he's going to do that, he wants to be sure he's given them a chance to back down first."

For a long moment, there was only silence from Klaus. An unsettling silence.

Then Klaus said, "You mean he's going to kill them."

Isabelle darted another look around the screen. Klaus sat in the same spot, in the same position. But there was a tension in his shoulders that hadn't been there before.

"If he has to," Isabelle said cautiously. She watched Klaus a moment longer, until he flipped another page in the paper.

"Maybe that's for the best," Klaus said.

Isabelle frowned as she tugged off her pajama top. She didn't disagree. From a certain vantage point, she understood Gryphon's reluctance to confront Viveca. He couldn't leave the castle anyway, thanks to his curse. But the fact was, Viveca wasn't going to give up her quest to get what she wanted from Gryphon. And if she *did* get what she wanted, she'd be a stronger, more powerful threat than she was now.

And she'd made it clear she had no problem killing innocent people. It was her *natural instinct.*

She couldn't be allowed to continue like this. Garrett was not the sort of person to allow it. This wasn't something he could walk away from even if Isabelle hadn't been involved. Especially now one of his own was dead.

The thought of young Evans brought a wave of sadness over her. He had been one of the soldiers who'd stayed at her house last autumn when Garrett came with his friends, seeking refuge from the monsters they'd encountered. She hadn't really gotten to know Evans, but she remembered him as unfailingly polite. And so young, somehow, despite the horrors he'd faced in the Mountain Kingdom.

The thought of Evans also reminded her of something she'd been meaning to ask. "Klaus." She held up her skirt. "When Garrett's soldier died—Evans—Gryphon mentioned he'd seen it before. That he'd seen someone die from the bite, I mean."

"He has." Klaus's tone was uncharacteristically sober. "We all have."

"When?"

"About a year ago. I found a woman in the woods. A trapper, passing through on her way to the mountains." There was a grave note in his voice. "She'd been bitten."

Isabelle swayed as she stepped into her skirt, and she reached out to steady herself against the wall. Klaus's conversation had distracted her from the throbbing pain in her head; she'd thought it was fading. Now it returned in a rush, encroaching on the corners of her vision. Isabelle squeezed her eyes shut and sucked in a breath.

"You all right back there?" Klaus asked sharply.

Isabelle released a slow breath. "Yes. Fine." Still leaning against the wall, she turned, pressing her forehead into the cold stone. "So what happened to the trapper? She died, I assume."

"Yes. I brought her to the castle. But it took her weeks to die. We had to lock her in the tower, like your brother."

Isabelle shuddered. "Did she become violent? Like Evans?"

"Yes." Klaus paused, then added, "It was terrible. I even met with Viveca to ask if anything could be done. But she said there was no cure."

Feeling a little steadier, Isabelle pushed away from the wall, reaching back to button her skirt. *I even met with Viveca.* Once again it struck Isabelle as strange, the thought of Klaus meeting with Viveca. When he'd nearly shot her less than a week ago, in the gully.

She remembered how defensive he'd become when she'd joked about him running into Viveca in the forest, when she'd teased him about the were-wolf allowing him free reign. Unease slipped through Isabelle, though she couldn't say why. She pulled her blouse over her head, shimmying to get the garment past her bony shoulders. "How often do you run into the wolves out in the forest?" she asked.

"What?"

"The wolves. You must run into them from time to time. What do they...do they speak to you? Threaten you?" The unease grew, some instinct pushing at the confines of her skin. She found herself awaiting Klaus's response with bated breath.

But all he said was, "I don't usually see them. They're out there, sure. But they know how to stay hidden. And they don't want a fight with me."

Some of the tension melted out of Isabelle. That made sense, she supposed. Though...she wondered that Viveca hadn't tried to use Klaus to get into the castle. Perhaps by taking the hunter and using him as leverage. Then again, perhaps she thought Gryphon didn't care enough about Klaus for that to work. But there were other ways she might have used Klaus. "I'm surprised Viveca never tried to make a deal with you," she said, "to get into the castle. Like she tried with me."

There was more silence from Klaus. Isabelle was on the verge of taking another peek at him when he said, "Even if she did, what makes you think my answer would be different than yours?"

Isabelle blinked. "I didn't. I just—"

"I'm going to see what's keeping Stefan with that tea," Klaus interrupted. Before Isabelle could respond, she heard the *creak* of the door as it opened and shut.

Isabelle cast a swift glance around the screen. Klaus had gone. And after all that about needing to stay *in the room* with her. Stepping back, Isabelle stuffed the ends of her blouse into her skirt—then doubled over as a thrill of pain shook through her, so intense she nearly blacked out.

It was an unbridled, all-consuming pain. Isabelle couldn't tell where it was coming from. It rolled over her like a steam train, flattening her, reducing her to nothing. Then it peeled back, just a fraction. Enough that she was aware of herself again, of her body, and she clutched at the sides of her head, fingers clawing into her temples and face, and it was that, she realized, that ache that had been plaguing her, that headache that was so much more than a headache.

It was going to kill her.

Her knees hit the floor. The bones in her face were screaming, begging for release. *She* wasn't screaming. She wanted to—she needed to—it was there, trapped at the base of her throat, fighting with her own breath to escape. But no sound left her lips; this pain, this *thing* inside her wouldn't permit it.

It radiated through her. Down her arms. She grew tight with it, so tight she thought she would break. All the bones in her body were going to break, they would shatter into a million pieces—

And then something pierced through the suffocating pain. Something startling. It was also pain, but a different kind—sharp, stabbing, yet laughably weak in the face of *this*. A pinprick, really, nothing more—

Something slick and hot ran down her cheek.

Isabelle ripped her hands away from her face. She looked at them.

Three of her fingernails were stained with blood. Only they weren't fingernails anymore.

They were *claws*.

Distantly, in the back of her mind, something rose to the surface. An unspeakable truth, dark and horrifying.

She was changing. She was *turning*.

They're not claws, a little voice inside her head piped up, trying to be heard past the horror. *Only sharpened fingernails—look—*

But the voice was small and tinny, the pain and darkness drowning it out. The pain, the *pain*. It ricocheted through her, splitting her apart. Splitting her *jaw* apart. The smothered screams in Isabelle's chest were desperate for a voice, but she could not scream because her teeth were growing, *shifting* inside her gums, and the bones in her face were breaking, mending, breaking, growing, breaking—

"Miss Isabelle?"

The sound of her name was like a gunshot. She clung to it. *Isabelle, Isabelle.* It tethered her, drawing her closer to that small voice inside her head. But a burgeoning dread woke in her too, a dread that knew what she barely held at bay—

The monster. The beast.

A mindless beast that would destroy anything—*anyone*—in its path.

Her arms flailed. She didn't even know what she was trying to do, only that she was trying to do *something,* and her windmilling arms knocked into the wash basin, sending it tumbling to the floor. It shattered into porcelain shards.

"Miss Isabelle! What—"

She whirled. *No, no, get away.* But her voice still didn't work. Her body felt unwieldy, foreign. It wasn't *hers.*

Her flailing arms connected with something else. The dressing screen. It went flying.

On the other side of it, Stefan ducked just in time to avoid it. Then he looked up.

The color in his face drained out of him.

"Miss Isabelle?" he whispered.

Stefan, Stefan. She knew Stefan. And Isabelle. Isabelle, *she* was Isabelle—

"But it's not the full moon yet," Stefan said. Dumbly. Shakily. He held his hands up in a helpless gesture. "Miss Isabelle...it's me. Stefan. You know me."

Yes, of course she knew him. But Isabelle's mind was preoccupied, caught on what else he'd said. *It's not the full moon yet.* Yes, he was right. The full moon was tonight. And that mattered because—because they thought she wouldn't turn until then, if she was going to turn at all—

"Miss Isabelle, please." The trembling, pitiful little creature that was Stefan gulped. "You're good. You're kind. You—you apologized for knocking me out, remember? You said you didn't want to hurt me. You don't want to hurt me."

No, she didn't. She didn't want to hurt him. She didn't really *feel* like hurting anyone, did she? She didn't think so. It was only just dawning on her that the pain, the pain she'd thought was going to kill her, had receded, leaving an empty soreness in its wake.

The pain had stopped. The *turning* had stopped.

Look, look.

She held up her hands. They were still hands. *Her* hands, human hands. What she'd thought were claws weren't exactly—they looked like fingernails, but thicker, elongated, sharpened to points.

She swept her gaze over the rest of her body. It was still...her. Arms, legs, everything else. She was still garbed in the clothes she'd just put on. She was still human. Nothing had reformed. She hadn't sprouted any fur.

There was just...her face. Her *face.*

Slowly—carefully—Isabelle raised her hands to her face.

It still felt like her face. Mostly. Her skin felt like her skin, smooth and a little clammy. And also—*ow.* Ah, yes, she'd scratched herself with her too-long, too-sharp fingernails. Leaving that raw spot for now, she explored the rest of her head. Her hair, her ears. Eyelids. Nose. It all felt like her. Her cheeks...

Her cheeks felt funny. Not quite right. Sort of *bumpy* and out of place. And her mouth felt strange too. Sore. She ran her hands over her lips, her fingers slipping inside her mouth.

She felt the length of one elongated fang.

A noise finally escaped Isabelle. A whimper.

"Miss Isabelle?" Stefan ventured. "Can you hear me?"

Yes, she could hear him. She understood him, but.... Dropping her hands from her face, she spun around. Behind her was the smudged mirror. She leaned forward to peer at her dusty reflection.

She looked like herself. Mostly. Except for her eyes—their tawny brown had turned a bright, glowing amber. And her mouth—her teeth—

She had the monstrous jaw and jagged teeth of a beast.

Another whimper escaped her.

It's not you, that small voice said. *You don't need it. Let it go.*

Let it go. Isabelle wanted to laugh in utter panic. She couldn't just *let it go.* She didn't know how. She had become this—this *thing*—this beast-human hybrid—

It's not you. Just let it go.

"Miss Isabelle?"

Isabelle. You're Isabelle. You are not a beast. You don't need the beast. You don't want to be a killer. You want to be human.

Just be human. Just let it go.

Isabelle closed her eyes.

Don't fight it. Let it go.

She felt for the beast inside her. Felt it raging.

She shoved it down.

As easy as that.

When she opened her eyes again—when she came *back*—she was herself again. Human. Isabelle.

A tremor shivered through her. She felt woozy, like she'd had one too many cups of wine. No, more like she had run ten miles in the snow, with bricks on her back. She was *exhausted.* She felt like something had been taken from her. She felt like jelly. Boneless.

But so very, very human.

Isabelle looked at her hands. They were normal again, her fingernails just regular fingernails. When she turned to look in the mirror, she saw the fangs were gone, her face returned to its normal shape.

"What just happened?" she croaked.

"I don't know," Stefan said.

Isabelle turned towards him. The poor boy's face was white. He gawped at her like she was something he had never seen before, which. She supposed she was.

"That just happened, didn't it?" she asked. Her voice was low and scratchy. As though she really had screamed all those screams. "You—you saw it. Or was it some mad dream?"

Stefan gave a wild shake of his head. "It happened. You—you turned into the beast! Or. A beast." He shook his head again. "But you weren't like Prince Gryphon. It was just your—your *teeth*—"

"And my hands—"

"Like just a part of you turned—and then you—" His eyes widened. "Did you stop it? Can you control it?"

"I don't know," she said slowly, but that wasn't quite true. Some innate part of her understood this thing inside her. She remembered what Adela said. *They became something. Their bite transformed the bitten.* The witch hadn't been certain Gryphon's bite would turn someone into a full beast like him. And she was right. Isabelle was not a full beast, but rather some...beast-woman hybrid.

And she had *controlled* it.

"I wonder...even though he's different..." Isabelle murmured. "I really think Gryphon could learn to—"

Before she could finish the thought, the door to the room *banged* open, and six people spilled inside. Garrett. Ellery. And all of Garrett's soldiers.

All four of the soldiers had their weapons drawn.

"Klaus," Garrett barked. His voice held a note of harsh command that was very unlike him. "Where is Klaus?" His green eyes swept the room as though he expected Klaus to jump out from beneath the bed.

Isabelle's chest tightened. "Garrett?"

"I saw Klaus on my way back from the kitchen." Stefan pointed towards the corridor. "I asked him where he was going, but he didn't answer. He was in a hurry."

Garrett gave a sharp nod, and all the soldiers except Spencer filed out of the room. They didn't lower their weapons.

"What's going on?" Isabelle asked.

"What's going on," said Garrett, "is that Viveca claims Klaus has been helping her. I wasn't inclined to believe it, but if he's left the castle—when he was supposed to be guarding you—then she might have been telling the truth."

23

BETRAYED

G RYPHON FELT HIS HEART sink into his stomach. "It can't
be." He punched a fist into his palm. "It just *can't* be."

"Look, I'm not making this up," Garrett said. He stood with
his hands clasped behind his back, his spine ram-rod straight. He
looked like a soldier, Gryphon thought, making his report, and
he supposed that was what Garrett was right now. A command-
ing officer, reporting to Gryphon.

With the worst news possible.

Garrett continued, "That's what Viveca said, word for word.
And when we came back to confront Klaus, he was gone. We've
searched the castle. Stefan and Ellery are certain we haven't
missed anything. He's not here."

Gryphon ran his hands over his face. The sun had gone down
half an hour ago. When he had emerged from the dungeons, he'd
found Garrett waiting for him in the entrance hall, a grim look
on his face. They hadn't had a chance to come to an agreement
with Viveca, Garrett said, because as soon as she told them about
Klaus's supposed betrayal, they'd hurried back to the castle.
Klaus had been left to guard Isabelle, after all.

Garrett swept his watchful gaze around the cavernous hall. "I figured Viveca was just causing trouble, but now...this doesn't look good, Gryphon."

"Klaus has risked his life for me," Gryphon argued. "Over and over again."

Garrett only looked at him. Gryphon turned away. His heart felt like a stone in the pit of his stomach.

Besides Isabelle, Klaus was the only person who was anything like a friend to Gryphon—or so he'd thought. When Gryphon first met Klaus, he'd been irked by the hunter's easy way—how he'd refused to show Gryphon deference, even when Gryphon told him he was a prince. But eventually, Gryphon had come to like Klaus's irreverence; in that way, Klaus was not so much a servant, but a confidante. Someone he could trust.

Had that all been a lie?

Gryphon rubbed a hand over his stubbled jaw. "What did Isabelle say?"

Garrett folded his arms over his chest. "Stefan had gone to get some tea. Klaus said he was going to check on him. She thought it was weird because he'd been so insistent he stay with her. And..."

"And what?"

Garrett sighed. "Are you aware there may have been some kind of...relationship? Between Klaus and Viveca?"

"Relationship?" Dumbly, Gryphon contemplated the word. In this context—*Klaus and Viveca*—he felt like he had no idea what it meant. He gave Garrett a blank look.

Garrett raised his eyebrows in a suggestive manner.

Oh. *Oh.* "That's...no. That's absurd. Klaus never..."

Gryphon trailed off. He felt horribly cold. *Viveca* had wanted Klaus, yes. She'd wanted him from the moment they'd met, the three of them, that day in the Black Forest. It had been the morning after a full moon. They'd come across her in a sunny, leaf-strewn glade. She'd just made the change into her human form. Her very naked, very beautiful human form.

Viveca had wanted Klaus. Was it so impossible to think Klaus might have wanted her back?

Gryphon shook his head. "Even if—that doesn't prove anything."

"What happened that day, last year?" Garrett clasped his hands behind him again, resuming the pose of interrogating officer. "When you escaped. What do you remember?"

"Nothing." Gryphon's eyes stung. He wanted sleep. "I went down to the dungeons as usual. We didn't have the portcullis back then—I just locked myself in a cell behind the iron door. I escaped while I was the beast, so I don't remember—" He never remembered. But that didn't mean Klaus was responsible.

He shook his head more vehemently. "Look, why would Klaus let me out of that cell and then risk his life getting me back? He tracked me for *days* in the forest, in near-freezing cold, and I—I attacked him before he got me under control. He nearly died. Why do that if he let me out?"

Garrett shrugged one shoulder. "Viveca didn't say that he did. Only that it was his fault and no accident. So." He spread his hands. "Any number of things could have happened. Maybe he regretted what he'd done. Maybe he let *Viveca* into the castle and she let you out." Garrett nodded, as though he liked this scenario. "He may not have known what she was going to do. Although..."

Although...why run away if he hadn't done anything wrong? *If he let Viveca into the castle, then he did do something wrong*, a dark, stubborn voice in Gryphon's mind insisted. "But why let

Viveca in to begin with?" he asked, still looking for holes in these theories. "If it wasn't to let me out—"

"Well, if they *are* in some kind of relationship," Garrett reasoned, "then maybe they just wanted a place to...you know..." He trailed off, raising his eyebrows again.

Gryphon looked at him, nonplussed.

"*You know*," Garrett repeated. He gave a delicate cough. "Er—don't you?"

"Yes, I know," Gryphon snapped. But would Klaus have really been that foolish? Surely the hunter would have known that inviting Viveca into the castle for some sort of tryst would have led to no good. "I just can't believe Klaus would have been that stupid."

"Well. There is another possibility." For some reason, Garrett looked distinctly uncomfortable, tugging at the end of his sleeve.

"Which is?"

Garrett sighed. "Maybe he wanted out, Gryphon. Of this castle."

"He leaves the castle whenever he wants. The pack leaves him alone." *More evidence of a relationship between Klaus and Viveca?* Gryphon wondered. He was feeling stupider by the minute.

"I mean...maybe he wanted out of this *life*," Garrett said quietly. "Maybe he had even come to resent it. Come to resent..." He trailed off.

But Gryphon understood now. "Resent me, you mean." Resent guarding Gryphon. Resent serving Gryphon. Well, Klaus had always made a point that he didn't *serve* Gryphon. But he was instrumental here, keeping them all fed and well-supplied.... He was their contact with the outside world.

Maybe he'd had enough. So much so that he'd allowed Viveca to talk him into something horrible, something he'd regretted...

But does it matter? that dark voice whispered. *Does it matter if he regretted it?*

Gryphon's heart had left his body. He felt wretchedly empty in its wake.

"Look, we're keeping watch tonight for the full moon anyway," Garrett said. "Two of us will be on the walls, and two patrolling the castle. Stefan and Ellery are staying with Isabelle. You should—"

"I'll be in my tower."

"Gryphon—"

"Just—tell me if Klaus comes back." Gryphon tried to summon his usual snarl, but his voice sounded small and pitiful. He turned his back before Garrett could say anything else, yanking open the front doors. A burst of brutal cold slammed into him.

Gryphon hardly felt it.

He didn't see anyone the rest of the night. Not Garrett, not Isabelle, not the servants. He didn't want to see anyone. Everyone was as safe as they could be. Garrett had seen to that.

They didn't need Gryphon. No one needed him.

He spent the night in his workshop but got very little done. Usually, he did his best work when he was riled up, itching to explode with frustration or loneliness. But he wasn't riled now. He felt vacant. Hollowed out.

He'd been a fool to think Klaus was loyal to him. That *anyone* in the castle was. It was the mistake he made again and again, thinking he could trust anyone...thinking they might trust him. They were all holed up in this castle, living in terrible danger, because of him. Stones, he'd uprooted Stefan's whole life when he was exiled. The boy had only been nine years old.

Gryphon closed his eyes. And there it was. He thought he'd left all this behind in the Glen Kingdom. But moving to another place hadn't changed anything. He was still a beacon for trouble and chaos. A cyclone, destroying everyone in its path. It was just who he was. He couldn't run from it.

He emerged from his workshop with less than an hour until dawn. For the second time that night, he found Garrett waiting in the entrance hall. He was alone, thankfully. Gryphon didn't feel like seeing anyone else. Well, he didn't feel like seeing Garrett, come to that.

"I'm surprised you're still up," Gryphon grunted.

Garrett ran a hand over his unshaven face. "I don't think any of us are sleeping until this night is over."

"Well, it nearly is." Gryphon looked at his brother and felt a strange surge of feeling. Almost like...concern. He looked ragged, his eyes shadowed and bleary. He'd been up for over twenty-for hours, Gryphon realized. Their conversation about Princess Snow had been this same time yesterday.

It isn't for you, said that dark voice inside his head. *He's doing all this for Isabelle. He doesn't care about you.*

"I'm sorry, Gryphon," Garrett said heavily. "There's been no sign of him."

"What?" Gryphon tore himself from his miserable thoughts.

"Klaus. He didn't come back."

Another surge of feeling. But different, painful. "It doesn't matter," Gryphon said shortly. "If he does come back, no one is to let him in. I can't trust him."

Garrett looked taken aback. "We don't know for sure what happened—"

"It *doesn't matter,*" Gryphon repeated. "He left his post. With no explanation. I'm done with him."

"Well. Right." Garrett's tone hardened. "Of course you are."

"I'm sorry," Gryphon said acidly. "Do you have something to say?"

"I'm just surprised you're not more worried about your friend."

"He's not my friend."

"You do realize—whether he betrayed you or not—Viveca only told us to drive a wedge between you?" Garrett stepped towards him. "She had no other reason to tell us."

"It doesn't matter why she did it."

"So that's it? You write him off so easily?"

"Pretty much."

"Stones." Garrett let out a bitter laugh. "How exactly like Father you are."

Gryphon felt as though Garrett had punched him. "What did you just say to me?"

"Well, isn't this what he did to you? Or so Isabelle says. Exiling you, without letting you explain or tell your side—"

Anger rose inside Gryphon, swift and hot. "It's *not* the same. If Klaus is working with Viveca, then he's put everyone here in danger. Even if he's not, he left Isabelle and put *her* in danger. But Father? Father only banished me to save face. To stop rumors spreading about me and ruining his reputation."

"If that's true, it didn't work. There are still plenty of rumors about you."

"Well, if you don't mind—" Gryphon turned his back on Garrett, starting across the hall "—I'd rather not hear them."

"I never wanted to hear them either," Garrett called after him. "I only wanted the truth. But no one would tell me. Will you? Or don't you want to set the record straight?"

Gryphon stopped in his tracks. He wavered, remembering what Isabelle had said. *You should talk to your brother. Tell him what you've told me.* At the time, that had seemed an impossible ask. But now...well, they were talking, weren't they? Working together, even? Albeit grudgingly, so far as Gryphon was concerned.

Gryphon turned back to Garrett. "You really want to know?"

"Of course." Garrett looked as though he couldn't believe he had to ask. "Gryphon, I've spent the past three years thinking my brother tried to kill me. If that's not the case, then yes, I want to know what really happened."

"I wasn't trying to kill you. However annoying you were."

"Well, this is off to a splendid start."

Gryphon sighed. He checked his pocket watch—over half an hour until dawn.

He had time.

He told Garrett everything. How he'd become involved with Malina, the witch. About the spell she'd wanted to cast to "protect" the kingdom. That she'd needed Garrett's blood. How it went wrong when Garrett woke up, how Malina disappeared, leaving him to take the blame.

Once he was done, Garrett let out a long breath. "I wish you'd told me all this," he said in a low voice. "Before you left."

"Yes, well." Gryphon's throat felt hoarse, as though he'd been talking for hours. "Father wasn't letting me near you, was he?"

"You could have tried, though."

"For what purpose? As though you would have believed me."

"I do believe you!" Garrett shot back. "If I'd only known—"

"You would have what?" It was typical, Gryphon thought, so typical of Garrett. He'd told him everything, and Garrett *believed* him, but he was angry anyway. He'd found something else to blame Gryphon for. "Fought for me to stay?"

"Maybe I would have," Garrett said quietly.

Gryphon's words died on his lips. Of all the things he'd expected Garrett to say, that wasn't it. "You hated me," he croaked.

"I was afraid of you," Garrett corrected. He rubbed a hand behind his head. "But I also...stones, I looked up to you, Gryphon. You terrified me, but even so, I just—wanted a brother." He turned aside, shaking his head. "If you'd asked me to help you and your witch with her spell, I would have *jumped* at the chance. Mind you, she was definitely up to something dodgy, so it's probably for the best she didn't get what she was after. But I would have helped you, Gryphon. Did that ever occur to you?"

It really hadn't. Because Gryphon *had* been awful to him. It had never occurred to him that Garrett would have helped him anyway. That Garrett—perhaps—had been as lonely back then as Gryphon was.

But this was too painful to dwell on. Certainly too painful to admit. Aloud, Gryphon said, "I didn't want your help."

"Well, great." Garrett threw his hands up. "I didn't want to be king either. But now I will be, all because of your stupidity."

"Yes, poor you," Gryphon snarled. "Because being king is so awful."

Garrett's eyes were resentful. "Well, it's not all roses. That's for sure." For a moment, Gryphon thought he was going to say more, but then he shook his head. With a glare for Gryphon, Garrett left the hall, his boots beating against the stone floor.

Leaving Gryphon to trudge down to the dungeons alone. As he always did. As he always was.

———————————◆◆◆———————————

When Gryphon changed back into human form roughly nine hours later, he expected to find Stefan waiting to raise the portcullis. He'd been the one to close it this morning. But instead, he found one of Garrett's soldiers waiting for him. He grinned when he saw Gryphon—stones, were all Garrett's people so cheerful?—and wound up the lever to raise the gate.

"Where's Stefan?" Gryphon scowled. It was unnerving to be met by a stranger down here. Unnerving to think of a stranger sitting here, waiting him out, listening to him roar through the iron door.

"Bringing in some wood for the fires," Garrett's man replied. He was tall and broad-chested, his skin a darker, richer brown than Gryphon's. He had a name like a bird, he thought—Falcon, that was it. His name was Falcon. "A big storm rolled in a few hours ago. There must be three feet of snow out there already, and still falling."

Gryphon strode past the man, trying to ignore the painful twinge in his chest. Usually, it was Klaus who made sure they had enough wood and supplies to see them through storms; of course Stefan had to pick up the slack now he was gone.

Falcon caught up to him quickly, undeterred by Gryphon's haughty demeanor. He climbed the stairs behind Gryphon. "Prince Garrett wanted me to tell you—though I don't know it matters now, with all this snow. He was planning to head out tomorrow, though I'm guessing it will need to wait another day or so now."

Gryphon cast a glance over his shoulder. In the dim stairwell, all he could see was Falcon's close-shaved head. "Head out? Has he given up on the wolf pack?"

"Not at all. He just wants to go to Spalding—the village we stopped by on our way here. Not sure if you're familiar with it. It's about a five-day journey. He can send a telegram from there to the Glen Kingdom."

Gryphon shot the soldier another look as they emerged from the stairwell. "Oh, not to your father," Falcon assured him. "He wants to contact Princess Briar. Make sure *someone* knows where we are and what's going on. Just in case a rout with the wolves doesn't go our way."

"Who's Princess Briar?"

"Oh, he's not mentioned her? She's the princess from the Mountain Kingdom—been living at Glen Castle for a few months now."

Gryphon was pretty sure this made no sense, as the Mountain Kingdom was a decrepit ruin devoid of people, but then, he also vaguely recalled Isabelle saying something about Garrett courting a girl who was a "half-dead rotting corpse." So clearly there was more to that story. "Right. Well." An idea occurred to him. "This village—it's where Isabelle's brother was, isn't it?"

Falcon nodded.

Gryphon considered. "Maybe Isabelle could go with you to visit him. If it's only a few days from here...she'd probably be safe enough with all of you." The wolves, after all, were at their weakest in the days after the full moon.

Falcon grinned again. "I'd wager she'd be safe enough on her own now, given what she can do."

Gryphon blinked. "What she can do? What do you mean?"

Falcon's smile faded. "You mean...no one's told you?"

Isabelle was not in her room. Ellery was there, changing the bedding, and she filled Gryphon in on what had happened. Yes, Isabelle had turned—sort of. Yes, before the full moon. No, she didn't become a beast. Not quite. Yes, it was only for a moment, because she...turned it off...somehow. No, Ellery didn't know why no one had told him; she had assumed Isabelle or Garrett would have.

All of this, it transpired, had occurred just before Klaus was discovered missing, which partly explained that last bit. After-wards, it seemed Isabelle had been exhausted and slept for about fifteen hours. She'd continued to rest today, Ellery said, but she was up now. She'd gone to the kitchen to eat.

That was where Gryphon found her. In the kitchen. One of Garrett's soldiers was with her—the tall, thin one; Gryphon couldn't remember his name—but he left the room when Gryphon appeared. Leaving him alone with Isabelle.

"Good evening," Isabelle said dryly as he joined her at the table. A mess of scents filled his senses—the caustic odor of the oil lamp on the table. The savory aroma of rosemary and basil from Isabelle's bowl of stew. A hint of spicy clove, steaming out of a jug of warmed wine.

And Isabelle. Beneath it all, Gryphon could still detect the rosy scent of her.

Her expression was far from rosy. The bags beneath her eyes were even more pronounced than Garrett's had been this morn-ing, despite her fifteen hours of sleep. Heart thumping in his chest, Gryphon swept his gaze over her, searching for any sign of distress or injury. But mostly, she just looked hungry. She sat hunched over her bowl of stew like she thought he might steal it from her. As he watched, she proceeded to wolf down its contents, using a hunk of brown bread to sop it up.

She caught him staring. "Sorry. But I'm starving. I feel like I could eat an elephant. I've never seen an elephant, but I'm sure I could eat one." She took a long sip of her wine. "What time is it, anyway? I honestly have no idea. I've slept most of the last twenty-four hours."

"So I heard."

She paused, bread halfway to her mouth, dripping gravy into her bowl. "Who told you?"

"Ellery," Gryphon said. "Explain to me how it is you turned into a beast—"

"Half-beast." She cocked her head. "No. Quarter-beast?"

"—yesterday *morning*, and I'm only just hearing about it?"

"Well, as I've said, I was asleep. Perhaps if you'd stopped to look in on me, you would know. Did you even think to, when the full moon was over?"

Gryphon winced. No. He hadn't. He'd been so consumed by thoughts of Klaus, by his own wounded pride and misery.

"And according to Ellery," Isabelle added, "no one has even seen you since they realized Klaus was gone. You've either been down in the dungeons or holed up in your tower."

That was also true. He supposed it didn't matter now. The sting of finding out about it from Falcon, of all people, was wearing off. "And I suppose you also think I should give Klaus another chance," he said, his tone rancorous. "Go looking for him. Just like my brother does."

Isabelle stopped eating for the first time since he'd entered the room. The look she gave him was almost injured. "I don't know what to think. I've had a lot on my mind, honestly, for the few hours I've been awake. But it's your call, Gryphon, whatever you decide to do. I won't judge you for it." She shook her head. "I don't *judge* you. When are you going to understand that?"

Gryphon's throat tightened. When would he understand? It was not that he didn't understand.

He didn't trust it. Couldn't allow himself to. Especially not now.

Isabelle resumed eating. As she lifted her spoon to her mouth, Gryphon's eyes lingered on her hand. Where he'd bitten her. The bandage had come off weeks ago, and now there was just a faint scar where the beast's teeth had punctured her skin.

"Tell me what happened," he said quietly.

"When I turned, you mean?" She...shrugged. She *shrugged*. "Well. I don't know what to tell. My headache came back. It was so bad I couldn't sleep, so I got up to dress. Then the pain just...intensified. It was overwhelming. And then my hands changed—my nails did. They grew into these...claws. And my whole jaw sort of rearranged itself. To make room for the fangs." She gave another shrug. "Then it went away. That was it, really."

Gryphon was incredulous. "That was it."

"Approximately."

He ran a hand over his face. "So I'm stuck in this castle. My entire body breaking to turn into a beast every morning. And you just...grow some fangs for a minute, and that's it?"

"Well, it's not *my* fault," she protested.

"It's terribly unfair," he muttered.

"Would you rather I become a full beast?"

Gryphon looked at her, suddenly sober. "No. I would not."

She caught his gaze in hers. They exchanged a long look, full of so many unspoken things. *I'm sorry*, her gaze said. *Don't be*, said his. *None of this is your fault*, said hers. *All of it. All of it is*, said his.

Gryphon looked away.

"It didn't just go away." Isabelle's voice was soft. She put her spoon down, letting it clatter against her empty bowl. "I controlled it, Gryphon. I just...let it go."

"How nice for you." He caught her narrowed gaze. "No. Really. I mean it. I'm glad, Isabelle." His eyes drifted away, fixing on the far wall. "I don't want you to live my life."

"Gryphon, what if *you* could learn to control it too?"

"I never have before. Don't you think, in over two years, I would have figured that out? If there was a way?"

"But Viveca made it sound like that's how it's meant to be. And Adela said—"

"Viveca. *Adela*. Now there're two people I can trust."

"Gryphon—"

"My curse is what it is, Isabelle." Gryphon's tone was short. "I've accepted it."

"You don't have to. You don't *deserve* this, Gryphon."

Gryphon bit back the automatic response. But Isabelle looked like she knew what he was going to say. She stretched an arm across the table and laid her hand over his.

It was a struggle not to flinch away.

"You say you don't want me to live your life." Her voice was clear, like a freshly melted pond in the first blush of spring. Rife with possibility. Rife with vulnerability. "But isn't it too late for that?"

She wasn't talking about the bite now. He knew that. Gryphon met her gaze. He saw everything in her eyes. Everything that was between them. Everything they'd shared, the good and the bad. The loneliness they'd faced together. The night they'd spent together.

He drew his hand back. "It doesn't have to be."

Isabelle stared at him. He saw cracks in her resolve. Saw her fighting to hold it in place.

He looked away. "Garrett is going to Spalding in a few days. As soon as the snow clears. You should go with him. Visit Ansel. You'll be safe with Garrett."

"Go with him?" Isabelle's voice sounded strangled. "And what about you?"

Gryphon stood from the table, evading her gaze. "I'll be here. As always."

24

ABANDONED

I SABELLE DECIDED TO GO to Spalding after all. To visit her brother, stones knew why. Garrett insisted that Ansel was worried about her. Granted, Garrett didn't know the full extent of the gulf between her and Ansel—he didn't know what Ansel had said to her all those years ago. Gryphon remained the only one who knew the truth.

But. But also. Isabelle remembered the look on Ansel's face the last day he'd been here. She remembered him trying to tell her something before he departed in that carriage. *You have to know. I never meant any of it. I'm sorry.*

Perhaps it would be worth it to hear her brother out, Isabelle thought. One last time. So she consented to go with Garrett.

"But you're coming back," said Ellery. She stood watching as Isabelle folded clothes into her pack. "Aren't you?"

Isabelle gave a tight smile. "Yes, I'm coming back. I'm only visiting my brother. Garrett says he's probably still recovering."

As Ellery helped her pack, Isabelle's smile vanished. She did intend to come back, if only because they weren't prepared for the month-long journey home through the Black Forest.

But she no longer knew whether there was any point coming back for anything else. After all, Gryphon had made himself quite plain.

You say you don't want me to live your life. But isn't it too late for that?

It doesn't have to be.

Isabelle closed her eyes. Those words had carved through her like a blade. And every time she recalled them, the wound bled anew. *You would think*, Isabelle thought glumly, *I would be used to this by now.* She'd bared herself to Gryphon. She'd let down all her guards, shared every secret.

So she shouldn't have been surprised he'd turned her away.

One of the reasons Isabelle enjoyed the study of history was because she loved to puzzle out the patterns. The chains of events that played out over and over again in different times and places. Influenced by culture and technology and belief, yes, but essentially the same designs enacted through different systems.

She enjoyed it. She was good at it. Yet when it came to her own life, she had yet to work out the obvious pattern. Or perhaps, yet to learn from it.

She wouldn't make that mistake again.

They left at first light, a few days after the full moon. As soon as enough of the snow had cleared. The morning they set out was brisk with cold. They were into the tail end of winter now, though if it was any warmer than it had been six weeks ago, Isabelle couldn't tell.

It was hard to believe she'd been in Gryphon's castle for six weeks.

As they set out beneath the canopy of trees, Garrett moseyed up beside her. "Did you say goodbye to my brother before you left?" he asked in a jovial tone.

"No. Did you?"

"Yes. But then, I was up a good hour before you."

It was true. Isabelle hadn't gotten up until it was nearly time to leave. "You try rising at the crack of dawn," she mumbled, "when you've been getting up at three in the afternoon for the past month."

"Really, though." Garrett raised his eyebrows. "Is there something going on between you and Gryphon that I should know about?"

"No." Isabelle's tone was a warning. "I can't think of anything going on between us that *you* should know about."

"He is my brother," Garrett pointed out.

"You don't even like him."

"And you're my friend..."

"Not for long, if you keep on with this."

Garrett laughed. "All right, all right. I only ask because he seemed very *concerned* about you. And you've been so bound and determined to help him with his curse—"

"I was." Isabelle heaved a sigh. "I don't know there's any point anymore."

"Why not?"

Isabelle hesitated. She wasn't willing to dive into everything with Garrett. She wasn't even willing to dive into it with herself. So she said, "Because Gryphon thinks it's a waste of time." Isabelle pushed aside a protruding spruce branch, the needles bristling against her gloved hand. "Trying to control the beast. He told me so."

Garrett was quiet for a moment. The wind spun through the treetops, shaking loose a flurry of dead leaves. "Well," Garrett said, his tone thoughtful. "That's Gryphon. That's not you."

"What do you mean?"

"Look, Gryphon likes to stew in his own misery," Garrett said. "I don't know if you've noticed. He either doesn't know how to solve his problems, or he doesn't want to. But you, Isabelle—you've never met a puzzle you won't try to solve." He quirked a smile. "No matter if someone is telling you not to."

"Yes, well." She took a deep breath, the cold air tickling her throat. "But that's because I don't care what most people think. This is...different."

It hung there between them. But Garrett did not make fun or ask her to clarify. He didn't make her come out and say it. *I care about him. I care about your brother. A lot.* He only said, "Look, no matter what he said, don't think for a minute he doesn't need your help. Just because he wants to brood doesn't mean you should give up. If you don't really want to," he added. "It's nothing to me whether you help him or not."

Isabelle eyed him sidelong. She wondered whether that last bit was true anymore. "Was he really so awful? When you lived at the castle together?"

Garrett hitched his pack up, looking rueful. "I suppose my first winter there was the worst—just after my mother died, you know. It was a bad winter—cold and wet and dark. We were stuck inside a lot. My father kept trying to get me and Gryphon together, playing and taking lessons, but, well..."

"Gryphon didn't want to?"

"Not so much."

"But what did he *do* to you?" Isabelle pressed.

"Well, mostly he just avoided me." Garrett scratched a hand behind his head. "But I was always hanging around him. I remember once I'd been following him all over the castle, all day, and he finally locked me in a broom closet. I screamed and cried, but it was hours before anyone found me."

"He locked you in a *broom* closet?"

"And another time," Garrett went on, "I was spying on him while he worked at the sword. When the master-of-arms stepped out, Gryphon found me, and he knocked all the armor onto the floor. Made a big mess, and when the master-of-arms returned, he told him I did it."

"He didn't!" Isabelle wasn't sure whether to laugh or not.

But Garrett did laugh. However he'd felt at the time, it seemed he'd put the hurt behind him. That was like Garrett. "There *was* one time. Later that year. Gryphon and I were out with the horse-master and some other lads for a ride. Gryphon was meant to keep an eye on me, help me out. Well, he did keep an eye on me. Long enough to spook my horse and send me galloping into the woods."

"On purpose?"

"Of course on purpose. Though, to be fair, I think he under-estimated how bad a rider I was. I couldn't stop the horse—it's a miracle I hung on as long as I did. Anyway, Gryphon came after me. Not out of concern, you understand, but because he didn't want to get in trouble. By the time he found me, I'd fallen off, my horse had disappeared, and we were a long way from the others."

"But you had Gryphon's horse, didn't you?" Isabelle asked. "Couldn't you ride back together?"

"Well, we meant to," Garrett said sheepishly. "But the horse was winded, and I was banged up. We'd stopped near this little pool, and the weather was so nice. I told Gryphon we should wait a bit, let the horse rest, before heading back. And I don't know if it was the fine weather, or if he just dreaded going back, but Gryphon agreed. So we lay down by the pool beneath some trees for shade, and ...we fell asleep."

"For how long?"

"Hours. It was dark by the time we woke. Father had fifty men out combing the woods for us. Some of them had passed right by, we were hidden so well by the trees." Garrett flashed a grin. "Needless to say, we were *both* in trouble—Father was fuming; he didn't even ask what happened or whose fault it was. And for once, we were in the same boat, and it was like...we were really brothers." He shook himself. "That was a long time ago. I doubt Gryphon even remembers."

They reached Spalding the afternoon of their fifth day out from the castle. It was a cold, clear day, the last of the sun's rays slicing through the treetops and slanting across the cobbled streets. While Garrett headed to the mayor's house to telegram Briar, Isabelle followed Spencer and Roy to the doctor's. The house sat on the end of the street, surrounded by bare-limbed ash trees and a few spruces. Spencer waited in the street out front, while Roy and Isabelle entered the house.

They were met by the doctor's wife, a woman with a round, pleasant face. She told Isabelle that Ansel was much improved as she led her down the corridor. "His infection's all gone, and his wrist is mending well," she added. "It was a small break. He's been talking about leaving, but I'm not sure he's strong enough yet." She left Isabelle alone outside Ansel's room, and after a tentative knock, Isabelle entered.

It was a small but clean, very tidy room, lit by a large lamp and the fading daylight coming in through two square windows. Ansel sat upright in bed, dressed in gray trousers and a soft wool shirt. When he saw Isabelle, his eyes went wide. "Isabelle! You're all right!"

"Yes, I am." Isabelle eased the door shut. "Don't get up—"

"But what are you doing here? No, I mean—*when* did you get here? How—"

Isabelle smiled at his astonished reaction. She was relieved too, for he did seem much improved. He had color back in his cheeks; gone was the awful gray look he'd had in the castle. His hair was even longer than before, grown out in thick, dark curls that nearly reached his ears. If she knew Ansel, he'd be itching to cut it back.

"You look so much better," Isabelle said.

Ansel gave her an incredulous look. "Never mind me," he said, his words clipped. "I can't believe you're here! When Klaus sent me off in that carriage, you said you'd escape right after me, and then you never showed!" He raked a hand through his hair, tossing it back with an irascible shake of his head. "Granted, it took me too long to get here. That damned carriage crashed and—"

"I know, Ansel. I know." Isabelle gingerly lowered herself into a wooden chair near his bedside. She'd not had much exercise all these weeks in the castle; five days of trekking through the forest had taken a toll on her body. She arranged her skirts around her to disguise her wince. "Prince Garrett told me they found you here. I'm sorry I never came to meet you—"

"So he did find you. Thank the stars. He got you out of the castle?"

"Not exactly. I—"

"But how did you escape?"

"*Ansel.*" Isabelle huffed a peeved breath. "Will you let me speak?"

Ansel broke off, jaw hanging open. "Sorry." He gave her a strange, close look as he leaned back, resting against the bed's headboard. "I just—I've been so worried about you, Belle. In fact, I was planning to head back to that castle myself. I even spoke to some of the villagers here, some of them said they'd come with me—"

"What for?"

"To rescue you, of course." Ansel shifted his head, as though trying to find a comfortable spot between the headboard's iron rungs. "Which, apparently, you don't need. Anymore."

"I never needed rescuing. Ansel, I *told* you I could get out on my own. I know I didn't come as soon as expected, but. It's not like I was being held prisoner."

Ansel stared at her. For a moment, he was silent, as though working through something in his head. Then he said, "Actually. That is what it was like. Or that's what I thought. You weren't locked in the tower like me, but the way I remember it, Gryphon said you weren't to leave."

Isabelle grimaced. It wasn't that she'd forgotten that. It had just been so long since she'd thought of herself as a prisoner there. "I told you, I could get out whenever I wanted. So it was not so dire as you make it seem. Anyway...things changed, Ansel. It's all rather a long story, but I'm here because Gryphon *let* me go. To come see you."

"But you have to go back?" Ansel's tone was suspicious.

"I'm *going* back. Of my own free will. I don't have to."

"Why the hell would you do that," Ansel said bluntly. It was not a question.

"Well, for one thing, I've left most of my things—"

"Why would you go *back* to that ruin," Ansel interrupted, "where you and I were *both* held prisoner—"

"I told you, it's not like that anymore—"

"Isabelle." The look in Ansel's eyes was urgent, as though he felt he needed to convince her how serious this was. As though *she* was the one who didn't understand. "Listen. I've heard some really disturbing stories about that castle *and* about Gryphon, since I've been in this village. I'm pretty sure some of those stories are superstitious nonsense, but it really seems there's something dark going on up there."

"Well, you're not wrong."

"What does that mean?"

"Look, I told you, it's a long story."

"I think you'd better explain it to me."

"Why?" Isabelle asked sharply. She wasn't opposed to telling Ansel what was going on—or she hadn't been when she'd first walked into the room. But Ansel's presumptions were making her angry. He didn't have any right to speak to her like this, as though she were some helpless—or worse, *stupid*—girl who didn't know what she'd gotten into. "What do you even care, Ansel?"

"What do I *care?* What sort of question is that? You're my sister."

"Am I? Because that's not what you said before. Three years ago. Remember? In the Mariner Kingdom?"

Ansel looked aggrieved. "Isabelle—"

"You said you didn't want me around. You said—"

"I know what I said."

"And? What, you didn't mean it?"

"No!" Ansel burst out. "No, I didn't mean it!"

The silence that followed his exclamation was charged with tension. Ansel's words rang in Isabelle's ears; she felt as though she'd been boxed around the head with them.

"What does that mean?" she asked, breaking the silence. "Ansel, *what does that mean?*"

Ansel's shoulders slumped. "Look. You must know what was going on in the Mariner Kingdom back then. I mean, afterward...you must have heard. It was less than a year after I took the job that it all went to hell."

It took Isabelle a minute to understand. "You mean, Princess Snow? Her family's deaths—"

"Murder," Ansel interrupted. His eyes were as hard as jet. "It was murder. They were all murdered by the queen."

"Yes, I know. But when you took the job, when you told me leave—that was months before any of that, before the king died—"

Ansel gave a hollow laugh. "Months before the queen's doings became public knowledge, sure. But that doesn't mean dark things weren't happening in that castle, Isabelle. They were. And when I became aware of it...well, the queen always made sure no one would tell her secrets."

Isabelle shook her head numbly. This was so beyond everything he'd said before, so beyond what she'd spent three years believing. "Made sure how?"

"She threatened you," Ansel said simply. "I don't even know how she knew about you. But she did. So...I did what I could to protect you. To get you out of that city." He swallowed. "I knew you'd never go without me, not if you knew the real reason."

"Yes, because you were in as much danger as I was! Ansel—"

"Well, it was my mess. I was already in it."

"But—" Isabelle couldn't absorb this. She couldn't make sense of it. It didn't fit the reality she'd lived for the past three years. All those cruel things he'd said...those words had *shaped* her. Changed the course of her life, and now....

Something clawed its way up her throat. Something awful and thick.

"How could you do this to me, Ansel?" she choked. "How could you make me think all this time—you made me think I'd done something *wrong*—" Just like their father had before him. "Ansel, after Papa l-left—Ansel, you were all I had."

"I know, Belle." Ansel's expression closed off. "Papa left me too, you know."

"But he left because of me," Isabelle rasped. She felt like she'd been punched in the stomach. All the breath was leaving her body. "He loved you, his *son*, his boy—"

"You must be joking?" The look Ansel gave her was one of disbelief. "Isabelle, if he left because of either of us, it was because of me. I was the one always getting into trouble, messing things up wherever we went. I was hopeless, and he was never afraid to tell me so."

Isabelle shook her head. That wasn't how she remembered it. She remembered her father heaping glowing praise on Ansel, his *boy.* Teaching him how to hunt, teaching him how to track, and all but ignoring Isabelle. If he'd criticized Ansel sometimes, well, that was still more attention than he'd ever paid her.

And then he left. Went off to hunt one morning and never returned. And when they went after him, they heard he'd taken off and wasn't coming back.

Isabelle's body felt rigid and airless. She couldn't draw a breath. She needed to get out of here; she couldn't be in this room. Looking out the window, she flinched in the glare of the reddening sun as it dropped below the horizon. "I need to go." She rushed to her feet, turning for the door. "I have to—"

"Isabelle, wait." Ansel's tone was pleading. "I'm sorry, Belle. Please don't go—"

"I'll be back, I—" She nearly stumbled in her haste to get the door open. She couldn't stand to look at her brother. She couldn't *breathe* in this little room.

She wrenched the door open and stepped out into the corridor. Roy waited in the front room, but Isabelle didn't want to see him right now, didn't want to see anyone. She just. Couldn't. Breathe. She needed to get outside.

Down the other end of the corridor was a back door, just a few steps away. Isabelle pushed it open and lurched outside into the cold.

She found herself on a tiny porch on the side of the house. A spruce tree towered over her, laden with snow. The sharp scent of the spruce filled her, a welcoming fragrance. Turning towards the tree, Isabelle leaned against the painted wooden railing and buried her face in her hands.

She wanted, so very suddenly, so very much, to be back at the castle. No, to be with *Gryphon*. Wherever he was, the castle or the forest or anywhere else, it didn't matter. Just...to be with him.

She wanted him. She missed him. He was the one, she thought. The one who just fit. He'd become a part of her. She had spent years alone, become accustomed to *being* alone. So how could it be—in the span of a few weeks—that he had become so integral? How was it that she felt so keenly the missing piece of herself? The missing piece that was Gryphon.

She had been stupid to think he hadn't wanted her in his life. To think there was something *wrong* with herself. How absurd that she'd ever believed that. Because the truth seemed so obvious now. Gryphon was afraid for her, just like Ansel had been all those years ago. And Gryphon—stubborn, lumbering, recalcitrant Gryphon—knew no other way but to run from his problems. To push them aside.

She'd thought her brother's confession had broken something inside her. But now, standing here, she realized she was not broken at all. She had never *been* broken. And she wasn't going to let Gryphon run from her.

Isabelle sucked in another breath, savoring the heady scent of the spruce. She was so engulfed by it, she didn't register the other scent creeping up on her. A mixture of soap and wool and incense. A very *human* scent.

"Hello, Isabelle."

Isabelle jerked her head up, spinning around.

A woman stood before the porch, a woman Isabelle recognized. She wore a midnight blue cloak, the hood pulled over her head. But not far enough to disguise her face.

It was Adela. The witch.

Adela cocked her head at her. "We've been looking for you."

Isabelle didn't bother to answer. *Run*, she thought, *run*, but something strange was happening. She felt woozy, a pungent fog encroaching on her brain. Too late, she saw the small, stone bowl Adela held in her hands, and the stream of smoke curling up from it. The odor of the smoke burrowed down her airway, burning her chest—making everything go *sideways*—

Isabelle swayed, her knees buckling beneath her. Then everything went dark.

25

EXCHANGE

GARRETT AND FALCON JOINED Gemma on the street outside after they left the mayor's house. It was nearly full dark. A wide swathe of sky was visible overhead like a dome covering the town, deep blue and full of winking stars. The air had grown colder, the temperature plummeting in the last half hour. Garrett pulled his long, thick overcoat on and adjusted the scarf around his neck. "Any trouble?" he asked Gemma.

Gemma pursed her lips. "Not *really*."

"That doesn't sound good," Falcon noted.

"Something happen?" Garrett pressed.

"It's just some talk I heard, sire." Gemma slung her rifle over her shoulder by its strap, shoving her hands into the pockets of her forest green coat. "A couple of men from the village asked me if we'd been up to the castle."

"What did you say?"

"Well, I told them that was your business and not theirs." Gemma shrugged. "They weren't happy about it, but they moved on. But I heard them say they were thinking of heading

321

up to the castle themselves. Something about 'confronting the monster' on their own."

"Doesn't sound good at all," Falcon said glumly.

"And they were definitely talking about Gryphon's castle?"

"Do you know any other castles 'round here, Your Highness?"

Garrett cursed. "I bet Ansel's been talking to the villagers. He was quick enough to tell us Gryphon was keeping Isabelle captive. I'm sure he didn't stop there."

"What should we do?" Falcon asked.

"Let's head to the doctor's and—"

"Your Highness!" Garrett, Gemma, and Falcon looked around as Roy stampeded up the street towards them. Garrett wondered at his stricken face before looking for Isabelle and Spencer. But Roy was alone. He skidded to a stop and bent over, panting heavily.

"What is it?" Garrett asked. "Where're Spencer and Isabelle?"

"Spencer's—injured." Roy struggled to straighten up and failed. He jerked a thumb over his shoulder. "He's at the doctor's—he tried to go after them, and they—knocked him out."

A chill ran down Garrett's spine. "Who?"

"The blasted—were-wolves." Heaving a deep breath, Roy finally managed to stand straight. "Sire—they've got Isabelle. I'm so sorry. I never saw her leave. But when I went to check, her brother said she'd gone. Spence was gone too—found him a few streets down, unconscious. He said they took her."

Garrett swore again. A couple of women passing by gave him startled looks. "How long ago?"

"I'm not sure how long Spence was out, but he said it wasn't dark yet—the sun was still up. Maybe fifteen, twenty minutes?"

"Then we're going after them," Garrett said grimly. "Spencer can stay here. Let's go."

It was full dark by the time they set out. Garrett stopped for a quick check on Spencer, while Gemma and Falcon commandeered a cluster of horses from a group riding into town, using Garrett's rank to persuade them.

They galloped out of the village, the horses' hooves clattering over the cobblestoned streets and splashing through puddles of melting snow. Once they left all the houses behind, they slowed to a walk, getting their bearings. Even once the sun had set, the town had been bright with gear-bulb lamps lining the streets and candlelight emanating through the windows of every house. But out here—not thirty paces from the village—the night was black and cold, the darkness dense. An owl hooted from the depths of the forest, its eerie call piercing the stillness.

"Spencer said they headed west. This way." Roy turned his horse from one side to the other. "Gemma?"

Gemma dismounted, her boots crunching into the ground. It hadn't snowed for the past couple of days, so the thin layer that covered the earth was packed, hard, and icy—and disturbed by many different tracks. Gemma examined several sets, most of which she deemed too old. She found a fresh set but of only one person—and then, finally, a second fresh set.

"These tracks weren't made an hour ago." She tilted her head. "Three people, all in thick-soled boots. One of them's walking quite heavily."

"Spence said Isabelle was unconscious." Falcon nodded. "They're carrying her."

Gemma got back on her horse, and they set off at a brisk walk, following the tracks. Gemma remained in the lead, Garrett close behind with a gear-bulb lantern raised high. The trees around Spalding were mostly ash and oak, tall but barren at this time of year. Out here, north and west of the village, the dormant trees gave way to clusters of evergreens, spruce and fir alike. The thick foliage shut out the light of the waning moon, so their handful of lanterns were all they had to light the way.

As the forest grew even more tangled and dark, Garrett's grip on his horse's reigns tightened. They had to come up on them soon, he wagered. They had to catch up to them, they just had to...

Suddenly, a dark figure stepped out from behind a fir tree, ten paces ahead. One of the horses let out a high-pitched whinny, stamping the ground as its breath misted the air. Garrett nudged his horse forward to make out the dark silhouette.

"That's far enough," the figure called.

Garrett came to a halt. Gemma glanced at him, swinging her rifle into her hands.

The figure before them let out a soft laugh. "I wouldn't do that if I were you."

It had to be one of the wolves. The white beam of Garrett's lantern fell over the creature. It was a woman—not Viveca, but around her age. This woman's frame was thinner than Viveca's, but she was tall, probably as tall as Garrett. Her brassy hair glinted in the light.

"Where is Isabelle?" Garrett demanded.

The wolf spread her arms. "Not here." She eyed Gemma and her rifle. "You can kill me. But you won't like the consequences."

"What consequences?"

"Kill me—kill any of us—and we'll kill the girl." The woman's voice was hard. "Stop following us. Come any further, and we'll kill her." She barked a laugh. "But don't worry. You know it's not her we want."

"As you can see," Garrett said evenly, "my brother isn't here."

"You'd best go fetch him, then," the wolf said. "We're willing to trade. The girl, alive and unharmed—for Gryphon. It'll take you, what, five days to get back to the castle? Maybe less on those horses. We'll send instructions where and when to meet." Her voice turned curt. "But if you follow us further, we *will* kill her."

Garrett stifled an oath. The wolf seemed to take his silence for assent and grinned, her teeth flashing in the darkness. Without another word, she turned away, slinking into the trees.

"Sire?" Gemma asked.

Garrett shook his head. "Leave her."

"What do we do now, Your Highness?" Roy asked.

Garrett's horse let out a nervous snort. He rubbed a hand over its neck to quiet it, thinking very hard. His soldiers, too, went silent, waiting for his answer. Then,

"We go back to the castle," he said, "and get Gryphon."

It took them three days to get back to the castle. Garrett had managed to broker a deal for the horses from their owners, shaving two days off the journey. In different terrain, it might have been more than that—but even horses couldn't travel all that fast through a wood so thick as the Black Forest.

By the time they arrived at the castle, a note with instructions had come from the were-wolves. They rode into the courtyard under a black sky, the moon a sliver so thin, it wasn't visible to the naked eye. In this darkness waited Gryphon, frantic and seething. While Garrett's soldiers coaxed their horses up the stone steps into the entrance hall—it was too windy to leave them outside with no shelter—Garrett rubbed a tired hand over his cold, weathered face, trying to keep his brother from storming out of the castle.

"This is the only way to get her back." Gryphon paced across the flagstones, his shoulders rolling. He'd never looked more like a caged beast, Garrett thought. "We have to trade me for her."

Garrett breathed a sigh, rubbing his gloved hands together. "Don't be stupid. We're not doing that."

"What else can we do?"

"I should think that would be obvious." Garrett flexed his fingers, trying to get some warmth back into them. Using his most reasonable tone, he explained, "We *pretend* we're going to exchange you for her, right? But instead, we blitz them, grab Isabelle, and run."

Gryphon stopped pacing. "That's your plan?"

Garrett put on a wounded expression. "I'm quite experienced in these things, you know."

"Don't you think they'll expect something like that?"

"Doesn't mean it can't work."

"And how do you propose to fake the exchange?" Gryphon's tone was still scornful, but his frown was contemplative. "I suppose we could tie me up, make it look like you're handing me over—"

"Absolutely not." Garrett waved the scrap of paper with the wolves' instructions on it. "This location is a three-hour ride from here. Even if we leave at dusk, we wouldn't be back 'til after midnight."

"Plenty of time before dawn," Gryphon said stubbornly.

"Yes, *if* nothing goes wrong."

"Which is why I need to go!"

"Gryphon, the whole point is to get Isabelle back without risking you." Garrett shook his head. "You're not coming." He took up Gryphon's pacing, though his was a calmer, more measured stride. "We'll take a cart with us, make sure it's covered, to give the impression we've got you inside. But you'll stay here in the castle, safely tucked away. I'll even leave a couple of soldiers with you."

"No," Gryphon protested. "You should take them all."

"The instructions say only me and you. Granted, Viveca would probably be suspicious if I comply with that order to the letter. But best keep it a small party."

"But you'll have to make it look like I'm there," Gryphon argued. "Otherwise, they won't let you within sight of Isabelle. And don't forget, even when they're human, the wolves have supernatural senses. They can scent like real wolves."

"So we'll take some of your dirty laundry in the cart. Let me worry about the details." Garrett glanced up the stairs, eager for a hot meal and a night's sleep. "I'll work it out with my people. You sit tight here and *don't* leave the castle, not for anything."

"Since when did you start giving *me* orders?" Gryphon grumbled. "In my own castle."

"It may be your castle, but I'll be king one day."

"I thought you didn't want to be king," Gryphon countered. "'It's not all roses,' isn't that what you said?"

Garrett drew his gaze from the castle and looked at his brother, remembering that conversation with a stab of displeasure. Isabelle had seemed to think once Garrett learned the truth of Gryphon's exile, everything would be mended between them. And certainly it was a step in the right direction. But learning the truth had also stirred up a great deal of bitterness within Garrett because it was all so *stupid*. All this mess, so far as he was concerned, could have been avoided.

Gryphon had behaved rashly, perhaps, but he wasn't dangerous. He had not tried to kill Garrett; he hadn't even wanted to
harm him. But if only he *hadn't* been so rash, if only their father
had listened to him, if only Gryphon had trusted Garrett—

If any number of things had gone differently, Gryphon might
never have been exiled. And then he, Garrett, would not have to
be king.

He had never thought he resented it, becoming king. He had
been a little intimidated at first, but he'd since grown comfortable with the idea. Or at least, as comfortable as one ever was with
that kind of responsibility.

But there *were* things he'd lost in becoming crown prince.
Much of his freedom, many of his own choices. The freedom to
be whoever he liked, become whatever he liked.

The freedom to be *with* whoever he liked. Whoever he loved.

And that was the crux of the matter. It wasn't fair to blame
Gryphon for his own exile when it was their father who'd banished him. King Victor should have been more understanding
with Gryphon. Just like he should be more understanding about
Garrett's feelings for Briar.

Gryphon cleared his throat. "You never did say what is so
terrible about being king."

Garrett blinked. He searched his brother's face, wondering if
this was a taunt or the start of another argument. But though
Gryphon wore his usual sullen expression, he also looked expectant.

"Well." Garrett shifted from one foot to the other. "There's
this girl."

Gryphon made a face. "Would this be...what did Isabelle say?
The girl who's a half-dead rotting corpse?"

Garrett grinned. "That's the one."

"You are so weird," Gryphon muttered. "Really, are we related?"

"Anyway." Garrett scuffed the toe of his boot against an uneven flagstone. "Let's just say...Father has some reservations about her."

"What kind of reservations?"

"Does it matter? He likes her well enough, but before I left for this trip, he made it clear he doesn't think I should marry her." Garrett rolled his eyes. "Not that I'm thinking about that yet—but—"

"But when you're crown prince," Gryphon said, "you have to think about that."

"Yes. Exactly."

Gryphon was silent for a long moment. Then he said, "Tell Father to go to hell."

"Gryphon!" In spite of himself, Garrett laughed.

"Really," Gryphon said flatly. "Tell him that's from me too, while you're at it."

Garrett folded his arms over his chest. "I could talk to him, you know. About you. *For* you."

"And tell him what?"

"The truth, for one thing. What really happened."

"I told him the truth," Gryphon said, his tone dismissive. "He either didn't believe me, or he needed to blame me more than the truth mattered. So why would he care now?"

"Because I do," Garrett said quietly. "I care."

Gryphon met his gaze. For a long moment, he just looked at Garrett. Then he nodded. Not, Garrett thought, because he was accepting Garrett's offer to speak to the king. But because he accepted Garrett's admission. That he cared about Gryphon. And that mattered, Garrett thought. It mattered to Gryphon.

As did Isabelle. "Garrett," Gryphon said, his yellow eyes pleading. "Get her back. Whatever you have to do. You have to get her back."

"I will," said Garrett. "That's a promise."

26

HOSTAGE

I SABELLE WOKE SLOWLY. HER head felt stuffed full of wool. A cloying odor hovered nearby, making her want to retch. But—as she took in a shallow breath—she realized the odor was not really there. It was only a remnant, the memory of the scent so visceral, it tricked Isabelle's senses.

Groggy, she opened her eyes.

Her vision swam. All she could make out were hazy colors and vague impressions. She blinked hard, then blinked again. Slowly, her surroundings came into focus.

She was in a kind of...cave. Her eyes traveled over rocky, beige walls and a low ceiling. Close quarters. There was a light nearby, but when Isabelle tried to sit up to find its source, she found her body sluggish to respond, her arms stuck fast.

That was when she remembered.

Spalding. Ansel. *Adela.*

The witch had used magic to knock her out. She remembered traveling in something bumpy—a cart, perhaps? She remembered coming awake long enough to swallow some bread and cheese, nearly choking as it was shoved into her mouth. She remembered someone feeding her stew at one point. And she remembered that biting, burning, *nauseating* stench—Adela's stone bowl, used again and again to put her to sleep.

And now she was here in this...cave. Her wrists bound before her.

How long had it been? Where had they brought her?

Every time they'd allowed her to wake—for brief periods only—she had been surrounded by the were-wolves. In human form, but still, they were more than a match for her, weakened by Adela's witchy herbs.

But now there was no one. She was alone.

Which meant...she had a chance to escape.

She would need some time. Not only were her hands bound, but her body felt heavy and tired, her mind still foggy. Which meant—if they came back—she couldn't let them know she was awake. She had to give herself time to recover.

Hopefully, she wouldn't need too much time.

She lay there for another fifteen minutes or so, fighting to stay awake. At one point, she heard voices, close but not close enough to make out any words. A shadow shifted, coming nearer—someone coming to check on her, perhaps. Isabelle kept her eyes closed, pretending to be asleep.

Then a voice said, "Isabelle? *Isabelle.*"

Isabelle twitched, barely keeping her eyes closed.

She recognized that voice.

"Isabelle. I know you're awake. Ferica put out those burning herbs over an hour ago." There was a soft scuffing sound, and then, the voice much closer. "I'm going to get you out of here, Isabelle, but we don't have much time."

Warily, Isabelle opened her eyes.

Klaus crouched beside her, shadows flickering over his pale face.

"Knew you were awake," he said, laconic as usual.

"Klaus." Isabelle's hushed voice came out scratchy. "What are you doing here?"

"I told you. I'm going to help you escape."

He shuffled back, giving her some room. After a moment, Isabelle twisted and shifted, trying to sit up. But it was difficult to move with her hands bound.

"Here." Klaus took a hunting knife from his belt. It glinted eerily in the darkness, and Isabelle tensed. But she needn't have worried. Klaus slipped the blade between her wrists, sawing at her knotted bindings. It took him a minute to cut through them, and then her hands were blessedly free. Isabelle let out a soft breath, flexing her sore, red wrists. They burned like a thousand bee stings.

That wasn't going to stop her though.

"Don't even think about it," Klaus said.

Isabelle kept her face blank as she levered herself upright, leaning back against the cave wall. She winced, her wrists giving a painful throb. "Think about what?"

"Trying to get past me."

A knot formed in the pit of Isabelle's stomach. "I thought you were helping me escape."

"I am." Klaus glanced aside, his face veiled in shadow. "But we have to time this right. Ferica will give us a sign when the coast is clear. Lotte is still prowling about somewhere. We have to wait for her to leave."

"Who is Ferica?"

"Viveca's youngest sister."

"And who is Lotte?"

"Viveca's cousin."

"And why," Isabelle asked, "is Viveca's sister helping us?"

Klaus rocked back, slinging his arms over his knees. That mysterious light danced over his face again. Peering past him, Isabelle discovered the source—two flaming torches set in wooden poles. They *were* in a cave, though it seemed man-made. Parts of the pitted wall had been smoothed out, symbols etched into these spaces. She and Klaus were ensconced in a small alcove. Beyond Klaus was a narrow corridor cut into the rock. The torches cast a warm glow over the alcove, but beyond the glare of the light was only darkness. Isabelle squinted into it.

Something moved in the shadows.

"Someone's over there," she murmured.

"It's Ferica. She's supposed to be keeping watch." Klaus clasped his hands together. "Viveca has two sisters. She *had* two brothers. Both of them were killed recently—the wolf you killed the night you fled the castle, and the wolf your prince friend killed."

"I think Gemma killed him, actually."

"Whatever. That wolf—his name was Alaric—don't you think it's odd he was so far from the rest of the pack? The prince said they killed him south of here, close to the edge of the forest."

Isabelle furrowed her brow. "I didn't even think about that."

"He and Viveca had quarreled, apparently. Viveca thought he wanted to challenge her for leadership. She told Ferica and the others he decided to go his own way, but Ferica thinks she forced him out. She thinks Viveca threatened to kill him if he didn't leave."

"And...she didn't like that? Ferica?"

"Alaric was her favorite brother, I guess. She's not happy he's dead. The way she sees it, it's Viveca's fault."

That's generous of her, Isabelle thought. Most people would have blamed the person who'd actually done the killing. Which, as Klaus had pointed out... "Well, I killed her other brother. And she's still willing to help me?"

"I don't think she cared much for *him.* He was Viveca's crony through-and-through." Klaus's tone was dismissive. "I didn't much like him either." The hunter glanced over his shoulder. "Ferica, you see, hasn't been happy with Viveca's way of things for a while. But she's too afraid to stand up to her."

"So she's helping me instead."

"That about sums it up."

Isabelle leaned back, the rocky wall digging betwixt her shoulder blades. "And you, Klaus?" she asked quietly. "Why are you helping me?"

Klaus's eyes darkened. "I can't believe you're asking me that."

"How did you even know the wolves were here? Wherever here is."

"Because I'm a good tracker. And because they've used these ruins before. We're not far from the castle, actually. Three or four leagues."

"And all that about Ferica and her brothers? You've gleaned all that from, what...being a good tracker?" The knot in Isabelle's stomach hadn't abated. She held Klaus's gaze, hardly daring to breathe.

But Klaus looked away, muttering under his breath. "Look, I'm not working with Viveca, all right? I never was."

"Then why did you leave the castle? When you were supposed to be guarding me?"

"Because I heard your prince and his people talking. Coming back into the castle. Viveca told them I was working for her."

A muscle worked in his jaw. "She told them it was my fault Gryphon escaped last year."

"And was it?"

Klaus's eyes went darker than ever. He rubbed his thumb over the back of his hand, the gesture betraying his nerves. But he held her gaze.

"Klaus." Isabelle took in a sharp breath. "It *was* your fault?"

Klaus closed his eyes. "Yes."

"But—you didn't let him out?"

"Of course not." Klaus's eyes flew open, and they were full of scorn. "I would never do that, all right? *Never.* But—" He blew out an explosive breath. "Look. Viveca and I used to meet all the time. Before I lived in the castle, before Gryphon was cursed." He cast her a wry look. "You asked if Viveca was *interested* in me. She was."

"And you were interested back," Isabelle deduced.

"Yes. Well."

"Did you...love her?"

"Don't ask stupid questions."

"Klaus. Did you?"

"It doesn't matter, all right?" Klaus twisted around, peering into the darkness past the narrow, twisting corridor. It was the cave opening, Isabelle realized. Now that she was more alert, she felt the icy air whistling past the torches. "It doesn't matter because we haven't been together for a long time. Not since—" His hands tightened into fists.

"Not since Gryphon escaped," Isabelle said, putting it together. "But what happened?"

Klaus looked grim. "It was a little over a year ago. Winter. Viveca told me she didn't want to meet in the woods anymore. She wanted someplace more comfortable. So I—I let her into the castle. Just the once." He ran a hand over his mouth. "It wasn't about getting to Gryphon—it wasn't *supposed* to be. I knew what Viveca wanted, but I'd always made it clear she would never get to him through me. And she understood. It was like a game to her. I protected Gryphon. She went after him." He kicked at a small, jagged rock with the heel of his boot. "But I overestimated her feelings for me."

Isabelle watched him closely. "So once she was in the castle, she overpowered you? Or slipped by you?"

"She *drugged* me," Klaus said bitterly. "I was out for hours. When I woke up, Viveca was gone. And so was Gryphon." He shook his head. "Thankfully, Viveca didn't get what she wanted from him. The beast was too much for her to handle."

"And you went after him. After Gryphon."

"Of course I did. It was my fault. I had to get him back, no matter what."

No matter what. Klaus's scars looked angry in the firelight, burning as red as the flames. He had done that, Isabelle thought. He'd gotten Gryphon back. And nearly died doing it. Ellery had told her, once, that the scars on Klaus's face weren't the only ones he bore from that attack. They were just the only ones most people could see.

Isabelle shifted her weight, stretching out her back. She looked past Klaus, gazing into the darkness. She realized that if she focused her eyes—looked long and hard enough—she could see much better. The formless shapes in the cavernous black became sharper, more distinct. Easier to identify—

"Isabelle?"

"Sorry." Isabelle squeezed her eyes shut. When she opened them again, Klaus was staring at her. He looked...spooked.

"What?" she asked.

337

"Your eyes. They were..." Klaus shook his head. "Never mind. Just the torchlight."

"Klaus," Isabelle said, "why didn't you just *tell* Garrett all this when you overheard him? I'm sure he would have understood."

"Maybe he would have," Klaus said darkly, "but Gryphon wouldn't."

"What? Of course he would!"

"Come on, Isabelle." Klaus gave her a knowing look. "Gryphon isn't big on second chances. Everything is black and white with him. I'm sure, just because I left, he decided he's done with me, right? And once he finds out I let Viveca into the castle..." He trailed off.

Isabelle faltered. There was nothing she could say. It was true. Though she was sure Gryphon had pushed Klaus away for the same reason he'd pushed Isabelle away—because he was hurting. Because, deep down, he believed he didn't deserve their love or friendship.

"Look, forget Gryphon." Klaus leaned towards her. "The question is, do *you* believe me, Isabelle? Do you trust me enough to let me help you?"

Isabelle glanced from him to the opening. "And you're sure we can trust this Ferica?"

"I'm sure we can trust her grief for her brother."

"Then yes." It was the truth. Though Isabelle had got the sense Klaus was hiding something, she'd found it hard to believe he was a traitor. And besides, if she was wrong, she had a few advantages. Advantages Klaus didn't know about.

A low whistle came from the front of the cave. Klaus jerked around.

"That's Ferica," he said, and indeed, Isabelle could see the girl's silhouette in the darkness. She saw her wave a pale hand for them to come. Exchanging a quick look with Klaus, Isabelle rose to her feet. Her legs were wobbly, but only from lack of use. She would steady out in a minute or two.

They joined Ferica at the front of the cave. Like Viveca, the girl was built like a warrior goddess, though she was much younger. Her hair was a darker red than Viveca's—or maybe it only looked that way in the dim light—and her features more delicate.

"Lotte's gone off to hunt," the girl said, "but you should go quickly."

"What will you tell them?" Klaus asked her.

Ferica shrugged. "That I fell asleep."

"Won't you get in trouble for that?" Isabelle whispered.

Another shrug. "I don't care. I'm always in trouble."

Isabelle felt an unexpected rush of pity for the girl. "Thank you."

"Just go before Lotte comes back."

They hurried away. Isabelle threw a glance at the cave before they left, and she realized it wasn't a cave but some kind of ruin, like Klaus had said. An old pagan temple, perhaps, most of it crumbled away. All that was left was an archway carved into the rock.

The ruins soon faded from sight, swallowed by the night's inky blackness. Klaus took Isabelle by the arm as they crept through the forest, the ground slick with mud and streaks of snow. "New moon tonight," he murmured, "but we can't afford a light. The others might be close by. The creek is just ahead though. So long as we keep it in sight, we'll know we're going the right way."

Unbeknownst to Klaus, Isabelle could see what lay ahead quite well when she focused her gaze like before. Looming gray shadows became yew and fir trees, glistening flashes became the mostly frozen creek. But she allowed Klaus to take the lead as they wound through the trees. "Where were the others anyway? The other wolves?"

"Ferica wasn't sure," Klaus murmured. "Apparently, Viveca was meeting Adela somewhere. The other three were preparing a place for the trade, I think."

"Trade?"

"You for Gryphon. That was their plan."

Isabelle's heart gave a worried tug. She hoped Gryphon wouldn't actually do something so stupid. "When is the trade meant to be?"

"I don't know. Ferica didn't know." Glancing over his shoulder, Klaus dropped his hands from Isabelle's arms. "I know it's dark, but we might want to run a bit, put some distance between—" He broke off.

"Klaus?" Isabelle's voice was little more than a puff of air in the darkness. "What is it?"

Klaus gave a single shake of his head, barely moving.

Isabelle closed her eyes and scented the air.

She did it without thinking. It felt...instinctual. And a little insane. But she'd been picking up scents like this for weeks now, she realized, detecting smells no human could. She hadn't even realized she was doing it. Now she scented something that had become familiar. Wolf. And human. Wolf-human.

The were-wolves.

But that was just Ferica, surely, she wasn't too far behind them yet...

The wind stirred, rustling through the forest, scattering dead leaves and fir needles over their boots.

No. Isabelle's eyes flew open.

It was more than one were-wolf.

Something moved in the darkness, darting from one tree to another. A shadow. "Klaus—" Isabelle said, but she was too late.

The wolf—woman—came out of nowhere. She burst from the trees, diving for Klaus with a snarl. Klaus went down, the two of them tumbling, rolling, wrestling. It was over in a second, before Isabelle could even think to move, and then Klaus was on his back, the woman pinning him to the sludgy ground. Her brassy hair fell forward, covering her face—but not the glint of the knife she held raised above him.

"Lotte," Klaus said, his voice strained. Had she been anyone else, Klaus probably could have hauled her off him, Isabelle thought, tall and lean as he was. But the were-wolf, Lotte, held him easily with her legs, one knee digging into his ribcage. She wiggled the knife in his face.

"Don't talk, Klaus," Lotte said. Her voice was low and rough. "I really can't stand you. It wouldn't take much for me to forget Viveca's edict that we don't harm you."

Isabelle balled her hands into fists. She could see Lotte well in the darkness, her enhanced vision making everything clear. A familiar, pulsating pain mounted in her temples. Migrating into her cheekbones. Sinking into her gums. Much quicker than before.

"Leave him alone," Isabelle said, her voice gravelly. "It's me you want."

Lotte laughed. She didn't even look at Isabelle. "Are you sure about that?"

"Yes," Isabelle breathed, and then she leapt for the wolf.

The beast was there. The beast was *there*, inside her, just waiting to be called. It emerged in a flash. Isabelle tackled Lotte. She dislodged her from Klaus, the strength of Lotte's wolf nothing compared to Isabelle's beast, and the two of them tumbled sideways. Lotte yelped, reaching back to swipe at Isabelle with her human hand, but Isabelle growled in her ear and batted her hand away, clawed fingernails slicing through Lotte's arm.

She tossed Lotte away from her. Spluttering, moaning, Lotte sprawled flat on her stomach. Isabelle remained in a crouch, lips drawn back from her fangs.

"Isabelle?" Klaus gaped at her, wild around the eyes.

Lotte, still facedown, made a grunting, choking sound. It was a minute before Isabelle realized she was laughing. Slowly, as though each movement pained her, she got one arm beneath her, and then the other. When she lifted her head, her brassy hair matted with mud, she was indeed laughing. A rumbling laugh that went on and on.

"Thought so," she rasped. "Viveca figured there had to be some reason Gryphon was keeping you around. Now we know."

Isabelle bared her teeth. "Good luck taking me back to her."

"Don't you get it?" Lotte shook her head and climbed to her feet. "We don't *need* you. Not anymore."

"You won't have anything to trade," Klaus said.

"There was never going to be a trade." Lotte looked at him as though he were deeply stupid. "We knew the prince would never go through with that. He came all the way out here for his brother, didn't he? He wasn't going to give him up. And we knew if we told him to come alone to the trade, he'd bring most of his people." She looked at Isabelle. "If you were so important, don't you think Viveca and Adela would be here right now? But they're not. Why do you think that is?"

Isabelle's protests that Garrett had not come to the Black Forest for Gryphon died in her throat. Her stomach churned. She looked at Klaus and found the same unease reflected in his eyes.

"The trade was scheduled to take place in, oh, another hour." Lotte's eyes glimmered like the point of her knife. "At the ruins. If you start back to the castle now, you might even meet the prince on your way. But you'll never get home in time. No matter how fast this—" She gestured at Isabelle "—can run."

She let out another laugh, this one short and sharp, like a bark. Then she turned and dashed into the forest, vanishing into the darkness.

Klaus scrambled to his feet, cursing. "Lotte—"

"Forget her, Klaus." Isabelle let the beast go, her teeth and fingernails shrinking back to human form. She was swimming with dread and fear. "We have to get back to the castle. *Now*."

27

CHECKMATE

G RYPHON DRUMMED HIS FINGERS against the smudged
table, his ire growing by the second. He shot a sidelong
glare at Garrett's two soldiers—the archer, Falcon, and the tracker, Gemma. They sat nearby at a large, mahogany table here in
the parlor, playing cards and talking quietly.

"You don't have to stay in the same room as me, you know,"
Gryphon griped. "No one's getting into the castle, and I'm not
going anywhere. You don't have to keep an eye on me."

They both glanced up. Gemma's face was inscrutable, but
Falcon grinned. He grinned a lot, that one, Gryphon thought
sourly.

"We're not keeping an eye on you." Falcon's face was the
picture of innocence. "We're just passing the time in here. It's
cozy."

"So if I were to get up and leave, you wouldn't follow me?"
Gryphon demanded.

"I wouldn't say we'd follow you, no," Gemma murmured,
turning back to her cards.

"We might decide we'd like a change of scenery though," Falcon admitted. "Get out of the room, stretch our legs a bit."

Gryphon snorted in disgust. "What is it about Garrett," he muttered, "that inspires such loyalty?"

"Well, he's the only noble I've met who'll take on women soldiers," Gemma said.

"I like his smile," Falcon mused.

Gryphon rolled his eyes. He rubbed at a deep gouge in the table. This was not *his* table, the one he usually occupied in the back corner. It was stupid, but he couldn't bring himself to sit there tonight—not without Isabelle. Instead, he sat much closer to the doorway, trying not to listen to the seconds tick by on the clock across the room.

He slouched in his chair. He'd tried to sketch, but he couldn't focus. It was half past seven. Garrett and the others would be well on their way to the meeting point by now, and Isabelle...hopefully Isabelle would be waiting for them, unharmed.

Gryphon felt sick at the thought of her. He hadn't said anything when she'd told him she was leaving, so...the last thing he'd said to her was that he didn't want her in his life. Well. He hadn't *exactly* said that, but it had been implied.

Now he just wanted her back. More than anything.

"I remember you, you know."

Gryphon looked up. Falcon pushed away from his table, wheeling around in his chair to face Gryphon. The opposite seat at his table was now empty.

Gryphon blinked. "Where did Gemma go?"

"Just to look around. Make a quick sweep of the entry points."

"For the Gift's sake!" Gryphon exclaimed. "No one is getting in this castle! We don't need to send out scouts. And what do you mean, you remember me?"

"From Glen Castle," Falcon said. "I was a new recruit in your father's army before you were exiled. I remember you came down to the practice yard one day. You didn't look too happy to be there, but. You tried a new crossbow and shot a target at a hundred paces. I was really impressed."

"I...remember that," Gryphon said. It was stupid, but it hadn't even occurred to him these soldiers were from Glen Castle—it hadn't occurred to him they might know him. "It wasn't so impressive. The whole point of that new design was that anyone could shoot it. I was never much for weapons practice. One of the many things my father found to complain about me," he added.

"Tell me about it, mate." Falcon leaned back in his chair, folding his arms over his chest. His cavalier pose reminded Gryphon of Garrett, but for some reason, he didn't find it so grating from Falcon. Maybe because he *wasn't* Garrett. "My father always wanted me in the king's army, so he didn't approve of my interest in the bow. He told me the king wanted snipers and gunmen, not archers. But I loved the bow." Falcon smiled, an appreciative gleam in his eye. "I told him I'd never join the royal army if the king wouldn't let me be a bowman."

"But he did," Gryphon said. "Let you, I mean."

"He did that."

That's more than he ever allowed me, Gryphon thought. He'd half-opened his mouth to voice this thought when the castle...*shook.*

Gryphon whipped his head around, wondering if he'd just imagined that. But then the castle gave another sharp tremor, the legs of the table stuttering over the paneled floor.

Gryphon looked at Falcon. The archer's face mirrored his alarm.

The castle gave another trembling shudder, and then a crunching, crackling *crash* exploded into the air.

Gryphon and Falcon leapt to their feet. "What the hell was that?" Falcon snatched up his bow.

"Nothing good." Gryphon licked his lips. That noise had been terrible. The closest he had ever come to hearing something like that was the time he saw lightning strike an old deadfall. The tree had shattered from the inside out.

Shattering wood, Gryphon thought, and then it came to him. *The front doors—*

The parlor door burst open.

This door did not splinter apart or shatter. It flew open with a great rush of wind, like a cyclone barreling through the castle. The gust hit Gryphon head-on, and he staggered back, losing his footing. Around him, the force of the wind sent books and lamps tumbling to the floor, glass shattering, pages ripping free of their spines. Gryphon realized, with a flicker of panic, that this could not be natural, and when he managed to lift his head, he saw he was right.

A woman bore down on them, coming into the room, her steps slow and measured. Gryphon recognized her—rosy cheeks and brown hair, the ends curling around her shoulders. But her eyes were usually dark, and now...

They were completely white from eyelid to eyelid.

The mark of a witch drawing on raw magic. A *great* deal of magic.

"Adela," Gryphon snarled. Viveca's witch.

Adela said nothing. With her eyes whited out, it was impossible to tell if she was looking at him. But she obviously knew he was there. She held one arm outstretched, her hand grasping towards him like a claw.

Gryphon's body grew rigid. The wind began to die, but the more it faded, the less he could move. He felt as though he was stuck in a bog, sinking, suffocating, losing control. His bones felt like lead; his legs wouldn't support his weight. He flung out an arm and clutched at the table, trying to stay on his feet.

Then Viveca was there. She stood in the doorway, her long, flaming hair streaming behind her, vestiges of the dying wind blowing it back. Though physically she looked the same, there was something about her—a terrible strength she hadn't had before. She loomed, seeming to fill the doorway.

"Hello, Gryphon," she said with a smirk. "It's been a while."

Gryphon struggled against Adela's magic. Falcon was on the floor beside him, trying to climb to his feet; that initial burst of wind had knocked him over his chair.

"It was very considerate of your brother," Viveca said, "to leave you alone for us."

"He's not alone," Falcon grunted.

Gryphon heard the *click* of the cocked gun before he saw Gemma. The tracker swung around the corner of the doorframe, her rifle leveled at Viveca. But Viveca heard it too; she spun around and smiled down the barrel of the gun.

"I never did like these things," she said, and before Gemma could let off a shot, Viveca grabbed the iron barrel and bent it back with a *squeal*.

Gryphon gaped, aghast. Viveca shouldn't have had that much strength in human form. But if Adela had worked some magic to enhance her—

Gemma's eyes went wide. Viveca snatched the rifle from the tracker, tossing it aside. In the next second, she had her long fingers wrapped around Gemma's neck, hoisting her into the air like a rag doll.

348

"No—" Gryphon fought against Adela's hold. "Don't—"

Viveca ignored him. She threw Gemma from her with a contemptuous flick of her wrist. Gemma flew halfway across the parlor before she tumbled to the floor, rolled back head over heels, and smashed into the wall, her head hitting the stone with a sickening *crack*. She lay in a crumpled heap on the floor and did not move.

Falcon was on his feet in a flash. He snatched an arrow from his quiver, putting it to the bow and drawing it back faster than Gryphon thought possible. The archer let off his shot, the arrow speeding towards Viveca.

But Viveca was faster. She whipped her hand up and caught the arrow deftly, inches from her chest. It wasn't possible, it *wasn't possible* that she could be that fast, and yet she was.

Falcon lowered his bow, stunned. Viveca snapped the arrow with one hand, baring her teeth. "You might have noticed," she said, "I didn't come alone either." She tipped her head towards the witch beside her. "And she packs quite a punch."

Then she moved. Faster than Gryphon's eyes could track. She was a blur of color, zipping out of sight.

Falcon let out a guttural, *tearing* sound. Gryphon turned his head to look. Viveca stood behind the archer—the cheerful, grinning archer, who grinned no longer. Falcon stood frozen, his face shattered, the tip of a long hunting knife peeking through his middle.

"*No!*" Gryphon howled. "Falcon—"

Falcon's glassy eyes found Gryphon's face. A torrent of grief hit Gryphon like a hammer, fracturing him from the inside out. He held Falcon's gaze, unwilling to look away. As though he could keep Falcon alive through sheer force of will.

But with savage pleasure, Viveca jerked the blade up. It ripped through Falcon's chest. As Viveca pulled the knife free, Falcon fell to his knees. He swayed upright until Viveca kicked him over with the tip of her boot.

Falcon slumped and fell forward onto the floor.

He was gone.

"No," Gryphon croaked. "No, *no*—"

"*Yes*," Viveca said, her voice filled with vicious triumph. "You should never have sent to your brother for help, Gryphon. You should never have let him threaten us. You know I don't like to be threatened."

Gryphon couldn't speak. The swirling storm of grief inside him was too much for words. Then Adela advanced, intoning her spell, her hand stretched towards him like he was a dog being brought to heel. As he slumped to his knees, a wave of darkness swept over him, and the storm broke apart as he sank into unconsciousness.

28

BEATEN

ISABELLE RUBBED HER EYES with the heels of her palms until her skin felt raw. She sat in the wrecked parlor in the castle, the remnants of Viveca's incursion scattered around. Splintered wood and broken porcelain littered the floor. Chairs had been overturned. Most of Isabelle's books lay strewn about, flung open, ripped down the spines, missing pages.

Klaus and Isabelle had indeed met Garrett on the way back to the castle. They might have missed him by half a mile had it not been for Isabelle's supernatural senses. As soon as they found him and his soldiers, they'd all made for the castle as quickly as they could.

But they were still too late—hours too late. Nothing had seemed amiss when they'd crossed the long bridge over the gully. The castle was immersed in darkness without any moonlight in the sky, but two flaming braziers were lit atop the ramparts. The silver portcullis was down, the stout gate behind it shut tight. Ellery, who was crouched behind the walls, raised the portcullis to let them in.

Then she told them what happened.

"Stefan said she *jumped*," Ellery said. "Viveca. Straight over the wall—cleared the silver. Then she opened the gate to let the witch in. They knocked Stefan out."

Inside the castle was even worse. They'd found Gemma in the parlor, crouched on the floor beside Falcon's lifeless body. Tilda, the cook, had whispered to Garrett that Gemma wouldn't let them move him, nor would she leave his side. But Garrett spoke a few quiet words to Gemma, and she climbed to her feet, wiped her eyes, and left the room. She'd only just returned a few minutes ago in clean clothes, all the blood scrubbed from her hands. Now she stood huddled against the wall, arms folded over her chest.

They gathered in silence around the fireplace. It wasn't lit; there were only cold ashes, giving the room a stale, smoky air. Spencer leaned over the back of a tall armchair, his eyes closed, but Roy stared dully into the barren fireplace. Isabelle knew he'd been good friends with Falcon.

Isabelle had collapsed onto a chaise. Her body felt bone-less with exhaustion, but inside, she was a mechanism of gears wound so tight, she thought she would break. Everything in her was screaming to get up off this chaise, leave the castle, and *run* until she found Gryphon. As though the beast inside her could track him by instinct alone. But that was foolishness; even with her honed senses, she knew she would need help to find him. And she would certainly need help to get him back from the entire wolf pack. So she sat here in this room, arms wrapped around herself, head resting on one knee. And she waited.

Everyone looked up as Garrett and Klaus appeared. They had gone to remove Falcon's body. Klaus looked grim and tired. Garrett's face was pale, but there was a light in his eyes Isabelle had never seen before, and it sent a chill down her spine.

"I'm sorry." It was Gemma who spoke. "I'm sorry, Your Highness—"

"You don't have anything to be sorry about, Gemma," Garrett said.

"I froze when she looked at me." Gemma's voice was a croak. "It was only for a second, but if I'd taken the shot—"

"It wasn't your fault, Gemma. And I won't hear any apologies, all right? There is no one to blame except Viveca, and believe me," he added bleakly, "I intend to blame her very much."

They lapsed into silence. No one seemed to know what to do or say. Isabelle folded her hands in her lap, squeezing them so tightly, they began to ache. Then—

"What do we do?" Isabelle asked, looking to Garrett.

Garrett's voice held a note of uncanny calm. "We get him back, of course."

"Sorry," said Isabelle. "I thought that was assumed. What I meant was, how? You're the one who always has a plan, Garrett."

"I know." Garrett rubbed the bridge of his nose. "I'm working on it."

"We don't even know where they are," Roy said, turning from the fireplace. His voice was gruffer than usual. "But surely they'll need some place to hold him? Once he turns, they'll have a time containing him."

"Maybe, maybe not." Klaus shifted his weight from one foot to the other. His dark eyes were distant. "I think I know what they plan to do."

Isabelle straightened. "What? You didn't say—"

"I know. I thought about it on our way back." Klaus surveyed the lot of them. "Ferica told me once there was a spell Adela wanted to try. But Adela said she'd never gather enough power to do it."

"She had a lot of power tonight," Gemma mumbled.

Klaus tipped a nod at her. "Exactly. This spell—it flips their curse. It's a new moon tonight. If Adela can cast this spell, they can take wolf form tonight. Until dawn."

"But why would they do that?" Spencer asked. "Just to control Gryphon and ward us away?"

"No." Isabelle met Klaus's gaze. "Viveca doesn't only want Gryphon's bite for her and her pack. She wants to create a kingdom of people like Gryphon. Or rather..." She cleared her throat. "People like me. A kingdom of were-beasts, I suppose. And since it *will* be hard to contain him, then her best chance is tonight—tomorrow. When the sun rises."

Another silence fell as they all contemplated this new horror.

Then Spencer said, "Well, I vote no to that. No to a kingdom of beasts."

"So she'll want him somewhere he can bite a lot of people," Garrett deduced. "A village? People live pretty spread out here in the Black Forest. The villages are the only places where people congregate. So where is the nearest village?"

Klaus considered. "The only one close enough to reach by dawn is ten miles south of here. It's small though. Doesn't even have a name."

Isabelle remembered it. It was the last village she'd stayed at before coming to the castle. She exchanged a dubious look with Garrett. "I know," he said, frowning. "It seems an awful lot of trouble for one pinprick of a village."

"There's no place else they could reach by dawn," Klaus insisted.

"Then that village is where we'll go," Garrett decided. "We need to leave now if we want to get there in time. Everyone meet in the entrance hall in twenty minutes."

"Question," said Klaus.

"What?"

Klaus rocked back on his heels. The look in his eyes was mulish. "Let's say we get there in time," he said, "what then?"

"Take Gryphon back, of course," Garrett said.

"What if we can't?"

"Can't?"

Klaus sighed. He dropped his arms to his sides and turned to face Garrett. "What if we get there, but we fail to get him back," he said frankly. "We should be prepared—if we can't stop them from unleashing Gryphon, if we can't get past them—you do have a sniper, don't you—"

"We aren't killing Gryphon," Isabelle cut in.

"Even if it's the only way to stop them?" Klaus asked. "If it's the only way to prevent a whole village from being turned into killer beasts?"

Garrett turned to Klaus. The two of them were matched for height, standing face to face. That dreadful light had returned to Garrett's eyes. "*No one* is killing my brother," he said, "and *I* will kill the man or woman who tries." He sent a sharp glance over the group. "Understood?"

He swept from the room without waiting for an answer.

———◆○◆———

They set out from the castle in less than half an hour, on foot. Some members of their party were not comfortable riding, and besides, traveling the woods at night on horseback would be nearly as slow as walking.

As they crossed the bridge to the clearing, a thick white fog leavened up from the gorge below, engulfing them. They were a small party, though not as small as Isabelle had expected. To her surprise, Stefan and Ellery had asked if they could come. Once he was sure they understood the danger, Garrett consented. Isabelle watched the two servants now as they emerged onto the clearing. She wished Gryphon could see them; she wished he could witness their willingness to fight for him. In spite of everything they'd been through because of his curse.

Their travel was quicker than the last time Isabelle attempted this trip—in a blizzard—but not much quicker. The woods were dense and difficult to navigate in the dark. Isabelle had the advantage now she'd learned to use her beast's eyes, so she took the lead with Garrett, pointing out knotted roots and small boulders close to the ground. The others followed, each carrying their own lantern.

It was bitterly cold. The wind sluiced through the forest, cutting through their coats. The spring equinox, Isabelle thought, was mere weeks away, but it didn't feel like it this far north. By the time they slowed to a halt, nearing their destination, Isabelle was stiff with cold and fatigue. Sweat dampened her clothes, and she shook and shivered, feeling clammy.

"Stones," Spencer swore. "My fingers are frozen solid."

"Where's the village?" Roy asked in a low voice. "I can't see anything."

"It's just below that rise," said Klaus. He and Garrett exchanged a glance. "Probably a good idea to scout it first. And the surrounding woods. We've made good time—still over an hour until dawn." Indeed, the sky was still dark, the forest grown misty. A sage gray haze hung over them all, the greenish gloom punctuated by their lanterns.

Before Garrett could assign scouts, there was a loud *snap* in the woods behind them. Everyone whipped around, reaching for weapons.

"Someone's there," Gemma said quietly.

"Wait," Isabelle whispered. She'd caught a familiar scent—a very familiar scent. "I know who it is." She raised her voice and called, "Ansel?"

The response was immediate. "Isabelle? Oh, thank the stars."

Ansel materialized from the fog, stumbling through the trees. He smelled of cold and woodsmoke and just the faintest trace of eucalyptus, lingering from the doctor's house. As he neared them, he raised his arms in a gesture of peace, for Gemma hadn't lowered her rifle. "I can't believe I found you," he said, breathless. "I thought I'd have to go all the way to the castle."

"It's all right, Gemma," Garrett told the tracker, who lowered her gun. "You came looking for us, Ansel? Why?"

"Because I've done something stupid." Ansel leaned over, hands on his knees, sucking in air.

"What else is new?" Klaus drawled.

Privately, Isabelle was glad he'd said it so she didn't have to. "What happened, Ansel?"

"It's about him—Gryphon." Ansel straightened. "A few days ago—just after you left, Belle—two people came to Spalding. A woman and a young man. They said they had Gryphon. They'd cooked up this mad story about him turning into a beast—"

Klaus coughed. "Not so mad."

Ansel didn't seem to hear him. "They said they would turn him over to the villagers."

"But Spalding is fifty miles from here—" Garrett protested.

"They're not taking him to Spalding." Ansel shook his head. "The villagers from Spalding have come here. Along with people from other towns." He indicated the village that lay below them. "They're taking him to an old stone circle. About a mile east of here."

"To do what?" Garrett demanded.

Ansel hesitated. "They're going to burn him. They mean to burn him at the stake."

Garrett swore loudly.

With much more calm than she felt, Isabelle asked, "When, Ansel?"

Ansel met her gaze in the darkness. "At dawn."

"This is Viveca," Klaus said immediately.

"Of course it is." Garrett put his hands behind his head and began to pace. "She's pretending to turn him over to the villagers. They'll truss him up to a bloody pyre, but before they can light it ..."

"He'll turn," Klaus said. "And bite everyone there."

Garrett swore again.

"Er—he's going to bite people?" Ansel sounded confused. "He *bites* people?"

"Ansel," Isabelle said, "do you know where this place is? The stone circle?"

"I do," said Klaus. "We need to get going. Now."

No one argued. They headed out, Klaus in the lead this time, with Isabelle. Isabelle could tell Ansel wanted to talk to her alone, but she couldn't focus on him right now. She was grateful he'd brought them this information, but then, he was also the one who'd riled up the villagers in the first place. And she hadn't forgotten their last encounter. What he'd told her about why he pushed her away.

She still wasn't sure how she felt about it.

Dawn was close—much too close, Isabelle thought—when they neared the stone circle. She watched the lightening sky as Klaus brought them to a hilltop covered in a copse of yew trees. As the others set aside their packs and checked their weaponry, Isabelle, Garrett, Klaus, and Ansel crested the hill, staying low to the ground.

Isabelle caught her breath as the stone circle came into view below them. A ring of flaming braziers surrounded the circle, giving light to the scene. Even at this distance, Isabelle could smell the braziers' smoldering embers, the charred scent carried by the wind. In the center of the ring was Gryphon, tied to a stout wooden beam amidst a pyre. Isabelle recognized his dark hair and brawny build, but she couldn't make out his expression. She couldn't even tell if he was conscious.

A mob of people surrounded him. The wind seemed to carry their frenzied energy as it did the embers, the low hum of their voices reaching Isabelle's ears. She swallowed her anger, glancing at the others. "Anyone see the were-wolves? All I can smell is all those people down there."

"They'll be surrounding the mob, I reckon—but sticking to the shadows. They'll try to stay out of sight of the crowd." Klaus rose to his knees, pulling out a pair of bronze binoculars. "But maybe I'll get lucky..."

"Amateur," Garrett teased. He pulled something from his coat pocket—a small, metalwork dragonfly built from old nails, springs, and bits of wire. Garrett wound up a tiny lever between its wings and then, to Isabelle's astonishment, it flew from his hand, vanishing into the darkness.

Klaus looked dumbfounded, slumping back on his heels. "What the hell was that?"

"A clockwork creature," Isabelle answered. "One of Briar's? But how can it tell us if the were-wolves are around?"

"It captures images," Garrett said. "Like a camera."

"A creature that small? But that's really advanced science!"

Garrett was nonchalant. "Briar's a genius." He turned back to the stone circle below. "Anyway. What about the witch? I wonder where she'll be?"

"I imagine she'll be in the crowd."

"About this witch, Prince Garrett," Ansel said. He crouched on Garrett's right, his dark eyes narrowed as he studied the scene below. Garrett, it seemed, had filled him in on the details on their way here. "Why don't you leave her to me? I think I'm best suited to handle her."

"What makes you say that?"

"I've made a bit of a...career, hunting witches." Ansel's voice was stony. "Since I left the queen's service. I've picked up a few tricks against them."

This was news to Isabelle, but Garrett only said, "Sure you're up to it?" He dipped his head towards Ansel's left wrist, which was bound in a thick bandage.

Ansel grimaced, waving the arm a bit to show its mobility. "I'm fine. The doctor wouldn't let me leave without this. But I'm up to it."

"You'll need to be careful," Garrett said. "It sounds like she's more powerful than usual."

Ansel's eyes lit with interest. "Then she's probably drawing on an outside source," he murmured. "Don't worry. I've got it handled."

"All right. Isabelle needs to get to Gryphon in case he turns. She's the only one who's ever managed to control him," Garrett said. "The rest of us will draw the were-wolves out. All in all," he concluded, a sliver of anticipation in his voice, "it should be a nice little rout to close out the winter."

Isabelle stared at him in the darkness. "Oh, stars," she groaned. "Your brother is about to be burned at the stake. Can't you act like a normal person for five minutes?"

"Isabelle, this entire trip has gone absolutely sideways," Garrett said in a crisp voice. "I set out on a rousing hunting trip, only to find the beast I was hunting was my brother. I'll be cursed if I don't get to shoot *something* before I go back home."

29

RAMPAGE

I SABELLE SHIFTED, MAKING A face as she adjusted her coat
over her skirt. Yanking her hair free of its pins, she began
braiding it back, trying to catch the evasive curls around her face.

"That's the third time you've messed with your hair in the last
five minutes," Ansel noted.

"Shut up, Ansel," Isabelle said scathingly.

The others had headed out a few minutes ago, sneaking down
the rugged hill towards the stone circle while Ansel and Isabelle
hung back, perched at the top of the rise. This close to dawn,
the air was at its coldest and dampest. There was very little wind,
but even so, the cold was cutting. Isabelle tucked her gloves into
her pocket, flexing her fingers to keep them warm. She and Ansel
would be setting out any minute, and she didn't want anything
hindering her should she need her hands.

So far, Isabelle hadn't heard any signs that Garrett and his
people had met the were-wolves. Briar's dragonfly had returned
with proof that at least *some* wolves were below, surrounding the
mob at a distance, out of the light of the braziers. So Ansel and

Isabelle crouched in tense silence, waiting for the all-clear. Or at least, Isabelle wished it was silent.

"How do we know when to head out?" Ansel asked.

"Ellery and Stefan will let us know." She hoped the servants were all right down there. They were neither of them fighters. They *were* clever though, and blessed with deft hands. The two of them had rigged something up in the dense boughs of the yew trees before they left, though Isabelle hadn't seen what.

Ansel was quiet for a moment—but unfortunately, only for a moment. "Isabelle?"

"What?"

"I...just wanted to say I was sorry."

"For?"

"For everything." Ansel ran his hands through his ruffled curls. He scowled as he picked at a particularly long strand, but his eyes were uncertain. "I don't know if you've noticed. But I have this tendency to find trouble."

Isabelle kept her gaze fixed on the blazing braziers below until her unblinking eyes began to sting. "I don't understand why you didn't just tell me. About the queen. That she'd threatened me, threatened *you*."

"I should have. I know. I wish—"

"Don't say wish," Isabelle interrupted.

"What?"

"Just...find another way to say it," she said. "Trust me."

"All right." Ansel sounded confused, but went on, "I should've found a different way to help you. Instead of pushing you away, being so cruel—I shouldn't have done that."

"Well...thank you for that." Isabelle took a deep breath. "But, Ansel—you didn't need to find another way to help me. You should have let *me* help you."

Ansel's expression was conflicted in the low light of their dimmed lantern. He opened his mouth to reply, but before he could, a low, vicious growl broke through the darkness, shockingly close. Isabelle felt her hair stand on end.

"What in the hell was that?" Ansel shot up straight.

Too late, Isabelle caught that wolf-human scent. She clutched Ansel's arm. "It's—"

A shining blond head appeared below, racing up the hill, coming straight for them. It was Ellery, Stefan a step behind her. Ellery looked up, her eyes widening as she spotted them. "Oh, damn!" she cried. "Move, move, *move!*"

Isabelle didn't understand until Ellery and Stefan raced past her. Then she caught a flash of yellow eyes in the darkness, and a second later, a giant wolf appeared, bounding towards them—

Ansel tackled her. They flattened to the ground as the wolf soared over the hilltop. It flew right past Ansel and Isabelle, fixated on its prey—Stefan and Ellery. Trembling and breathless, Isabelle pushed herself onto hands and knees, looking for the servants. Stefan had disappeared, but Ellery stood a short distance away, facing the wolf.

"Ellery—!" Isabelle scrambled to her feet.

"Stefan, *now!*" Ellery shouted. As Isabelle watched, something large and glinting flew from the treetops, crashing over the wolf. It was like a blanket—a blanket threaded with silver. As the wolf fell beneath its weight, whining in pain, Stefan appeared from behind a tree, panting.

"Silver-linked net," he said to Isabelle. "We'd been working on it for a while back at the castle."

Isabelle watched the wolf squirm within the net, its shrouded form undulating like a bag of cats. "Will it hold it?"

"It should." Ellery wiped a hand across her forehead. "It won't kill her, but she's not going anywhere. You two should head down there—they're routing out the rest of the wolves now."

The hill sloped steeply, but there were plenty of rocky ledges to grip onto, so Ansel and Isabelle scurried down at a near-run. Isabelle stumbled over the loose, pebbly ground at the bottom, barely catching herself before she pitched forward. Ansel was close behind. The edge of the mob was a good fifty paces ahead. Even still, the hum of their mingled voices swelled, their fervor radiating clear across the clearing. Isabelle and Ansel jogged towards them, their steps light and wary.

About twenty paces from the crowd, a huge shape hurtled across their path, snapping and snarling. Isabelle skidded to a halt, ready to draw on her beast as she faced down the colossal wolf. But then a shot *cracked* the air, and the wolf shuddered and whined, collapsing to the ground.

Garrett appeared in the darkness as he ran towards them, pistol in hand. "You two go ahead!" he called. "I'll follow!"

The sky was still a deep violet as they dove into the crowd. A few people at the back had looked around at Garrett's shot, but amazingly, most seemed unaware of the disturbance. There was too much noise, the crowd growing thicker and louder as they raised their fists and shouted. Isabelle turned her head, overwhelmed by the smell of so many bodies, warm and rank. As she and Ansel melted into the crowd, she glimpsed a wooden platform near the pyre. A balding man stood upon it. He was shouting and waving a burning torch, whipping the crowd into a frenzy. Isabelle also caught a fleeting glance of Gryphon, but he looked like he was unconscious, his head sagging against his chest.

Ansel peered at the lightening sky. "All right," he murmured. "You get to the pyre, and—"

"Ansel!" Isabelle grabbed her brother by the arm. "The witch, Adela—*there*, she's there!" The witch was somewhat conspicuous in the crowd, her midnight blue cloak concealing half of her face.

"I see her," said Ansel. As they watched, Adela turned, weaving her way through the throngs of people. "I'm on it. Be careful," he added, grasping Isabelle's hand. "We've still got time—try and wait for Garrett before you go for Gryphon, all right? Someone will need to distract the crowd, they're not just going to let you cut him down—"

"I know, Ansel, just go." Isabelle pushed him away.

Her brother sidestepped a gaggle of women and disappeared into the crowd. Isabelle looked around, still hovering near the back of the mob. There were a lot of people between her and the pyre. The mood was growing crazed, the energy high and frenetic. Isabelle was jostled as the people around her shrieked and waved their arms. Maybe she *should* wait for Garrett; she judged there was another twenty minutes until sunrise—

Then something heavy knocked into her from behind. Isabelle's flailing arms smacked into the people around her as she sprawled to the ground. A cry stuck in her throat, her hip smarting, one bruised arm pinned beneath her.

The shouts nearest her turned to screams. For a moment, Isabelle couldn't move, her chest aching, her vision darkening. The heavy weight pinning her down shifted. Isabelle gasped a ragged breath; she felt like her ribcage was going to crack. Then a hot breath dampened her cheek, a menacing growl grazing her ear—

Isabelle jabbed back with an elbow, making contact with a soft, meaty flank. The growl sharpened, the weight shifting again, going slack this time. Isabelle managed to roll onto her back.

She found herself face to face with a were-wolf. This close, the wolf's scent filled Isabelle's senses, and she knew who it was: Lotte, the wolf who'd pursued her and Klaus last night.

Lotte loomed, saliva dripping from her canines. She pinned Isabelle with one burly forepaw, digging into her breastbone, crushing all the air out of her. If people were still screaming, Isabelle couldn't hear them; the noise had been drowned out by Lotte's deadly snarl. Even in wolf form, there was something taunting about that snarl. *Who's stronger now?* she seemed to say.

Isabelle didn't know. It would be interesting to find out. But she didn't have time for that.

She called for the beast inside her, and the beast answered. Lotte growled as Isabelle's face morphed, fangs protruding from her mouth. But it wasn't the fangs she needed now.

Isabelle reached up with one clawed hand and tore straight into Lotte's exposed flank, her fist rupturing flesh and splintering bone.

A strained yelp escaped Lotte. Her yellow eyes bulged, her massive body trembling. Then she collapsed atop Isabelle and lay still. Dead.

Isabelle grunted. *Maybe not the best idea,* she thought, struggling to get the were-wolf off her.

"Isabelle!"

Isabelle recognized the voice with relief. She felt the weight of the wolf carcass lift as Gemma appeared above her. Together, they shoved Lotte's corpse away, and Isabelle rolled to her knees, panting. Her throbbing teeth and nails shrank back as she released the beast.

"You all right?" Gemma asked.

Isabelle nodded, though she was still gulping in air. "Ugh." She grimaced at her human hand, covered in dark, gunky blood. Shards of bone and chunks of sinew slipped between her fingers. "That was really disgusting!"

"Pretty much." Gemma helped her to her feet. Most of the villagers nearby had given them a wide berth, but a few inched towards them now, fearful, angry. Gemma shook her rifle at them with a murderous look, and they scurried away. "This is getting out of hand. We need to get to Gryphon before the crowd decides they're not going to wait for dawn."

Isabelle climbed to her feet, wiping her hand on her skirt. She was surprised to see that only a few stragglers had noticed her altercation with Lotte; most of the mob was fixated on the pyre. But then, they were still at the back of the crowd, just beyond the light of the braziers. Gemma was right; they needed to get closer. They needed to get to Gryphon.

They pushed through the throng. Some of those who *had* witnessed Lotte's attack ran from the stone circle, vanishing into the darkness, but others, heedless of danger, shoved closer to the pyre. Isabelle breathed shallow breaths, trying to close out the stench of so many people, trying to move through the tightening press of bodies. She caught another glimpse of Gryphon over the top of the crowd. She couldn't be sure, but he seemed to be stirring, lifting his head as the mob surged around him.

"*Move!*" Gemma snapped, knocking a hollering villager aside with the barrel of her gun. "We need to—*ooph!*" A man in front of them whipped around, his elbow catching Gemma in the face.

Isabelle grappled for her, but the tracker went down, and Isabelle lost sight of her as a mass of people swarmed in.

"Gemma!" Isabelle cried. "Gemma—"

Someone knocked into Isabelle, the jut of their shoulder slamming into her chest, and she stumbled back, tripping over several others. By the time she righted herself, fighting against the eddying tide of people, she realized she was close to the pyre—maybe ten paces away.

Shots rang out behind her. Isabelle looked around, but she couldn't tell if it was Garrett and his people, or the panicking mob. She caught sight of a group of men beside the pyre, shotguns and pistols in their hands. One of them was the man who'd been leading the crowd—a tall, balding man in furs and a black overcoat. He was still waving his torch in the air, dangerously close to the pyre. Isabelle's pulse spiked, fearful for Gryphon, and she shouldered her way forward, shoving and elbowing where she couldn't get through.

More shots rang out. Isabelle looked towards the armed men at the pyre. One man gestured wildly towards the crowd, speaking to the balding man. The balding man leaned towards him to listen, then straightened and nodded.

He lowered his torch to light the pyre. The tangle of piled wood caught quickly, flames leaping as they spread beneath Gryphon's feet.

"No!" Isabelle screamed. She pushed through the last of the mob, finally lurching free of the crowd. The heat of the growing fire enveloped her; she'd nearly tumbled into it. She looked up, billowing smoke stinging her eyes.

Gryphon was right above her. It was hard to see through the haze of smoke, but she thought he saw her. His eyes met hers. Isabelle stretched a hand towards him—

Then someone grabbed her by the arm, yanking her away. "Get back, girl!"

Isabelle staggered. A man spun her around to face him, but Isabelle wrenched in his grip, dealing him a backhanded blow. He cried out and released her.

"You have to stop this!" Isabelle screamed, facing the armed men. "This is madness! You're murdering an innocent person! You have to put it out!"

"That's no person!" One of the men sneered. "That's a monster!"

Isabelle wasn't going to argue with insane people. She looked left and right, spotting pails of water nearby. She lunged for one, lifting it with some effort. She could hear the men shouting at her, but Isabelle ignored them. Shoulders straining, the metal handle biting into her palm, she wheeled around, emptying the pail onto the pyre. Some of the wood sizzled and smoked, but it wasn't enough. She turned for another pail, but her hand had scarcely closed around it when a shot rang out, deafeningly loud.

Isabelle felt a heavy blow, like a hammer smashing into her. She dropped the pail, water sloshing everywhere. All at once, her body went numb, from the core of her chest to the tips of her toes.

Isabelle looked down. Her black coat was violently torn below the collar. Something wet spread across it, quickly staining the fabric. *The water from the pail*, she thought, but no, it wasn't water. It was thicker, warmer. Blood.

"You—shot me," Isabelle said dumbly. Or she tried to. But the pain was overwhelming, burning, *burning* like the flames engulfing the pyre. A wave of darkness swept over her, and she fell, slumping face-first onto the ground. Then she knew no more.

30

SURRENDER

G RYPHON HEARD THE *CRACK* of the shot over the thundering flames and screaming crowd. At first, he thought *he* must have been shot, the bullet meant for him. But after a confused moment, he realized he was all right—well, as all right as a person could be while tied to a stake, fighting for air and sweating buckets from the heat of the flames licking at his heels. He coughed and looked around through the thick fog of smoke, fighting to stay conscious. But his head rang, his eyes and nose burned. His throat felt full of ashes. The terrorizing heat drained what little strength he had left.

When he'd first realized what was happening, he'd been desperate to escape, to get away from these people before the sun rose and he transformed. But then they lit the pyre, and his worry turned to lasting long enough to change into the beast at all.

And then Isabelle was there. He saw her fight free of the crowd, lurching dangerously close to the burning pyre. For one, hopeful, terrifying moment, they locked eyes. But then she'd been pulled away. Gryphon lost sight of her. Smoke blistered his face. He squeezed his eyes shut, gasping for air.

Then the shot rang out. Gryphon managed to open his eyes.

He saw Isabelle. Stumbling, unsteady. And Gryphon saw the man standing opposite her, and he saw the pistol in his hand, pointed at Isabelle.

They hadn't shot him.

They'd shot *Isabelle*.

Gryphon tried to shout, but smoke clogged his throat. He watched, helpless, as she slumped to the ground. He pleaded silently for her to move, to get up, but she did not stir.

A storm of grief woke inside Gryphon. It was the same storm that had raged within him when Falcon died, but ten times stronger, overwhelmingly violent. Grief turned to fury. It spun inside him like a hurricane, flooding his veins, electrifying his bones. He lifted his head to the sky. It had turned a deep slate blue, but dawn was still several minutes away. The sun was nowhere to be seen.

Gryphon had never wanted to become the beast, but he did now. He reached for it, calling to that creature of pain and savagery. He reached and found it within him, clawing to get out.

He surrendered to the beast.

Something gave way. The beast burst free. The storm inside him reached a whirling crescendo, and as his body gave a great *shudder*, he felt his bones begin to break.

31

RETRIBUTION

G ARRETT HAD JUST REACHED the back of the mob when
someone lit the pyre. After a rout with one of the
were-wolves, he'd lost a pistol and been forced to stop and reload
the other—in the dark, no less. He'd finally run to join the
crowd, just in time to see the pyre light up like a solstice bonfire.

Garrett cursed. It wasn't dawn yet. The sky was still dark,
the blue-black expanse dotted with fading stars. The mob must
have panicked. Garrett ran, ducking and weaving through the
thinning crowd. Many people had broken away and run for the
woods, and those that were left surged forward, closer to the
pyre. There weren't many people left back here near the ring of
braziers.

He'd nearly reached the thickest part of the mob when his
breath froze in his chest. Literally. He couldn't breathe. Garrett
clutched his throat, but it was as though a stone had lodged in
his airway. Choking on nothing, he clawed at his neck, pressure
building in his lungs—

"You aren't going anywhere, Your Highness."

Garrett staggered around in a half-circle. A woman in a midnight blue cloak stood before him, next to a brazier. Her arm was stretched towards him, her hand clenched in a fist.

The witch. Adela.

Adela opened her hand, spreading her fingers wide. The stone in his throat turned to pins and needles. Sharp little points jabbed and scratched at him from the inside as a coppery, metallic taste coated the back of his tongue. Garrett coughed and fell to his knees, putting a hand to his mouth. It came away red with blood.

"Leave him alone, witch."

Garrett looked up to see Ansel duck out of the crowd. He grabbed Adela, spun her around, and punched her, hard, in the nose. Adela's arm fell to her side as she reeled back, and suddenly, the pins and needles were gone. Garrett sucked in a breath, sweet air filling his lungs. He breathed in again, his throat raw, and tried to still his quivering limbs.

Adela righted herself, stumbling away. She was closer to Garrett now than before, but all her attention was on Ansel. She looked furious. Her mouth was smeared with blood, her nose twisted and malformed. Broken, Garrett thought.

"You're going to regret that, little boy," she spat.

"I'm not a boy," Ansel said coolly. "Though now you mention it, I *did* kill one of your kind when I was little. My sister and I cooked her in her own oven."

"I'm going to cook *you*." Adela raised her hand. As Garrett watched, struggling to his feet, her hand burst into flame. "You can't fight me, you wretched cretin. Tonight I have the power of a thousand suns behind me. I have stores of magic you can't even imagine."

"Yes, I know. That's why I have this." Ansel held something up in his hand, pinched between thumb and forefinger. Garrett had to squint to see it. It was a tiny sphere of glittering black clay about the size of a ball bearing. Garrett glimpsed veins of something silvery in the clay—and something red. Adela's blood, smeared over the sphere.

Unlike Garrett, Adela seemed to know what this was. All the color drained from her face. "No!" She reared her flaming hand back.

But Ansel was quick. He leaned over and dropped the blood-stained sphere into the burning brazier.

The brazier emitted a tuft of spitting smoke. Sparks sputtered, giving off an acrid stench. Adela launched her flames at Ansel, but as they arced towards him, they guttered and died, burning out mid-air.

Adela sent one terrified look in Ansel's direction. Then she turned and ran, vanishing into the darkness beyond the braziers.

"What did you do?" Garrett wiped a hand over his bloody mouth.

"Turned her magic on her," Ansel said. "That was a ball of elarium—you know, the ore. She must have found another source of magic to tap into, something besides fairy blood. A direct connection to the land. It's always temporary—like a fire that burns hot and fast—but it granted her a lot of power. Burning the elarium and her blood together severs the connection. Not sure why, exactly." He looked sharply at the pyre. "Garrett, your brother—"

"I'll get him," Garrett said. "See if you can catch that witch!"

Ansel complied, running away from the crowd. Garrett took off in the opposite direction. The flames on the pyre had grown higher, leaping into the air. It was hard to see through the black, billowing smoke, but it looked like Gryphon was conscious and struggling to get free—or perhaps contorting in pain, if the flames had already reached him—

Then Gryphon burst into a hulking beast.

Garrett stopped in his tracks, struck dumb. It was like Gryphon's human body had exploded, exposing the beast within. When he'd seen Gryphon transform down in the dungeon, the change had been much slower, working through him bone by bone. It didn't seem right that he'd turned so quickly now. And not only that...

Garrett tilted his head back, looking up at the sky. It was still dark, no sign of the sun on the horizon.

But somehow, Gryphon had become the beast.

Garrett watched with wide eyes as the beast gave a violent twist of its body, snapping the stake at its back. His bindings fell free, bits of rope whipping through the air like writhing snakes. Then, with a thundering roar, Gryphon launched himself into the air. He leapt clear over the flames, landing on his hind legs in front of the pyre.

"Curse me," Garrett swore. His relief at seeing Gryphon free was short-lived. Letting out another roar, the beast began to advance on a group of armed men. Some of them ran, while others leveled their shaking guns in Gryphon's direction.

None of them got a shot off. Gryphon swiped at them with one massive paw. The guns—and most of the men—went flying.

Swearing under his breath, Garrett started forward—or he tried to. The violent mood of the mob had turned to panic, horrified screams filling the air. All the people turned to flee, and now they streamed past Garrett, their momentum pushing him in the wrong direction. Garrett dug his boots into the mud, trying to push back, but it was no use. He yanked his pistol from his holster, intending to shoot into the air and clear a path, but a flailing arm knocked his hand aside. The pistol fell from his grip, disappearing into the crowd.

"Curse it!" Garrett hollered. Up ahead, Gryphon was wreaking havoc. Garrett watched, his chest caving in dismay, as the beast tackled a man and pinned him to the ground. He couldn't see what Gryphon did next, but he heard the man's tearing screams.

The crowd finally thinned enough for Garrett to stumble free of them. He surveyed the scene of carnage before him. The armed men had all fallen or fled. Black streaks of blood stained the ground. Garrett raced forward as the beast set its sights on another man, tall and balding. His thick overcoat was already rent, but he'd made it to his knees and begun crawling away. When he saw the beast coming, he screamed in terror.

"Stop!" Garrett shouted. He moved without thinking, throwing himself in front of the beast. "Gryphon, stop! Enough! You don't want to do this!"

The beast stopped dead, its glowing eyes focused on Garrett. *Oh, curse me to the ends of the earth*, Garrett thought, mentally kicking himself. *How do I get myself into these situations?*

The beast tossed its head, snarling at Garrett. It was a hair-raising, resonant snarl that shook Garrett so deeply, he felt his bones rattle in his body. Rearing back on its hind legs, the beast towered over Garrett, a good three feet or more taller than him.

Garrett gulped a breath. He fought the urge to run in the opposite direction. He thought of Isabelle, facing down the beast in the snow, charming it.

If only he knew how she'd done it.

"Gryphon," Garrett said in a calm—albeit quavering—voice. "It's me."

The beast's eyes were merciless. It gave no sign of recognition.

"It's me. Garrett. Your brother." It occurred to Garrett that maybe he wasn't the best person to do this, considering Gryphon didn't much care for him, even when he was a person. But Isabelle was nowhere to be seen. There was no one else. "I know you hate me, Gryphon. But you don't want to hurt me."

The beast let out another snarl.

"Or, maybe you do," Garrett said quickly. "But you don't want to kill me. You told me so, remember? You explained about your exile. You said you never wanted to kill me. No matter how annoying I was. Am. How annoying I am."

The beast regarded him. Then it lunged forward, dropping to all fours. Given how much closer this put Garrett to the beast's maw, he did not take this as a good sign. A low, steady growl emanated from the beast as it bared its teeth in Garrett's face. But Garrett didn't flinch away.

"Gryphon, please." Garrett's voice was hoarse from the smoke and the cold and Adela's hex. "If you've ever cared about me—if you've ever once thought of me as your brother—" He thought fervently of the afternoon they'd spent in the woodland together, dozing by that pond. Did Gryphon even remember that? he wondered.

Suddenly, Garrett realized the beast had gone quiet. Its yellow-eyed gaze was fixed on Garrett, but no growl issued from its throat, no snarl twisted its face. It only gazed at him.

"Gryphon?" Garrett whispered.

Then another violent snarl tore through the air. But it didn't come from the beast. Garrett whipped around and saw, his heart pounding in his chest, a giant, russet wolf bounding towards him.

Garrett reached for the pistol at his waist, only to remember that it wasn't there.

The wolf leapt for him, jaws snapping—

—and with a deafening roar, the beast dove in front of Garrett, knocking the wolf aside with a swipe of its paw.

Garrett stumbled back, falling to one knee. The russet wolf flew through the air and tumbled, rolling away. As Garrett watched, the wolf gave a great shudder. Its reddish fur retracted into its skin, its claws and teeth began to shrink. Garrett glanced behind him and saw the first rays of the sun, streaking over the treetops.

When he looked back, the russet wolf was gone. In its place was Viveca, very much human and very much naked. Even though there were *much* bigger things to worry about right now, Garrett felt himself flush. He fought to keep his eyes on Viveca's face.

The beast stalked towards Viveca. "No, please." Viveca scrambled to her knees, hunching over. Her shoulder bled freely where the beast had cuffed her. "*Please*, Gryphon. Don't kill me. I'll leave you alone, I swear. I'll leave this forest. I promise."

Garrett frowned. This cowering woman was very different from the one he'd met outside the castle two weeks ago. He wasn't sure whether to believe this plea for mercy.

Evidently, Gryphon felt similarly doubtful. The beast leaned towards Viveca. He opened his jaws wide, rows of jagged teeth on full display, and roared in her face. The sound was so loud, the nearby trees quivered, dropping needles and swaying in their roots.

Viveca recoiled, ducking her face. "Please." Her voice was so low, Garrett could barely hear her. "You'll never see me again. I swear."

379

Gryphon's eyes were like cuts of amber. Garrett wasn't sure how much the beast understood, how in control Gryphon was. But the beast let out one last snarl, then stepped back, sitting on its haunches.

Viveca shot him a terrified, disbelieving look. Then she scrambled to her feet and ran into the forest.

Garrett let out a long breath. His shoulders felt suddenly heavy, and his head rang with exhaustion. He looked around.

The bright morning sun cast a stark light over the scene. The burning pyre still crackled, though it creaked and groaned, beginning to collapse in on itself. Really, Garrett thought—feeling just a little punchy as the adrenaline seeped out of him—these villagers needed to learn how to build better bonfires. Charred wood scented the air, and hazy gray smoke swept across the stone circle. Most of the villagers were gone, likely hiding in the trees or still running. Some of them would probably run all the way back to their villages, Garrett thought wryly. A few people remained—injured and groaning on the ground, or else just in shock.

He saw Spencer, bending to talk to one of the wounded. Ash covered one side of his face, turning his ebony complexion gray. Gemma was there too, squinting in the sunlight as she made her way towards Garrett. Half of her dark hair had pulled free of its braid, and a small, bleeding cut marred her forehead. But otherwise, she seemed uninjured. As she reached him, Garrett clapped a hand on her shoulder. "You all right?"

"Yes. Nearly got trampled by all those mad people, but I'm fine." She looked around, smoothing a hand over her frazzled hair. "I lost Isabelle in the crowd. Have you seen her?"

"I haven't. I—" Garrett broke off, a pained whine drawing his attention. He turned around.

The beast stood by the dying pyre, veiled in a cloud of smoke and ash. Wondering if he was injured, Garrett picked his way towards him, cringing as he sidestepped the bodies of the men Gryphon had killed. The beast stood beside one of those bodies, gently nudging it with his snout.

But it wasn't one of the village men.

It was Isabelle.

"*Isabelle!*" Sprinting the last few steps, Garrett threw himself down beside her, his knees thudding into the dirt. She was almost unrecognizable, prone on the ground, her wool coat dirtied with soot, her braided hair loose and strewn about her. "Isabelle, Isabelle—" She could not be dead, *she could not be dead*—

Shoving down his fear, he took her by the shoulders, carefully turning her over. She was not conscious. Propping her in his lap, Garrett searched for a wound. Her face was horribly gray, her body limp and cold. One of her hands was sticky with gore, but a quick examination showed no injury there.

Then he saw it. A dark stain across her front—just above her heart. Dried blood, crusting around her shoulder. A rough gouge in her coat where the fabric was torn.

"She's been shot!" Garrett cried. "Roy! *Roy*, where are you?" He looked up, frantic, as Gemma knelt beside them. The tracker took off her coat and wadded it up, pressing it to Isabelle's wound.

"You're going to be all right," Garrett told Isabelle, though he had no idea if she could hear him. Her eyes remained closed. Cradling her in his lap, he cupped her face in one hand. "You're going to be fine. Do you hear me, Isabelle?" His voice cracked. "You're going to be fine!"

Gryphon stamped a paw, letting out a huff. Garrett started; he had forgotten the beast was still there. As Garrett looked on, the beast threw back its head and let loose a mournful howl.

Then it turned and sprinted out of the clearing, vanishing into the woods.

In less than half an hour, they had a tent erected and Isabelle laid up inside it as Roy performed surgery to remove the bullet. The bullet missed her heart, Roy said, and any major arteries. She would likely pull through. Even so, Garrett would have sat outside the tent for as long as he had to—until he *knew* Isabelle was all right—but someone had to take charge and clean up this mess.

The pyre had been put out. Garrett stood beside its blackened remains, keeping clear of the smoke. His eyes tracked Spencer, Ellery, and Stefan as they moved among the wounded, tending the lesser injuries. Gemma stood beside him, making a report. "We've got four dead wolves," she said. "There were six of them, weren't there?"

"Six of them met with us." Garrett nodded. "But I don't know if that was all of them."

"Klaus might know."

"Klaus." Garrett glanced around. He'd completely forgotten the hunter. "Where is Klaus? I haven't seen him since the fighting started."

Gemma looked uncertain. "Me neither. He's not among the dead or wounded though."

"Klaus?" echoed a voice.

Garrett turned. Stefan stood behind him, a bundle of rags in his arms.

"I saw Klaus before," Stefan said. "After everything was over, I mean. I should've said, but Miss Isabelle was hurt, and—I forgot."

"Where did you see him?" Garrett asked.

"He went into the forest," Stefan said, pointing towards the trees. "After the naked lady—Viveca."

Garrett and Gemma exchanged a quick look.

It took the two of them about fifteen minutes to track Klaus. Once Gemma located his footprints, fresh in the icy mud, they followed them through the woods. The forest here was rife with towering spruce trees, their evergreen branches a canopy, blocking out the morning sun.

Abruptly, Gemma came to a halt. The footsteps had vanished in a great swathe of snow and mud.

"It looks like there was some kind of fight." Gemma turned, examining the gouges in the ground. "Or some kind of—"

"Listen." Garrett raised a hand. Gemma went silent, lifting her head like a bloodhound pricking its ears. For a moment, there was nothing—only the wind sifting through the trees, and cheeping songbirds, calling to each other—and then—

A soft, mewling noise. Like someone crying. Or someone in pain.

"This way." Gemma's voice was low. She indicated Garrett follow her, and they set off, their steps slow and silent, their breaths shallow and soft. As they wound through the trees, the crying grew clearer, closer, until—

"Klaus, *please.*"

Garrett and Gemma stilled. It was a moment before Garrett recognized Viveca's voice, whimpering through tears.

"If I ever meant anything to you—if you ever loved me—"

"That's the problem." This was Klaus's voice. He sounded like he was speaking through gritted teeth. "We both know I loved you. But I don't think you ever loved me."

Garrett held a breath, listening. It sounded like they were just beyond the cluster of spruces ahead. Without waiting for Gemma, he crept closer, brushing up against a prickly tree.

"Gryphon let me go." Viveca's voice was desperate now. "Gryphon spared me—"

"Yes, well." Klaus's voice was hard. "I don't serve Gryphon."

There was a *clicking* sound. The trigger of a gun, cocking back.

Garrett's eyes widened when he realized what Klaus was about to do. He darted forward, cursing as he slipped on a patch of mud. Viveca might have deserved death, but he didn't think any man could recover from killing the person he loved. Catching himself on a flimsy branch, Garrett hurled himself around the tree.

Then he slid to a halt. Viveca knelt in a bed of dead leaves less than ten paces away. From his position, Garrett couldn't see her face, but he could see Klaus's. The hunter stood facing her, his pistol trained on Viveca, ready to fire. But Klaus's face was a frozen mask of pain. His clenched jaw trembled with the struggle to hold it in. He didn't want to do this; Garrett could tell by the look in his eyes.

Klaus dropped the pistol to his side.

"I never—" Klaus's voice was little more than a harsh breath "—want to see you again."

"You won't." Viveca shook her fiery red head. "I promise."

Garrett slumped, stepping back to give Klaus his privacy. He saw the hunter turn away from Viveca, his shoulders hunched.

Viveca climbed to her feet. And—too late—Garrett saw the small blade concealed in her palm.

She lunged for Klaus's unprotected back.

"Klaus!" Garrett cried, fumbling for his pistol.

A shot rang out, snapping through the forest. A flock of birds burst into the air, squawking and screeching at the disturbance.

Garrett stepped out from behind the spruce tree. He faced Klaus, who looked as stunned as he was. Between them lay Viveca, spread-eagled, blood slowly pooling beneath her, soaking into the pile of dead leaves. Her glassy eyes stared at the treetops, unseeing.

Klaus looked at Viveca for a long time. Then he lifted his gaze to Garrett.

Then he looked to his right.

Gemma, rifle steady in her hands, stepped down off a massive boulder. Her dark eyes were inscrutable, her mouth set in a grim line. She looked at Garrett. "I took the shot."

Garrett nodded.

Klaus was still staring at Gemma. His pale face was numb. In that moment, Garrett could not have guessed what he was thinking.

"You're welcome," Gemma told Klaus, her voice as toneless as ever.

But when she turned and stalked past Garrett, he saw her eyes were filled with tears.

32
BEAUTY

Isabelle woke with a terrible ache in her shoulder. There was a bright light nearby, blinding her with its glare. She tried to turn aside, but the ache in her shoulder became a shooting pain, arcing down her arm like lightning. Clamping her lips shut, she let out a muffled whimper.

Then a dark silhouette appeared above her, blocking out the light.

Isabelle blinked. "Roy?"

"That's me." Roy grinned. "How do you feel?"

"Like a train ran over me," she mumbled.

"Well, that's not what happened," he said cheerfully. "You were shot. Close-range, but it was a small round. Shattered your collarbone though. You'll be sore for several weeks."

"Why," Isabelle groused, "do you look so bloody happy, then?"

"You're alive, aren't you?" Roy stepped back. "I'll tell Garrett you're awake."

When Garrett came in, he shifted the light—a gear-bulb lantern, hung from a pole—so it wasn't shining into her face.

Isabelle saw she was in a large canvas tent, lying atop a cot and tucked beneath several thick quilts. The air was chilly, though Isabelle thought the tent must have been surrounded in braziers, for she could feel a warm draft wafting in. Even still, she felt strangely cold. As though her body was sucking up every drop of energy to heal itself.

As Garrett pulled up a stool, Isabelle asked, "How long have I been out?"

"Almost thirty-six hours." Garrett lowered himself onto the stool, moving tensely, as though he was as sore as she was. "You've been in and out. Roy gave you morphine, so you might be a little hazy. Do you remember what happened?"

"Roy said I was shot." Isabelle cast her mind back. Garrett was right; everything felt fuzzy. She was so, so tired.

"Mmm," Garrett agreed. "I hope you're comfortable here. We thought about taking a few rooms in the village, but funnily enough, we didn't seem welcome there. In fact, some of the villagers were downright hostile when we went to get supplies. You'd think we were the ones who tried to burn *their* friend at the stake." He sighed. "I suppose they're just upset we spoiled their bonfire. And *hopefully,* a little ashamed of themselves."

Burned at the stake.... That's when Isabelle remembered. "*Gryphon.* The villagers—they lit the pyre, and I tried to put it out, and they *shot* me—but Gryphon—is Gryphon all right? Did you save him?"

"He's all right," Garrett said, but he evaded her gaze, fiddling with something on his belt. "He escaped the fire. Viveca is dead. One wolf escaped—" He glowered "—but Klaus said it was the youngest sister, Ferica. He's not worried about her, so I suppose I'm not either. Everyone else is a little banged up, but basically all right." He laid a hand over her arm and gave it a squeeze. "You should get some rest, Isabelle. We've settled here to camp—Roy reckons you'll need a week to recuperate before we head out. So—"

"Hang on," Isabelle interrupted him, annoyed. "Where is Gryphon? Is he here?" It had not escaped her notice that Garrett had glossed over him.

Garrett dropped his hand. "You should really rest."

"*Garrett.*" Alarm pushed against her ribcage. Something was wrong. "What is it?" she whispered. "Just tell me."

Garrett sighed and met her gaze. "Isabelle—Gryphon is gone."

———◆———

For a whole week, Isabelle was laid up in that tent, resting, allowing her wound to mend. And for a whole week, every day, she waited for someone to tell her Gryphon had returned. That he'd been found. Man or beast, she didn't care. She just wanted to know where he was.

But there was no word.

Garrett told her he'd changed before the sunrise, then disappeared into the woods. They hadn't been able to go after him right away, Garrett said, and by the time they did, there was no sign of him. Gemma had found a short trail, but it disappeared at a nearby stream.

Garrett thought maybe he'd gone back to the castle. "Perhaps he still needs to go there to turn back," he'd pointed out. But though Stefan and Ellery had returned to the castle, they'd sent no word that Gryphon was home.

Ansel left camp as soon as Isabelle was in the clear. "I'm going after the witch," he said darkly. "Adela. She got away. I'll find her though."

Isabelle gave him a faint smile. "You will be careful, won't you?"

"Isabelle, I'd wait for you." Ansel's eyes were glum. "But if I don't go after her now—"

"It's all right, Ansel," Isabelle cut in. "Look, I...it's all right. You know?"

Hope stirred in Ansel's eyes. He seemed to understand what she couldn't quite say—she forgave him. For pushing her away. For trying, in that wrongheaded way of his, to protect her.

"So you go hunt witches," she told him. "I've got my own things to see to." She hesitated. "I've been doing some research on witches, actually. Perhaps we could...meet up some time. Compare notes."

"Yes, we should." Ansel looked pleased. "Definitely we should."

And so, with those plans made, her brother set out. Off to hunt his witch.

At the end of the week—when Roy *finally* pronounced her fit to travel—everyone packed up to leave. But they weren't all going the same way.

Garrett was going to the Glen Kingdom. Isabelle was going to Gryphon's castle.

It was a cold, blustery morning. It had snowed just a few days ago, but only a few inches, most of which had already melted. All that was left were patches of ice, clinging to the tree branches and glittering over the forest floor. Which was just brilliant, Isabelle thought grumpily. Slipping and falling over a sheet of ice would do wonders for her mending collarbone. Her left arm was in a sling.

Garrett sidled up to Isabelle as she clasped her pack shut. He asked, "Are you sure about this, Isabelle?"

"Are you?" she returned.

The look Garrett gave her was rueful. She was a little disappointed he wasn't coming to the castle with her. She'd thought—after all he'd been through with Gryphon, after Gryphon *saved his life*—that Garrett would want to find him. But a telegram had come from King Victor, delivered by messenger from Spalding. It seemed word had reached Garrett's father about what happened at the stone circle—garbled word, anyway—and Garrett had been ordered to return at once.

"You know I'd go with you if I could," he said. "To see you there safely."

"But not to find Gryphon?" Isabelle protested.

"Isabelle." Garrett took her gently by the arm. "There's nothing I can do for him here. But maybe back home—maybe I can talk to my father. I doubt he'll restore Gryphon's title, but perhaps I can persuade him to lift his exile."

"Well. If your father will listen." Isabelle's tone was droll. "Because it sounds like you're in *trouble*."

"I doubt it." Garrett made a face. "It's just, you know. I was meant to be off hunting beasts, not riling up the locals in the neighboring kingdom. I'm sure he just wants to know I'm all right." A sigh rumbled through him as he looked across the clearing. "Isabelle—if you *do* see Gryphon, if he's at the castle—"

"Yes?"

"Will you tell him something?" Garrett gazed down at her. He looked oddly young, his eyes soft and troubled. "Tell him...I've decided to take his advice. About Briar. About my father."

Isabelle raised her eyebrows. She didn't know what that meant, but she assumed Gryphon would. *If I get the chance to tell him.*

She banished the thought. She *would* tell him.

She could not so easily banish the ache in her chest.

"Of course I'll tell him," she said.

Garrett smiled. It was such a jocular smile that Isabelle couldn't help but return it. Even though she was sad to see him go. Even though she wished he would come with her.

Garrett wrapped his arms around her, giving her a very careful hug. Then he shouldered his pack and set out, his soldiers following behind. Four figures, growing smaller in the distance, until they disappeared into the frosty woods across the clearing.

"About time we head out too."

Isabelle looked around. Gemma, the tracker, slung her rifle over her shoulder as she approached. She turned and eyed the gnarled forest, her expression unreadable.

Klaus had decided not to go back to the castle either. Isabelle had begged him to come, assuring him that he and Gryphon could mend things. But Klaus had been firm. The way he saw it, Gryphon was either gone for good—in which case, there was no point returning to the castle. Or he was there, waiting—but not for Klaus. Gryphon, Klaus was sure, would not give him a second chance. And the hunter was ready for something new. He was going to the Glen Kingdom with Garrett, to join his company. Isabelle could not really see Klaus as a soldier, but that was for him to figure out.

She understood his wanting a new life, far from this forest. Gryphon was not the only person he'd lost.

As Garrett did not want Isabelle traveling alone while she was still recovering, he'd decided one of his people should accompany her back to the castle. Gemma had volunteered. Garrett agreed she was a good fit, since she'd grown up in the Black Forest and would be fine making her way home on her own.

Isabelle thought she was a good fit for another reason.

Their travel was slow. They took breaks often so Isabelle could rest. Though they'd set out early, it was nearly dusk when they emerged into the clearing before the gully. The sky was a deep, pewter gray, the sun still shedding some daylight, though it had disappeared below the trees.

As they crossed the long bridge over the gully, Isabelle eyed the castle walls. She wasn't sure anyone would still be here. If Gryphon had not returned, would the servants have stayed?

But as they neared the end of the bridge, Isabelle spotted a familiar, sandy brown head on the wall. Stefan gave her a quick wave, then disappeared to raise the portcullis. Isabelle waited with hopeful anticipation. But when she and Gemma stepped into the courtyard, her hopes were dashed.

"We knew you'd be back," said Stefan. "But, I'm sorry, Miss Isabelle. Lord Gryphon isn't here."

Isabelle's heart felt as heavy as a stone. "He hasn't been back at all?"

"Well, he was," Stefan admitted. "But only as the beast."

"What? When was this?"

"A few days ago," Stefan said. "I was manning the wall. I've been manning it every day. He turned up on the bridge around noon—the beast, I mean. He seemed—he just sort of looked at me. So I let him in."

"And?" Isabelle pressed. "What happened?"

"It was weird." Stefan made a puzzled frown. "I was ready to run, but he didn't attack me. I asked if he wanted to come inside, but I don't know that he understood. He didn't follow me in. He stayed out in the courtyard all day. And then night fell and—" He hesitated.

Isabelle guessed what he didn't want to say. "He didn't turn back? Even once the sun set?"

"No," Stefan confessed. "He never turned back. And the next morning, he banged on the gate until I opened it. He ran across the bridge and disappeared into the forest." He gave a helpless shrug. "I'm sorry, Miss Isabelle. That was three days ago."

"But why didn't he turn back?" Isabelle asked in dismay.

"I don't know. I don't know how it works."

Isabelle bit her lip, turning it over in her head. Garrett said Gryphon had controlled the change when he turned before dawn at the stone circle. So why couldn't he change back? What had happened to him?

Gemma gave her a knowing look. "I don't know what you mean to do next. But we should rest here tonight. You need to pack your things anyway."

Isabelle agreed with reluctance. They met Ellery inside, who helped Isabelle to her old room. Isabelle ate a warm dinner of venison stew and nutty bread, then retired early. She was exhausted from the travel, her muscles like lead, her shoulder aching.

She fell asleep at once. But her dreams were vivid and fretful, and she woke abruptly in the middle of the night. She couldn't say what woke her. She lay still for several moments, eyes flicking up towards the high window. The sky was clear, the light of the waxing moon gazing in.

Isabelle sat up. Her eyes swept the dark room. There was no one there, of course. She tried to go back to sleep, but she felt wide awake. Her shoulder throbbed, and she was a touch too warm beneath her quilt but too cold without it. Rising from her bed, she slipped into her boots and shrugged her good arm into her coat, pulling the other side around her shoulder like a cloak.

She set out into the castle.

Isabelle felt strange as she wandered the gloomy corridors at night. She didn't see anyone, and so few candles were lit in their sconces. In only a week without Gryphon, the servants had returned to a normal sleep schedule. That was only natural, she supposed, but it felt wrong. Like Gryphon had been forgotten.

She wandered past Gryphon's room, which was shut and locked. She remembered sitting on his bed there, listening as he'd told her the story of the last Forest king. She peeked into the parlor, thinking of the nights she'd spent reading while Gryphon sketched. She tip-toed down the grand staircase into the entrance hall, spotting the door to the dungeons, and recalled how she'd crept down there when she first arrived, thinking she'd find Ansel.

And found the beast instead.

Isabelle stopped before the great front doors. They were not the same. The old doors had been destroyed when Viveca breached the castle. In their place were doors of thinner wood, hanging awkwardly in the frame. They clearly had not been made for this entry. A draft of cold air slithered in through a gap between them.

She opened the doors, letting in a rush of crisp, frigid air. The moon lit her way as she descended the steps, crossed the back of the courtyard, and stopped before the squat tower. The door there was unlocked.

Isabelle stepped into Gryphon's workshop.

It was very dark. She took slow steps, fumbling until she found a gear-bulb lamp and wound it up. It flared alight, casting a shallow white halo. By this scant light, she peered around. Everything was in shadow, the easels and sculptures creating murky shapes in the dark. She could have used her wolf eyes to see more clearly, but she was tired again after wandering the castle.

She crossed to the bed in the corner and crawled on top of it. The thin, folded quilt there was cold, but Isabelle scented traces of Gryphon on it, as though some part of him was still there.

Suddenly, she felt unbearably sad. It shouldn't have been sudden, because the sadness had been building in her as she traversed the castle corridors, as she stepped out into the courtyard. It was what had woken her, back in her own bed. But she hadn't recognized it until now. Her sadness swelled inside her, pushing to get out.

She was afraid she knew why Gryphon hadn't changed back when he'd returned to the castle. At the stone circle, he'd managed to turn on his own, just like she could. He'd broken the cycle he'd always been stuck in—beast by day, human by night. Now, if he wanted to turn back, he'd have to do it himself. Release the beast. Let it go.

But he might not know how to do that.

Isabelle lay her head on Gryphon's pillow, tears leaking from the corners of her eyes. She fell asleep.

When she woke in the morning, the lamp had gone out. Daylight strained in through the glazed window. Isabelle sat up slowly, taking a minute to remember how she'd come to be here. She glanced around, wondering what time it was.

Her gaze fell upon a marble bust on the worktable. Isabelle stared at it, preoccupied with a memory. That night she'd burst in here—when she'd discovered the truth about the bite—Gryphon had been sculpting something. It looked like he'd finished it.

Isabelle climbed from the bed, holding her shoulder awkwardly, and went to examine the sculpture. It was a two-sided, two-faced bust. Isabelle bent to look at one side and gasped.

Her own face gazed back at her. The likeness was impecca-ble. Her expression was serene, even stern, her eyebrows drawn down, her lips in a cool line. It was a face she knew well, for it was the face she set in the mirror every morning. The composed, implacable young woman. The mask behind which she locked everything away.

She shuffled around the worktable to see the other side of the bust. Her breath caught. This second side depicted her again—but it wasn't the same face. Her expression here was raw, passionate, vulnerable. It wasn't a sad face, exactly. But her eyes were huge and brimming with feeling, the good and the bad. It was the face she *never* showed the world, the face she had shown only to him, even though she'd never meant to.

The swelling inside Isabelle had grown beyond what she could contain. She felt like she couldn't breathe. He had *seen* her. He'd seen what her past had done to her—the rejection, the abandon-ment, the loneliness. The search for belonging.

He'd seen it all and made it beautiful.

Or maybe that was just how he saw it.

The door burst open and Isabelle sprang back. For half a second, she thought she'd see Gryphon standing in the doorway.

But it was only Gemma. "There you are!" Gemma's cool voice was tinged with exasperation. Her dark hair tumbled over her shoulders in tangled waves, as though she'd just gotten out of bed. "Ellery said you weren't in your room. We looked *every-where*, and then Ellery said maybe you'd come here—"

"Gemma," Isabelle said, "I want to find Gryphon."

Gemma fell silent. Her gaze surveyed the workshop, impassive as ever. Then she looked at Isabelle. "I thought you would. But you've no idea where he's gone, Isabelle."

"But you can track him." Isabelle didn't suppress the pleading in her voice. "Please, Gemma. I know you can find him. And you have duties elsewhere, I know, but—" She broke off, glancing at the two-sided bust. "I have to find him, Gemma," she said quietly. "Please tell me you understand that."

Gemma stared at her. Isabelle swallowed. She remembered how they'd found Gemma after Viveca took Gryphon. How she'd crouched over Falcon's body, unwilling to leave him.

Gemma let out a low breath. "I do understand. And Prince Garrett never gave me a timeframe for returning to the Glen Kingdom." She paused. "I'll help you find him. When do we leave?"

33

LOVED

G RYPHON RAN UNTIL HE couldn't run anymore. He ran
until his legs buckled. He ran until his lungs were fit to
burst, his heart racing in his chest. He ran as hard and as fast as
he could. Trying to outrun the images haunting his mind.

His world had become a confused jumble. The beast's stark
world of absolutes melded with bursts of color and distinct lines
the beast had never known—memories of his time as a human.
The beast didn't like the visions invading his mind, the sudden
stabs of *feeling* that cut through him as he hunted a rabbit or
drank from a cold brook of water.

He remembered going back to the castle. The sun had been
pleasant that day, glimmering overhead. He'd settled into the
courtyard and stayed all night. But when the sun rose the next
morning, a feeling of *wrongness* came over him, and suddenly,
he'd wanted to be gone from the castle. It wasn't his home anymore. He wasn't sure what home was, but he was sure of that.

He was running from something. His past life, and all the hurt
that came with it. He remembered surrendering to the beast,

letting it take control. In that brief moment, he'd experienced a freedom he'd never known before.

But it had been fleeting. Now he could barely remember it.

Night fell. He stopped running, exhausted. A chilly drizzle fell from the black sky. He found scant shelter beneath an oak tree. Tufts of dark leaves had begun to sprout from its sturdy branches, giving him cover from the rain.

That night, he dreamed of a human. She had huge, curious eyes, beautiful brown skin, curly hair that felt soft to the touch. But it was her scent he truly remembered. A scent that made him feel safe and warm, even as the beast.

He woke from the dream, a new day shining over him. It was an awful *wrenching*, coming awake from that dream, like plunging into icy cold rapids. He let out a low whine, wishing he could fall back asleep. He tried to recall the girl, tried to remember her face, but it wouldn't come.

A terrible bleakness opened inside him. It grew and grew, threatening to consume him. It surged up his throat. He was going to choke on it. He couldn't breathe. What was wrong with him?

"Gryphon?"

The beast leapt to his feet, all four of them, and whirled about. He'd drawn his mouth back in a defensive snarl before he realized he knew the scent of the creature before him. It was the scent he'd dreamed of. The human he knew. He couldn't make out her face in this form, but he knew her.

He was still choking on that terrible feeling, but now he remembered. He knew what to do. This pressure building inside him—it was something to do with his eyes. He just needed to change his eyes somehow, and then he could let it go. He could breathe again.

He looked at the human, took in the scent of her, and let it fill him.

His bones began to crack. It was painful, but in a good way, like stretching a tight muscle. He began to shrink, his bones knitting back together. The dark fur covering his body vanished. His claws retracted. He was looking at his hands, splayed across green grass. *Human* hands.

He was human again. A great shudder spasmed through Gryphon. A sob broke from his lips. His eyes stung with tears that streamed down his cheeks. He felt at his face—his wet, human face—and rocked back on his heels. Another sob escaped him, and it felt horrible, and wonderful, his whole body shaking as he wept.

And Isabelle was there. "Gryphon," she murmured, kneeling beside him. She threw a large cloak around him—he hadn't even felt the cold until then—and tugged it around his shoulders. Then she wrapped her arms around him, bringing him close. "Gryphon, it's all right."

"I couldn't remember who I was," he gasped. His head fell against her, and he inhaled the soft, rosy scent of her hair. "I couldn't remember you."

"It's all right. I'm here."

She was here. He didn't even know where *here* was. He shifted, laying his cheek against her shoulder, his eyes traveling over his surroundings. They were in a low glade by a babbling stream, surrounded by mossy boulders and twisted, majestic trees blossoming with new growth. It was a beautiful place, but not one Gryphon recognized. The landscape was nothing like the Black Forest.

He'd come a long way.

"How did you find me?" he asked.

"Gemma," Isabelle said simply.

"Is she here?"

"She's nearby. Scouting the area. I told her I was safe with you." Isabelle squeezed his arm. "It's been over a month since you ran off. Since you changed. I was beginning to think I'd *never* find you."

Gryphon's tears slowed, drying up, but he went rigid as he remembered the change. At the stone circle. "They shot you." He leaned back to look at her, his eyes searching her face, her body. "One of the villagers shot you—"

"I know. You killed him though. You...killed a few of those men."

"Yes, well, I won't lose much sleep over that," Gryphon muttered. Still holding Isabelle's hand, he climbed to his feet. He shivered, clutching the cloak about him. He'd forgotten how cold it was, being human.

Isabelle rose with him. "And then you ran off. Into the forest."

Gryphon remembered it all. Killing those men. *Not* killing Garrett. Sparing Viveca. Finding Isabelle, bloody, injured, her life draining away. It had been more than he could bear.

He remembered that pain. Isabelle had been shot because of him. She'd been there, mixed up in that mess, because of him. He'd inflicted his bite and curse on her, confined her to that miserable ruin of a castle. He'd separated her from her brother. She'd been kidnapped by the were-wolves, used to get to him—

Yes, seeing her so hurt had been more than he could bear. And even the beast had realized what he needed to do.

Leave before he could hurt her again.

He looked at her now, his throat tight with the words he didn't want to say. "Isabelle—"

"No." Isabelle laid her fingertips over his lips. "No, Gryphon. I won't let you say it. I won't let you push me away." In the soft, dappled light of the glade, her eyes seemed to gleam like a hawk's eyes, unyielding and fierce. "I'm done with all that."

"Isabelle," Gryphon said weakly. Even as he protested, Isabelle took his hands in hers. Making this so much harder. "I won't say I don't care about you. I do. I—" His heart was in his throat. "I think I love you." He ran his thumb along the back of her palm. "But that's why—"

"Why what? Gryphon, what do you think is going to happen?" Isabelle tucked his hands against her chest, bringing him a step closer to her. "Don't you get it? I'm *like you*. In more ways than one."

Gryphon looked into her face. And that's when he realized. Her eyes *were* gleaming. But not like a hawk's eyes.

They were a wolf's eyes, yellow and bright. They were like his.

"You call it a curse." Her voice was a gentle breeze, ghosting along his skin. "And it was for you. But it doesn't have to be." The gleam of her eyes slowly faded, muting into the coppery brown he remembered. "You think I'm not safe with you, but you're wrong. There is nowhere safer because...there is no one who sees me like you do. And I *won't* give that up. Because I love you too."

Gryphon closed his eyes, but he could not shut her out. Even when he couldn't see her, he was surrounded in her heady scent. Even when he couldn't see her, he could feel the warmth of her seeping into him.

Where could he run that she would not follow?

She was right. They were the same, they two. Not just in form, but on the inside. He'd known it all along. Ever since she'd told him about her brother, and he'd seen his own pain reflected in her. Ever since the night they'd shared, coming together in loss and loneliness.

But now, he could leave all that behind. The guilt, the fear. He could let it go.

He surrendered it to the beast. To Isabelle. To the promise of a new life.

He was free.

He breathed in his first breath, the first breath of this new life. Opening his eyes, he gazed down at Isabelle.

Isabelle tilted her head. "I don't think I've ever seen that before."

"What?" he asked.

"You, smiling." Her voice held a note of mischief. "It's a little weird."

Gryphon only smiled more. He couldn't help it. "So, what do we do now?"

"Well. I think we should go back to the castle one last time. To get all our things. And collect Stefan and Ellery. And then…" She shrugged one shoulder. "We go home."

Home. The word awoke such wonderful longing inside him. He found his gaze lingering on her shoulder, appreciating its slender grace. "Do you have a place in mind?"

"Yes, actually. I'd never really thought of it as *home* until recently, but. It does have a very nice library. With all my books. I suppose I *could* even spare a room for your workshop."

"Kind of you." He squinted at the sky. A cloud shifted overhead, and a shaft of sunlight pierced the leafy boughs of the oak tree, shining over him. For the first time in years, he glimpsed the light of the sun—as a human.

He dropped his gaze. "I do think there's something we should do first. Something you've forgotten."

"Oh? What's that?"

Gryphon cupped his hand over her shoulder. "This."

He bent his head and kissed her. As he slid his hand down the slope of her shoulder, she wrapped an arm behind him, pressing her fingers into the curve of his back. The sun beamed down, enveloping them in its warmth.

There was no fear in this kiss. No desire to lose himself. He knew exactly who he was, and nothing—not even the beast—could ever steal that from him again.

He was hers. And he was home.

DON'T MISS THE NEXT
HORRIFIC FAIRY TALE!

THE
LITTLE SEA
MONSTER

After losing everything he loved,
Prince Demetri embarked on a quest to
find a new life. But while on a ship out at
sea, something finds him... a beautiful
creature with a monstrous appetite...

TURN THE PAGE
FOR A SNEAK PEEK!

Demetri squinted against a splatter of sea spray as another violent wave crashed against the side of the ship. The salty water stung his eyes. His fisherman friend, Mason, made his way to Demetri's side, using the rigging to get across the deck. Mason was only about an inch taller than Demetri, but he had a broad chest and thick arms that gave him the appearance of a much bigger man. His white cotton shirt was soaked through and plastered to his skin.

"What did I tell you?" Mason asked, grinning widely.

Demetri managed a weak smile. It was early summer here on the coast of the Mariner Kingdom, and quite warm during the days. But here on the sea at night, with a storm raging nearby, kicking up the waves and bolstering the wind, Demetri was freezing. His fingers, wrapped tightly around the scratchy rigging, had gone numb. He couldn't even feel the rope biting into his skin.

Raising his voice, Demetri asked, "Any sign of the sharks yet?"

"Remy says no." Remy was the ship's lookout, a short, skinny girl with the bluest eyes Demetri had ever seen. She was the only girl on the crew. "Anyway..." A dark look passed through Mason's eyes. "That's assuming they *are* sharks."

"What else could be killing people besides sharks?" Demetri asked. That was why they were here. There had been an uptick in shark attacks lately. People out at sea—sailors, fisherman, and bathers alike—had gone missing. Bloodied body parts had even washed up on shore.

Mason cast him a glance. "Mermaids," he grunted.

"Mermaids?" Demetri stared at his friend, wondering if he was serious. Mason did like his jokes—almost as much as he liked doing reckless things, like going out into violent waters at night. Demetri supposed he'd found a substitute Garrett. He wondered what that said about himself, that he always sought out mad thrill seekers for company.

"That's right, mermaids." Mason ran a hand through his dark beard. "Don't believe all those pretty stories you hear. My mother always said a mermaid was what killed my father."

Demetri opened his mouth to respond—not that he had anything more eloquent to say than "Huh," because he wasn't sure if he believed mermaids were even real, let alone vicious killers—but before he could say anything, the ship gave a violent lurch. Demetri gripped the rope so tightly, he thought his frozen fingers would fall off.

As the ship rollicked, Demetri saw the bow dip dangerously low towards the water. A massive wave tumbled over it, breaking against the ship like glass shattering into a thousand pieces. Sailors shouted and scrambled to grab onto something, but when the bow rose up again, water billowing down the sides, there were several cries of "Man overboard!"

Mason swore and ran for the bow. Some of the sailors began unraveling a buoy to throw out. Someone else bellowed over all the other voices, "Stop the ship! Bring her 'round! Tell those boys in the engine room to stop the cursed ship now!"

Demetri followed the rigging as best he could, lurching down the deck towards the bow. Once he ran out of rope, he staggered to the side of the ship and gripped the slick steel railing. He half-ran, half-fell the rest of the way, wayward waves lapping over the side and drenching him more than ever.

As he joined the sailors at the bow, he addressed the one closest to him. "Where is he?" he called over the roar of the sea.

The sailor cursed in response. "He's gone under. Must have. He was right there, and then—"

Whatever he meant to say next was drowned out by an ominous, earsplitting *cr-a-a-a-ck*. Demetri mirrored everyone around him as he clutched at the railing, for the ship gave a sharp lurch. It felt like the hull had caught on something. Alarm rushed through Demetri like a tidal wave. Something about that sound had raised every hair on his head, as though he'd been struck by lightning.

"By the Gift!" the sailor next to him swore. His face was pinched and white as he stared down the ship. "That sounded like—"

He was interrupted a second time as the ship began to rattle, *k-thnk-k-thnk-k-thnk-k-thnk*. As though it sat upon a warped axle. Then there was another *crack*, louder this time, the sound as thunderous as the nearby storm. The next thing Demetri knew, he was on his knees as the ship gave another great lurch.

"Breach!" someone shouted, and the cry cut Demetri to the core. "Breach in the hull!"

Sucking in a breath, Demetri reached for the side of the ship and looked up. Even amidst the thrashing sea, he could tell the ship had stopped moving, no longer cresting forward over the water. But the ship was not still. Instead, it shuddered around him as though resisting a great pressure. He could imagine the sea swelling into the cracked hull below, filling the ship with water.

It was a terrifying vision.

Screams rent the air as sailors dashed across the deck and clutched at the railing, driven by panic, rushing to save the ship. As Demetri stumbled to his feet, the ship dipped perilously, the port side—where Demetri stood—sinking low. Demetri saw Mason running, shouting about lifeboats, but then the port side dipped again, and Mason fell towards him. Demetri spun to avoid being flattened by the man, but he lost his footing as the deck heaved beneath him and he pitched backwards.

His head slammed into a sharp edge. Everything went black.

It couldn't have been for more than a minute, but when Demetri came to, he was in the water, his head slipping beneath the surface.

———◦———

Perpetua watched the ship break apart with little satisfaction.

The truth was, she liked ships. She liked the way they looked moving over the sea, like giant swans gliding across the roiling waters. She liked the way their sails billowed in the gusting wind like clouds in a pearly sky. She loved to watch the little sailor up in the crow's nest, looking out over the world. They must really feel like a crow, she thought, perched so high above the water.

What she really loved about ships, though, was their very existence. It was a marvel that humans could build such things, that they'd discovered a way to traverse the sea without fins. Even though they couldn't breathe underwater or swim very well. The sea was not a natural habitat for a human; the sea often *killed* humans. But they braved it anyway.

Which made it all the easier to hunt and eat them.

"Imagine seeing you here, Perpetua."

Masking her shock, Perpetua twisted around, sea water spattering the rocks beside her. She hadn't realized there was anyone else nearby. Naiads were solitary feeders; they rarely sought out company at mealtimes. "Candelaria," she said evenly, recognizing the blood red scales glittering beneath the water's dark surface. "What are you doing here?"

Candelaria flicked her tail fin in a nonchalant gesture. "I believe I just asked you that."

Refusing to be cowed, Perpetua adopted a cool tone. "I was at the docks earlier. I saw Alamena set the sabotage."

"And you decided to help yourself?"

Perpetua fixed her eyes on Candelaria's too-pretty face. "Am I not welcome here?"

Candelaria's eyebrow hitched, but she didn't press the issue. Perpetua turned away, satisfaction burning hot inside her. Although naiads preferred to hunt alone, they did sometimes hunt together out of necessity—taking down a big ship took more than one, and the amount of food that ship would provide was far more than a single naiad needed. Others were always welcome to take their fill, even if they hadn't helped with the sabotage.

"I hate to hunt like this," Candelaria said. "It's degrading. Letting them kill themselves, really. And we are just the scavengers picking at the wreckage."

"We have to be careful," Perpetua said. "The Ternion dictated we should limit taking prey from the docks. The humans will start to notice if too many of their own disappear."

Candelaria laughed scornfully. "The humans. They always talk. That doesn't mean they're clever enough to hunt us."

Perpetua could feel Candelaria's gaze on her, smoldering with anticipation. This, Perpetua thought, was the real reason Candelaria had confronted her here—to rile her up. It was her favorite pastime. And Perpetua wasn't about to let her enjoy it. Striving for a bored tone, she replied, "If you say so."

"You're not going to defend them?" Golden moonlight arced over the rippling water as Candelaria swam around, placing herself in Perpetua's line of sight. "Your precious humans? Isn't that what you do all day in your cave? Sit around and write poetry about them?"

Perpetua didn't deign to grace this ridiculous jibe with an answer. She did not think humans *precious*. Humans were prey, humans were food. If she was a bit curious about them, well, humans were very different from other food, like a bed of oysters or a school of coal fish.

"You probably have one picked out." Candelaria nodded, indicating the wreck. "Seeing as you were there when Alamena set the sabotage. You've probably had your eye on one since it boarded the ship." She laughed quietly. "I only ask so I know who to stay away from. I don't want to get into a fight with you over food."

"Then stay clear of me," Perpetua growled, "and you won't."

Candelaria snarled back, her eyes bleeding red from eyelid to eyelid. Perpetua stifled a flinch but didn't back down, meeting the naiad's scarlet gaze without allowing her own vision to redden. She wasn't afraid of Candelaria, but she would *not* allow the naiad to provoke her.

Candelaria backed away. With one last sneer, she dove into the water and vanished beneath its inky depths. Perpetua watched her go, her eyes trailing those crimson scales until they disappeared. She only relaxed when Candelaria did not return.

The truth was, Perpetua *had* picked out the human she wanted from that ship. She did that sometimes. She could not explain why, not even to herself. It was just that humans were *more* than just another meal. Sometimes, Perpetua wondered why they ate them. On a physical level, she understood—she'd seen what happened to a naiad who went too long without consuming human prey. The hunger became unbearable; it became a *need* burrowed deep inside. As though the hunger, unsated, turned on its host, feeding on the naiad instead.

A naiad who went too long without consuming a human went mad. Perpetua knew that.

She just wondered why.

It was time to go. If she waited too much longer, all the humans from the wreck would be dead and drowned. The timing was important. Naiads preferred their prey alive when they ate them, but the entire point of sinking the ship at sea was to draw little attention to themselves. If any of the sailors saw them and escaped on their little boats, the Ternion would not be pleased.

Perpetua dove a fin's length below the surface and swam towards the ruined ship. As she neared the wreckage, she heard screams from the floundering sailors, filtered through the water; she felt the disturbance in the sea from their splashing and flailing. She glanced around to make sure Candelaria was nowhere near her, then set off in search of the human she'd seen boarding the ship.

She'd watched the sailors board one by one, but this one had drawn her attention because he was *not* a sailor. At least, she didn't think he was. He hadn't been dressed like the sailors in their white uniforms. He'd worn a dark coat and carried a weapon, something long and thin with a glinting edge—a sword, Perpetua thought.

And he'd had a quiet, serious face. Even when one of the sailors had said something to him and he'd laughed, there had been a careworn look in his eyes, as though he could see something the sailor couldn't. Ghosts, hovering at the edge of his vision.

Perpetua couldn't forget that look.

As she reached the midst of the wreckage and swam through it, she searched for him. She wove around sinking netting and steel beams, she ducked beneath bobbing shards of the ship's wooden exterior. But she focused on the humans. The sailors were easy to spot in their white uniforms; they stood out like phosphorescent algae in the black sea. Perpetua bypassed them all—drowning, unconscious, or dead. She passed one whose eyes bulged in their sockets as he choked on sea water, sinking fast.

Then another shape caught her eye, off to her left. A dark, flailing shape—a human. And not a sailor, not in the white uniform of the ship's crew. This was him—*her* human. The one she'd picked. She couldn't see his face, for he clutched at something holding him above the water, but below the surface, his torso twisted, his legs kicking frantically.

She remembered his serious face from the docks, and her mouth began to water. She could feel every one of her teeth lengthening, sharpening to a point, her jaw unhinging and stretching wide to accommodate their growth. Her vision reddened, a filmy scarlet veil dropping over her eyes.

She hated this part, right before she fed. When she was on the precipice of losing her mind. Most of the other naiads gave into the furor that welled inside them, relishing the burgeoning rage and madness. But Perpetua always resisted it. It had overtaken her once or twice, and she couldn't understand why the others didn't experience the shock of terror that came with it. So she struggled to hold the madness at bay as she swam, pivoting up towards her chosen human.

She was three fin lengths from her prey when a glistening shape darted in front of her, snatched her human, and dragged him beneath the water's surface.

Perpetua stopped short. Some of the red faded from her vision as she took in the scene before her, trying to make sense of it. A shaft of moonlight pierced the dark ocean, casting dazzling light over garnet fins and golden hair.

Candelaria. Candelaria had taken her human.

COMING SUMMER 2024

ACKNOWLEDGEMENTS

Everyone always says that the second book is tougher than the first. I don't remember feeling that way when I wrote the rough draft of *Beast By Day* ten years ago. But bringing this book from rough draft to final draft was incredibly tough. So I must thank the following people who helped me.

Thank you to my beta readers: Sarah, Allison, and Emilie. Your invaluable feedback helped elevate this tale into the story it is today, and your endless enthusiasm for this series bolstered me when I most needed encouragement.

Thank you to the Miblart Cover Design team for bringing this story to life through another beautiful cover. Thank you to Saumya Singh, who created the wonderful map of this world.

Thank you to my family, who have all tirelessly supported me in the pursuit of this book. Thank you to Rachel and David, the earliest readers of this story. Thank you to my parents, without whom none of my stories would be possible.

Lastly, thank you to all the readers. Thank you to everyone who has shown support for this series through reviews and social media, through buying and reading and spreading the word. Most especially, thank you for cheering me on over these last few months. It has meant so much to me and helped me through the difficult times. Thank you.

CONNECT WITH THE AUTHOR

Visit the author's website for excerpts, book playlists, and more.

WWW.ELIZABETHKKING.COM

Follow the author on Instagram.

@ELIZABETH_K_KING

Follow the author on Facebook.

@ELIZABETH K. KING, AUTHOR

If you enjoyed this book, please support the author by leaving a review!

Milton Keynes UK
Ingram Content Group UK Ltd.
UKHW040134130324
439347UK00013B/165/J